DEATH IN THE SPACE BEYOND

Atkill suddenly stiffened as a red light began to glow in the panel before him. "Damn!" he muttered. He snapped on a screen that glowed in dark, somber red, and black. Three strange long-necked Bay-Raonii were training some sort of a weapon on the ship. Atkill stepped to the open lock and through it, and looked toward the men. He could not see them in the dark, but suddenly they began to glow in weird, greenish colors. Their startled faces looked up.

"Your masters are stupid," said Atkill calmly, in perfect Bay-Raonii. "I am ATKILL!"

The figures of the men began to glow more vividly. They stiffened suddenly immobile. The one on the left began to shake violently; his outline grew hazy and a scream rang out from his open mouth. Presently it stopped, and he slumped suddenly downward; but as he fell, the light that shone from him grew brilliant, and the clothes he wore, and the flesh of his body, melted like snow in the path of a heat-ray, and a skeleton fell to the ground surrounded by bits of metal and glass and crystal . . . .

THE
SPACE
BEYOND

John W. Campbell, Jr.

Introduction by Isaac Asimov
Afterword by George Zebrowski

WILDSIDE PRESS

CONTENTS

BIG, BIG, BIG

by Isaac Asimov

The thing about John Campbell is that he liked things big. He liked big men with big ideas working out big applications of their big theories. And he liked it fast. His big men built big weapons within days; weapons that were, moreover, without serious shortcomings, or at least, with no shortcomings that could not be corrected as follows: "Hmm, something's wrong—oh, I see—of course." Then, in two hours, something would be jerry-built to fix the jerry-built device.

The big applications were, usually, in the form of big weapons to fight big wars on tremendous scales. Part of it was, of course, Campbell's conscious attempt to imitate and surpass Edward E. ("Doc") Smith. The world-shaking, escalating conflicts in Campbell's stories, as in *The Space Beyond* in this collection, is a reflection of the escalating conflict on the printed page between John and Doc.

A great deal of Campbell's science is sheer gobbledygook that you must not take seriously. You have to read it as a foreign language that the characters understand and for which the action and the astronomical background serve as a translation.

In some places, Campbell is deliberately and bullheadedly *wrong* and one can never be sure whether he actually believes the nonsense, or whether he is doing it just to irritate and provoke his readers into thinking hard.

In the December 1934 *Astounding Stories,* John Campbell, writing under the pseudonym, Karl van Campen, published "The Irrelevant," in which the heroes were rescued from a deadly interplanetary dilemma by working

7

out a method for creating energy out of nothing. In this way, they defied the law of conservation of energy which, it can be argued, is the most fundamental law of the universe.

Campbell did this by arguing that the quantity of energy produced by a change in velocity was different according to the frame of reference you chose for it, and that by switching from one frame to another you could create more energy than you consumed.

This is dead wrong. I won't argue the reasons here because I don't want to start a controversy. The argument that began with "The Irrelevant" continued in the letter columns of *Astounding* for an incredible length of time, with Campbell (always writing letters under the name of Karl van Campen) maintaining his views against all attacks—as in later years, he would maintain, with equal unswerving vigor, all attacks against his equally indefensible views in favor of dianoetics the Hieronymus machine, the Dean drive, and so on. He might stop arguing points and allow them to drop into oblivion, but he would never openly admit he was wrong.

"The Irrelevant" was the only story that John ever published under the van Campen pseudonym, but *Marooned* was a sort of never-published (till now) sequel under the same pseudonym, and it made use, in the end, of the same fallacy of a broken law of conservation of energy. I don't even feel guilty about giving away the climax in that story because I don't want anyone to be fooled by it. It doesn't work. You have been warned!

Yet, on the other hand, John's incredibly vivid imagination would sometimes strike gold and would inspire other writers into striking gold also. The great writers of the Golden Age in *Astounding* were more Campbell than themselves. I admit, freely and frequently, that this was so in my case. Other writers are perhaps more reluctant to do so.

Campbell's hand is, I believe, quite obvious in the early work of the greatest of all writers of the Golden Age, Robert A. Heinlein. *All*, included in this volume, became "Sixth Column" by Heinlein, published under the pseudonym of Anson MacDonald, in the January, February, and March 1941 issues of *Astounding*.

The example of Campbell's golden prescience that struck me most forcibly in the stories of this collection occurs in *The Space Beyond*. There, Campbell mentions that lithium bombarded with protons gives off alpha particles and that beryllium bombarded with alpha particles gives off protons and that the two mixed together can keep each other going in a "self-maintaining atomic explosion."

Actually, this is not so. It takes a high-energy proton to initiate the lithium reaction and beryllium releases low-energy protons; at any rate, protons with too low an energy to break down the lithium. And the same is true in reverse for the alpha particles.

Nevertheless, the suggestion is remarkable. It was made in the mid-thirties and surely not many people were then thinking of the possibility of a nuclear chain reaction, which is what Campbell was suggesting. Eventually, not many years after *The Space Beyond* was written, a practical nuclear chain reaction *was* discovered, that of uranium fission. It was practical precisely because it worked under the impetus of *low*-energy neutrons.

Campbell's brightness in seeing the importance of the nuclear chain reaction may well explain the most remarkable of his predictive visions. During World War II, he kept insisting that nuclear power would be developed before the war's end. Once he heard of the discovery of uranium fission, his understanding of nuclear chain reactions made the atomic bomb seem to him a natural consequence. This was also true for the physicist, Leo Szilard, but for practically no one else.

Campbell went on to inspire a series of stories by other authors on the subject of power through uranium fission, the most notable being "Blowups Happen" by Robert A. Heinlein, "Nerves" by Lester del Rey, and "Deadline" by Cleve Cartmill. (These all appeared in *Astounding*, in the September 1940, September 1942, and March 1944 issues respectively.)

Campbell was eventually investigated by a suspicious American government for knowing too much, but it was easy for him to demonstrate that he didn't know too much —it was the world that knew too little.

With characteristic cosmic-optimism, Campbell carried nuclear power forward to its extremes without ever considering its danger. To control nuclear power meant, to him in *All*, the ability to cure disease miraculously; although, alas, the reality has shown us that radiation is the most deadly potential *producer* of disease the world has ever known.

In fact, there is a peculiar blind spot in prediction that affects us all, even Campbell. One sees the extrapolations of the present in a straight-line way. One misses the surprises.

In *All*, Campbell lists the few chemical specifics humanity had developed by the early 1930s and moves directly forward to nuclear panaceas—without ever foreseeing the antibiotics. And yet, I distinctly remember sitting with him in his office once, before antibiotics had been discovered, and listening to him tell me that since almost all pathogenic bacteria were destroyed in the soil, there must be substances in soil bacteria that would destroy harmful germs and cure disease.

In a way, Campbell's vision of nuclear power was self-defeating. Lured by his success there, he went on to attempt to lead the way into a morass of semi-mystical pathways, through psi and related subjects, from which he never entirely emerged.

Campbell's love of bigness showed itself at its most glamorous and remarkable in his tendency to describe astronomical bodies of the largest variety in dramatic but utterly realistic prose. It is here, for instance, that he shines in *The Space Beyond* and in *Marooned*.

But there, Campbell was, at times, betrayed. In the forty years since these stories were written, astronomy has made strides (thanks to radio telescopes and planetary probes) that not even Campbell could have foreseen, and the result has been to dwarf even the most liberal imaginations of earlier generations.

Campbell describes the super-giant stars vividly and beautifully in *The Space Beyond* and, indeed, they steal the show in that novelette. Making them Cepheids adds to the supernal glory (even though Campbell has the notion, it seems, that the more massive a Cepheid the shorter its period, when it is the reverse that is true).

However, no such super-star could exist by modern notions—or, indeed, by the astronomical notions of the time at which the story was written. In the 1920s, Arthur

S. Eddington advanced the mass-luminosity law which made it quite clear that stars very much more massive than our Sun could not exist. The radiation pressure from within would cause them to explode at once. In the case of a star as large as those Campbell describes, the result would be an immediate supernova.

Furthermore, even if a star as massive as Campbell's super-giants could be imagined to hang together, the rate of consumption of hydrogen fuel that would be required to keep it glowing at its incredible level would probably drag it through its entire stay in the main sequence for a hundred thousand years. It would only be during that stay that planets could form and evolve in a fashion that would produce life as we know it and if they had formed when the star itself had (at the appropriately colossal distance), there would simply have been no time for the planet to evolve any life at all, to say nothing of advanced intelligences.

Imagine what Campbell could have done had he been able to write the story a generation later. In place of such super-giant stars, even groups of them, he could have had a quasar—an entire galactic center of millions of stars interacting in some fashion to form something as far beyond a star as a star is beyond a planet.

Or he could have imagined his stars collapsing (as they would surely have done) into black holes. Given an area in space where there were black holes by the dozens, whatever problems would have arisen, as sure as Campbell was Campbell, they would have been solved.

Or perhaps, he would have had his environment filled with a white hole—that area in space where the matter endlessly pushing into a black hole somewhere else is emerging in great gouts of radiating energy. Perhaps a quasar is a white hole and he could have combined concepts and driven through space and time by using the cosmic ferry of a black hole.

And if, since these stories were written, our knowledge of the Universe has increased a thousandfold, our knowledge of our own Solar system has been refined ten-thousandfold. We have mapped, in detail, the hidden side of the Moon, and men have stood upon our satellite's surface. Unmanned probes have landed on Mars and Venus, and the surfaces of Mars and Mercury have been mapped in detail, as well as those of the tiny Martian satellites, Phobos and Deimos. Jupiter has been seen at short distances, and a probe is gliding its way to Saturn even as I write.

How does *Marooned* seem in the light of all this?

We must begin by forgetting about "synthium" that beautiful example of one mainstay of early science fiction—the wonder-metal. Element 101 has indeed been discovered since Campbell wrote *Marooned* but it is named mendelevium and it is unstable, as are all elements beyond atomic number 83. Even if it were stable, we know what its properties would be like, and they would be nothing like those of synthium. In fact, the properties of no conceivable metal in the real world would be like those of synthium.

Next, there is another old standby—the difficulty of getting past the asteriod belt. I used that one myself in my very first published story "Marooned Off Vesta." The asteroid belt, however, is a paper tiger. The material in it is strewn so widely over so vast a volume that any spaceship going through it is not at all likely to see anything of visible size. The Jupiter-probes, Pioneer 10 and Pioneer 11, went through without trouble and detected *less* dust than had been expected.

Still a third commonplace of science fiction was its tendency toward water-oxygen chauvinism. Almost every world encountered in science fiction stories had its water ocean and its oxygen atmosphere.

Campbell needed an atmosphere for Ganymede, so he gave it one, but I think he knew better. Any gases in the vicinity of that satellite exist only in traces. However, Campbell was probably correct in placing quantities of ice on its surface. The low density of Ganymede and of its sister-world Callisto make the presence of such materials very likely. Campbell makes the ices those of water and carbon dioxide. It is likely, however, that frozen ammonia is there rather than frozen carbon dioxide.

And what about Jupiter? Campbell suggests that this could only be explored with something like synthium since without it, ships could not pass the asteroid belt and could not even penetrate to the depths of Earth's own ocean. Not so, for within a quarter-century after the story had been written, not only had the asteroid belt been shorn of its terrors, but human beings had made it down to the deepest abyss of the ocean in bathyscaphes—and without synthium.

But Jupiter itself is a harder nut, and Campbell portrays its giant intractable nature gloriously well. He is wrong in details, inevitably. He describes its atmosphere as mostly nitrogen and water with helium and "some hydrogen." Later on, he describes the hydrogen content as "a minute trace" and places a rather larger quantity of free oxygen there.

Undoubtedly, there is water in the Jovian atmosphere; it has been detected. So has helium been detected, but not nitrogen, and certainly not oxygen. Ammonia and methane, which Campbell doesn't mention, are present, but the major component is *hydrogen*. In fact, all of Jupiter is at least 90 percent hydrogen, mostly in the liquid form.

Campbell correctly assumes there is a greenhouse effect in Jupiter's atmosphere; that solar radiation is trapped and that the temperature is higher than it might otherwise be. But he has his heroes in the arctic zone where he describes it as fiercely cold.

Thanks to Jupiter-probe data, gathered in 1974, however, we believe that the temperature of Jupiter rises steadily as one penetrates the atmosphere. Six hundred miles below the cloud layer, the temperature is already 3600 C. It seems quite likely that by the time the ship had penetrated to a depth at which the atmosphere had become dense enough to resist further penetration, the problem would be heat and not cold.

But what's the difference? Whenever a story is placed at the edge of science as it is known at the time, and whenever the author allows his imagination to steer him forward as best it can, making intelligent or dramatic extrapolations—the advance of real science is bound to outmode him in spots. This must be accepted, and to be wise after the event, as I have been here, or to shine in hindsight, as I do, is of no significance.

The question is this: Were Campbell's extrapolations, whether right or wrong, nevertheless intelligent and dramatic? And the answer is: A thousand times, yes!

Campbell might be outwritten by many others, in and out of science fiction, in terms of characterization, plot, and dialog, but no one ever outdid him in visualizing the grandeur of the Universe.

MAROONED

I

In August 2133, Robert Randall discovered *synthium*. He announced simply that he had created element 101, which had, according to his modest report, "unusually interesting properties." Since civilization has been based on metals for the past seven thousand years, and synthium's "unusually interesting properties" included such things as its unheard of (and, because they had no machines at the time capable of determining it) undeterminedly great tensile strength, and its crystalline, transparent allotropic form with a strength only slightly less, Randall was most unnecessarily modest in his claims.

That was several years after the last expedition to Jupiter had been destroyed by the customary meteor, and the last of Stephenson's three ships was tastefully draped over an asteroid. Naturally there were half a dozen expeditions trying to get the Interplanetary Committee's consent to a new expedition. Bar Corliss had been trying patiently for four and a half years. Jimmie Mattorn had been trying to get permission for four of their "Explorer" type ships. They'd been turned down regularly and with punctuality by the Committee, because *parium* was the latest word in strong materials at the time—something like two and a quarter million pounds to the square inch. Good, but not good enough to stop a really determined meteor, of course—and most of those found out Jupiter's way were very determined.

Then too, parium fuel tanks had a nasty habit of "failing" when one of the overanxious explorers loaded a twenty-ton tank with thirty-seven tons.

All in all, Jupiter kept pretty much to himself. Only one ship got past the asteroid belt—they couldn't dodge out of the plane of the ecliptic in those days, because that meant taking more fuel for the dodging. Erickson did it. He fell back into the Minor Orbits some six years later, and the bodies of the crew were retrieved by the tow-cruiser "Maximum," which pleased the widows to some extent.

But Randall's mild "unusual properties" hid a world

of high-explosive punch. Since all of the explorer's gang was looking for the slightest thing in that line, undoubtedly they all read the line. Somewhere or other, though, Bar Corliss had met Randall. He read the thing, and he suddenly got a mental picture of Randall: a little sandy-haired man with pale-blue eyes and a pale-sandy mustache, rather moth-eaten in appearance, slightly stained by weather and his favorite pipe, wearing clothes apparently made by the American Packaging Bag company, fitted by the oldest of tailors, Guess and Gosh, and dyed by Laboratory Fumes. And he remembered him as the discoverer of triconite—familiarly known as "tricky-nite" and described by him as a "rather powerful explosive."

So Corliss wandered down to Pittsburgh and American Metals. Randall had a piece of the stuff, paper thin and impossibly strong. Corliss looked at it, and grunted. It was the early product, not the refined stuff they turn out today, and it looked like a poorly tanned pig's hide with the measles. Randall went into one of his quiet raptures about it, and tried to demonstrate its strength. He was rather handicapped, because he'd already broken most of the testing machines trying it out, and they hadn't built a new one yet. But Corliss wasn't slow in getting the possibilities. Corliss had more money than he could spend then anyway, so he found out what American Metal's total possible production of synthium would be, and ordered it for the next six months.

Jimmie Mattorn got there two days later, and Norddeutscher Rakete, two and a half later—they couldn't get in touch with their American representative. So Corliss wasn't without competition on the thing. Norddeutscher, finding they couldn't get more than a scrap of synthium from American Metals, bought German rights to the stuff, and wanted to start making it, and get a rocket under way.

Corliss was already moving.

That was probably why the things happened as they did. When Corliss built that ship, he hadn't the faintest idea of the strength he put in it, because he didn't have the ghost of an idea of the strength of synthium. Besides, he had carefully drawn plans for a parium ship—four of them actually—and so he just made them out of synthium instead. He did make a test tank, and broke down his pumps trying to break the tank. That was all he cared about though, so he let it go. He was in too much of a hurry.

He'd probably have forgotten something in the rush if he hadn't planned on his parium ships for so long. If he'd known how long he'd have for planning afterwards, he'd probably have spent less before. He certainly wouldn't have backed out.

You can weld synthium—they could then. But you *can't* cut it with any saw, or tool. So the "Mercury" was slapped together in a remarkable hurry. The synthium plates had to be cast and heat-treated because Corliss wouldn't wait while rolls and machines were built of it to bend and work it. So he allowed a little extra size over his original parium blueprints—he found out two years later that cast and heat-treated synthium was stronger than rolled—and plowed ahead.

The Germans were at his heels all the way. But his crew—with plenty of money and no budget—got four ships together in slightly less time than the German crew did. They loaded them up so fast that they had to get some of their supplies at the terrific rates prevailing on old Luna.

But the Committee didn't know that; they saw four new ships, of a very strong metal, with very strong fuel tanks of unusual capacity, and a remarkably different course laid out that would take men around the asteroid belt— and the plans were stamped.

Automatically, they turned down the Norddeutscher people when they applied "until the success or failure of the present expedition has been determined." The Norddeutscher people had a long wait. And then, of course, when Corliss' fate was settled they couldn't get approval of their ships, or, for that matter, any Jupiter-bound ships. Corliss settled that for once and for all with the result of his expedition. They couldn't have gotten men anyway, probably, for none had the desire to have their ship christened "Mahomet's Coffin" for so excellent a reason.

Corliss got off Earth in May 2134. The Corliss Jupiter Expedition was underway. A fleet of four tiny ships, each of five-thousand-ton mass, each looking, with their raw, unpainted synthium, like a farmer-boy's unsuccessful effort toward a home-grown and tanned football, mottled with green and yellow and pink.

They were remarkable looking things, stubby, thick-bellied, and quite hideous, with their weirdly-shaped wing-attachments sticking out forlornly at a broken angle.

But they lifted off at ten A.M., May 17, 2134.

Bar Corliss looked at Brad Warren, second in command, with a sour, exaggerated grimace. "Great gang of planners we are," he commented.

Brad Warren grinned back at him. "Forget something, Bar?"

"Only a few minor things—like soap, and coffee extract and antiseptics. Nothing really important of course—" Bar chuckled. "Wouldn't the Norddeutscher crowd like to know that!"

Brad gestured out the port toward the blinding light and the sharp shadows of Luna. Half a mile distant loomed the dome of Lunar Metals and Mines No. 3. "When do we break loose?"

"Don't say the words," moaned Corliss. "Break loose, I mean. That's what the clerk in the L.M. and M. keeps saying. And, dear God, has he been breaking me loose. I've *got* to have the stuff. It's my own fault we haven't got it—and is he 'breaking me loose' from plenty of cash. Only 22.50 a pound for coffee extract. Only a dollar a cake for five-cent laundry soap. And as for the water we've got to have for fuel—!" Bar shook his head and looked piously upward. "May God bless him—nobody else ever will."

Brad grinned without sympathy. "You knew it was coming on that score; how else could you get away from old Earth? Even when the famous 'Irrelevant' disproved the law of conservation of energy in interplanetary work, she didn't disprove the fact that you needed a lot of kick to climb away from Earth. We've still got to climb out most of the way from Earth, so far as gravity goes."

"Uhmmm—but considering they generate power here directly from sunlight in the Davison photocells, get their water by cooking out the water of crystallization of the deeper rocks, and have plenty, you'd think they could sell it for less than thirty-two cents a gallon.

"What's the latest figures on water at Phobos? Interplanetary Minerals sent anything yet?"

"Uhm," said Brad. "It's down. It seems they found it

wasn't selling well. Three and a half a gallon on Mars, and seventeen and a quarter on Phobos."

"That's not so stiff. It'll change, though, by the time we get there. And we need tens of thousands of gallons of it!"

"Well, you still won't be broke," grinned Brad, "and you know damn well the kick you get out of this is worth it. Anyway—we lift off here any time you say now. We're loaded with everything, I guess."

"Make it two hours then. That is—two hours and whatever more is needed for aligning of orbits and so forth. How long did you say we'd have to wait on Phobos?"

"Randall was very timely in his invention. Jupiter and Mars will be right, in about three months. If we take off as you say, we ought to wait about three months, three days and four hours."

"It could be worse," sighed Bar.

Two hours, forty-seven minutes and thirty-three seconds later, the "Mercury" and her escorting squadron of three ships got underway. Pale-blue flames flared for a few seconds as they trembled, soundless in the vacuum of Moon's surface; then they rose in slow sweeps, rocketing upward, and away. They were visible to the men watching in the protecting glass and steel of the L.M. and M. company. But finally, they were lost in the haze of stars that obscured almost all the heavens, flaring brightly despite the glaring yellow sun.

The steady drone of the great rocket tubes of infusible tungovan grumbled and echoed and murmured to itself in the metal shells of the ships. The rockets were marvelously well-designed. There was little wasted energy here, and therefore, little noise. Noise is the audible warning of waste energy. They could not afford wastage of the precious burden of fuel, so there was almost no noise, only the smooth, carefully engineered flow of gases rushing through ground, honed and polished rocket tubes, designed as nearly as possible for absolute stream flow.

To all new spacers, rocket tubes are flimsy-looking things. The metal is less than an eighth of an inch thick, flimsy, tinny in appearance. It would seem that those incredibly powerful and light engines, rocket engines, would certainly burst anything so slight. That again illustrates the refinements of rocket engineering. It is a well-known fact that the greater the velocity of a fluid stream, the less the side-pressure. Those tubes were designed for the greatest possible velocity, naturally, and since that meant almost no side-pressure, tons of metal could be shaved from the rocket tubes. Only the great pressure blocks seemed, and were, capable of resisting strain bracing the egg-shaped combustion chambers.

Hour after hour the tubes moaned and droned. They were running almost white hot, but they were polished more carefully than the finest telescope mirrors, and they were in vacuum jackets equally polished, so that almost no heat escaped from them—for heat, where it isn't wanted, is not only a nuisance, but a warning of inefficiency.

Presently, the song of the fuel pumps started. They had been feeding the tubes on the original pressure in the tanks at first, but now this was falling. Pure hydrogen and oxygen were being taken from the tanks at seven tons, pressure, and stepped up to the necessary eight for efficient running in the tubes. It was a gas—but under that pressure, denser than water.

That might have warned them, had they stopped to think then. But it was a hastily conceived and carried out thing, throughout. They'd raced against time all the way. When, after seven days they landed on Mars North City field with wings spread and the parachute air-brake spread to stop them, the ships needed repair and final adjustment, so much so that the three-month wait on Mars was no ordeal of monotony. There were plenty of trained mechanicians at Mars North City to help them, and still it was more of an ordeal of labor. And still there wasn't any time for recalculation that might have stopped the expedition then and there.

They loaded up with water-fuel—that is, hydrogen and oxygen gases, at Mars North City where the gases were cheap, and pulled out to Phobos running heavy. They replaced the burned fuel there, and at last the "Mercury" and her companions pulled out on the real trip.

So far they had gone. This trip out to Mars and her moons was old, charted and laid out by a pair of generations and more of space travel. Over a hundred and fifty years of exploration, over seventy years of commercial exploitation of the Minor Planets, and still no human being had passed beyond the magic ring of the Planetoids.

You have seen a scale map of our system. You know the dimensions. Forty, seventy, one hundred and one hundred-forty millions of miles are the orbits of the Minor Planets. Then—the Great Gulf. It's five hundred million to Jupiter, nine hundred million to Saturn, a billion and three quarters to Uranus. When the Lord made this system, he used two scales. Maybe he started out with one, and didn't like the looks of the dinky little system he got —planets with diameters measured in thousands of miles, orbits with diameters measured in millions. Maybe he threw that scale away, and decided to start all over with something worth while. The dust specks he had, he just forgot, and worked with a scale reading in billions instead of millions for the orbits, and he used tens of thousands of miles for planet diameters.

At any rate, there are two systems really, the Inner System, and the Outer System, and they're as different as two entirely strange systems might be. Four, seven, ten and fourteen tens of millions for the Inner System. Four, eight, seventeen, twenty-eight hundreds of millions for the Outer System.

The "Mercury" was trying to be the Messenger of the Gods, from the Lesser Gods to Mighty Jove. And she was the first ship that really stood a chance of crossing that gulf.

That's quite a hill, there between the Inner and Outer systems. Nearly four hundred million miles—and every blasted mile of it uphill—with old Sol dragging, dragging, dragging on the other end. Four hundred million miles of uphill climb had stopped exploration for a hundred and fifty years and more.

The "Mercury" lifted off Phobos, with her train of three service ships, distinctly heavy. She staggered as she pulled loose of Mar's gravity. Then she shifted into high for the climb. Hour after hour the tubes moaned. Then day after day they coasted, slowing their pace steadily as Sol pulled with his infinitely untiring grip to stop them. Then for more hours, the tubes droned and hummed, and then they began to spit and bark unevenly, and the ships lurched and staggered like mad motes in a beam of light, skittering and dancing lest some unheeding, trundling rock, weighing perhaps a thousand quadrillion tons, brush them along with it.

And all day long and all night long, though the only

night here was the nose of the ugly foot-ball thing they called a ship, there was a steady rain of terrific, sharp *pings* as tiny, invisibly small planetoids crashed against the synthium wall. They were going at almost the same speed—as space speeds go—so the incredible, never-tested strength of synthium turned those shocks. They were going at almost the same speed—there wasn't much more difference in their speed than the speed the mightiest shells of Man's armory attained, about a mile and a half a second. But they were made of only plain, high-grade nickel-steel armor-plating, the natural alloy of meteors, and the ships were made of synthium.

So somehow, after three horrible days in there, the men took off their space-armor suits again, and gobbled a little food (they couldn't eat with those suits on, of course) and then flopped down to rest.

And through the ships the steady, peaceful thrum and drone of the smoothly working tubes made sweet music to them. The soft regular *chuck-shug-pssiii* of the air circulators and the fuel pumps sounded steady and sweet.

For the "Mercury" was through the Magic Ring, and cruised at last in that *terra incognita,* the no-man's-land beyond the Inner System.

When sleep had restored them, their watches were sharp, sharper than ever before. For they began to sense the *difference.* This space was different—it was the Great Space, the space where things the size of Mars were satellites, and gravitative control-fields of planets reached out thirty million miles. It was the Space of the Giants.

And day by day, the Sun dwindled, grew tinier. And day by day they saw the pinpoint of Jupiter sweeping into position. Jupiter was huge—but this was the Great Space. It was still a pinpoint to their eyes.

They let a bit of hydrogen into the vacuum surrounding the rocket tubes now, so the shields weren't such good insulators, and they put a special soft black paint on the outside sheath, so radiation was better, and the ships began to warm up a bit.

And the sun dwindled four hundreds of millions of miles behind, and Jupiter became a respectable disc, an unchanging disc.

They shut off their rocket tubes then, because most of the fuel was gone. In fact, they had enough left to permit a landing on one of Jupiter's little satellites, and, by putting all the fuel in one ship, the smallest, enough to fall back to Earth safely. But the ships began to get cold. Out there, a planet like Earth would have a temperature in the neighborhood of two-hundred and thirty degrees below zero. Those ships were well insulated—but they had to burn a good bit of fuel to permit life in them, even so.

III

"Yes, I agree that Ganymede has an atmosphere," Bar argued tensely, "and that it may be thick enough to permit us to halt almost entirely by atmospheric friction instead of by rocket power—highly important saving of fuel of course. But—Ganymede's only six hundred and sixty thousand from the surface of the blasted planet, and with the gravitative field Jup's got, that's no distance. If we go in so far before we stop, we might not be able to get back at all, if we can't find water there."

"But, Bar, we can save enough fuel by air-braking to a stop to permit us to pull out from that close approach with our little ship, if necessary."

"Uhmmmmm—maybe. I suppose we'd better. I know there's no real chance of collecting water on that chunk of rock called Number Nine, fifteen million miles out from Jupiter though it is." Then in sudden decisiveness, after a moment of thought, he said, "Shift'er over."

Brad turned to his calculated data, and presently the rocket tubes on one side moaned loudly, a driving acceleration came again as the weight-warning bell echoed dully through the ship. Bar Corliss was calling off figures into the microphone, sending instructions to the three other ships, now within ten thousand miles of the "Mercury."

The Mercury turned, and the great disc of Jupiter shifted till it was more nearly straight ahead once more; almost directly before them, the tiny disc of Ganymede, three thousand two hundred miles in diameter, loomed. It was ringed with a fat, bright ring, the halo of an atmosphere.

"That atmosphere must be pure hydrogen," said Corliss thoughtfully. "It's cold as the hinges of hades out there."

"Hydrogen, hell. That planet's too light to hold pure hydrogen with the tug and cross tug of old Jupiter down there. It's more likely something heavy and useless like nitrogen."

"We'll know quick enough. We ought to get there in eighteen hours the way Jup's pulling us now."

The rockets were silent, yet the ships were moving faster

and faster. Mighty Jupiter was dragging at them. Slowly
their course bent, and Ganymede shifted across the windows till it was directly under the nose of the ship. It
was enlarging swiftly now—more and more swiftly.
Slowly, slowly Jupiter's pull dragged the ship over till
Ganymede passed the center spot of the windows, and
hung off to the other side. The ship seemed destined to
pass between Ganymede and Jupiter. Then, the throw
hesitated, as Ganymede began to loom; a great round
moon, dimly silvered, it hung for a moment as it grew
swiftly, and abruptly the ship was being pulled to the
satellite. Ganymede's gravity was greater than Jupiter's
at last!

The thin bright ring of atmosphere expanded, the satellite grew till it seemed evident the ship would touch the
atmospheric rim, and plow on.

"Wings," called Corliss at last. Motors hummed into
action, and a slow grating squeal of gears and racks
sounded in the ship. The rocket trembled to the push of
the motors. It was rotating slowly as the powerful col-
lapsible wings thrust out.

"Put her on high-lift angles, and throw out the air-
brakes," suggested Brad. "I think we're a bit high. We'll
need a lot of resistance in the first passage to cut our ·
speed to an orbital velocity."

For an instant the rockets flared again, pushing the
ships back into a path closer to the satellite. Then, soon,
there came a thin high scream, the first sound to penetrate the walls of the ship from the outside since the
asteroids had been passed, a scream so thin and cold and
shrill the sleeping men woke and joined the active watch.
There was a new acceleration now, an acceleration due
not to the rockets, but to the great metal wings, spread
and screaming in the thin air outside, an acceleration actually that thrust them to the side away from the planet,
for the wings, cutting the thin, thin air at more than three
miles a second, were helping to hold the ship down to
the planet where there was air to stop them, while behind, the great air-brake was tugging, tugging to stop
them.

They couldn't hold the planet the first circle, and swung
up, away again, falling out of the atmosphere as their
grip on the thinning air weakened, weakened, and finally
broke.

But they'd broken their hyperbolic orbit to an extended ellipse, and turned the ship so their momentum fought not only Ganymede's strain, but mighty Jupiter's as well. They were back in Ganymede's atmosphere in two days, screaming through the thin fringes again, deeper this time, till the strain on the wings became almost unbearable, and their angle of incidence was decreased to nothing, and the air-brake cable screamed in thin-noted protest. Then, their parabola rounding again, they started up—out toward space.

"Cut the wings in again," called Bar. The screaming of the air changed once more, and "weight" returned to them as the wings began the attempt to turn the ship to the planet. Still the tremendous throw of their orbital speed was hurling them up—up—

"If we don't hold it this time," said Brad, "we'll have to stop on rockets. The orbit's so broken now we'd fall right on into Jupiter. If we stop on rockets, we'll *have* to find water to get back home."

"Do you hear that creaking?" asked Bar softly. "We had to use steel gears and racks, you know. We couldn't cut synthium gearing. If we add another degree to the angle of those wings they'll break those racks off."

The ships reeled slowly, they seemed to be turning, the "Mercury" echoed to a still thinner howl of air. Corliss advanced the angle of the wings a bit more, let a bit more of the air-brake come into play. There was a terrific resistance back there—and a limit to what strain the ship could endure.

Suddenly Brad was making observations again. Swiftly he ran the figures into a calculator. "Bar—Bar," he called, "she's turning in now."

They couldn't fly an hour later, at less than 2,000 miles an hour, at their high level, so they descended with the air-brake pulled in again. Gradually, the rockets glided around the little world, around again, and slowly they settled to the northern pole, landing finally at almost dead-rest on the rocket blasts.

The cold started to creep in then. The rockets were off. Ganymede they'd seen as a white planet, covered with barren, cold black rocks and shadows of deepest black, for the air was cold, colder than anything earth knew, and there was a thin atmosphere but not enough for real diffusion. And there were fields of unbroken whiteness, with a strange blue tint in them.

It was the air, what had once been, perhaps, a dense atmosphere long since frozen. When they had settled down on that field of frozen cold, the ship had hissed, and vapor rose in spurting streams. The ship chilled swiftly. Before it had been heated by the air friction. Now they began to know cold—real cold.

In an hour they were sleeping, all save a few on watch. Two hours later they waked to the roar of the rockets as one of the companion ships landed nearby. Then, one after the other, the two others landed. The Corliss Expedition was encamped. Three of those ships were loaded almost solely with photocell equipment. Only the "Mercury" was really an expedition ship. Work was to begin now.

It was strange, the people who had applied for membership back on Earth, and the qualifications they listed. A professional "strong-man," because he could stand the heavy weight on Jupiter; another man, "because he loved adventure," and a professional guide in Africa and South America, "because he understood wild country."

Tad Martin was one chosen, a little man with a heavy body, and fingers as long and slim and sensitive as a surgeon's, a ready grin and slightly-faded thatch of thin hair. Tad Martin was chosen because he had a sound constitution, an extremely cheerful personality; he was a born optimist, and he handled a monkey wrench and a pair of pliers with the genius Fritz Kreisler once used with a bow and a wooden box known as a violin.

Tad Martin was a super-mechanic. His type is known as a mechanician, not a mechanic, and calls itself "tinkerer."

Karl Thrumann went because he was a born optimist, and a chemist. He could play half a dozen different instruments, was a fairly good actor, and an excellent raconteur.

That's the type it takes in an expedition bound to be away from all humanity for at least two years. Every one was an optimist. They had to be. But—expeditions aren't adventure. They represent an unexampled amount of extraordinarily hard, dreary work with the wrong tools in the wrong places under unfavorable conditions. Expeditions are largely made up of fine chemists peeling potatoes and expert physicists washing clothes, of trained mechanicians fixing the plumbing, which never could be made right anyway, and, most of all, sitting and waiting. Sitting and waiting to do something, anything at all.

It wasn't hard to find something to do at first. There were the great cells packed in the "Corliss I," "II," "III" and the "Mercury" to be set up. The sun was weak here, and it was inconceivably cold, far far colder than night on the Moon, or even on Phobos or Deimos. Not because the sun was so much weaker, though that of course counted, but because there was not merely a lack of heat coming in, but an actual withdrawal of heat by the cold substances, the frozen gases, the almost-frozen atmosphere. Cold? No human had ever before known the like. Why, on Luna, elsewhere in empty, shadowed space they used *rubber* suits. Here, a bit of rubber exposed to that air was as hard and brittle as so much glass in twenty seconds. They used storage batteries to heat the suits on old Luna. Storage batteries!

Men had to go out the first day of landing. They divided the time into "days" and "weeks." Weeks was a sensible division, a natural one, because Ganymede revolved around Jupiter in almost exactly a week—seven days, three hours and forty-two point two minutes to be exact. They set one of the chronometers to mark that week into sevenths, and worked on that basis. They had three and a half "days" of sunlight, and three and a half of darkness, except that, having landed on the Jupiter face of the satellite, their days were broken by the great shadow of the Titan of the System.

But explorers had to go out, and they went out in the special suits provided for them. They were made of woven asbestos, because that was both an insulator against heat loss, and flexible. They were padded with powdered asbestos fibers, and covered finally by an inner lining of airtight, finest rubber, impregnated in tough canvas. But between the layers of asbestos padding were heated coils, not powered by any mere storage battery, but by the main power lines of the ship, run by the powerful, light steam engines on board her.

Those engines were *designed*. The flames of hydrogen and oxygen gases, taken from the fuel tanks, ran the steam engines, by boiling water. They were one hundred percent efficient, because the energy that wasn't used in generating electric power couldn't escape save as heat that warmed the vessels. The condensors were nothing but radiators.

So there was plenty of electric power generated while the ships rested on that cold, cold world.

They went out first to set up the sun-power cells. They were wonderfully light things—they weighed scarcely an ounce apiece because they were made of that transparent form of synthium, the transparent allotropic form. Like all transparent solids, synthium-beta, as it was known, was an insulator to electric current. And they were wonderfully rugged and strong, despite the ten-thousandth of an inch thickness of their walls.

Rack after rack of them appeared, set in chronometer-driven frames that kept them always pointed toward the sun. The sun was weak here, horribly weak, yet still it had power, and they had a great, great deal of area exposed. "Corliss I," "II" and "III" had been loaded almost exclusively with them. Those three ships were never intended to go back to Earth, nor to leave this system of Jupiter's.

It took a week to set them up. In the meantime, the chemist and geologic parties had been at work. They found some gypsum here, but didn't need its water of crystallization. They found water, ice. Ganymede was very light to have much water, yet it had nearly as much as Mars had, for it was so very, very cold here the water never got a chance to escape. And it was overlaid almost everywhere by great masses of carbon dioxide.

Corliss stared when he saw their find. A great, rugged mountain of glistening, beautiful blue and faintly green, transparent, beautifully clear solid. "Is that—solid carbon dioxide?" he gasped into the transmitter.

"It sure is," laughed Karl Thrumann. "It's clear, because it's lain there for half a billion years, just slowly packing, and, under the direct sun, melting ever so little till it packed solid. There's a white snow on top, where the pressure couldn't solidify it, crystallize it thoroughly into a whole block. We're looking at a side where something broke it off.

"The lower vein there is hydrogen oxide. I think that's a better name for it than water, considering."

"It is," agreed Corliss. "I've seen glaciers—but they didn't look like that."

"No—that's because they weren't really cold. They melted at the base, where all the millions of tons of weight rested on them. Ice will melt at a fairly low temperature if you press it hard, remember. That's how a glacier flows. The bottom melts under the pressure—heat runs out as liquid water, escapes the pressure, and instantly re-freezes, because without the pressure it's solid at that temperature. Here, the temperature is so low even the pressure won't do it."

"Uhmm—suppose we have glaciers of CO_2 here?"

"No, not carbon dioxide. Water, remember, is a wonderful substance. Unique in a thousand ways. Dissolves more different things than almost any other single solvent, absorbs more heat in melting and boiling than almost anything else, holds more heat per pound-degree of mass and temperature than any other thing save hydrogen. And—it contracts on changing from ice to liquid water, and then further contracts as the temperature *rises* to four degrees centigrade. Unique, really. And because it *expands* on solidifying, pressure liquifies it because it occupies less room then. That's not true of CO_2. Therefore you can't get moving glaciers."

"Uhmmm—but it's cold enough for them. How much more cable have we, Ben?"

Back in the ship, Ben Riley, the electrical engineer-electrician-mechanician-radio-expert-physicist-electronics engineer, answered over the telephone sets, "About five hundred feet, Bar. Then unless you want to run without heaters, you'd better stop."

"May the good Lord preserve us from any such situation. We'll stop. I'm half-frozen with the heaters. Can't you send any more juice?"

"No—not without danger of burning them out altogether. It's your own cock-eyed calculations that said you'd lose only five horsepower of heat out there."

"All right!" laughed Corliss. "I admit it. How many are we drawing?"

"Ten right now, if you want to know. What are you doing? Rolling in the snow? I can't figure where it's all going myself."

"I can't either," said Thrumann sourly. "You'd never guess it from here.

"But that's all right. There's plenty of water here, so we can set up a quarry and get our fuel. How much power coming in from the cells?"

"Five thousand horse—and we need one and a half to warm these blamed ships. We can break down some water for you though. They've got the cells set up in Two."

"Check. We'll bring in a load now. I brought some cotton along."

"Cotton?" asked Corliss, mildly surprised. "What for?"

Thrumann chuckled. "I didn't trust your explosives in this temperature any too much. Wait and see."

Thrumann had an electric drill with him, and Tad Martin had some other apparatus, as well as the sledge they'd hauled over. In five minutes, the electric drill was humming almost inaudibly in the thin air, and cutting swiftly into the brittle ice. In five more, a series of ten holes had been drilled, slanting into the clear "rock" of this world. Carefully Thrumann packed plain cotton batting into them with a little rod. Then Martin produced his flask. "Oh," said Corliss grinning. "We're well below the critical temperature here, aren't we?"

"Brrr—" said Thrumann. "I'm not, but I'm damn near it. It certainly is outside." From the flask he poured a stream of clear blue liquid into the holes, generously. Then he inserted caps in each, and the party backed off. The clear liquid oxygen they had poured in was thoroughly soaked up in the cotton in ten seconds. In thirty the thing was quite ready. In forty-five, Thrumann sent the current through the caps and wires—and a thousand tons of the rock-hard ice shattered off. There was an explosive born of cold and as safe in this temperature as in the coal mines of Earth where it had originated two centuries before.

The sledge was loaded with a will—and consequent warming work—and hauled to "Corliss II." The lumps of ice were hurled into the lock, and the door closed once more. The men went back for another load of ice. They passed the laboratory ship—"Corliss I." The research laboratories had been set up in this ship, now that the cells had been placed outside. Corliss hesitated as he passed, and asked Ben to connect him with Porter, in the lab.

"Hello, Bar," came Porter's voice finally. "What is it?"

"Got the air analyzed yet?"

"Oh, yes. Some time ago, we finally got the last constituents. Nothing new. No helium to speak of, but it was all rare gas. Mostly argon, neon and Xenon. There's one tenth of one percent oxygen, and a detectable trace of water vapor even at this temperature. The rest, as Thrumann told you, is nitrogen, carbon dioxide, a fraction of one percent chlorine, and lots of rare gases. Everything else seems combined with something to make a solid.

"That chlorine had us going for a while; still I guess it's as logical as the trace of oxygen. There's no life here of course—probably never was, and when you consider how active oxygen is, it's no wonder so little of it is free, and probably the combination of the oxygen meant some chlorine couldn't find a partner."

"You're wrong in saying it combined to a solid," said Corliss. "I saw a nice little river back a way. Know what it was? Just a nice, cool swimming pool of Xenon, so Thrumann says."

Porter whistled softly. "Nice planet. No wonder we found so much Xenon in the air."

The work was started then. They quarried for their water, and, of course, for their air. But they were mighty glad to have that work. To Bar Corliss it meant that the millions he had sunk in this expedition were not lost. For the whole success of the thing depended on finding a source of water—hydrogen and oxygen for fuel—on this satellite, or on Callisto. Hurling the rockets across space had required all but the last dregs of fuel. No ship could be designed which would have been otherwise. The sheer work of lifting the fuel across the four hundred million miles of space against the sun's pull prevented that. They *had* to find water—or return at once, immediately, before those last dregs of fuel were used in heating. Not even two months could have been spent investigating after all those millions of miles of travel and those millions of dollars spent.

That was most of the expedition, that. That was the adventure of exploring the planets, digging and working and sweating even in that cold, to dig out the water they must have, and the slow, slow waiting while the electrolysers took the electric power obtained from the sun and converted the water to hydrogen and oxygen fuel. That and cleaning, polishing, selecting, weighing, repairing, cooking. Cooking, and living in the air that was already heavy with the odors of meals a month past, for the rectifiers would *not* remove those last faint traces which the unhappy sensitivity of the human nose detected.

IV

"It would be an immense advantage—" sighed Bar. He looked across at "Two." There were two feet of "snow" on it now, and the light that shone on it was weak and dim and red, the light of enormous, magnificent Jupiter, mighty in the sky, almost full. For six months they had waited here while the fuel tanks of the ships filled slowly —so slowly. They were nearly full now. The men for the last dash had been selected, the trip planned to almost the last detail—as though the years on Earth had not been calculation time enough for this particular feature—but now Brad proposed to change it.

"It can be done. Refueling in space has never been done—but I think it *can* be done if we do as I suggest. To do it would mean the 'Mercury' could land on Jupiter with tanks completely full, not nearly full. The original plan to establish a fuel depot on satellite Five, tiny though it is, and close to Jupiter, still means *some* fuel would be needed in escaping its pull. We have fuel enough on hand now, and it would save twelve hours wear on your tubes, and on the tubes of 'Two' and 'Three' to do it. Also, it would save the work of gathering that much fuel again."

Bar stood looking out of the port. They had had a "cold snap" two weeks before. It had snowed Xenon, a wind had sprung up in the thin air to howl with horrific threats about the ships and their apparatus. The cell frames had been well anchored, and resisted till the blizzard had covered them over, and banked snow two feet deep over them, and made drifts ten feet deep on the windward side of the ships. It was a strange scene now; it had an air of permanence, of stability.

Finally Corliss spoke. "I don't like the idea of using those magnets. We don't *think* they'll disturb any instruments. But we don't *know*. Still—I suppose we may as well."

The men cheered. "Attaboy, Bar. We start tomorrow then?" asked Brad.

"Uhm—I guess so."

37

There was no sleeping that "night." They were preparing. Goodbyes. So-longs. And hungrily gazing at the ship that was to make the crossing. There were thirty-two men in the expedition. And there were just five who were on the "Mercury" when she took off the next day, and shook off her burden of snow, to sail out again into space. Five men.

No more, because every man breathed precious air, and ate heavy food; and on Jupiter that would represent another five hundred pounds of force to be overcome in climbing up. They had to calculate close on this trip. Their fuel would just about make it. And even so, the other ships, "Two" and "Three," would have to be sacrificed to pull them free. Satellite Five revolved at only 112,000 miles from Jupiter's center, and only 70,000 from his surface. On Five, "Corliss II" and "III" were to wait, with fuel for the "Mercury" as she climbed up from Jupiter's cloud-wrapped atmosphere. And they would never leave Five.

No less, because it took two men to operate the ship, and they needed—a spare. Dr. Louis Lombard was their physician, and spare. He was a Doctor of Medicine by vocation, but an expert geologist and paleontologist by avocation, and camp-chief and mechanic by necessity. Rather an unusually useful man? Every man in that ultra-select group *had* to be, had to be in deadly earnest. He was small, too. He weighed only 135 pounds, all bone and muscle, because weight was important—and incidentally, appetite was, too. They'd have to learn to get over wanting food when their stomachs were empty, because they would always be nearly empty. Concentrated, ashless food *had* to be used, and it wasn't either tasty or filling.

Ben Riley was going along, because he was another handy man, an electrical engineer, and radio engineer among other things, with an avocation as an artist and photographer. These five had to be a dozen things in one. And he weighed 137 pounds.

Karl Thrumann was going. He was the chemist—among other things, and Tad Martin, artist of the monkey wrench and lathe.

Only Bar Corliss didn't belong, really. Not because he wasn't versatile. He was the mathematician, the physicist, the rocket engineer. But he was big, and powerful. He weighed 197 pounds—all muscle and bone. He tried to make it 195, and couldn't.

They were the selected five. Brad didn't go, because he was second in command, the most thankless position of all. He had to remain in charge of the group on Ganymede, so he couldn't leave. The others didn't quite equal these five.

For all the good it did them, Corliss might as well have taken the whole crew. They didn't stand a bit better chance of returning because they took only five, and shaved the weight by taking no razors, since shaving equipment meant weight, but they didn't know it then.

So the "Mercury" took off from Ganymede with five aboard. She plowed her way up through space, and toward Jupiter, behind her trailing her faithful escort diminished by one, "One" remaining on the satellite. They went on, the blue flames of her rockets trailing out, till the ship was well away from Ganymede, and falling freely to Jupiter. Then the rockets of the "Mercury" stopped, and as she fell, the other two ships maneuvered and twisted to approach the falling ship. Presently a black, snaky cable reached out with a great round lump on the end of it. The two ships were moving slowly relative to each other, and presently the round lump began to accelerate of itself toward the "Mercury." It struck with a thump and a jar that the men aboard the ship felt to their bones, and clung.

The magnet was on. Slowly, those aboard the "Two" reeled in on the braked winch, braking their relative speed. Twice the magnet pulled loose, to jump back as the strain was released on the cable. It took an hour of maneuvering before the feed pipe could be sent across. Then the "Three" made fast by the same laborious process. Two hours later, the "Mercury," her fuel tanks full, was falling all alone through space. Far behind her, two dots of blue flame marked the "Two" and the "Three" returning to Ganymede. The Great Adventure had really begun—the final dash for which they had spent five years in preparation.

Alone, a dust mote in infinity, the mottled football of synthium dropped. Bar Corliss was about to learn something of the strength of the wonderful stuff Bob Randall had invented.

It didn't take very long. They reached Jupiter's outer

fringes of atmosphere in only eleven hours, on a long, long slant. They were forty-five degrees removed from the Red Spot, and forty-five degrees south of the north pole. Before they slowed to a stop, relative to Jupiter, they would be ninety degrees removed from the danger that might lurk in the Red Spot. They were more interested in learning something of Jupiter and returning with it than in learning all—and not returning.

The shriek of air sounded again in the spread vanes on the wings, high and shrill and thin. The "Mercury" was going more swiftly now than it had been when it touched Ganymede's atmosphere. But there was unlimited room to maneuver in this atmosphere. There was no fear of darting out of it again.

Five thousand miles they shrilled through that air, their speed slowly dying, the friction warming the ship. They weren't falling any more, no longer a free fall, and they didn't have orbital speed any more, so the wings began to support them against Jupiter's pull.

Corliss looked at Lombard, standing beside him, looking anxiously over the pilot's shoulders, through the ports. There was a vast darkness, and below, a vast sheet of sheening clouds, scudding, racing. There was no horizon. It was level, just a distant point so far no eyes could see it. Jupiter was too huge.

"Doc," said Corliss softly, "do you feel the way I do?"

"I don't know, Bar. I don't know how you feel, but I feel awfully tired."

"I think Jupiter's taking hold of us, Doc." Bar looked solemnly at the accelerometer. It stood at one point two. Only twenty percent greater than Earth's pull—and they were feeling it. "Six months on that pebble out there didn't prepare us for this, exactly, did it."

"Not exactly."

"She's not obeying the controls too well, Bar," said Tad Martin, piloting now, as the most expert of them. "I think we're getting in to wind."

There was a different note in the squeal of the air now, a deeper note, a throaty cry, and a pulsing howl was coming in, a gustiness to replace the steady-high-noted fluting of the air as they split through it at twenty-seven thousand miles an hour. Their speed had dropped to about six thousand miles an hour now, and it was falling rapidly, more rapidly than the airplaning rocketship.

There were pushes now, little jabs and jerks. They were getting out of the clear, straight streaming of the uppermost air levels into something slightly turbulent. Only thirty miles below them now lay the cloud level.

At that particular moment, the "Mercury" could have pulled out. Fifteen minutes later, it was tossing, jumping, leaping wildly, horribly in a screaming tornado.

"I can't do a thing," snapped Martin, struggling with the controls. "They don't affect her—she's too heavy for them, and the wind's too much."

"Can they stand the strain?" asked Corliss anxiously.

"They're synthium. They won't break, but—" As if in answer to his words came the harsh grind of the control racks, racks of molded parium, not a tenth as strong as the synthium wings. It was a harsh, grating squeal of tortured metal.

Corliss dragged himself back. It was labor, for the terrific accelerations of the wind's force, doubling and tripling Earth's gravity, made him near helpless. Finally his voice called out. "The main rack's sprung half an inch. If it gives another half it'll strip the teeth on the left pinion, and break the shaft on the right pinion."

The "Mercury" was heavy, very heavy, and the winds were terrific. The ship was still traveling close to five hundred miles into the atmosphere since detecting the first faint screams of air. It approximated stratospheric density, and the wings gripped well and solidly in this air.

Almost abruptly they descended from what we know as the "supersphere" of comparatively calm air into the stratosphere of Jupiter. Jupiter's stratosphere isn't like ours. There are clouds in it for one thing. And it has winds. The "Mercury" was now in forty-five degrees north, and so unfortunate as to be right near one of the junctures between neighboring "belts."

Martin had a chance to look for a second. Below, off to the left, he saw the clouds tumbling, tossing, rolling by him at terrific speed, nearly seven hundred kilometers per second. On the other side, off to the right and below, he saw them racing back in the opposite direction at nearly two hundred. And right in between was a vortex effect.

Martin's face turned white as he suddenly jammed home the firing lever. The rockets thundered deafening defiance; for an instant the "Mercury" righted herself, and steadied, then started slowly to climb upward.

From somewhere, Jupiter thrust up a giant hand. The flea that had been buzzing around him apparently planned to leave. The mighty hand smacked the flea on the back; there was a horrible rending shriek of torn metal, the grinding bumping thump of broken beams thrashing about. Martin turned owlishly to look out of the ports. A great broad flat thing went skating down the wind, turning over and over. Presently another one joined it. Simultaneously the rockets stopped operating as the fuel pumps gave up trying to operate in the wildly pitching accelerations aboard the ship.

Ten seconds later the men were relieved of the weight that had been crushing them down, and some fifteen later the great broad flat things were flapping dismally upward past the ship. They were dropping much more rapidly than the wings.

"Happy landings," said Corliss grimly. "I wonder if synthium bounces?"

"We won't know, I'm afraid," sighed Martin. "I'd like to leave this place but—well."

Abruptly they had fallen through the area of terrific winds. The clouds that still wrapped them seemed less turbulent, save where their rapidly mounting speed tossed the vessel. The ship seemed calm and almost motionless; only an almost-earth-normal gravity affected them. "We're approaching stability," said Corliss. There was a limit to how fast the football-shaped ship would fall—though Corliss knew it was a very high limit, for the ship was streamlined.

"Is the air-brake out?"

Martin snorted. "The cable snapped like a thread when the wings went. The rudder's off too. I don't know how much the airspeedometer means, but it says we're making about two thousand an hour. Still climbing, I see."

There was heavy silence for some seconds, age-long seconds. Then a soft laugh from Martin broke it. "We're thirty thousand feet below sea-level according to the barometer." He reached over and closed the synthium valve connecting it to outside pressure. They were fortunate it was welded synthium, really. It would have been so easy to make those tubes of brass, or steel.

They began to feel again the sudden heavy weight of

Jupiter. The ship had reached its maximum speed, and was going down now at a constant velocity. "Stability," said Corliss. "Does the radio work?"

"No," replied Riley. "It quit shortly after the storm began. I guess we passed the reflective layer. The waves bounce back, and we can't reach out, nor they in."

"Too bad—we could have told them not to send the rescue ship in six months. They'll wait six months now."

"Hasn't most of it gone already?" asked Thrumann, slightly green. "It seems that way."

"The air must be—we've hit!" gasped Corliss. Then he realized he was wrong. There was a steady, terrific bombardment, a shattering, bone-jarring series of colossal smashes. *"Hail!"* he gurgled ten seconds later. "My God—everything's on a giant scale here!"

"They sound like asteroids, they may puncture us—"

"Let's hope not, and thank God for transparent synthium ports!"

As suddenly as it had started, the hail stopped. And the clouds vanished. They were out of the clouds. And outside was only a tremendous, driving sheet of rain. It washed back across the ship with a driving, thudding, thundering wash of water. For an instant, they thought they had struck, by chance, in a great ocean.

"We're slowing still. I wonder—will we strike so terribly hard?" Corliss labored nearer the instrument panel under more than three Earth-gravities, crawling on hands and knees.

Martin looked at the airspeedometer. It showed now, only two hundred and fifty miles per hour—for what that might mean.

"I wonder how far we've fallen now, and how deep the air is?" he asked.

"Only God knows how far we've fallen now, or how deep the atmosphere actually is." Corliss sighed. "We must be near bottom, though. Well, boys, it was a grand fall, while it lasted."

"It lasts too long," moaned Thrumann. "I—I can't bear the suspense—the waiting for the inevitable."

"It won't last much longer," said Martin bleakly. "We've slowed to one-seventy-nine now."

A strange look came over Corliss's face. He looked out. The rain seemed to have stopped, momentarily; they were no longer rushing through it. There was something else out there, though. Suddenly the ship jarred slightly, and a great, sprawled thing hung limp and brown across the ports—obscuring the view. Corliss looked at it thoughtfully for the instant before it was ripped away by the air streaming past.

There was a new sound, growing slowly. The howl of torn air was growing deeper in tone now, heavy and thick, almost a groan. And—intermingled with it a slow, heavy creak and groan, a straining settling, a slow, jarring vibration through all the ship. The fabric of the ship was creaking with the colossal strain upon it. Corliss was first to recognize it.

"Martin—Martin—" he said softly. "Open the barometer valve—just a trifle—let a little air in." Silently, Martin did it. The needle crept over on the gage—over and over and over. It struck the stop pin at five times atmospheric pressure. Some fifteen seconds later there was a dull explosion; the barometer shattered, and a roaring, terrific thunder of incoming gas sounded from the synthium valve. Martin closed it as the ship's atmosphere became permeated with a thick, heavy smell of musty plants, and cold dankness.

"What's the air-speed, Martin? Have you noticed? I did, just now. It's almost zero—thirty-five according to that instrument. We've almost—God!" They saw it too then. They had been watching and listening to Corliss, but now they saw the horizon-reaching water-surface!

It seemed ages the ship fell—fell—fell toward it. Then —a bone-cracking jar as they struck it. It seemed to splash about the ship in thin, airy froth; then they were plowing slowly through it. "We'll float," groaned Corliss. "My arm—but our density's only .94, thanks to synthium."

Martin suddenly yelled; he yelled in horror, amazement, sudden fear of the impossible and unknown. They had penetrated the water and were on the under side. Below them was air, just clean air, except—perhaps fifteen miles down—they saw rocks, great boulders, stones, and pebbles, a little higher there was dust. And the boulders, the rocks, and the pebbles were floating in the air.

Corliss spoke. His voice was very calm and disassociated. "We've stopped falling, haven't we, Martin? Yes? I thought so. We'll rise now, presently. You see—this is Mahomet's Coffin. The ground won't take us, and we can't reach the sky, so we will float, float just as those boulders and the water do—in the air.

"You see—we were too hurried. We didn't make our investigations properly, because we knew that Norddeutscher would be on our heels in six months; the Interplanetary Commission knew synthium ships could cross the Asteroid Belt.

"So we didn't make the observations we should have. If we had, we'd have learned quickly enough from the elasticity and the gravitational vectors what the atmosphere was like. How deep it was.

"We've come down nearly eight hundred and fifty miles. I wonder how far the atmosphere does extend? It can't go very much further, or it would become terribly dense. See —in some ten miles more it is dense enough to float rocks.

"The upper part must be less dense than Earth's. You know even under Earth's light gravity, the air pressure doubles in three and a half miles. And at the surface of Earth, the atmosphere is 1/800th as dense as water. You have to double it only a few times—let's see—it mounts so rapidly—2;4;8;16;32;64;128;256;512; and then 1024. That's ten doublings. If Earth's atmosphere were just thirty-five miles deeper—it would be denser than water. If it were fifty-five miles deep, it would float anything known—platinum, iridium, mercury.

"You see we didn't consider that. The atmosphere here —ah, that's the hydrosphere again. We'll rise through it slowly this time. We'll float above it somewhere—a few hundred feet. The atmosphere right here is as dense as water. Water—good lord—it must be warm here!"

Martin stared blankly at the instruments for several seconds, then shook himself like a dog emerging from a swim. "It's—it's three degrees above zero, centigrade."

"Yes—it would be. The air blanket. What is the composition of this air, I wonder. We can't really test it, you see, because the test bottles wouldn't stand it. And— try the rockets, Martin, ever so gently."

"My arm hurts. Look at it, will you, Lombard?"

Martin touched the rocket feed control. There was a soft thud, then a very muffled, heavy, laborious whoosh. The ship stumbled slightly, and moved under a very, very faint acceleration. They were out of the hydrosphere now, and again in the air above. Martin looked at his gauges.

"Impossible," he sighed. "They won't work at all."

"Oooh—I was afraid they wouldn't. You have only eight tons pressure in the fuel tanks, the atmospheric pressure must be close to that. You can't get any rocket kick that way—and we aren't equipped with propellers. Propellers would work fine in this stuff." He jerked slightly as Lombard felt his shoulder gently.

"It's dislocated," said the doctor. "I'll have to splint it and wrap it a bit. I wonder what effect this gravity will have on it."

"I don't know. We're oscillating now, aren't we, Martin?"

"Yes—going down again, slowly now."

"We'll reach rest rather quickly—and rise and fall with the barometric pressure. But I think we're—parked."

"Can't we get out?" asked Thrumann softly.

"Well—the rockets don't work, and the wings are gone, and we haven't a propeller."

"Can't we—can't we make one?"

"Difficult, Karl. I really don't know what kind of a diving suit we'd use. They never made a suit—or a submarine for that matter—that could get down to the bottom of the Six Mile Deep of Japan—and that's no worse than this is. We have some idea of the strength of synthium, anyhow. Remarkable stuff. I'll have to calculate the stress on those beams—" Corliss looked up at the great cross-girders in the ceiling of the room. They'd been made heavy—intended to resist the shock of meteor and asteroid impacts. They'd groaned under the awful load when the air pressure hit them, but—somehow they'd held.

Probably, had those early explorers had any real idea of the immense strength of the stuff they worked with, the "Mercury" would never have gotten so far as the hydrosphere layer. They wouldn't have used such heavy stuff. But there were two-inch plates of welded synthium as a hull, and immense girders in that ship. The old "Mercury" would look enormously clumsy and heavy to us today, like the old twenty-by-twenty solid oak beams they used to use in the old settler's homes for reef-trees when America was settled. Vast, unnecessary strength.

Well, it served them well. The "Mercury" hung, still a mottled, bloated football of metal, stuck on dead center in Jupiter's impossibly dense atmosphere. Even the rockets couldn't build up much more pressure than that atmosphere had. There simply wasn't any discharge velocity —the gases drifted out slowly from the center of burning— and the ship stuck where she was.

An hour later, Corliss was in bed, sleeping under a mild opiate, his arm bandaged and reset. Martin was looking at his controls, only half intelligently. He was trying to accept that they couldn't move.

He *knew* they couldn't. He'd always known that someday he'd die, too. But dying is an act *always* performed by someone else; no conscious person ever performed the act—so it remains the unexpected, a rather mythical thing you believe in; you agree it *will* happen—but not now. And since all time is only a succession of *nows*, Man never really believes in Death.

Martin had always come back, he'd never been stuck, hopelessly, utterly, eternally stuck. So he was trying to realize simultaneously the two unrealizables—personal catastrophe and personal death. Because Death was at hand now, actually this particular *now*. There was a limit to the food. There was a limit to the air. But there wasn't any limit to time. Time would just go on, in its usual way. Only *he* wouldn't be part of it. He'd be gone. He'd be gone because he couldn't go.

Martin was too much of a mechanist to hope to move. He knew there wasn't a hope of working on the outside of the ship, of getting out for even an instant. And of course they couldn't do a thing from inside.

Ben Riley had given up that angle. He was fussing with the radio apparatus. He was timing echoes now. The echoes were sharp, and definite. The reflecting layer was turning back everything he sent. He couldn't get a note through that layer. And there was a terrific, washing static, like ocean breakers snarling on a rocky coast. He tried timing the cycles of the interference, began to plow it carefully, found its wavelength of maximum intensity. Riley had settled to more or less routine work.

Thrumann was in the laboratory. The reagents were limited, and he didn't have enough of any of them. Reagents were heavy. But the gyroscopes were working now, holding the ship in position. They were too light and small to resist the turning, bouncing winds up above, but they held the "Mercury" nicely now, and Thrumann began setting up his laboratory. Presently he began looking at the sample bottles. Quietly he put one with a trip-seal in the special test-lock. He opened the outer valve and watched through the clear synthium port as the outside air came in. There was a barometer connected with the lock, and suddenly it exploded. Thick, dank, foul-smelling air rushed into the room as Thrumann shut off the intake valve. The trip valve was closed on his test bottle however. Then—suddenly it exploded too.

Thrumann went to work. Under the heavy gravity he laboriously removed the wrecked barometer and put a heavy brass cap over the tube. He fished out the wrecked test bottle, and put in another, empty one. Carefully he ran the pressure up inside the little lock, till he felt he had enough. Then he started the pump that would force the excess air back into the outside atmosphere, and permit him to let in the ship's air, without contaminating it further. For a few moments the pump chugged heavily—then it stopped at the lower end of a stroke. It couldn't handle the difference in pressure now.

Thrumann valved the air into the ship. But he got his test sample, and began checks on it.

Monotony set in that day. Within three hours of their final coming to rest, they had seen all there was to see from the ports. Below, the vast sheet of floating water, extending infinitely into the distance. Above, the murky, clouded air, and finally the clouds. A very long twilight came, and the dark grey clouds turned darker, till they were only a luminous belt in the utter, unbelievable black of Jupiter's night. The light of nine moons and a billion stars was falling on them—and stopping there.

At about the same time, the cold set in. It was just a very little above freezing outside, and slowly the cold crept through the hull of the ship, and into the insulated rooms. It was a persistent cold, a dankness rather than anything else, because there was an enormously dense atmosphere outside to drink out the heat, and the metal insisted on getting down to that temperature and staying there. Naturally, a spaceship uses vacuum heat insulation because it is obviously the lightest. The "Mercury" did. But while she could maintain that vacuum nicely between her hulls on Earth, no matter how perfectly metal is joined, even if it is synthium, it leaks a little. The vacuum, originally obtained by exhaustion into space through the usual bilge-valves of a spaceship, was breaking down. Air was leaking in. The vacuum gage mounted on the instrument board was slowly falling toward zero. And when the insulation went, the walls grew cold, and colder. Presently the inner hull began to show beads of moisture, and the heating of the ship had to be increased.

The chill leaked in. The air temperature showed 94° and the men put on heavy sweaters, because the cold metal walls soaked up the radiated heat from their bodies and didn't return it. There was no way to heat those walls satisfactorily, and the hot air cooled on them, and ran down in puddles of cold air on the floor, so their feet felt frozen.

They started electric fans to stir it up.

Corliss woke after twenty-four hours of sleep, and looked about him. There were heavy blankets over him, and the room was cold, for they had shut off the heat in his cabin bunk. He joined them presently in the motors room. They were watching an exhaust pump, designed to clear the inter-hull insulation when needed, and mainly to clear the locks. It had a seventy horsepower motor to drive it, and three cylinders, one of steel, one of parium and one of molded synthium. It was laboring terrifically, thudding horribly with every stroke, and the heavy steel of the first stage cylinder was bending visibly outward against the pressure.

It worked for some five minutes as he watched silently, unnoticed. Then there was a rending crack, and the crankshaft of the pump broke off. The synthium piston slammed down against the lower head of the cylinder, and started all the studs. Air whistled through the gasket. But the synthium valves and pipe lines held when they closed off the pump.

"Have we any spare synthium plates?" asked Corliss softly. They turned to look at him.

"Oh—hello, Bar. How's the arm?" asked Riley. "We have plenty of synthium stock, I guess, but we haven't any bigger motors so it wouldn't do much good to make it. I suppose you were thinking of a synthium pump?"

"Yes. We'll have to make it. A little one, so that motor can handle it. Because if the vacuum has been broken in the inter-hull, the pressure there will build up till it leaks into the inner hull here. And we can't live under any such pressure. We've got to make an exhaust pump that will keep the pressure here down. It's cold as blazes here. The heaters on?"

"Uhmm—full. The steam engine won't handle any more. We could rig burners, of course—but the fuel won't last indefinitely. I wonder if it wouldn't be better to be cold, and have the fuel last as long as we do?"

"Why?" asked Martin glumly. "I'd rather be warm for a while, anyway, instead of half-frozen all the time."

Riley gestured out of the port. It was raining now. At least, what passed for raining. There was evidently a slight current in the dense air, too, for the water surface below was passing under them. They could see that in the light from the ports, for it was night, and utterly black outside. Great rounded globules of water drifted slowly, slowly downward past the windows. "We need electricity for things other than warmth. Hot coffee tastes damn good."

"We should have used asbestos insulation, or something like that," muttered Martin.

"It wouldn't have done any good. That air's too dense. If we'd used cork, the stuff would have been pounded flat under that pressure, and the air in between the asbestos fibers would have carried heat almost as well as so much cold water."

"Could we pump that inter-hull vacuum back with a stronger pump, instead of using it inside here?" asked Corliss.

"I doubt it," replied Riley. "The leakage is too fast. If we pump the inside, we have two slow-leaking dams between us and the outside pressure. If we pump the inter-hull, there will be faster leakage, though it would of course keep the pressure down in here just as effectively. It'll be a hell of a job making a pump work on that pressure. I'll use a cam instead of a crankshaft, and make it a radial pump. I'll have to start right away, if we don't want to get squeezed first. The pressure here's up a pound and a half."

"Yes, but some of that I'm afraid I let in," admitted Thrumann. "I got a sample of the air out there though. It has nearly one percent oxygen. And a hundredth of one percent carbon dioxide. There must be lots of plants here. The rest of the air is water, mostly."

"Huh—the rest of the air is water," quoted Martin. "Is that how you say it in German?"

"No, stupid. The rest of the air-pressure is due to

water vapor, largely, and most of the water vapor seems actually to be liquid water droplets. There's lots of nitrogen and helium and some hydrogen and lots of rare gases. But most of it is nitrogen and water."

"One percent oxygen—that'll do us a hell of a lot of good," grunted Martin. "A louse might live on it."

"A louse does. I tried it, only it was a fly rather than a louse, and so does a mouse—for a while. There is one hundred and twenty pounds pressure of oxygen in this air—forty times Earth's oxygen pressure. I think I can get it out. By solubilities. If I can just get pumps that will handle it." He looked at Riley, and the engineer groaned.

"How?" he asked. "We have only one seventy horse motor, and the next is the thirty horse on the hydrogen fuel pump. Then there's a twenty on the oxygen fuel pump, and a pair of twenties on the fuel-tank charging motors. And the main power plant won't handle any more than 175 horsepower."

"Have you got plenty of synthium stock?" asked the chemist.

"No. I haven't got such a heck of a lot. Remember we had to shave weight."

"Could you tear out some partitions?"

"Not a chance. Those partitions are probably bearing a few thousand tons of load right now—helping to hold out the walls of the ship. I wouldn't touch them. I might consider the inner lock door, if it was absolutely necessary. The lock doors aren't leaking, by the way. There's a rubber gasket around them, you know, then a machined steel seat. Well, under the pressure, the rubber got hard, and the steel flowed, so that it is the gasket now, confined between rubber on one side, and the synthium plates on the others. That's the tightest joint in the ship."

"I thought we might make a water pump that would kick the water out into the little chemistry test-lock, throw it up in a stream, then let it come in again, and work a water-motor on the in trip that would help push the pump that boosted it out. To overcome losses in that system we wouldn't need more than a few horsepower."

"Lord—" said Corliss, and fell silent, thinking swiftly. Finally he spoke again. "Thrumann, do you remember how heat-operated refrigerators work? The kind that freeze by heat? They circulate a liquid in a balanced-pressure system, with vapor-pressure on one side, and absolute pressure on the other side of a pool of liquid ammonia, or rather, a U-tube of ammonia, in liquid form. I wonder if you could use a similiar system with water? Somehow have an absolute pressure of oxygen and nitrogen on the outside balanced by a pure nitrogen pressure on the inside, and circulate it, taking out the oxygen on the inside. What we need is some kind of a valve that would let oxygen through, but not nitrogen."

"Ahhh—I see what you mean—yes, and then we would need less than half a horsepower to keep the liquid moving, and agitate it thoroughly on both sides! I think it could be done—I must see—not a valve—a metal plate, permeable to oxygen, and impermeable, or almost so, to nitrogen. I must work—"

So Thrumann had his work. Riley had his, and Martin had to help him. And Corliss had only the responsibility of the expedition, and a dislocated arm.

Martin and Riley had no cinch, the task of making a pump that would handle a pressure of over six tons. It had to be synthium, and they couldn't machine the stuff, so they had to cast it. They had available a flame that would melt it, but they didn't have casting beds, nor the materials to make them. So they did the next best thing, they cut them out of blocks with their flames, and smoothed them with delicate welding, and final polish on a synthium disc, roughened and abrasive, driven by an electric motor.

It took them two weeks, and then the air pressure was up to two atmospheres, and the air was rank and musty and foul, and the men couldn't eat because they were sickened by it. Finally, though, they had a two-stage radial pump of synthium, and they welded the tubes on to the broken tubes leading from the old exhaust pump, for these were synthium, fortunately, and they started the contraption. It wasn't quite true, and the bearings squeaked, no matter how much oil they put on them, but it ran. They didn't know how much it would have pounded on a normal load, with a synthium-on-synthium bearing, but it thudded terrifically on this load—but it worked. In twelve hours the pressure inside was down again, and Thrumann, with his deodorizers and perfumes had the air smelling breathable again.

They had to run the pump a good deal, and they

couldn't sleep while it ran, and it was cold all the time, which made sleep uncomfortable anyway, till Riley rigged some electric blankets out of a cut-up space suit. Then they could sleep, but when they were awake, their fingers and their feet were frozen, and it was hard to work.

Then Thrumann announced he had found that a silver alloy would pass oxygen, and not nitrogen, but it had two difficulties. They didn't have a pound of silver on the ship, and even if they had, silver could never have withstood the pressure, save if they used a series of at least ten silver-walled chambers. That would have needed at least half a ton of the metal. Thrumann had known silver "blisters" were formed by the solvent action of melted silver on oxygen, and had worked in part from the idea of that selective action.

The air kept getting bad, and the cold drained them, for only near the heaters was it at all warm, so most of the time they had to sit near the heaters, and think. Only Thrumann had anything to do now, and his task seemed hopeless. When the pump worked, they couldn't stay in the same room, and that was the only room that was comfortable, so they froze most of the time, with the motors room door closed to stop some of the noise, the clanking and pounding and thudding.

They were beginning to get used to that horrible, monotonous life at the end of a month. Then, apparently, Jupiter entered another season. The weather changed. It had been rainy most of the time, and now it rained all the time. Day and night great round gloves of shining water drifted slowly, slowly past the window, and they sat and watched them drifting by in the light from the ports. They glowed and sparkled like gigantic jewels at night, and by day they were lusterless, dim miniatures of the leaden black sky above and the leaden black water below, and the leaden, limitless view beyond. For two weeks that continued, for fourteen endless periods of twenty-four hours. Then a change came. The air grew rough. The sea below began to heave gently first; then they realized the ship was beginning to move. It heaved gently up, then fell gently down. Like a giant breathing. The balls of rain, big as basketballs, heaved up and down too. The motion grew worse as the "season" advanced. In another month they were continuously seasick from the queer, choppy motion. The ship heaved and pitched and rolled. Then—slowly it eased off. The motion grew less, as the men slowly regained some strength.

They began to be active enough to be moody and quick-tempered. They were optimists, chosen for even tempers, smooth dispositions and perfect agreement of temperaments. But they began to snarl at each other. Thrumann cursed Riley for not building the pumps he needed, or even trying to. Riley cursed Thrumann as a fool for thinking of an idea so insanely impossible, for his false-hope silver plate.

And Thrumann—found the answer. He finally found a way of imparting silver's selective absorption to a synthium allotrope, the clear, transparent type.

Instantly, tempers changed. A new hope had come. They could, perhaps, get air indefinitely, it was something to do at least, and the remaining pitching motion was dying. They guessed, wrongly as they learned, that the "season" had changed. There never had been a season. They'd drifted over the equator.

But they set to work with a will, while Thrumann made more of his plates, bigger ones, more of them. Finally, better ones, and then started all over again. With 120 pounds of oxygen pressure on one side, he could get seven and a quarter pounds of oxygen pressure on the inside, and a flow of half a pint per square inch at three pounds oxygen pressure. Nitrogen pressure didn't affect it in the least.

The laboratory test-lock was opened from the inside, the inner door dismantled, and the apparatus set up in the lock. Then the synthium retorts in the lab were connected to the apparatus in the lock, and a new door fitted in the inner lock-seats. And the apparatus was ready to function just three weeks after the start of the work. There were two washing retorts, where outside Jovian air entered, was washed, and the pure gases dissolved in the water; the water was agitated so that it passed under a partition that dipped into it, and into a second chamber, where the dissolved gases came out, as the apparatus was slowly brought up to working pressure. Nitrogen and oxygen and carbon dioxide. Presently the pressure on both sides was equalized, and outside pressure was the norm. The apparatus held. And—a soft, gentle breeze of pure, cold, odorless oxygen gas swept into the room. There were twenty of the rectifier plates, evolving gas so swiftly a steady breeze of the intensely invigorating gas passed in.

They ran the oxygen concentration up in celebration, delighted that there was no odor leaking through the plates and the water solution system. A reserve water system was available for use while the main one was cleaned.

And Thrumann grew inspired by his success. He tried using both systems at once. Rapidly the oxygen concentration built up to a dangerously high point, and an over-exhilaration was produced among them. The seven and a half pound limit was reached, for the oxygen supply from the fuel tanks was cut off, and the process stopped. Thrumann set up new apparatus, and collected oxygen from his second apparatus. Three days later he pointed with swelling pride as the pumps forced new oxygen supplies into the fuel tanks. Oxygen stolen from the atmosphere of Jupiter!

Martin deflated him. "We can't burn oxygen though. It's no good without hydrogen."

Thrumann glowered at him, and swore he'd produce that too! "We shall escape! We shall get so much fuel we can escape anyway. There is hydrogen in this atmosphere—a minute trace, as in all atmospheres, but some. We shall isolate it till we can go!"

"I'm afraid we can't, Karl, even then. The rockets just won't work well, and unless you could isolate your fuels faster than the rockets burn it—"

It was manifestly impossible, so Thrumann returned disconsolate to his laboratory. He had hoped for an hour they might break free.

Thrumann was asleep when the last disappointment came. Riley was on the useless watch, and stared somewhat as he noticed the rain start—and it was not rain. Then he thought it was hail, and for some minutes it was. He looked at the thermometer outside, and read with surprise that the temperature had fallen to five degrees blow zero, centigrade. In amazement he looked out—and in utter astonishment he rose from his seat and glared through the port. Very, very slowly, skating back and forth like a bit of dropped paper, a great, white hexagonal thing dropped gently past the window. It was night, and it shone like a marvelous jewel in the light of the window. It was two feet across, a thing of wonderful fairy-land beauty. A snowflake, six-sided, wonderful crystal of water. Another dropped into sight, and another. It was snowing heavily in half an hour, and Riley called the others. Flakes as big as dinner plates, all magnificent, perfect hexagons dropped past, all different, all alike. There were always hexagons, but some were like fish-bone patterns, like the vertabrae of a herring, and some were solid pale plates, and some were two crystals united.

It was snowing on Jupiter. And it was colder, noticeably colder.

Day came later, and it was the brightest day they had known, for the air was full of whiteness. And not until then did they notice the air was growing stale and thick in the room. They had been fascinated by this miracle of beauty.

Thrumann guessed the cause instantly. The water in his apparatus was frozen, solid, and the little agitator motor was humming and smoking hot. He shut it off, and looked blankly while the others gathered. "Can't you just set your plates directly in the wall of the ship—wouldn't they pass the oxygen directly that way?" asked Corliss.

"I tried them that way. They will—till they get clogged with organic products. The water was the best. I can still work that, and I will, for a while. We must heat the water and melt it. Then we can add calcium chloride. That will be all right, because synthium is very inert. But I am afraid. We will see, however. But first—the flames."

They worked on it, and forgot the miracle of the snowflakes. The flames roared, and slowly the stubborn apparatus heated, and the water thawed. They had shut off the pipes leading in, and presently the pressure was released on both sides, and the tanks opened. The whole supply of calcium chloride was added to them, when they had been flushed and cleaned, and the stench killed. "The chloride will kill the plant-life forms that have infested the water, and it will be even cleaner now—I hope," said Thrumann.

All day they worked, and the next they finished it,

and the apparatus was ready for working again. They opened the valves, and after a single heavy clank, the pressure came up to normal. Presently clean oxygen was pouring into the room from both machines. Thrumann worked them at full power, anxiously it seemed, and kept the pump working on the one machine that was charging oxygen into the fuel tanks; so much so that the output fell off, as all the oxygen was drained to the other apparatus, where the pressure on the room side of the plate was less than a tenth of an ounce.

Twenty-two hours later, the snowstorm was still going on, and the biting cold had grown more intense, more unendurable. And twenty-two hours later the apparatus stopped again. The tanks were not frozen this time, the inlet pipes were. Moisture had collected in them, and blocked the flow of gases. They probably had been frozen before, but when the full difference of pressure between Jupiter's atmosphere, and that of the ship rested on it, the ice broke down, naturally. Now there was only the difference of oxygen pressure on them.

They thawed them out this time by sending an electric current through them. But it was getting colder. Thrumann started pumping on both tanks, so that he got the maximum rate of flow, for he knew that soon this would be impossible. It was getting colder.

The snowflakes got smaller, smaller and smaller till they were no larger than flakes on Earth or Mars. But still they drifted in majestic slowness past the window.

The beads of moisture on the walls of the ship froze that day. The walls were below freezing. And the men were colder. The heaters were working at full capacity, but Corliss ordered them turned off, and the men put on the electrically heated suits. They could not move about so much now, but it was warm, and they needed less heating power. They had to put heating coils in the water tank.

What happened next came so slowly, they did not realize it at first. The snowflakes were melting slightly on the ship, because it was heated somewhat. They melted and froze, and more came and froze on. It built up a layer over the ports so smooth and transparent that, where nothing but a uniform whiteness was to be seen, they did not notice it at first. Air and all about was white suddenly—and the ship was ice. The oxygen apparatus was plugged up, and no amount of thawing the tubes would clear them. The ice was outside.

That was how they found the ice. Day after day passed, and the ice remained. A week went by, and the uniform whiteness was all there was outside. Two weeks went by—a month.

Corliss guessed it finally, and ordered a slight trial of the rockets under very low power. There was a sudden explosion, the roar of a ruptured rocket tube. "Turn it off, Martin. It's no good. We're stuck more than ever. I wonder—how thick is it?" He looked out of the port.

"How thick is what?" asked Riley blankly.

"The ice, Ben, the ice. We're the center of a block of ice, and we probably always will be. I think I know what happened. You know we figured that Jupiter was above freezing because the blanket of atmosphere was so deep that the sun's heat and light that got in as short-wavelength light never got out because it was turned into long-wave heat, and stopped, held prisoner on Jupiter. That keeps the equator and temperate zones warm. We're in the arctic zone. The temperature's forty-two below, centigrade. We were carried here by the air drift probably. And the snow settled and froze on us, and more froze on us, and more, till so thick a shell was formed we sank, due to increase in density. We probably sank till now we're resting on the great polar icesheet. We thought it was just that the snowing kept up. It may have, at that. Probably it stops sometimes. But we're stopped always, because we're stuck on the polar ice sheet, and can't drift away to warmer climates where the rain would melt this ice off. Oh, probably there is some motion of the ice, but too little to do us any good. Maybe in a million years it will reach the tropics again.

"That does not matter. We are here—forever. The rockets can't melt us out, because they are plugged, and will simply explode, and unless we had an engine more than one hundred percent efficient we can't melt the mass of ice around us with our limited supply of fuel."

"Always—here! No more air—" Martin said it very softly, and sighed. "That engine would have to be more than ten thousand percent efficient, I guess, to get us loose now."

"No—just 101% would be enough—because we would

get back what we started with every time. But there ain't no such animal," said Corliss. And stopped. Because he'd suddenly remembered there was one—a rocket ship! Then he shrugged his shoulders, and sighed, for *this* rocket ship would never again be even one percent efficient.

"But the air-lines are plugged. We'll never get any more air," protested Martin.

"Martin, there is not one single thing we can do about it. They're plugged. What of it? What good did they ever do? You knew that eventually we'd run out of food, and there always was more air than food."

"It's cold," said Riley. "We'll need a lot of fuel for warmth—if we never get back where it's warm."

"We won't," sighed Corliss. "You can depend on that." There was a resigned hopelessness in his lean, seamed face. "But we've been here a good while now. Can you tell whether or not you can send a radio message?"

"Yes, I can tell—and we can. I've been fussing with the set for days. There being nothing else to do."

Nothing else to do. That was the situation of the Corliss Jupiter Expedition. Days followed days, and merged into months. Thrumann puttered and read and sulked and tried to think of chemical schemes. He converted all the excess paper and cloth into sugar, and ran out of reagents. The men wouldn't touch his results, but he ate it, and seemed to wax fat and happy, or at least fat.

They grew strong. The eternal crushing weight seemed to affect them less as they grew accustomed to it. And the ship was stable now, very stable. It was anchored by unknown millions of tons of ice. The ship had merely served as a nucleus for a gigantic hailstone, and now, here on the floating ice mass in the air, it grew heavier. Day and night grew to have less and less differentiation. The layers of ice, translucent though they were, finally blocked all light, and the ship lay in a mass of dark, lightless ice, with only the glow of her lights showing what lay beyond. The temperature never varied; it hung at forty-two degrees below zero 'week after week, for they never moved, and Jupiter's air is too massive to change rapidly in temperature as Earth's does.

Riley watched the calendar, and played with the radio, and Corliss watched the calendar, and worried. The six months was rapidly dwindling to a matter of days. There was nothing they could do about it. The "relief" ship would come. That was inevitable. But they *might* be able to stop it before it got so far down into the atmosphere that retreat was impossible.

And, deep in Corliss's mind, a single thought began to rankle, the thought that went with those words he had spoken hastily when he first realized they were forever imprisoned in the icy floating continent of Jupiter.

Corliss was sleeping; he woke with difficulty to the shaking of Riley's hand on his shoulder. "Bar—Bar—wake up. Brad's calling."

Corliss sat up with a start. "Brad? Brad's on Gamymede!"

"He's not any more. He's on Jupiter," said Riley grimly. Corliss was up in a second. In another he was in the radio room. The speaker was rattling to a human voice for the first time in all the months they had been here. There was the background wash of static—but there was a human voice.

"Riley—Riley—hey, what's up?"

"O.K., Brad—I went to get Bar. He's here. Now listen. Have you stopped?"

"No, I haven't. I'm going to bring you out somehow. You may have had tough luck but—"

"Brad," said Corliss slowly and calmly, "if you haven't reached the region of storms, turn on all your power, and get out. You haven't a chance, and we know it better than you do. If you have passed the first layers of the storms, fold your wings at once, and let it fall freely till you pass them. You'll hit the thick air, and slow enough to partly open the wings again. Ours ripped off. But go back. The air is denser than water. We've floated in it for months."

The speaker rattled softly as Brad's voice came through. "God," he said aloud, then, "they've gone mad," softly, as though he had turned away from the microphone to speak.

Bar laughed softly. "It won't do any good, I see. You won't believe me. But fold your wings, and you will be that much better off. When you get down, let us know. And watch out for the hydrosphere. It isn't very thick, but it may strain your plates to the breaking point. Close off all barometers, too. They'll explode."

The voice of Brad suddenly became jumpy. They had reached the level of the storms. An order rang out sharply: "Level off, if you can, and shut off the gyroscopes before they break a mounting. Are you using full lift on the wings?" A moment pause. Then: "Good—then take a straight dive. This storm area isn't very deep evidently. And you might cut the wing-lift down, for now."

"Why not do as I say, and fold them, Brad? I'm not nuts, even if I do say funny things. The air is denser than water. The rocks float in it down a little lower. We're frozen in a hailstone now, and can't break loose. But if you aren't going to use the wings, why not fold them?" Corliss spoke ironically. There was no answer. Finally he spoke again. "All right, go ahead. But close off the barometers when they start exploding. Synthium's the only stuff that can stand the pressure."

"That pitching's pretty severe—God—that pinion gear is strained. Pull in the wings!"

"They won't move now, sir," a faint voice replied. "The rack's—" The voice was drowned in a rending, crashing thunder.

Silence returned in a few seconds. "The wings go off?" asked Corliss sweetly. "Ours did too. Right about where you are. Will you order the barometers closed off now? And don't try to fire your rockets when you get any lower because the air's too dense. It will burst the tubes, and if you melt a hole in the synthium rocket-housing, you'll die in a thousandth of a second, and we *would* like someone to talk to."

"Close all barometer valves," conceded Brad's voice at last. "Where are you, Bar? I thought you must be mad."

"We're frozen in a hailstone about a mile thick, I guess. We're on the south polar ice cap. Where are you?"

"Forty-five degrees north. It doesn't matter because we're falling freely, and we'll smash when we hit."

"No you won't. The air's too thick. If you just had your wings, you could stop like landing in a featherbed. You'll float as it is. Take my advice and drop some kind of an anchor in the hydrosphere. What ship are you in?"

" 'Two,' " replied the radio voice. "But we haven't any anchor."

"Heave out that magnet if you've still got it. It might do some good, though I doubt it. But stay north. The equator is a region of storms—bounces and heaves. It will make you sick. If you get in the snow regions, use the rockets to push out. But you won't hit. You'll float in the air."

Two hours later the "Corliss II" was bobbing slowly in Jupiter's atmosphere, in just about the position the "Mercury" had occupied. And there she stuck.

"Isn't there anything we can do, Bar?" asked Brad, from the "Corliss II."

"Well, maybe you can, but we spent six months and didn't get far. Our food, by the way, will give out in about a month. Not that it will make much difference."

"But there must be some way out?"

"Straight up," said Corliss ironically. "But don't use your rockets. They'll burst, as ours did. Thrumann has a system for getting the oxygen out of the air if you're interested. Personally, I don't think its worth while. I've got something rankling in my head, and I'm going to start working on it to pass the time. It's impossible of course, so it's just the sort of thing to get us out of this impossible situation on this impossible planet. It's so impossible I'm going to work on it. Goodbye. Talk to Riley for a while. Personally, I'm rather disgusted with you for being a rather complete nitwit, and for disobeying the orders I gave you. You knew we must be wrecked; you might at least have waited till we gave you the details. Then, if you didn't believe us, you could come on in, with some reason."

Corliss turned disgustedly from the microphone and looked slowly at the men around him. "Don't get all hot and pepped up about what I said. It's impossible to begin with; it's impossible to do any work here because we haven't anything to work with, and I think it would still be impossible to get out if I made what I want to."

Corliss retreated to the motors room, and locked the door. Then he sat down and started calculating, and playing with a pencil and paper, and drawing diagrams. Gradually, as hours went by, the diagrams started to become modifications of one general pattern. Ten hours later there was one, finely finished little diagram, with pages of notes explaining each little arrowed and numbered part. Corliss had seen daylight—and was beginning to dissolve the word impossible out of his vocabulary.

He ate finally, having locked everybody else out of the motors room, and went to sleep. When he got up, he ate again, and returned to the motors room. The men in the radio-corner were carrying on a lengthy talk with the "Corliss II," giving advice. Aboard the "Two" they were building a pump now to force the leakage out again. Riley and Martin were trying to explain just how it was made, but they couldn't give diagrams, and they couldn't point with their fingers, and they had to develop a whole new nomenclature. There was too strong a tendency to use the words "this," "that," and "gadget." They were well occupied all the morning.

And Corliss worked in the motor room, looking up data and working the calculators. About four hours after he went in, he stuck his head out of the door, and spoke for the first time that "day." There was a broad grin on his face.

"Riley—come here will you? I think—well, come here anyway." Riley came. And the door was locked again. Martin looked after them sourly, then spoke into the microphone.

"Bar's hauled Riley in with him now. He had a grin on his blasted face, but he won't share whatever it is with us. Maybe he's inventing more ways to use that pet 'impossible' of his."

He wasn't though. He and Riley were discussing actively, swiftly, their words clicking out like the clash of rapiers. And two hours later, a group of apparatus was being set up, the machines were turning out new pieces, and the room was being *warmed* so that they could work without clumsy heated suits.

The super-efficient engine wasn't really complex. It was simply the science that led to it, that had stopped all men who went before. Man had already defied the law of conservation of energy in one way, on a grand scale which was still a small scale. They had learned to defy it on a small scale which was actually a grand scale!

Whoever had first discovered the principle that made rocket ships possible had overlooked the fact that they were irrelevant, relative to nothing in the universe. Since the work they did was the product of the distance traveled times the force applied, a formula known to physics for a thousand years, nearly, it worked out in the rocket peculiarly. The first second it might travel 1,000 feet, and use a force of 1,000 tons. That would be a million foot-tons of work. But later, when it reached a speed of 10,000 feet a second, it would do ten million foot-tons of work, and yet burn the same quantity of fuel. This led sooner or later, by the steady building up of this mathematics, to a condition where the ship was getting more work out of the fuel than was originally in it.

It had originally been shown to the physicists of Earth in this form: A ship moving one mile a second relative to Earth is, at the same time, moving ten miles a second relative to Mars. It accelerates at a velocity of one mile a second, and so moves two miles a second relative to Earth, and eleven miles a second relative to Mars. How much work has it done? They knew how to calculate kinetic energy: $K E = \frac{1}{2} MV^2$. But if they calculated the work with respect to Earth, it was three units, while calculated with respect to Mars, the ship had done twenty-one units of work!

In hopeless mathematical confusion, they were forced to admit that the rocket cannot be justly related to anything, until it actually comes in contact with it. Then, and then only, can it be calculated on.

So rockets had sailed through space, super-efficient engines landing with more energy than they began with.

And Corliss, remembering that rankling statement of his that they needed an engine more than 100% efficient —had built one! The first Corliss Energy Generator. In principal it replaced Earth with one electrode, where power was fed in the rocket ship by a charged atom that dissipated its charge in propelling itself, and Mars with a second electrode that absorbed the kinetic energy of the moving atom to electric power.

The first engine wasn't completed till nearly nightfall of the third Jovian day, twenty-four hours after they started. They had swallowed a few tablets and cubes of the compressed food, and worked steadily.

They opened the locked door finally, and called the others in. Corliss was laughing, almost insanely. Riley was standing with blurry eyes looking at it and shaking his head. Neither one would talk sensibly. The others came in and stared and wondered what the thing was all about, and looked at the roaring three-inch arc that thundered and thudded and threw out heat that warmed the whole room. Corliss actually told more in his laughter than Riley in his dumb incomprehension of his own handiwork.

"It's super-efficient—super-efficient!" Corliss chortled.

"The dry-cell there is running it—a thousand amperes at twenty thousand volts from a six-volt dry cell! The current goes in, and it is multiplied, because the thing's more than 100% efficient; then it is sent in again, and through again, and each time, because this model is 198% efficient, it gets nearly twice as powerful—and finally it's that!"

Lombard gave Corliss some amytaline to make him sleep, and Riley got some more, and the others sat and stared at the instrument, afraid to shut it off, and afraid to let it run, for fear it would burn itself out, so it ran on, and thundered and roared, and they sat and gaped at it. Presently they took off their heated suits because it was getting too warm! And the beads of ice on the walls had accumulated till they became a layer of clear slippery ice a half inch thick, and a wet, dank layer on the floor, began to melt and run down. And the flame roared on and on.

They called the "Corliss Two," and told them about the flame, and worried, and ran around helplessly because they were afraid the power would be used up! The inexhaustible, everlasting, infinite power of the first Corliss Energy Generator!

Corliss woke finally, to a ship that was stifling hot, and stank with the sharp, biting tang of ozone. He woke, forgetful of what had happened the previous "day," and heard the roar of the arc, and almost ran to the motors room. The arc roared on, the terminals glowing almost white hot, a fearful heat flooding out, for the tungovan terminals were radiating at a temperature close to that of the sun's surface.

"Thank God—Bar!" said Martin. "Can you shut it off?"

"Certainly," said Bar, remembering suddenly. And he opened the circuit to the little dry cell. Instantly the arc stopped, and their ears, deafened by hours of the noise, rang in the silence that followed. "The battery ran it," he explained. Then, slowly, as the enormous thought of it came home to him. "The battery—ran that! How long?"

"Thirteen and a half hours, Bar," said Lombard softly. "The ice outside the ship is melted for two feet around."

"We'll melt it!" Corliss almost shouted. "We'll melt it for a thousand feet around—we'll drill our way out of here!"

"Can we, Bar," begged Martin, *"can* we? We can't work outside. Even with power, we can't work outside."

"We *will,* now. Somehow we will," said Corliss. "But first we've got to make a bigger generator. By Great Jupiter, it *is* a generator—the first, for it *generates* energy!"

Martin and Riley and Corliss started making it, and they started telling the men in "Corliss Two" how to make one, and in five more days, they had it finished. They ripped out the old steam "generating" plant, and cut it up to make the new power plant. Then they connected it, one great lead to the stern rocket tube, and one great lead to the nose of the ship. One million amperes they pounded through it, till the leads turned dull red, and the skin of the ship grew warm to the touch.

And the power came from a storage battery! They charged the battery from the power lines, and Corliss roared in laughter as he saw the impossible being done! They charged a storage battery from the power it generated, and heated the whole ship so hot, the water outside melted the ice. And they ran the pump as fast as they could, with two motors, and pumped out the inter-hull. They lightened the ship by that much, and slowly it floated up, up, up through the ice and water.

In two days it worked its way through the ice ball that held it, and rose slowly, grandly, nearly two hundred feet till it struck a balance again. They were free! Free—and with power unlimited, and infinite.

"We'll work the rockets—gently, very gently—oh so inefficiently—and we won't give one single little hoot in all Hades *how* inefficient they may be! And we'll reach the 'Two'!

"And in the meantime, damned if I can't work out *some* way to use the power we've got now." Corliss laughed in vast triumph as he looked at the little twelve-volt storage battery that was emergency power for the radio set—turning out a power that fused a great block of ice, and raised the ship—running a hundred and fifty horsepower of motors as a minor job.

Oxygen was pouring in again from Thrumann's apparatus. Corliss walked slowly through the ship, looking vaguely about him, seeking, seeking, seeking . . . an inspiration. Riley watched him steadily, saying nothing. Corliss looked, and finally spoke, half to himself. "We *could* get out—we could make a diving bell—or rather sphere—like the famous bathyspheres before they used parium submarines. Synthium—we've got enough now, since we cut up the power plant. But how—how to work. A propeller would do fine down in this air—but we haven't any wings, and we'd get into thinner air pretty quickly. But—how to work out of the thing—it will require mechanism—outside mechanism controlled from within—somehow.

"But—what to use—what to use— Are we no better off now?" Corliss stood looking at the greater generator they had made, working only lightly now, discharging to some extent at high voltage. A switch stood open, and the knife-blades were brushed with little blue fuzz, luminous blue like iron filings hanging stiffly onto a magnet. And then Bar Corliss saw the whole, complete answer, and laughed softly. It was so beautifully simple, effective—and inefficient. But he didn't mind *that*.

He just went on laughing when Riley asked for the secret, and showed him what he needed for the diving sphere. Riley and Martin started making it, and the men in the "Corliss Two" announced their generator was working, and started on a diving sphere too.

That took nearly two weeks, with all the magnets and motors and little gears and grips and welding arc apparatus. And Corliss made experiments in Thrumann's laboratory air-lock. The big lock was full of diving sphere. Riley wasn't too sure they could open that lock, with the steel gasket that had run like warm tar.

They sent the diving sphere out alone, first. It was more mobile than the ship itself! It had the little Corliss Generator and a dry cell for a power plant, and four motors and propellers for mobility, and it was made of solid synthium. They *could* open the lock—and the diving sphere resisted the pressure safely.

So they were ready for the things Riley had been cutting out of synthium at Corliss' directions, little Venturi tubes a foot long and three inches in maximum diameter, with electrical connections. He was making hundreds of them, making them till the synthium stock was gone, and then he cut up the furniture—made of synthium because synthium was stronger per pound than anything else ever began to be—and when that was gone, he cut up an empty water tank, and used that. Finally he had to stop. But he had a lot of the little things made. Corliss was

working still on Thrumann's lock—to the German's disappointment, because all his oxygen apparatus had been
torn out.

Martin and Riley had the job, and they hated it. In that
bubble of metal, steadied somewhat by a motor used as
a gyroscope, driven by four little propellers, they had to
maneuver around, and with a queer thing Corliss called
a "mechanical hand," place the Venturi tubes as Corliss
had directed, weld them onto the synthium wall with a
sudden spot of energy (they had let the entire pressure
of the outside atmosphere into the inter-hull again, so
that the outer wall was bearing little strain) and place
them correctly. Then—the leads, power leads of copper
wire supported in synthium beta insulators, welded finally
through the synthium-beta port in Thrumann's air-lock,
into the ship itself. Then—they were done.

That was all.

It was rather difficult, the last few days. Because there
wasn't any food at all left now, not even one of the cubes
of concentrated nourishment.

It took them a month to do the final modifications,
because the thing was incredibly difficult, working in
a bubble of metal that turned and spun and jiggled un-
predictably, no matter how they anchored it magnetically.
Magnets on the end of mechanically jointed arms held the
things they wanted to weld, and the electrodes always
bobbed the other way, and when they were in the right
position, the Venturi had twisted in the wrong orientation.
By the time they had two of them in place, they had to
go back to the ship, and have their leaky bubble re-ex-
hausted, as the pressure crept up.

It was misery those last days, slowly starring.

They did it though, and the "Mercury" was ready. The
ship turned around at 11:30 P.M., 221 days after she
first touched Jupiter's atmosphere—under her own power
now. At nearly thirty miles an hour she started on her
long trek north. Two days later, the "Corliss Two" started
south to meet her, also under her own power, and moving
nicely. And behind each ship they'd spun long streamers
of electric fire. They glowed beautifully. The "Two"
reached the Equator first, and had the pleasure of plowing through the "heaves and bounces." It was not so bad
though, because it made good time, and had some control.

They joined in about ten days, because they rose soon, out of the exceedingly dense lower atmosphere to a greater height where the air was not so dense. They had no wings to add drag, so they made good time—180 miles an hour up there.

That was speed. On Earth, they'd have circled the planet in less than seventy hours at their combined speed of 360 miles an hour—yet they spent 240 hours en route —and those in the "Mercury" were very near dead when the two ships joined, and food could be obtained. Then Lombard and Corrier from the "Two" worked together, and in three days, the men were well again.

And then—in all the little Venturi tubes, the electric flares started again—the little brush discharges that Corliss had visualized as he watched the brush discharges from the knife switch—that day long called, at times, the "electric breeze," never before used. But now the electric breeze started again, grew in power as the inexhaustible energy of the Corliss Energy Generator flowed stronger, and the two ships swung slowly upward, then faster and faster as they left the thicker air, faster and faster . . .

The region of storms had little terror for them now— they had control. They pounded up, at rising speed, for the electric breeze, a drive less than one percent efficient; but what matter, it was capable of thousands of miles an hour.

It was as good as a rocket, really, while a trace of atmosphere removed, for as they reached the last thin traces of Jupiter's atmosphere, the electric breeze became a terrific electric tornado from the electro-static discharge points, the ionized molecules flying out at thousands of miles a second.

The "Two" reached Satellite Five in ten hours. The "Mercury," with one burst tube, took twelve.

But they worried little about that. They made it, and Ganymede too.

Corliss looked out of the ports. Jupiter hung gigantic, steamy above them. Outside, terrific cold prevailed. Jupiter hung giant—and still mysterious.

"I'm going to go back there," said Corliss, "and it *won't* be the last thing I do. I can move there now, and by Great Jupiter, I will! I'm going back to Earth now— for a good ship.

"But that's all right, Jupe," he laughed, "the score's even! You knocked me about a bit—but you taught me.

"Brad—this expedition cost me thirty-seven million, five hundred and forty-two thousand, and several hundred. Brad—what do you think an energy *generator's* worth to the world?"

ALL

I

John Reid rose slowly as the radio clicked into silence
under Grant's fingers. The nine other men at the table
moved restlessly. John Reid the younger snubbed out a
cigarette with a grinding, heavy persistence, slow and in-
exorable.

"It is done," said old John Reid slowly. "America, last
to fall, is fallen to Asia." He shook his massive white
head slowly. "And by Fate's unkindest mockery, we reach
our goal, reach it at the end of a course as difficult and
as long as the course Asia's Nijihua led her men to reach
their goal—the Asian World, simultaneous in birth with
America's death.

"Our goal is reached, Scientists. Before you the atom
burns to silver light, silver energy, so safely, so control-
lably, so irresistibly when we choose. The world needs it,
needs it infinitely for peace as America needed it for war.

"Now—shall we sell it to Nijihua—and the world? Give
it to the world—and Nijihua?"

Young John Reid rose slowly. His face was keen and
his eyes intense; there was in his slowness of movement
not the slowness of defeat and age and despair. His was
of absolute determination, and known power. Blue eyes,
young and strong, starred in the silver star-flecked light
of the golden lamp, looked down the table to blue eyes
under silver hair, thin and silky. "No," he said, soft and
cold, "we will not sell, we will not give. At the crook of
our finger, at the whisper of a word Nijihua would heap
honor, power, on the one who mentioned the secret of
the Atom to him. But Asians will come. They will find us
here, even here. But it will be months, three months, six;
for this Research Department 7–A was chosen by the
American Government not unwisely, not without secrecy.
We will have time before they find this lone, lost canyon.
And when they come this will not be American Research
Department 7–A. It will be something very, very different.
And that we must work out. For we have tools, we have
machines, and we have that Lamp of the Atoms, which
is not a lamp alone. Inadequate they are to strike direct

73

at Nijihua and the Asian World we know, and useless when the spirit of America's unity is crushed.

"One thing we have done, we have lighted the lamp. Two things we must do; rebuild America into a unit, and strike at Nijihua. Now for this we have a tool, and the lamp we have lighted lights unguessed caverns of knowledge. Three days it has burned for us, and in that time we have seen lead melt to gold, raw rock to flaming radium, seen tearing bolts that shattered rock and metal. But does any man know this infinitely important thing; why, three days ago, when Warren Lewellyn first lit that lamp, seven of us died in sudden silent rigidity while we eleven, who stood beside and among them, are here this hour?

"I know, radiations, radiations we have stopped by brute shielding, and brute ignorance. But we did not die, and they did. We know nothing of the thing we have found. But—I have thoughts on that.

"We will do much invention in these three months, and some will be artistic and some will be fantastic, some will be—the exploration of the caverns the light of the lamp reveals.

"We must have men, men of our own race to back us and aid us and hold what we conquer for them. And we must have something that will withstand the might of Nijihua's armies, and nothing will do that. Therefore we must deflect their fury until the time comes that we are ready.

"Now we would build a firm-knit political union of our people, and Nijihua would build a firm-knit union of all peoples for the benefit of his own. To do this, Nijihua has taken a leaf from the ancient books, and from Rome he has learned and from Persia, from Macedonia and Egypt who ruled world-girdling empires. All these have taught him many things, and the first of these is this: it is not swords which hold or overthrow empires, nor mighty leaders alone, but emotions and mobs and mass. It is the race, not the man. A well-fed and sheltered slave is a safer companion than the freest of starving wretches. The freedom man wants, is freedom to work and eat and live and think as he wills. To rule an empire then, each man must have his way in those things that matter no whit to the empire, and matter so much to the man. You have read the promises of the Emperor. What does he say?"

"To each man a home, a wife, a living, and peace to enjoy these things. To each man the right to learn, to think, to live, to worship as he will, so only he does not disturb the peace of the Emperor," old John Reid quoted slowly.

"To worship as we please! That, and that alone I shall demand!"

The nine men looked from father to son in puzzlement. John Reid the younger pointed to the star-flecked silver lance of light that leapt in frozen grace from the golden lamp, and slowly their eyes deepened, and their faces set in a grim, sure knowledge.

"We want no converts of an alien race," said David Muir slowly. "How, John, do we turn them away?"

"If my guess be more than guess, though he come in skin-dyed white as ours, with hair like golden grain and eyes blue as liquid air, set straight and true across his face, though we make him gladly welcome, still no convert shall slip through to spy and warn and reveal!" said John Reid. "We have a thousand thousand inventions yet to make, and a hundred days to make them."

"Whom do we worship?" asked big, slow Tornsen.

"And that is not the least of our inventions," answered John Reid. "Let it be—All, Lord of Things that Are and Are to Be!"

"We build, then, the shrine of All, in whom everything that is, is." Old John Reid nodded slowly. "And All is manifest in the Flame. Yes. We must invent the Service of All. Which will be the Service of America.

"The Temple will be built."

"But not too swiftly, not too swiftly," said young Reid softly, leaning forward. "We must study All. All has many faces, and His star-flecked flame is but one. By the lightest touch we show another phase of All—Lord of Destruction!" His long, slim fingers touched the base of the lamp, and in the instant the lancing flame darkened, shown iridescent, and was abruptly twin-forked, snake-tongued, crimson as new-let blood, so the dimmed cavern was washed with red that dripped from every rock and puddled on the great table, and the gold of the lamp itself was dark and red with it. The cavern was a place of terror, scarlet and black, for what would not reflect that angry terror-stirring red, must needs be black, for there was no other light save that to reflect. And every shining surface threw back the snake-tongued flame that moved and waved so slow, so slow, so sinuous there, to some strange breeze unfelt by man, feeling never the stirring of the air in the great chamber.

"And," said Reid as the lithe, white fingers moved again, "All—Lord of Wisdom!"

And his color was blue, blue as the purest sapphire, cold and clear and gemlike, a tetrahedral flame, perfect as a mathematician's formula, straight-ruled as a clear, clear crystal of light. And the cavern walls were cold and blue as vast antarctic ice-caves, and black as spatial night, and every polished thing gave back the tetrahedral flame of blue, the flame of All, Lord of Wisdom.

II

Major Nashiki halted—in surprise that did not show on his hard-lined, immobile face. "Halt!" he snapped softly. Then he advanced over the low ridge of rock before him, scoured, beaten sandstone, red as the dust of Mars. A great gash in the hide of Earth fell away below him, red as the stone he trod, blue as distant hills, yellow as sea-sand and riotous with cloud and sun and shadow. Three quarters of a mile it dropped to some forgotten riverbed, deserted aeons since when a mighty slide had dammed the stream that carved that gash. But the bottom ringed by Titan columns of jutting rock—isolated island-pillars half a mile tall—was sand as smooth-and-white as silver-dust.

And that had not halted him. Country such as this, in miniature, he and his scouting party had traversed for three long weeks. But he halted, for on the farther wall, half a mile to his left, was a great patch of the rock wall that was not rock, but threw back the long rays of the sun in blinding light, white as salt. And in it were glints of purest raying color, blue, green, pearl and somber scarlet.

"Captain Tiashi, bring the American scout."

A trimly uniformed captain, a weary, dirty American in tattered rags, light chains on his arms, came forward.

"Tucker, what is that?" demanded the major.

Tucker looked silently for a long time. He answered slowly at length. "It's new to me." He folded his long legs, and settled down wearily. The small major glared at him.

"Dog, what is it?" His hand struck out like a flash of light; the echo of the slap died out in infinite space.

The American looked at him through narrowed eyes, his face unmoving. "If I did know, I might and I might not tell you. As it happens I don't, and I can't. If you want real bad to know, I'll show you how to get down there. But you'll have to take these gee-gaws off, because you get down there with your fingernails, and you pull your ears in so you don't blow off. Or you use wings."

"Captain, remove those irons. We will go down. Captain Tiashi, you will make camp here, and remain with your men. Shurimi, Hitsali, Kushkiani; you will come."

Five men started down. The American went first, long arms, long legs reaching for known holds, the little brown Orientals silently stretching themselves impossibly to reach holds easy for the lank American. Tucker led them a merry chase.

Far below, they struck an angling shelf that led down and down, then a short climb down bare, crumbling rock. Then a great slide, a terraced pillar. They walked the fine, white sand of the floor. Tucker looked about slowly, and moved on.

They were three miles from the dazzling whiteness of the strange wall; the sun was setting now, and in this deep canyon the dusk was coming. But there was light across there, silvery light that streamed through door and great carved windows. Tucker slogged wearily along. Behind, the others marched, the slipping sand making their instinctively assumed rhythm uneven.

A half mile from the great doors, the major halted. The intense sheen of the white wall had abated, and he saw now it was a perfect square of white. The square was edged with five-foot bands of crystal, crystal above that shone like a mighty sapphire, five hundred feet long, five feet wide; at the right, green as new-grown leaves. Light in it was swiftly growing, softly lambently gleaming. At the left, a vast, luminous and softly pulsing light like an acre of pearls. But across all the bottom was red, not ruby, but deeper, sullen crimson.

Nashiki pushed on. The light died in the canyon, and by hand torches they plodded on across the silver sands, while dim stars showed the mighty, black walls, and ahead the great crystals pulsed, and the whole vast face of the wall was faintly luminous, as though bright light shone within. The great doors stood open, and silvery light cascaded down the majestic steps.

Boldly Nashiki started up the great stairway, and it rang to his tread like mighty bells, deep and slumberous. Half up their fifty-foot climb he was, he and his little troop, when a figure appeared at the peak.

"Who comes?" The voice of the silhouette was deep as the voice of the stair.

"Major Nashiki of the World Imperial Army, Scouting

Division. Who are you, and what is this place?" he snapped.

"This is the Temple of All. If you be of Oriental blood, stop at the last step. It is the way of All, Lord of Life."

"The Temple of All? What sect is this? I do not know it."

"All is Lord of Life, and his phases are Dis, Lord of Death; and Mens, Lord of Wisdom; Tal, Lord of Peace; and Shan, Lord of Fulfillment. And his phases make All, Lord of Life."

Steadily Nashiki mounted the Singing Stair, and as he mounted, his troop behind him, the song became a welling melody. "It is new to me. This property lies in the Province of Colorado, and is unregistered. Why has it not been listed as the Emperor commands?"

"All, Lord of Life, alone commands. Nashiki, you have reached the top. Halt, for the Lord All admits none to his Temple save those of All."

"I shall enter," snapped Nashiki viciously. "The wrath of the Emperor shall be upon you if any interferes with my way." He strode forward.

The man loomed before him, enormous. A cloak of silver lined with a strange cloth of woven metallic threads, blue and red, silver and green, wrapped him. A strange headdress, set with a one-inch ornament of crystal, diamond-clear, sapphire, pearl and sullen crimson and green that held a bound silver cloth, gleamed in the light of the Temple. In his hand he carried a curious staff, wrought of silvery metal, three feet long and tapering from one inch upward to the four-inch cubed crystal at its head set flush with its sides, a strange crystal that glowed with sparkling light, silvery with star-flecks at the top, sullen red and iridescent pearl, green and sapphire on its sides. The man stood massive and unmoving, six feet three in height, as Nashiki halted to inspect him.

"Who are you?" demanded the Oriental.

"Tornsen, Server of All," said the man quietly. "No man shall halt you. But there is death in the air of the Temple of All for all save the People of All."

As he spoke, the staff in his hands glowed brighter. The silvery flame leapt in the crystal's crest a foot tall, silvery with bursting stars that floated and vanished in an instant, and from the glowing side of sullen red a vaguely seen, vaguely stirring snake-tongued flame of deep crimson wavered and died as the brighter silver waned again.

Nashiki laughed softly. "So no man touches me, I have no great fear of Gods," he said. He strode forward again.

The giant blocked his way by a slow step. "It is Death," he said. And Nashiki looked through the great doors. Before him was a great cubed chamber of light. Five hundred feet on a side, it was, and the far wall was dark jet, against which stood a great graven altar, a mighty staff of gold, fifteen feet thick and topped by a Titan's crystal such as the man carried, cubed as his, colored as his. And from its peak lanced a silver flame, sparkling, coruscating. The right wall was green as the crystal's light, the left a vast pearl, the roof more luminously blue than a summer sky. And the floor was a sea of waving blood.

For a moment the sight had stopped Nashiki. He stepped forward again. "That is gold," he said. "All gold is the property of the Emperor, alloys are to be used for decoration."

Again the man was in front of him. "That is Death," he answered slowly. "That gold is the property of the Lord of Life."

Nashiki stepped back, and his movement was swift as the darting tongue of a chameleon; his revolver was in his hand. "Stand aside," he said. Tornsen stood away, his head bent slightly.

Nashiki stepped forward, across the threshold, to the sea of blood.

And fell dead.

He uttered no cry as he fell, nor did he twist; in all the Temple there was no sound nor change, save only that on the floor was a lax, empty sack, discarded by life.

His little troop started forward, rifles suddenly raised, and their voices were high and sharp with anger. Tornsen spoke again, his staff upraised. "Hold! I did not touch him. Dis, Lord of Death has destroyed him. I will bring him to you, for it is death for you to cross the threshold."

A man was thrust forward suddenly, a disheveled, ragged man, weary and emaciated. Three rifles pressed his back.

Tucker looked up into the broad calm face of Tornsen. "Is that—true?" he asked slowly. "I can cross."

"So you are American, All welcomes you," said Tornsen.

Slowly, reluctantly, Tucker crossed the line, his eyes

fixed on the great cubed crystal of the altar. He crossed, stepped over the dead Oriental, and walked down the broad floor to the mighty crystal.

Tornsen stepped behind him. At twenty feet from the great crystal Tucker halted, and turned to look at the man behind him.

"All—All—" he said, "I never heard—"

"All, Lord of Life, one weary, worn stands before your altar. All, Lord of Life, cleanse him with your flame, give him of your life! Tal, Lord of Peace, one distressed stands before your altar. Bring Life, Lord of Life. Bring Peace, oh Tal."

The motionless, silver flame washed higher, till, like a great fountain, it spilled over and fell in soft-glowing stars of light about them. The crystal turned with a vast majesty till the green facet shown toward them. As the silver died, green washed and spun within the crystal, soft green, restful emerald that reached out and through and about the two, and returned to the crystal.

In a moment Tucker turned, very slowly. His face was clear, his eyes bright with new life, new hope; his weary body stood straighter now, stronger. "All—All—" he said. Slowly he knelt before the softly glowing green of the crystal. "I have hope again—hope—something I thought gone for all time. Oh, God—let me stay, let me stay—"

The green washed out in a sudden whirling fire that wrapped him, and very slowly he sank to the floor, arranging himself comfortably.

Tornsen turned to the door. The Orientals stood staring, rifles lowered. But suddenly they lifted them. "We are coming, we are coming, for there is no death—some weapon—"

"It is Death for you," repeated Tornsen steadily.

"Come here," snapped one, "we will see! You will stand beside me, close to me—"

Together, side by side, they stepped across the line. Soundlessly, the smaller man sank to the floor.

"It is Dis, Lord of Death," said Tornsen again. "I will bring them to you, and you must believe, for to not believe is Death. Tell me, then, what man can kill as these men died? Look at their eyes, look at their flesh."

He picked up the limp Nashiki, and bore him across the threshold. The two remaining Japanese bent over him quickly, with little half-smothered twitterings, their watch-

his eyes, the eyes of a long-dead fish; they examined his
his eyes, the eyes of a long-dead fish; they examined his
flesh, and it was like boiled flesh, stiff and strangely white.
They backed away suddenly, twittering more intensely.
Then abruptly their rifles were flung to their shoulders,
centered on the white-robed man. Behind him, abruptly,
the great crystal whirled noiselessly, instantaneously, and
from its sullen red, a monstrous flame licked like a great
rope of congealed, luminous blood, a snake-tongue of
death that wrapped suddenly about the nearer Japanese,
and flamed about Tornsen.

It flicked back, and the second Japanese stood frozen
as his companion wilted slowly. Tornsen, bathed in the
heart of the red flame, stood calm, unmoving.

"I thank Thee, Dis," the Server said as he bowed his
head slightly.

He raised his eyes to look at the remaining Japanese.
"Go," he said. "Bring your companions, and take these
bodies."

"I cannot leave," wailed the Oriental suddenly, "I cannot. I know no trail, he—the American—led us. It is
night, I do not know the way."

Tornsen looked at the broken man. "Where are your
companions? I will take you to them."

"No—no—I will not betray them—"

"We hurt no man. We serve All, Lord of Life. Those
who trespass against All, beware. I would help you."

The Oriental looked up at Tornsen's broad, calm face.
"They are at the top of that great cliff. There—their
fire—"

"Oh Tal—bring peace!" Tornsen called softly. The staff
in his hand spun, and the small man screamed as the
green face glowed, a lapping green reached toward him.
He tried to run down the steps, but the great song of the
stair echoed in his ears as lethargy overcame him. He
slept.

He woke. His captain was shaking him, looking at him
with angry eyes. "Shurimi, answer! How are you back?
Where is your officer?"

Shurimi leapt to his feet. Hard red sandstone, age-old,
lay beneath his feet, the great canyon swept out to the
left. "Dead—" he gasped. "Dead, in the Temple of All!"

Sunlight, still faintly red with dawn, fell on the camp.

III

Three vast feathers falling silent through the blue sky, great wings turning slow through still air, they settled vertically to silver sand between vast upflung walls of rioting color, sullen reds and slate blues, dull golds that shifted infinitely with shifting, lancing sunlight and cloud. Three great helicopters, the striking dragon of the Asian World flung bold across their sides. They touched and halted; slowly a stream of men came out to look across the gorge to the salt-white Temple of All with the bordering blue of Mens, the Green of Tal, the shifting pearl of Shan, and the sullen scarlet of Dis, Lord of Death.

The Commanding Officer came out a moment later, and behind him came thirty women in shabby clothes, torn and patched, half a dozen ragged children with them. He spoke swift orders to the men, then presently Lieutenant-General Hitsohi started up the mighty silver treads of the Singing Stair, glinting lancing light under the sun. The great treads echoed slumberously to his steps, a growing carillon as the eight men under Captain Chu Li followed, and a private, one Shurimi. And finally the American women came, and the peal of the Stair became a mighty chant that echoed infinitely through the rock-walled gorge.

At the top, Hitsohi halted as before him loomed the majestic figure of Tornsen, Server of All.

The Oriental turned to Shurimi. "This is the man?" he snapped.

"Yes, General."

"You brought about the deaths of Major Nashiki, and three men of the World Imperial Army?" he demanded, turning again to the giant.

"All, Lord of Life brought their deaths, Warrior. This is the Temple of All, and before the Cubed Crystal of All only ours may stand, for such is the will of All. No man may sway the will of God, Warrior."

"Never yet have I seen a God that killed, save through the hands of men. Further, there is report that aside from the violation of the Registration Edict, you have metallic

83

gold stored here, against the will of the Emperor and the laws of the Empire. Is this too, true?"

"Such is the base of the Cubed Crystal. All wills it. It will remain," said Tornsen simply. "Now I warn you, as I warned Nashiki, there is death on the Scarlet Floor of Dis. You do not believe, but believe me thus, that you, ignorant, cannot safely venture within the domain of mighty forces unknown to you, be they such things as man may understand or those things forever beyond man's finite mind, the will of Lord All."

Hitsohi stared cynically. "You are violating the Edicts of the Emperor, and you and your companions are under arrest for these things, and for the assassination of Major Nashiki. The mighty forces of the Empire, priest, are within the limits of any man's finite mind!"

"We violate no Edicts. This is the Temple of All, and so reads the Edict of Nijihua; that any temple or major religious edifice, not saleable, is not to be Registered or taxed. This is the Temple of All, eternal, unchanging. Never can it be sold. So it is not to be registered.

"And so reads the Edict of Nijihua; that any man or organization may retain and use gold for such purposes as gold alone may serve.

"We violate no Edict."

"You need gold because no other will serve! That is not true, you will use alloys, alloys which have the brilliance, the color, the incorruptible beauty of gold. No nobler metal is needed for ornament."

"Give me then, some bit of metal, Warrior. I will show wherefore the Temple of All uses gold."

"Shurimi, your bayonet. Pass it to him."

Reluctantly the man walked forward and handed the bayonet to the white-robed giant at arm's length. Tornsen took the metal, wrapped one end in a fold of his cloak and held up his cubed-tipped staff.

"All, Lord of Life, let thy flame play upon this metal, test Thou its baseness!"

The silver flame of the staff leapt and died, lanced upward eighteen inches and burned clear and cold, the dying stars of silver light tinkling very soft, tiny crystals shattering.

Tornsen drew the metal of the bayonet through the flame, and it washed about it, through it. He handed the weapon back to its owner.

"This is the way of All, Lord of Life. Test your blade, Warrior."

Reluctantly Shurimi received it back. In his hands he twisted it. With a note high and sharp, the death cry of shining crystals, the metal vanished, gone, a powder settling very slowly from the air.

In the silence the Server spoke. "The Edict says: 'Man may retain and use gold for such purposes as gold alone may serve.'"

Shurimi slowly opened his hands, and a rain of finest dust fell downward, sparkling silver rain in lancing sunrays. Hitsohi looked askance at the fear-struck private, then at the Server.

"Your staff is silver," snapped the Oriental suddenly. "Then gold is not irreplaceable."

"My staff is of iridium and platinum," Tornsen answered. "Gladly we shall relinquish our gold if platinum, iridium, osmium or rhodium or other noble metals be given us. None others long endure the Flame of All, and even swifter is their vanishment beneath the snake-tongued flame of Dis, Lord of Destruction and Death.

"We violate no edicts, we obey only the command of Nijihua, the Emperor; that every man worship as seems good to him, and fitting."

"You are guilty of the assassination of Major Nashiki," insisted Hitsohi, but his voice was softer and less harsh. "For this the Temple must be confiscated."

"I am not guilty, I warned Nashiki as I warned you that Death lies on the floor of Dis, and in the flame of All for all save the people of All. I laid no hand on him, but under the threat of his weapon I was ordered to admit him. He did not know the powers of All, and being ignorant entered, as would the savage to the mighty powerplant of the civilized engineer, not believing in death he could not see. I have no guilt."

Hitsohi's gaze was cynical. "So," he smiled, "so will you be forced to admit me. And my troop. But we guard against hidden members of your priesthood.

"Captain Chu Li, place the squad as ordered."

The pattern shifted like running sand. The thirty American women stood dull-eyed, hopeless in a rough circle about the Oriental troops, a living shield, shoulder to shoulder, through which no weapon could reach.

Hitsohi looked at the Server, and a tight smile crossed his thin lips. "Forward," he ordered.

They crossed the slate-white threshold and entered to the sullen crimson floor of Dis, Lord of Death. Three steps the women took before Captain Chu Li, in the lead of the Orientals, reached the Barrier of the Threshold. He stepped across, and soundlessly, so soundless they scarcely noticed, he slipped to the floor and rolled to his back, so his eyes stared up, white and dead, the eyes of a long-dead fish. Two men behind stepped over, and died before the others could halt.

Dull-faced, hopeless beyond caring, the women walked on unharmed, unhalted, unnoticing.

"It is death," the Server spoke soft in the hush. "There be powers here man may not understand, the will of All, Lord of Life. But it is the will of All that the woman cross and it is not his will that you should cross."

The women crossed the threshold, stood silent, looking at the crystal with faces strangely peaceful and calm after the long months of agony, the years of terror the war had brought.

Tornsen stood beside them. "Tal, Lord of Peace brings strength again and refreshment."

A woman spoke, low and tense. "Can—can this All bring—health to the sick?" She held up her son, a six-year-old with spindly legs, scrawny neck and arms, his head a boney case far too large for his weakened body. "It—it is tuberculosis, brought on by the war-gas."

"All is Lord of Life. Come forward, woman." The silver fountain sparkled, silent and steady as Tornsen led her around a great crystal to a flight of golden stairs that chimed soft and deep to each tread, till they were on a level with the top of the crystal and it lay a vast sheet of diamond-clear light below them.

Tornsen took the child in his arms, a frightened child that clung to the strength of his great arms. "Lie here," said the Server gently, and the boy lay amidst the pulsing silver light, breathing in the shining star-bursts. "All, Lord of Life, one weak and enfrailed by the wastage of disease lies on your crystal, bathed in your flame. Let Thy great forces play through him, let health return!"

The silver flame rushed up and through him, soundless beauty of light, till the boy was hidden in its shining sheath. Then it was gone, and the boy sat up slowly.

"Mother," he said, "Mother, take me down! I'm—I'm hungry—" He began to cry softly.

The woman looked at Tornsen half afraid, half worshipful, as she took the boy back in her arms. "All brings health, he brings strength and refreshment. Carron, Lord of Time, who is another phase of All, brings full healing." The crystal in his hands spun till the shifting, swelling pearly light of Shan, Lord of Fulfillment and Happiness faced the mother, reached out to her and bathed her. Suddenly her tired face broke into lines of relief; she laughed.

"He—he's well. He's hungry again!"

The Server smiled. "The child is healed. Come closer, women of All, that the Flame of All may bring you strength."

Slowly the women came forward as the great silvery flame gushed up to fall in star-sprinkled spray over and through them. A new strength came to them, weariness dropped from them as water from the swimmer's back as he reaches the farther shore.

Tornsen went toward the gateway of the Temple, and the Japanese woke to life from their brooding melancholy as Tornsen stood before them, the blue flame of Mens pulsing in his staff.

Hitsohi stared suddenly, and his revolver whipped up. "What weapon is that you bear?" he demanded. "Give me that crystal."

"It is the Crystal of All. To you, it would be the Crystal of Death."

"Give me that crystal," snapped the Japanese. His revolver muzzle trained on Tornsen's eyes, steady as the rocks of the canyon.

Tornsen smiled. "Fire, Warrior. No shot can reach the bearer of the Staff of All."

Hitsohi fired. The Server stood unmoved. Again the Japanese fired, and again. The men behind him muttered and pointed. Hitsohi looked, and saw at Tornsen's feet three leaden pellets, rolling slowly, unharmed, undented, moving lightly on the salt-white stone.

"The crystal is Death," said Tornsen quietly. "I tell you this, and because you insist, I will hand it to one of your men, for you must report this thing in truth. Therefore I hand it not to you, but this I tell you; not five full seconds will he hold it in safety."

"Shurimi, take the crystal," snapped the officer after an instant's pause.

"He speaks true—it is a God—a God—" wailed the man, turning away, pleading.

Hitsohi's revolver spoke again. Shurimi spun, rolled, and the Singing Stair echoed and spoke softly as his body rolled from tread to tread till the whole great stair sang its carillon song of mourning.

"Tashistu, take the crystal," said Hitsohi softly.

The man stepped forward as though to death, and took from Tornsen's hand the flaming crystal. The staff was warm in his hand, and heavy, very heavy. It seemed to hum softly, a growing, echoing hum that soothed and was music, soft and deadening like heavy smoke of the poppy, till his arm grew numb and his legs, and his eyes were heavy—heavy—heavy—

Tornsen tore the staff from the man's grip as he fell to the threshold. "It would be Death, he has not deid, for not two seconds did he hold it, and it may be that I can revive him."

The Crystal of All in his hands flamed silvery, and its filaments writhed and twisted to the man. He twitched and writhed with them, and rose suddenly crying in pain and terror, crying out in his native tongue and rolling on the salt-white stone.

"The radiance of All burns those not of our race, and even at best is painful. But it heals for all that. The pain will go in a day, and the healing will last," said Tornsen slowly.

"Now go, and may Mens, Lord of Reason, bring you wisdom."

The staff in his hands spun till the cold blue of Mens' tetrahedral flame looked into Hitsohi's eyes and its radiance bathed him. Very clear seemed all things to Hitsohi, and he caught a glimpse of an infinite understanding, so that the Temple was transparent to his mind, and within it mighty beings moved, and their bodies were streamers and flames of unguessed force, immense and irresistible, and the vast Temple was too small for them, looming, thousand-foot Titans who watched over it and its men.

And to his understanding, the patterns of the atoms were clear and precise, and the workings of men, and the meaning of radiation. And he was infinite and all-understanding, watching this scene from afar. And the thoughts of his men and the calm assurance of this man before him were known. All Earth, all Infinity was a well-laid pattern, clear to his mind. And he knew that All was space itself, in whom all things that are, or are to be, have their being.

He turned without word or backward glance and marched down the Singing Stair and the men behind followed him slowly, so that the gorge rang to the melody of the Stair.

IV

Nishaki looked blandly upon Lieutenant General Hitsohi, and smiled. "The report is interesting, General Hitsohi. But it is quite meaningless. The details you have given me are of no interest, their hypnotic methods do not in the slightest interest the World Empire. You will answer, please, accurately and concisely three questions? Yes?

"The edifice is a major religious building, not to be sold, and hence not taxable, nor registerable?"

"Yes," said Hitsohi, softly. "That is true."

"They have gold ornaments, but the nature of their use is such that under Section twelve-B of the Edict of July, the gold is irreplaceable by alloy?"

"Such would be my report, made, perhaps under hypnosis, as you suggest. But the metal was dust, and it floated in the air. The gold was claimed under the Edict's exception; the investigator is satisfied."

"Is the investigator satisfied that the deaths in the building do not make the edifice confiscate under the World Empire's laws?"

Hitsohi stood before the Council, and he was silent, his face motionless as weathered stone. The stone-walled room grew silent, and the men stared steadily at the testifier. At length he spoke, and his words were audible only for the stillness of the place.

"No hand of man, or weapon of man that is known or conceivable to the investigator brought their deaths. They crossed the threshold and—died. Beside them crossed the Americans, and—lived. And they that died, died without sound or move, and their tissues were as though boiled. The science department has reported every nerve and cell and tissue coagulated. The investigator believes— no man brought about their deaths. Is the investigator's report complete to the best of his poor ability?"

"The report is complete," said Nishaki pleasantly. "The Council does not accept nor approve the report. The investigator is dismissed."

Hitsohi bowed stiffly, straightened and walked from

the room. In his barracks office, he did as the Council expected of a Japanese officer under the circumstances, and he died with fear and sorrow in his heart, for All was very real, and not for him or his race, as he had known and understood in the Flame of Mens, Lord of Wisdom.

V

Tornsen, the Server, stood upon the great Crystal of All, and the silver Flame of All washed up and through and about him. His voice was deep, and rolled softly in the great Temple.

"In the Temple of All, only the sworn servants of All may remain. This, then, I must bid you. Who will, may enter the Temple. Whom All wills may remain in the Temple for his prayer. Them, he will welcome to his Temple, and to their prayers he will listen, though not always will he answer them in full, nor ever is this to be hoped, for the plans of All and the judgments of All must remain true to the judgment of His phase, Carron, Lord of Infinite Time. The good of the moment, and the good of the man, All will not uphold if it be the sacrifice of the Infinite Time, and the race.

"They who enter the Temple must go forth again. Always there is refreshment and sanctuary and healing, All will bring you health, Tal, Lord of Peace shall bring you comfort.

"But now you are refreshed. Tal has brought hope again to your eyes and hearts, and All has brought strength to your limbs. Return now. Amos Tucker will guide you, and the trails are smooth and the way easy. For this night and the next and the next, this Crystal of All I give you will glow, but on the fourth night the crystal will be dark, and its flames will die. Leave it then, for on the sixth night it will shatter and blaze fiercely as Dis the Destroyer takes leave of it.

"Go now, to your homes. All be with you."

"We—we can return, Server?" a woman's clear, anxious voice echoed in the Temple.

Slowly the great crystal on which the Server stood rotated, the green face of Tal turned past, and the red face of Dis, the pearly light of Shan, till the sapphire light of Mens, Lord of Wisdom faced them.

"The temple of All, and Mens is ever open to you," said Tornsen, and the crystal glowed till all the temple was cold, and every detail lined with a certainty and clearness unearthy. The assembled company breathed quickly once—and the blue of Mens, Lord of Wisdom and Understanding died.

Slowly, silently they turned and made their way from the Temple, each bearing with her a little pack of silvery metal threads, and in each pack were half a hundred tiny rounded nuggets of very heavy, very beautiful metal, for gold was forbidden the people, though the other noble metals were not.

Tucker, lean and rangy, browned in the sun and wind stood alone and last in the Temple. Alone before the mighty, glowing crystal.

"Tucker," said Tornsen softly, so that the great room whispered in his voice, "you will lead them?"

"I will lead them, Server."

"You will protect them with your life?"

"I will protect them with my life, Server."

"To you I will give the crystal. Though, if it should that you and the others must die, the crystal of All must not fall into the hands of the enemy. It would explode with deadly flame. And this more I tell you. If danger threatens you cannot overcome, hold the crystal so that the eye of Dis faces this danger, and call unto Dis that he may protect you, saying only, 'Protect thy people, Lord Dis!' and Dis shall serve you then five times.

"When the sun sinks, the silver light of All shall rise to guide you and light you for two hours yet, and for the dark hours his warmth shall beat forth so that cold night nor dark shall oppress you. Remember these things then, and that on the coming of the sixth night, the crystal shall disintegrate. Do you remember this, Amos Tucker?"

"I shall remember, Server. I—I may return? Bring others here? The weak and the ailing, the tired-of-life?"

"So they be of All's people, they shall be welcome. You may go your way, Amos Tucker."

From the platform of gold beside the crystal of All, Tornsen, the Server, lifted a crystal, cubed, four inches on a side, silver and sapphire, pearl and green and sullen scarlet, resting on a graven base of silvery metal. It was lifeless now, but as he held it in the star-fire of All he spoke low words over it and the fire of All leapt in a mighty tongue of lancing light, and as it died, the crystal in his hands glowed with life of its own. He handed it down to Tucker and stood silent, watching the man across the sullen scarlet of the Temple floor.

"They have gone, John Reid," he said softly at last. The cubed crystal sank to a faint glow, the shining walls of Temple faded till a vari-colored dusk crept in, and the blue of Mens across the ceiling became a midnight sky, crystal clear. From a scarcely visible doorway in the wall of jet, John Reid the elder came in a robe of sapphire blue with cloak of azure metal threads, his silver hair hidden under a headdress similar to that which Tornsen, Server of All, wore save that it too was of blue metal, and the tiny, cubed crystal set in it was the five-faced cube of All, changed only in that the sapphire tetrahedral flame of Mens, Lord of Wisdom shone directly forward, blue as the steadfast eyes in the lined old face. Behind came the green-clad figure of Robert Blake, Tal, Lord of Peace. Tall as Tornsen himself, but leaner, and the face under his headdress was lined and graven with the thousand marks of Carron, Lord of Time, cut deep and sharp with a chisel that Tammar, Lady of Mercy, had tempered and guided. His deep-set eyes were green as the cloak he wore, with a glow of human understanding behind them.

Young John Reid entered, his bronze hair hidden under the sullen color of Dis, Lord of Destruction, his stern, determined face gave warning of the character of the man, just to the ultimate but lacking somewhat in understanding of human failure. To him, where success belonged by all law of science and probability, no excuse of human weakness was sound. A man himself unlimited in endurance and determination willing, ready to drive his iron-muscled, iron-nerved body beyond human endurance in a cause he found just, he looked in others for the same, and catalogued it weakness when they failed.

John Reid wore the scarlet of Dis.

Behind him the others entered in the costumes of Temple Servers, simple robes with cape and headdress of spun metal. They wore the cubed crystals of All in their headdress, but their robes were of a simple white cloth.

"There were none satisfactory, Tal?" asked Tornsen, turning to Robert Blake.

Slowly the psychologist shook his head. "None, there will be others who come within the week."

"I suggested to none of them that they spread word of Temple of All."

"Wherefore the word will spread more swiftly, if that may be. And the lad, Charles Sherman went away healed, active. The simple cold men have disregarded too long to note as a miracle the cure that made three small girls stop coughing in five minutes time. But tuberculosis they know and dread, the aftereffects of the gas. There are many who suffer that and will seek this temple with all speed when Charles Sherman returns."

"They will scoff."

"And come that they may see through the trickery, and thus scoff louder. We need yet a Tammar, Lady of Mercy and Shan, Lord of Fullfillment. Grant Murray of the Station is dead, dead in the mob that felled America at last, or Shan would be with us today.

"But it is not wise to make hasty choice."

"We are fortunate to find four who fitted so well," said old John quietly.

"We are fortunate, we built the Gods." Blake looked toward the old man, smiling. "We built to fit two patterns, a pattern of men and a pattern of forces, but there are limits to our molding. We will not lack for choice soon, I swear that."

"That is the need that created the gods," old John sighed. "Let they who come be strong, though, if we would do our work well and quickly."

VI

The sun was warmer when they came, not the strong, but the weak, for the strong of America were gone, or imprisoned workers rebuilding wrecked factories and drowned mines. They came down the dry gash of many colors along the silver sands as the sun sank and deep shadows crossed the gorge. Before them the shining crystal front shone, a mighty beacon, and the Singing Stair was a silvery cascade that shone in the light from the great doors of the Temple of All. Multicolored shadows lay on the sands, shadows in blue and green and pearly light.

Amos Tucker led them, a poor straggling of blasted men and broken women, and weary women with racked children in their arms or crying at their sides. These, the weak, believed, for it was hope, the only hope there was for them. The medicine of the World Empire was not for them yet. Their own medical men were gone, dead at war or concentrated in the hospitals of the workers by the World Empire's will and Nijihua's. There was no help for them, save here, and they did not truly believe it could be even here. But they would try.

The Singing Stair rang again to the tread of Amos Tucker, and the men behind him, and the women with them. Tornsen stood at the threshold and welcomed them as they entered. The Crystal of Shan, Lord of Hope and Fulfillment faced the entrance as they entered and their hearts lifted to its glow. As they entered their shoulders straightened, and the load of fatigue fell from them. In the empty air in the center of the great Cube Temple sound began to vibrate, soft, scarce audible minor notes that rose and rose from key to key, became joyful trumpetings with a vast chorus of half-understood voices shouting their joys. And where the music sang its crystal notes a light grew and increased as the music, a light pure green, green as fresh spring forests, and it waxed and waned slowly in the empty air as the people watched, quiet and untroubled.

From the jet wall, merging through it seemingly, Tal himself came, tall and clad in green, sparkling clear, and

96

his crystal glowed with his cool green light as he stepped up to the high altar, up the golden stair that sang, a great golden xylophone to his tread till he stood on the crystal in the silver of All, and the silvery light tinged slightly to the green of Tal, Lord of Peace.

Tornsen, the Server joined him, and as he stepped to the silvery light, the jet wall faded behind the sapphire blue shape of Mens, Lord of Wisdom. Slowly he climbed the stair, till he too stood on the Crystal of All. The music of the air became crystalline, precise movements of notes that marched and countermarched in ordered ranks in the air, precise and perfect as the immutable laws of Truth. The Temple glowed in the blue light of Mens, and the blue crystal face shot out a tetrahedral crystal of light in salute to its Lord.

From the top of the crystal, Mens lowered his staff till the tetrahedral flame pointed toward the people on the Temple floor, and the blue light swept over them.

And in their minds came the understanding of the infinite Lord of Infinity, All, Lord of Life. They glimpsed the myriad worlds of infinity, and understood them, and they understood in that instant their own longings, their own needs, and the infinite justice of All.

And the Flame of Mens died, and they were content in their understanding. The Server spoke.

"Amos Tucker has led ye here?"

"I led them, Server," the man bowed his head slightly.

"It is a long road for many. Have ye food?"

"We have food, enough for now. But there is no water, nor any we could find. Server of All, is there water for our many?"

Tornsen raised his staff slowly. "There shall be water. Amos, there are sick and crippled amongst these who have come?"

"Many, Server, and many more who would come, could they make this journey."

"Let those ailing of disease come forward first."

Eagerly a man who stood apart from the others hobbled forward, and the crowd made way hastily to his approach, his filthy rags flapping about his scarecrow frame. "Is there—is there hope for—even me?"

Tornsen looked down at him slowly, and smiled so his broad face welcomed the hideous outcast. "Not hope, Leper, health. In ten seconds your horror shall be done with, and in ten days the sound flesh shall grow again. Come up, Leper, to the Crystal of All."

The man came forward, up the stair, faltering and afraid at the last, till Tornsen reached down and took the hideous, rotting thing that served the man for hand, and helped him up. All's light flamed silver, and the sparkling stars seemed angry as they beat at the man, and little tinkling vibrations of sound rang through his body. He sank to his knees, then rose as the Flame retreated.

"You are healed, Leper," said Tornsen. "Go down now, and join your fellow men. In a score of days, come once again to the Temple, and if the new flesh has not filled in those scars that make you a monster, All will aid you further. Go."

Half uncertain, half doubting, the man went down and as he reached the base of the stair, walked away. Tal, Lord of Peace turned his staff upon him and the green glow pierced him. Gently he sank to sleep on the crimson Temple floor.

A woman called out, her hands at her breast. "I came to be healed of cancer, Server—and the pain left me between my crossing of the threshold, and my standing here. Am I—will I have life?"

"All, Lord of Life, has destroyed your cancer, woman. You can go home to your family now, if you so will, and never will cancer bother you."

So they came, and in the Temple of All were healed of disease, or the Crystal the Flame of All washed them and they lived again. Three hours they came, till all the diseased were gone forth again, whole or healing once more, and only the crippled remained.

Through the wall of jet they went, one by one, and behind the wall came to a chamber walled complete with the silvery crystal of All, and to two clad in the silvery cloth of All, carrying staffs like that of the Server, save that theirs were smaller, lighter. As one ailing entered the room, the green of Tal bathed him, and he slept deep, deep beyond all pain.

Then very swiftly, without mask or glove, with only clean, shining scalpels and instruments the two worked, cutting tissue and bone and sinew and re-arranging it as was right, and from the silvery walls of All came silvery light that tinkled and rustled eerily in the whispering silence of the chamber. Then the staffs in their hands glowed with strange lights, violet and amethyst, rose and pale amber that played and interplayed on the tissues. Before their eyes the life-stuff grew, the stretched bone thrust out swift new cells that knitted and built firm incredibly. New flesh grew on severed muscles, white threads of nerves shot out and lengthened under soft-glowing amethst.

Half an hour, and the crippled walked out, straight and strong, rejoicing. Thin white scars, silvery sands outside they made camp, a full hundred of them, then two hundred, and little fires glowed; they spread blankets as the chill night crept through the valley on soft wind-rustled feet.

The Server came down the Stair, his Staff in his hands. Amos Tucker rose at his coming, and stepped forward to meet him. "They have had food, but there is no water?" asked the Server.

"They have had food, but no water. But they miss it not greatly. For each who came, ailed and is whole. They will not sleep this night for they must talk."

Tornsen looked about him, at the silver sands, and where a low, rounded shoulder of grey-green sandstone thrust a rugged mass upwards, he looked. "They shall have water," said Tornsen. He walked to the sandstone and climbed its three-foot dome. Fifty feet across it was, lowly rounded.

"Lord Dis, lend thy strength. Let there be a vessel that thy people may drink!" The sullen scarlet face of his staff brightened, murmurous light washed through it, then leapt out in a fifty-foot snake-tongued flame that hissed like monstrous serpents. The tongue split to many, many that circled and swirled, hissing spitefully, redly brilliant. The rock boiled upward in blue-shining luminescence, pulled softly and licked higher in hot, almost invisible blue flame. Softly the flames hissed, swirling and licking, and the rock glowed brilliant red and violet. Then abruptly the flames died. A soft sigh escaped the watching people, for in the sandstone mass was a hemispherical cup, smooth-walled, clean-cut, ten feet deep, ten feet across. Amos Tucker started forward.

"Hold," said the Server. "It would leak, thus, and it is not filled." Then soft words he spoke to the crystal, murmurous words they could not hear. Again the crystal glowed, but now but a single tongue of flame leapt forth, needle-fine, a thread of intense, sullen scarlet. And its end crashed against the rock with shrieking lightning that swirled and circled in to dance over all the surface of the cup till it glowed white with the heat of the lightning. The flame died, and the white light of the cup died. It was a greenish milky cup of glass now, deep and smooth, very clear and clean.

"The cup is made, Lord Dis. Lord Mens, Lord of Knowledge and Wisdom, fill for us this cup!" The staff in Tornsen's hands seemed to leap of its own volition, spinning abruptly till the crystal of Mens faced the cup. Cold was his flame, cold and blue, and the soft radiance that spread from its tetrahedral crystalline faces crackled in the air suddenly chilled to an arctic cold. The people shivered in the chill that swept them, shivering in their light clothing. The air grew blue misty, and the hot glow of the cup faded abruptly. Very slowly a mathematically precise line extended itself from the apex of Mens' tetrahedron and bent a mathematically exact image to strike the geometric center of the cup. It rustled softly as it extended itself through the glassy wall, through the hard, age-old sandstone, down and down. Abruptly a new rustling came and the flame of Mens died. A soft, gurgling rustling that whistled a note higher and keener, stronger growing constantly—till it jetted clear water up and out, over the cup, till it was filled.

And a little stream led away down the silver sands, to sink presently in its dry thirstiness.

They camped there that night, and the next morning those who had families, those who felt their friends must know, went back. But many stayed. The next day more came, and more. In three days, the men came bearing the tents, and shelters, and behind them old, half-wrecked ammunition service cars, their tractor treads skimming over the sand. But they were loaded with food and materials. Fuel, too. But they threw out the fuel, save the gasoline they carried, for by the Cup of All stood a Crystal of Dis, Lord of Destruction—and fire. It glowed with sullen scarlet, warm and red at the top, but cool as the desert night at the sides, and the women cooked their food on that, and warmed the water and as night came on it glowed very dull over all its sides, so the entire gorge was faintly warmed and comfortable.

And more came in other trucks, and the needy went

away with metal nuggets that brought them food, and health that brought them strength to earn. Only once might any man be helped with gifts of wealth by All, but health was ever ready for him who asked.

They came to ask, and more, till the Gorge of All held a small city, served by the ancient ammunition service cars. Then Amos Tucker came before the Crystal again, with seven men of the little community.

"Server, we ask aid of All, gifts of platinum and precious metals."

"Once may men ask that of All, Amos Tucker. You, All has already helped, these seven who come with you may ask and receive."

"Server of All, we ask it not for ourselves, nor in amount that buys food and shelter till work is found. We ask twenty pounds of metal that roads may be built and trucks purchased that more may know All and reach Him and be healed. Americans have no wealth left, Server, and can earn it but slowly. The Empire favors the Emperor's race, and they may earn more swiftly, and have capital. We have no capital, for it is gone in the defense of America.

"We would bring more to All, those who cannot walk, or ride the rough trucks we have been able to buy and run."

The Server nodded slowly. "For that, All grants capital. It is a loan, and must be repaid to All's people. As He helps those who have fallen to regain their feet, but will not carry strong men in His arms, so All will help enterprise to its feet, but will not carry it in His arms. Those who have must help those who have not. The loan shall be repaid in this way; that they who have not and cannot reach the Temple shall be carried here; they that have shall give to aid the others. It is understood?"

"Yes, Server. We thank All that this thing can be." Tucker nodded.

From the jet wall came blue-clad Mens, Lord of Wisdom, and in his old arms an iridescently beautiful bar of metal, small and very heavy. This he gave to Amos Tucker, who saluted him with bowed head and took it.

"The roads shall come, and many who need the help of All," promised Tucker. "We thank Thee."

And they left.

It was three months before the first cars rolled in,

bearing freight of paralyzed and sick; and some that came died, for All had so decreed in his infinite understanding of what must be. "Change is the order of All, for as the pool that has no inlet nor outlet grows to a stinking slime, so would the race that had neither inlet of birth nor outlet of death. All may not let all live, for that way lies stagnation and rot. The pool that has inlet but no outlet grows salt and bitter and becomes sterile so no worthwhile thing may grow there.

"There must be birth; Shan, Lord of Fulfillment is a phase of All, Lord of Life. For these things are the Filler and the Emptier of Life, lest Life grow stagnant and bitter.

"Thy Father lives on, Son, in thee, and shall live on in thy children, as in you lives the First Father of all life, passed on an undying torch whose fire is elder brother to the mountains which come and pass as must men, yea, not even the mountains are so eternal as life, nor is their shifting less rapid, for as surely as Death must empty thy own vessel of life eventually, so surely must this rocky gorge pass on to form new valleys of green and fertile land that life may continue its way, a thing more constant than the hills, and more immortal. Change is the order of All's universe, for All himself is Lord of Life and Change."

The City of All grew, and its fame spread among the people of All, so that many came and were healed. Five months after his first coming to the Temple of All, Amos Tucker entered it in the Service of All, and did not return to the city, and the people of the city did not see him for three months longer. Then Tucker appeared in the White of All's novitiate, beside some dozen others who had joined the Temple, some five women and seven men. Tucker's face was more kindly, yet more stern, and in its graven lines was a far deeper understanding and a strong light of resolve in his eyes.

Amos Tucker had been introduced to the Mysteries of All, and knew All for more, and yet less. And on the pearly throne of Tammar, Lady of Mercy, there sat a woman now, some twenty-seven years of age, yet possessed of that ageless beauty of face and feature suffering can sometimes bring.

Her hair was glass wool, purely white, but live and

sparkling in the golden light of Tammar, Lady of Mercy. Doris Shane had come to the Temple in one of the first of the motor ambulances, pain-racked, tortured through seven long years, paralyzed beyond possibility of hope, so the doctors found, by a flying needle of metal from a bursting bomb. Seven years of agony had turned gold to silver, had lined and softened her face, had forced upon her and into her soul an understanding and a human philosophy that made her—Tammar, Lady of Mercy.

Thus was the Fourth Lord come to All; so they sat when Amos Tucker saw them. They were five now, the Five Lords, and the Server of All. Old John Reid, Mens, Lord of Wisdom. Robert Blake, Tal, Lord of Peace. John Reid the younger, Dis, Lord of Death. Doris Shane, Tammar, Lady of Mercy. And Grant Loman was Shan, Lord of Fulfillment.

They were the Five.

And they were Six, for the Dread Lord, Barmak, the Black Lord of Nothingness was there, ever beside the Five, invisible, unmentioned, unknown even save to the Five Lords and to Tornsen, the Server.

Grant Loman had come an old man, nearing seventy, his sparse hair grey and stiff, his face lined and seamed with a half-century of winters in the high ranges, a staunch old man who followed the trail Amos Tucker had carved out first seeking this fabled Temple of healing. It promised things he had ever hoped one day to see, healing all diseases and banishment of crippling ailments. Half a century he had worked among the lonely people of the high ranges, an apprentice doctor learning as they did before medical schools had been invented, from his father before him. Then medical colleges had brought him some new skills, but there was no science then of drawing back from Death those whom no chemical or drug could aid. So he had known better than all the schools and had healed, he and his high ranges and his God, Nature. He'd seen the souls of men stripped bare by calamity and death, and healed those wounds too. Half a century he worked with the souls and bodies of his people, and longed for such things as the Temple of All had shown.

Grant Loman sat on the throne of Shan, and the Lords were Five to the people.

VII

Chu Liang nodded slightly to his pilot, and the ship began to settle slowly, vertically downward. Li T'sang spoke softly as the ship neared the settlement below. "The Americans seem to believe at any rate, Dr. Chu."

"Yes. There is probably some reason. The reports we received are unscientific in the highest degree, but I think I can trace a semblance of a highly ingenious plan. Obviously, any such organization must have political meaning, since the Asiatic Empire has conquered these people so recently. I think perhaps there exists some weapon which is aimed from above. From the condition of the bodies, I have hypothesized a radio-frequency heat-beam, an explanation of such startling simplicity that, of course, the warriors overlooked it completely. Undoubtedly the threshold is so equipped."

"I had thought of such a possibility. It is for this reason you brought the three condemned deserters?"

"Yes, and further experimentation. There will be Americans enough here. We will go out. Li T'sang, you will bring the recording instruments, I think. Pie Chan, the direct reading instruments. Captain Shikani, if you will see that the prisoners are brought under guard—"

Chu Liang stepped out to the silver sands, and looked across at the great Temple front. A score of Americans from the city of All were watching narrowly, and followed at a little distance as they crossed to the Singing Stair. Bright sun dimmed the glory of the Temple somewhat, but the flashing light on the great stairs was near blinding. Chu Liang looked upward to the giant form of the Server, wrapped in robe of silver cloth and silver cloak, his crystal staff gleaming slightly, lambent flame playing about it.

Chu Liang halted at the head of the stair, and looked through the mighty doorway of the Temple.

"All holds no welcome for your race, Scientists," said the Server softly. "That you know. You cannot analyze All, for reason as basic as that which prevents experimental measuring of the contraction of matter at extreme

104

speed. All is part of your instruments, as your instruments are part of All. You cannot measure the contraction, for your measuring stick contracts with it. So it is here. You will find nothing, nothing save Death for such of your men as cross to the crystal floor of Dis, Lord of Death."

Chu Liang looked silently into the Temple, and his breath whistled softly over his teeth. "Your edifice is truly magnificent, Server, for so I understand you to be. Your lighting effects are exquisite. I am very stupid and lack finer understanding; I cannot believe in Gods, for such is the mind of science that always it must feel in some way to believe; that is the necessary basework of science. If I feel nothing, it proves nothing. If I can feel this God, then will I believe wholly. If it so be that it is compatible with the will of your Deity, I would make certain tests here, for even though the Deity enter into our instruments' construction, still it may be possible to discover his presence, as iron compass discovers hidden iron."

"Halt!" snapped the captain's voice. The ringing of the great Stair quieted slowly to a rolling echo as the tread of the little squad ceased. "This is the place you choose, Dr. Chu Liang?"

"If it may be?" asked the Chinese softly, indicating the spot he preferred his assistants to set up the instruments.

The Server nodded slowly. "All may give you some sign of His presence, Scientist; I know little of your instruments. Upon the Singing Stair, all men are welcome, and to all it is sanctuary. But All welcomes none save His own within the Temple."

Chu Liang looked within the temple, and the multi-colored dusk of scarlet and blue and pearl and blue was very cool and very restful. The great Crystal flamed softly, and the stars that winked and lived and died in the Flame of All caught his eye, and his mind. From the wall of jet the Five emerged, slowly, and mounted the golden stair to the face of All's Crystal, to stand silent.

Dr. Chu Liang turned back to his assistants, and spoke softly to them as their instruments were unpacked and assembled on the salt-white stone at the peak of the Singing Stair.

"There is radio-activity here," said Li T'sang softly.

"That may have something to do with the reported feeling of increased well-being. It is known that radio-active waters bring temporary feeling of health, before the blood-building tissues are destroyed."

"All the rock, I know, is radio-active. Sandstones are not normally so. It surprises me, yet the radio-activity cannot explain either the deaths of our Army Officers, nor the cures of disease. It is a surprising development. But not, I think, an answer. Try the radiation bolometer."

The younger man adjusted his instrument carefully, and set a small motor humming very softly. On a strip of white paper, a thin black line stretched out, rising and falling and shaping itself as the intensity of the varying wavelengths radiated varied.

Chu Liang looked at it silently for a moment, till, finally the snaking line dipped, reached zero, and remained. "It is interesting, Li T'sang. Focus the instrument on the floor nearby, that no light reach it from other sources."

Again the line traced, remaining on zero for long, then rising suddenly to a great peak, and falling as sharply. Then again it rose to a waving line at an extreme range.

"The red light is monochromatic," said Li T'sang in some interest. "I would expect more spectral lines. Only in the red and in the ultra-violet are there lines. There is strong ultra-violet, which may explain the healthy tan of the Americans here. But it neither cures nor kills save in vast concentration, where normal light would be near as effective, killing by sheer energy alone."

"It interests me, Li T'sang, that I have spent weary hours adjusting apparatus that I might receive a beam of monochromatic energy. The blue is pure, and the green is pure. The Line is confused by the radiation of the white wall and the white light of the top crystal." He turned to Tornsen slowly.

"Server, we have heard of this Flame of Dis that is said to bring death. How may we see this, then?"

Tornsen's face became stern. "Lord All does not parade his might in vain display. If you would see the Flame of Dis, attack the works of All, and it shall play, and play unhindered, unstayed, thru any screen or instrument you may turn upon it."

The Chinese consulted quietly, and looked upon the

records of their instruments. The captain joined them, and Chu Liang spoke to him. "There is no ray or radiation of death here. Let the prisoners earn their freedom as was ordained, and let two children of the Americans be brought, that they may be carried, as was ordained."

The captain moved. A score of Americans stood on the Singing Stair, quiet and watchful, a half-dozen children watched, intent-eyed.

The captain's orders were spoken in Japanese, and his men turned instantly to obey. The Americans roared in anger and stepped forward menacingly as the troops seized two small children. The Server called out once, a strong, sharp syllable of command, and they halted, Oriental and American alike.

"To the people of All, I promise that the children will not be harmed or even frightened, for see, they shall be at peace." As he spoke, Tal, Lord of Peace, raised his staff on the distant Crystal of All, and green radiance shone over the group, so that a feeling of lethargy stilled them, while suddenly the children slept in the arms of the troops. Chu Liang's voice was soft and intense as his assistants worked swiftly to mark the recording instruments.

The Server spoke again. "To the people of the World Empire, I promise also that the children will not be harmed, for the Lord of Life guards his own, whether he appear in his phase of Dis, Lord of Death, or Tal, Lord of Peace. But no act of yours shall harm the children."

The Chinese bowed slightly. "So let it be. Two men shall carry them. That is all."

The prisoners took the children in their arms, two sleeping children, and held them above their heads. At a snapped order they stepped forward. Tornsen stepped forward to meet them, staff upraised. "It is Death," he said softly. "All permits no enemy to cross to the Crystal Floor of Dis."

The Chinese said, "Unfortunately, it is death for them outside, a death they understand very well, and do not desire. They will enter, for they are condemned, and inside lies their only hope of life."

Tornsen looked at the two silently. "Carry the children, then, less high, for the fall might injure them."

Chu Liang felt in his heart a sudden triumph, as he

knew his guess was true. "They carry them high or die!"

"Let the two put down the children, for there is Sanctuary upon the Singing Stair for all men," cried Tammar, Lady of Mercy. "They shall be free upon the Stair, and none there shall hurt them."

The strong, deep voice of old Mens, Lord of Wisdom spoke. "Such is the law, for those who seek sanctuary for justice. These two have sought justice, and justice finds them condemned. They be not seekers of justice, but refugees from it. The Sanctuary of the Stairs is not for them, Lady Tammar."

Tammar bowed her head. "Aye, Lord of Wisdom."

"Step forward, and if you would live, carry the children high, for the weapon that kills is above!" cried Chu Liang. And the two stepped forward as the Server stepped to meet them. They stepped across the threshold, so that the sullen scarlet of Dis lay beneath their feet—and died. From their lax hands, softened suddenly by Dis, Lord of Death, the Server caught the children in his great hands, and lowered them to the floor.

"Lady Tammar, bring awakening," called the Server, and the golden staff, tipped with amber light that was the staff of Tammar, Lady of Mercy dipped, a lancing flame of golden light touched the children. They rose, and hurried, frightened, away and down the Stair to their homes.

"There is death in the Temple for all save All's people."

Chu Liang bowed his head slightly. "Yes," he said softly. "We go now. Give us those we cannot reach, if such be the will of your Deity."

Two Americans stepped forward into the Temple at the Server's gesture, and the troops of the World Empire carried the lax bodies down the Stair in the thrumming silence. Chu Liang and his assistants packed the instruments into their cases and marked them carefully.

"It is quite useless," said Chu Liang quietly as the great stair sang its triumph in their ears and through the gorge. "I do not in any way understand, but this I know; there is a god there, and a much greater god then ours. We have a god. It is Science. Theirs is a greater god."

Li T'sang looked at him thoughtfully. "A greater Science you mean, Dr. Chu?"

"I did not say," Chu Liang replied softly. "We will examine the bodies of the men at once, upon reaching the plane. Li T'sang will perform microscopic sectioning work on the tissue of the muscles, skin, hair and such cells as have the lowest forms of life. I will examine and test the muscles for galvanic effects. There remains physical examination of the bodies, which Pie Chan will perform."

"Will you not examine the recording instruments?" asked Li T'sang in some disappointment.

Old Chu Liang shook his head. "Science is our god, Li T'sang, and gods have infinity to work. Their work must not, then, be hurried and spoiled by their hurry. Our recorded films must be developed under optimum conditions, which we do not obtain on our laboratory plane, complete as its facilities are. The body of the smaller one, you may take to your laboratory, Li T'sang."

"Yes, Master." The younger man signaled to the two warriors who carried the body and followed them to his laboratory. Presently he brought Chu Liang certain muscles, very white-seeming, cold and yet with the appearance of freshly boiled tissues, completely coagulated. He returned silently.

Chu Liang entered his laboratory some time later, as the helicopter rode smoothly east to the American Department Capital at Chicago. Li T'sang looked up at the elder man and shook his head blankly. "It is very peculiar, Master. There is no living cell in all the body, neither skin, nor muscle, nor even lowest hair cell. And that is perhaps understandable. But in all the body there is *no* living thing! The bacteria of mouth and nose and intestine are dead, the bacteria of skin and feet are dead. Only a few very small colonies on the surface of the body live, implanted perhaps by the hands of those who carried the body here. But I think that as it lay on the temple floor it was more sterile than any surgical instrument."

Chu Liang looked silently through the microscope at the slides his assistant had prepared. "Not even in the tartar from the teeth is there any living thing. Man needs certain bacteria for healthy existence. You know this better than I, Li T'sang. Tell me then, were all living organisms save those human organisms that make up and defend the body, the corpuscles of blood and tissue, the cells of nerve and muscle and brain, were all save those destroyed, could man long survive?"

Li T'sang looked thoughtfully at the microscope for many seconds then his voice came hesitant and thoughtful. "If in all the world this were done, man could not live, for there are many non-human organisms needed, the many life-forms in the intestine that break down the foodstuff we eat but cannot digest, to a form we can digest. There are very many others. But if only the individual man were so completely sterilized, he would quickly regain his natural balance thru inevitable ingestion of these bacteria, as must the new-born infant. Man enters this world near sterile, yet within hours the baby has gathered those necessary, bacterial colonies. Probably no man would even know that this sterilization of his body had taken place, were it possible. But it is not, for any chemical strong enough to destroy the bacteria would destroy man as well, unless a degree of specificity almost never attained were possible for an almost infinite horde of invaders, while leaving the body untouched. We have but three species of this type, one furnished by nature's accident, quinine, which is hundreds of times more poisonous to the malarial parasite than to human tissue, one by the blind experimenting of man, salvarsan, hundreds of times more poisonous to the syphillis organism than to man, and one developed by years of laborious analysis of the human antibodies, kappasol which is vastly poisonous to typhoid fever, but harmless to man. And these are one third the gift of nature, one third imitation of nature, and one third blind and infinitely laborious research. Now in the centuries of chemical medicine, if but three have been found, how then, could man find the specifics for thousands, and compound them in half a decade?"

"But there exist, then, chemicals which have the property of destroying only non-human life-forms?"

"No, only those three, an exception as unimportant as oxygen of atomic weight 17. Oxygen atoms have a weight of sixteen, save for one in millions."

"But the principle is vastly important. What man has done once, man may do not only again, but many times. Even, perhaps, improve to such an extent that specifics that differentiate between native Americans and Asians might be found. Is it not so?"

"In a thousand centuries, yes. But even if analysis of all the anti-bodies were achieved, which is not the work of a man, but a thing to be done in an historical era, and the vaster task of synthesis as well, there is no anti-body which destroys Orientals but not Westerners. And even if this be so, no anti-body produces the effects we have witnessed. It may poison, it may dissolve, but it does not fry. The explanation of the Temple is not there, Chu Liang, I fear."

"There is a greater god than ours, Li T'sang, and the day will come when our god can understand the God All. Our report to the Science Committee will be as unsatisfactory as the report of General Hitsohi's to the Rebellious Activities Control Commission."

"But of what importance is this temple to the government of the World State? To science its meaning may be profound, since we have no understanding of observable results, but of what importance is it to the State, this hidden temple in the wildest mountains of the American Province? There are hidden temples in the high passes of the Himalayas, the temples of the Tibetans, we do not investigate."

"There are hidden temples on all the Earth the Empire rules, but they are old beyond memory of man. This is not old. These other temples do not regularly make cures of hopeless paralysis by operations incredible and impossible, with healing in a day that cannot take place in a year. These temples do not regularly cure cancer in the last, hopeless stage, nor tuberculosis of lung and bone.

"That is something of it. But this is more important. Few temples of the world forbid entrance to Asiatics. This temple not only refuses, but brings mysterious death. This you do not know, nor do the people of that temple city. Kimishti, one of the Empire's best men, has circulated freely through Occidental countries as an operative of the Asian State through all the years of the war. He has behind him respected standing of home and family, all standing. By operations, by hard work, he had become Occidental, his skin pink as an Englishman's, his eyes blue, his hair blonde and curled. He entered the Temple, suffering as he showed, from scarlet fever, feeling safe in their welcome. He was accepted and brought up to the place by one of their ambulances. He died as he was carried across the threshold by a temple novitiate.

"I had thought he was recognized secretly perhaps, and executed. I know that the god All knew his difference and exacted toll of Death. The members of the Temple prayed over him, and read over him the Service of Dis and Shan, their burial service, and he was buried as an Occidental dead of heart disease, the after-effect of scarlet fever. The Server there knew him for Oriental though, since his tissues were—coagulated.

"And that is something more of it. It is a temple of death, with a god of power who acts. A god who does things so indisputably has never been since the world began, and was not expected when the Edict of Free Worship was given forth by Emperor Nijihua.

"But there is yet more in this: Nijihua seeks to make a true universal state, wherein all men recognize a common destiny and a common center of interest and leadership, the World State, in which each sees his only nationality. Nationalism of the most intense he desires, patriotism of the highest—but toward the World State. It is not oppression which will bring this, for that brings only revolt. Only common leadership, respected and honored, can unite men. Whether Oriental or Occidental, the leadership of the World State must be *the* leadership, the only common reality which men can form themselves about.

"Half he has succeeded. All Orientals today recognize him, and many Occidentals. And—in all the world today, there lives not one Occidental capable of political leadership. Every man with such abilities was killed in the general uprising of the mobs that brought the wars to an end, or he has died of cholera. The only leaders Nijihua has allowed are the leaders of the World Empire, since men generally *must* have leaders to be happy— the only leaders there are are the World Empire.

"The Temple of All has arisen. To it Occidentals turn for health and advice, comfort in life and death. It becomes more and more a center of man's many interests, and a center of *Occidental* interest, perforce not *common* to *both* Oriental and Occidental. It makes them separate peoples, divided by All, a God of power who acts positively for the benefit of his people, who favors them. Inevitably then there is crystalization of the loose, leaderless mass of Occidentals about this new god, and his priests. Yet, they do not realize that they are being led, being separated from the World Empire, a race and a class apart. But they are! They are soaking in the pleasant idea that they are superior, god-chosen.

"Nijihua must act. He has acted. The Empire needs money. In a day and a day now, the World Empire issues a new Edict, the Edict of New Worshipers. It is a tax of one thousand dollars on each new worshiper to a religious faith—and must be paid in metal!"

Li T'sang nodded slowly. "The Temple of All will gain no new worshipers. No American can gain metal. In America alone has this new religion gained power, thus none of the rest of the Empire will greatly revolt, since growing families can, I imagine, enter their children to their church untaxed."

"That is right. The Temple of All will be deserted in a week."

VIII

The Lords sat on their high thrones, the sapphire of Mens in the center, the golden of Tammar on his right, and Shan on his left, the rich deep scarlet of Dis beyond pearly Shan; beyond Tammar the cool, freshening green of Tal, Lord of Peace. And unseen, below and in front of their semi-circle, visible only to the eyes of the Lords and the Server, sat Dread Barmak, the Black Lord on his lightless, rayless throne of black deeper than the night of Space itself.

For this was the inner Chamber of the Lords. Mens spoke, his voice deep and low in the multi-colored dusk of the Chamber. "This Edict is a weapon at the throat of All. For the people of All are oppressed and poor. All is possessed of vast treasures, and it comes to me that it were better that All disdain the collections of the tax, and give of his treasures to meet this imposition."

"Aye," said the Lords softly. "The treasures of All are infinite as is All himself. Let this be the rule."

Shan, Lord of Fulfillment spoke. "This is the rule then, but let it be thus applied; the people of All who have wealth and ability to pay, shall pay, lest the infinitude of All's treasures be measured and beget covetousness in the heart of Nijihua.

"Now further, it seems the Emperor, wishing a healthy subject people, has decreed that only those who attend more than five times in the course of the year are true members of any temple. But he who speaks with the Server of a temple is not a member thereby unless he attend that temple. Thus we shall apply it; that there shall be Servers who go forth, and the members of the temple shall be selected by the Lord that they be good, else they pay the tax of their own ability. Thus shall the doors be open to all, and yet be closed to those of the people of All whom we don't find worthy."

Tornsen spoke, and his voice rumbled in the small, cubed, crystal chamber of the Lord. "The Edict harms All little thus, and All pays the tax from the infinite resources of the earth. The impost collector comes on the

114

morrow, and the Lords shall assemble then on the crystal, and the Server and the Novitiate shall bear to him the impost for the eighty and nine members who have joined the Temple."

The next day brought the plane of the World Empire, glowing golden, with scarlet dragons in the sun, as it lighted on the silver sands, and the Collector of Imposts mounted the Singing Stair before a squad of armed men.

"Halt there, man of the World Empire, for the Temple of All is closed to you. The tax shall be brought out."

"What is the roll of your temple?" snapped the Oriental.

"The roll is one hundred and three, and of these are the Five Lords and the Server, and certain others who have been here long. But there be eighty-and-nine for whom the tax is to be paid. There be many who have not joined, and cannot. But for the eighty-and-nine, tax shall be paid."

The Oriental looked at the man a bit surprised. "It must be paid in metal," he said warningly. "No goods save precious metals."

"And the metals shall be rhodium and palladium, which are in the Empire Catalog of precious metals."

"Bring them forth, then," said the Collector, and on the salt-white stone his servant set up the small case which opened out to a work bench and a pair of scales. The Server brought to him the first ingot, two inches square and a foot long. The man looked at it, weighed it in his hand, for its mass was great, and spread upon the stair-top a sheet of fine-woven silk, then with a small saw he cut it through in six places and gathered the dust. The dust he dropped into a small tray and two pinches he tested with his reagents. Then with a tiny spectroscope of high power he examined the lines of the metal. Softly he drew in his breath.

"Your metal is pure, pure within the limits of the spectroscope, which is very pure indeed. While the metals are exceeding difficult to separate, the weight is such that four such bars exactly meet the tax."

Silently three of the Novitiate came forward bearing in their hands bars of metal of absolute purity and great weight. The tax impost collector gave to the Server a small sheet of paper bearing the crest of Nijihua and the quick brush-strokes of his signature.

"The impost is met, and so must be met with each

new member of the Temple, Server. This you will remember under the penalties of Nijihua's Empire."

"Aye," said the Server, "we understand."

And the Collector left to go to another Temple, for such was his duty and not the understanding of the tensions that built about those four bars of utterly pure precious metal so readily supplied. Chu Liang understood, for to him came the metal for analysis, and he analyzed the ingots to one sole element each, and he fused the two elements together, nor all his science could draw the rhodium from the palladium with utter purity. For the metals were exceedingly intractable. And he frowned somewhat, for rhodium, in which the greater part of the payment was made was not as useful to him as was palladium, platinum.

IX

His silver robes shimmered in the sun and wind like the ruffled surface of a clear lake under slanting evening sun, his turban-like headdress gleaming. In his hands he carried a Staff of All, silvery and intricately chased, mounted by the softly-glowing cubed crystal, greater mate to the crystal of his headdress.

The ambulance driver looked at him in some doubt and awe. "Then the Servants of All are going to leave the Valley?"

"Certain of them, the Teachers, that the people of the cities, unable to reach All, may be able to have his help. There will always be the Five Lords and the Server to aid All's people at the Temple. But the impost makes it needful that certain ones of us go out."

"Amos Tucker, where will you go?"

"Amos Tucker no more; a Teacher of All. I go by foot that more may know, first to the city whence you came, then on to the coast, probably to San Francisco. It is not determined by the Lords, since each is sent on his mission. But delay no longer, Driver, since those who ride behind go in need of help. Stay, I will bring a moment's peace to them; then you must go your way, and I mine. Farewell, in the grace of All."

The Teacher stopped a moment more to step inside the low ambulance body and let the green crystal of Tal shed its rays on the sick. Their harsh breathing relaxed and the soft moan of one died way in deep sleep. Then he stepped out and the vehicle moved on.

As it disappeared from sight, the Teacher raised his staff to his lips and spoke softly. "Sick come, seeking aid, Server."

The Crystal whispered reply. "We are ready for All. You are well."

"Yes, scarcely a day's journey out. I will reach the city by evening, however."

"Good. All aid you." The Crystal's slight hum died, and the Teacher strode on easily with the long lope of a trained desert man. The endless sand over which the road

ran glared in the sun, and presently the Teacher rested
for a moment. The staff in his hand sent out a licking
tongue of ruby flame and a patch of sand two feet across
fused in blinding heat, sinking to a slight depression. The
Teacher scooped a bit of sand into it, and the flame of
All licked at it with shrieking, crashing star-dust. The
depression boiled with white vapor-fumes, hissing and
bubbling. For some seconds it continued, then burst into
sharp blue flames, while the flame of All changed strangely
violet. Instantly the rolling vapor vanished and the flames
licked slowly and seemed to struggle against an opposing
force. Presently they died and a moment later the Teacher
knelt beside his cup and drank his fill of cold, clear and
somewhat tasteless water. Then with a rested body he
started on his way.

Toward evening the natural desolation gave way to
man-made desolation, torn and racked, the deep craters
in the sand stained with red of iron and black of
smoke, green virulent stains of exploded XR-78 gas-
shells. More cars passed him now, and curious hybrids;
an automobile chassis stripped to four wheels and a frame
with weather-stained broken planks as a body, drawn
by a decrepit horse, or a slow-moving ox. Tires too
old and weak for automobiles shod them, tires in the last
stages of decay, as with all the country. Broken buildings
appeared and here and there a light, tinnily shiny, factory-
made dwelling.

The Ranchers were filtering back, such as lived, or
their women and children. Chinese and Japanese lived
here now, they lived in the broken houses and farmed
a few acres in their immemorial way. To them, no vision
of the infinitude of rolling land brought relief from
pressure, still they farmed to the fence-posts, and planted
beans to climb the posts themselves. There was vast
plenty, to them, and in their old way they ate the plenty,
making no reserve against the time it might vanish.
The men worked, and the women pulled the crude plows
while the children set out seed. Other gangs of men
worked at clearing the irrigation ditches for the water
that would come when the engineers finished the restora-
tion of war-blasted dams.

The Orientals paid no attention to the curiously garbed
stranger, the Americans little. They looked, and then
looked back to the work that engaged them, wearily.

America had no reserves, and they must compete with the Oriental mode of life. They used better tools, better methods. But the Oriental called the American's direst poverty vast prosperity.

The Teacher went on, into the city where more people looked at him. An Oriental policeman pacing his beat eyed him narrowly, and passed on; a few Americans turned to stare, and an expression of interest and sudden remembrance stirred in their eyes. Finally one stopped, turned and came to him.

"Server—" he cried.

"No, not the Server, John Graham. I am a Teacher of All. You are well?"

"Well and able, Teacher. The tuberculosis is gone from my lungs and my bones. I have been better and stronger than ever in my life before I stood in All's Temple. But —I did not know the servants of All left his Valley."

"Never have they, before. But the impost makes this necessary to the best good of All, so the Teachers go forth. I am the first. Many more will follow me across this road, till the robes of All become a familiar sight in the city here."

"It is near evening, Teacher. Can you—have you made arrangement for the night? Can you stay with me—and my wife?"

"My only arrangement was that I find some man who knew All and might take me in. Gladly then, I accept your offer."

"Come then," said the man eagerly, "It is but a block or two—I was just leaving my store for the evening—"

The man's wife greeted the Teacher timidly, uncertainly. "We have little for tonight—even among the merchants it is hard to get enough, but what we have we are glad indeed to share, for all we have we owe to John's health, which All gave him. I—I—I scarcely know how to address you—Your—But come in, come in and rest at any rate, for I am tired myself, and you who have been walking in the heat all day."

The Teacher smiled, and with his smile the pearly light of Shan waxed in his crystal, and the green of Tal. The women stood surprised for a second, then a stiffness went from her body, and a brighter light came to her eyes. "Oh—oh—" she cried. "There was truth in what John said. I could not believe, myself, despite John's health. I feel—feel as though I'd slept for hours!"

"The Peace of Tal and the Fulfillment of Shan be on your house, John Graham. The Powers of All and the Phases of All are not easily credible, I know, Mrs. Graham. But they are more real than even John Graham who lived through them believes.

"But let us go in. I am not weary, for All goes with me." He smiled, raising his Staff slightly. "But I am a Teacher of All. Address me only as 'Teacher'."

"I did not know, Teacher. Will you be with us long?"

"Not long, for I must go on."

And in the morning, when they woke, he was gone, and in his place they found a little cube of silvery metal, very heavy and very beautifully iridescent in the morning sun. And amazingly heavy, more than twice as heavy as lead.

John Graham took it that morning to the little office of the Real Estate agent, John Mackenburg, who spent half his time interviewing those who would make the trip to All's Temple, and to him he gave the cube of metal, explaining how he came by it.

The Teacher stayed that night, and another and another at the homes of people who had heard of All or had reason to bless All's Temple; and the fourth evening he came to San Francisco. It was not so badly ruined in appearance, rising now as an Oriental city from the ashes of the blasted city they had captured in the early years of the war. The busy city paid no attention to the Teacher as he wandered about, but evening found him staying in the home of a man who marveled still that he walked on two legs of flesh and bone where but one had been left him when he left the hospital of the American Army Medical Corps.

The next day he went down to the Empire building in the heart of new San Francisco and attended an auction that was going on, the selling of certain lands in the neighborhood of Golden Gate Park. And some of his friends went too, and purchased plots of land.

In two weeks the land was as level as it had been before the great shells of the Empire Fleet had reduced it to churned rubble. Five men seeded it and planted it, and a sixth walked about in curious robes bearing a curious staff of crystal. In two weeks, foliage more green, more luxurious than San Francisco had ever seen grew there, and curious people stopped to look at it. And more curious Orientals examined the grass and the soil, and did not understand.

A building appeared, of white marble and red granite and curious blue, intensely blue stone that came from hitherto unknown quarries along with an intensely green stone. A great crated mass, five feet on an edge. Men came too, and set the stone and the crystal mass on a golden column that had come, and other thin crystal plates and curious lighting devices.

In six months, the House of All was built, and shone white and sapphire and emerald on the broad sweep of landscaped lawn. At first a few curious ones came. Then the sick, and then more ailing in streams, till every Westerner in San Francisco had visited it, and come out well and strong, and the Orientals complained slightly. But the Orientals who were in power took no notice of it, being too intelligent to be deluded by faith healers, and since their people were not a race used to complaining, but oppressed for countless generations by a dull drudgery, they merely looked on with envious dull eyes as the Occidental crippled limped in, and returned whole, and the pallid, feverish were carried in to walk out, eyes shining.

But the rulers were intelligent and paid little attention to faith healers, being far too busy attempting to establish a very new political control over a vast area.

And their work was not to complain and object to a religion that obeyed the Edicts of the Emperor in every way, and turned in nearly two hundred and forty thousand dollars of precious metal in the course of six months from the House of All in San Francisco. And those originally interested lost interest as time passed, and nothing new or startling developed, save amazingly good revenues.

Another House of All rose under the direction of the First Teacher in Denver, and another in Seattle. And hundreds of thousands of dollars were paid, while tens of thousands of sick were healed. The stores of precious metals in Nijihua's treasury were augmented by the receipts from nearly seven hundred members of the House of All, in that year.

X

The Server stood before the Lords, and the First Teacher stood beside him.

"Lords, you have heard the tale. Eleven Houses have been established in these two years, and the First Teacher has worked fairly and well, these two years. Now he grows weary of this work, and would, if it meets the approval of the Five Lords, rest in the House of All in Chicago as the Server of All."

Mens, Lord of Wisdom spoke from his great, crystal throne. "The First Teacher has done well, and no one of his sending has been excluded from the Works of All, whereby is shown his wisdom of human understanding. The Lord of Wisdom is pleased."

Tammar, Lady of Mercy spoke. "Many he has helped, and through his spreading of All's houses, many have learned of All's works. Tammar, Lady of Mercy is pleased."

Shan, Lord of Fulfillment spoke: "In no way has he failed in his words given us, the Lords of All. The Lord of Fulfillment is content."

So they spoke, and agreeing, Amos Tucker, the First Teacher, was made Server of All in Chicago, the American Capital of the World Empire.

Lord Mens spoke again. "Your work, Server, must not cease, for you must instruct many and introduce them to the Mysteries of All. You have shown complete competence in the handling of these things which a Server of All must understand. But every man of our race whom you believe competent must be sent here for final education in All's Mysteries. We have but two Houses east of the Mississippi, and you, who have done so much of this work must aid others in the work, not by your presence but by your constant advice. The Crystal of the Server reaches to every Crystal of All, and speaks with it at will. This remember, and aid in every way, as we know you will. Your work has been exceedingly good."

The Second Server bowed to the Lords. "I cannot understand fully these mysteries, as I know better even than you. But to the utmost of my abilities I will apply the knowledge and understanding of the human mysteries, to the betterment of All.

"I go now to Chicago, but I will pause at Denver, where the Seventh Teacher is setting out soon for Boston that a new House of All may be built. He has purchased, through his agents, Corey Hill, which overlooks all Boston. I find his plans good."

The Lords nodded agreement. "I know the city," spoke Tammar, Lady of Mercy. "It is an excellent position."

The First Server stepped forward again. "Now there comes to me that a more pressing business yet demands attention. For a year and a year we have escaped great notice from the Empire, the work of consolidation being very great for them, and their need of revenue being very pressing."

"They sought to destroy us with their tax," said Lord Mens softly, "which was not the way of wisdom, with All of infinite resource, and they have sold themselves for a bribe instead. They fear to harm us now, who have in two years brought them eight and one third millions of dollars in precious metal, metals very rare and difficult to collect. This year we build our membership by eleven thousand men and women. They will not quickly destroy the bringer of so much revenue, nor the source of so much excellent health and good-nature among the people of the country they own.

"But therefore I say this: The work of consolidation nears its end, and the need of our revenue becomes less pressing as normal industry swells, and its revenues swell, and some measure of prosperity returns. This third year, therefore, let us expand to the limit Lord All may permit us.

"The Council of Lords is ended?"

"Aye," said the Lords.

And now Amos Tucker raised his new Staff of the Server, and held it before his eyes, by chance, and he started back, his face frozen in sudden surprise. There was a Sixth Lord! The Black Lord, Dread Barmak, a silhouette of utter jet that seemed to stare straight to his heart, and dip slowly his massive head in greeting to the new Server of All.

Frozen fingers gripped the heart of the Second Server as he turned stiffly to the First Server. Tornsen smiled gravely, and for an instant Tucker caught a fleeting twinkle in the kindly old eyes of Shan, Lord of Fulfillment ere he filed away with the others to his chamber.

"Come," said Tornsen, "there are further things that the Server of All should understand."

"Aye—Aye, indeed," sighed Amos Tucker unsteadily.

XI

Chu Liang sat with unmoving face as the Shaman of the Western District bored in upon the curiously garbed witness in the Testifier's Stand. There had been little result of the Shaman's persistent questionings.

The Shaman's voice was growing sharper. "How old, though, is this sect, Server?"

"A religion, Shaman, is ageless. A deity is everlasting, without knowable beginning, without knowable end. These exist in the mist of creation and the mist of the ultimate dissolution."

"The religion is not older than men, for without man there is no religion. This is not as old as man, and therefore I ask its earliest inception, Server."

"The earliest inception began about three thousand years ago in Greece. It developed very slowly, till this day came when the better understanding of All, and his message to men, the great need of his race all combined to make his understanding of man and man's understanding of him better."

"The active spread of the religion is but three years old though, Amos Tucker?"

"I have no name, save that of Server, Shaman. It has become my title and my name. The great growth of All's Initiate has taken place in these three years of stress, but his understanding has increased greatly and steadily over the period of a hundred years, since the year 1890 of the old calender."

"Eleven thousand, nine hundred and eighty-seven members have joined the church during this year, and paid the initiate tax of one thousand dollars. It is said this tax is paid in large part by the Temple, yet no known source of revenue is in evidence. How then, has this revenue been gathered, this sum of over eleven millions of dollars, and the greater sums spent in the construction of the Temples, thirty-seven this year, and investment not less than seventy millions of dollars I am told."

"The resources of All are infinite. I am of the Server

125

class, and such is not within my province. I cannot answer you that, Shaman."

"Who then is responsible for this thing?"

"That is the province of Mens, Lord of Wisdom."

"He is forbidden by the religion's laws to leave the valley?"

"Yes. He does not leave the Temple."

The Shaman's face was not so smoothly impassive as it had been. "We have heard the testimony of Chu Liang upon the destruction of life within the temple, and upon the complete sterilization of the bodies."

The Second Server interrupted smoothly and gravely. "The works of Dis, Lord of Death are not understood by men. As the people of All are welcomed within the Temple, unfortunately the other peoples are not. That is the will of All, which I serve, but do not influence."

"The Hindus have entered, an Oriental people, dark of skin," said the Shaman softly.

"The understanding of All's will is not to men."

"You understand sufficiently to make efficient use of the Crystal of Life, and the Staff which you bear with you so constantly."

"That is an achievement attained after three thousand years of study and thought and deepest sincerity of purpose. The day may come when the entire will of All is understood. To us, these things are greatly valued, and not to be cast aside, for in them, in the crystals, resides something of the living All, The Infinite, perceptible in his living flame."

And as he spoke, the silver Flame of All lanced upward, the dying stars coruscating and vanishing.

"You and your people have been consistent in your refusal to part with this symbol of All."

"Only once, under the order of an officer of the Empire has any man of All parted with his staff. The report has been read in this room that All whispered in the crystal, and the man dropped dying saved only by the beneficial effects of All's crystal in the hands of its owner, Tornsen the Server. All is not a destroyer needlessly, and the people of All attempt to prevent such suffering as the release of the Staff brings. Such is the will of All."

The Shaman tried for long hours, and at the close of the long day's session dismissed the Server, who had appeared voluntarily, and exasperatedly watched him leave the room, to be joined by a dozen Novitiates of the House of All. A dozen others appeared around him, calling softly. Gently his voice floated back, clear and sharp. "It is not wise that the Flame be used here, since there are those other than All's who would suffer by it. The House of All is open to all men of his race, and the Teachers of All will come at any man's call if need be." And the Shaman spoke softly to his colleagues. "I am informed that the Council of American Military Affairs wishes us to cease inquiry at this time," he said.

Chu Liang went quietly from the room to the building at the other end of the Empire Park, and into the small room where two dozen men sat quietly supping. Dark fell presently and they sat talking softly of many things. And a man came in quietly, his face very white and his eyes seeming glazed and unseeing. He was guided by the hands of two who stood on either side of him, uniformed guards, and he was not alone in his paleness. The two at his side saluted, but he in the center stared only ahead, dull-eyed.

"Yokishi, you report?" asked Commander Torisuti.

"Yokishi, yes. Yes, I report Commander. The thing was done, and I am done."

"You apprehended the Teacher who went out?"

"Yes, yes, we apprehended the Teacher. From the Singing Stair of the House of All he went down, to the call of the one who demanded aid, as was ordained, and Lieutenant Tsi Chian accompanied me to the mean dark streets of the American Section. The darkness closed in as we closed in, as noiseless as we. The lights of the street grew further apart, and the houses more cramped and decayed, and the Teacher continued but about him shone light, for the Staff he carried glowed with silver light and green, and sapphire blue and pearl, and was very beautifull to look on, but tore at the nerves and deadened them. Lieutenant Tsi Chian went forward as was agreed, and with the silent pistol fired at him, but as was known the Teacher was not stayed nor hurt nor even aware of the firing. So then did I advance with the apparatus Chu Liang had designed for me, and did as he had directed in the starting of it, and as he directed I tried its power on a dog that appeared slinking through the alleys, and he died as was told to me, lying down without a sound.

"I advanced upon the Teacher, and trained the projector upon him, and the tubes glowed properly, and the meters were correctly set upon the base of the weapon. Then I depressed the contact, and the Teacher before me did not stumble or halt, nor even seem aware, for behind him, directly between him and the weapon I bore, appeared a soft glow of violet that seemed a wavering disc of light, and slightly brighter the Flame of All glowed on his staff. The sparks were sharp and hot in my hands, so I was forced to drop the thing."

"The clatter warned him, for he turned slowly, and we stood revealed in the silver light. Lieutenant Tsi Chian made to dart away as did I, hoping to escape recognition in the foul clothes we wore, but from the staff he carried green light reached out, and we were overcome by a lethargy and a paralysis such as made us slump to the ground while he came back to us. He smiled as he saw the weapon I had carried, and from his staff a snake-tongue of scarlet lanced to touch the thing Chu Liang had fashioned. It touched it, and it was gone, only an instantaneous glow of intense violet light lingered for a moment to mark its passage, and a shallow depression in the hardpacked earth of the roadway."

" 'All protects his people, Warrior' he said quietly, looking upon us. 'It was not the will of All that your weapon should injure me, so it did not. Go now, back to Commander Torisuti who awaits you in the room of Decisions in the Hall of War.'

"He pointed his staff upon us, and the pearly light touched us, so we rose and darted into the shadows. He walked on."

"That is your report?" asked the Commander silkily.

"No, that is not my report, Commander, for we knew then that his diligence would be at low ebb, having overcome one attack, and would not be strong to aid him. We followed him then to the house of the ailing one, and the Teacher was inside for half an hour. Then we knew, as he came out, his Staff must be at low ebb also, and no protection against material things since he must move through the narrow doorway of the squalid place.

"His silver light came before him, bright upon the darkness of the place. As he followed through, Lieutenant Tsi Chian stood upon the right, and I upon the left, and Tsi Chian had a section of heavy metal he had found, and I a broken beam, hoping that great mass might accomplish on his weakened screen what no bullet might.

"Tsi Chian struck, and his metal bar shot lightnings, so that he was hurled to one side, writhing. My wooden beam was slowed, as though striking water a foot from his head, and ran aside, but so great was its mass that it moved still, and struck him upon the shoulder.

"He fell to his knees, dropping the Staff of All, but it dropped not swiftly, but slowly to the ground as though feather-light. I leapt upon the Teacher as he kneeled, half stunned while Tsi Chian leapt upon the Staff. Tsi Chian grasped it, and I rose to follow as he went swiftly down the roadway to a place of safety, for there are many Americans in the Section. I was close behind him when he stumbled to the ground, turned over—and slept with the staff beside him.

"I grasped it and ran on, but a numbness came into my arms as I ran, a great numbness so that presently I felt my feet as those of another, and it seemed I ran on for many hours while a single house dropped back. And for many more hours till, weary, I stumbled as Tsi Chian had, and lay with the numbing creeping from my arm to my heart and my eyes. The silver light grew dimmer to my eyes, then vanished, and suddenly a searing, unbearable pain shot through my arm, so my eyes opened again. All the Staff glowed violet, and the Crystal was shattered.

"Lightning gushed from the end of the staff, so that the ground fused, and the air rocked at the roarings of them. The crystal was gone, and as I watched, helpless to move, the Staff glowed more intensely violet, then blue flames rushed up from it and the heat seared me and my hand. But the hand felt no pain now, nor did my side presently, and the lack of pain was spreading, while the blue flames rushed higher—and then were gone. Commander, it had vanished utterly, so that no scrap of metal or ash rested in my hand."

"That is your report?" asked the Commander again.

"That is my report, Commander, save that presently the Teacher came again, and stood over me. He spoke again and said: 'Your hands, and the release of the Spirit of All within the Staff, which is the Spirit of the Lord of Life, brought a false life to you. You are dead, Warrior. Now I will give you the peace of Tal, that you may endure to reach your commander. But it is not the will of All that you, who have attacked a Teacher of All, shall live, nor can any of us of All bring life to you, into whom the Fire of All has penetrated.'

"And as he spoke, the fire was eating at me, so that my body burned, and all of me from my skin to my innermost part flamed with the agony of it, like the Death of a Thousand Cuts, so that I groaned. From the crystal of his headdress, a pencil of green light reached down, and touched my head so that the fire died there, and in a moment I felt no fire, or any other thing in all my body.

" 'Now the fire is not dead, but your senses are dead,' he said softly, 'nor will they ever return. Your eyes see, and your ears hear, but neither touch, nor taste, nor smell is with you. For an hour and at most another hour, the Fire of All will leak from you, then when it is gone you will be dead indeed. Now for those who speak with you, know this; when the Fire of All is gone from you, and you die, there yet remains an hour while the Fire of All is within the atoms of your body. Then this fire too returns to All, who is the essence of the Infinity, so that it be best your body be far from men. Go now, to your commander.'

"And now he turned on me a ray of red, such as that that had licked at the weapon of Chu Liang. The ground beneath me hissed to it, and shrieked; it dissolved so that I felt myself sinking, and the snake-tongued flame wrapped about me and clung like the cocoon of the silkmaker. Then blue fire licked from my body, and fought with it, and presently I felt strength come to me again, save in the arm and the side where the staff had lain and touched. Then blue flame and red, snaked-tongued ray died together, and I stood up and came swiftly away. I ran, and was tireless. A fence was before me, and I grasped its top with the hand which would act to my will, and lightly flew over it to the strain of my muscles, while the planking dented between my fingers.

"Now look, and say you whether I am as before." The young Oriental grasped the oaken door-frame, and between his fingers it splintered as though in the grip of a vise. Suddenly they knew he was shining over all his body, with iridescent whirling rainbows, luminous oil on water.

"The strength is going from me, and I know that All, Lord of Life, is leaving me. Oh, All, Mighty Lord—I believe—I understand—let me—take me—"

And the men of the Council started abruptly to their

feet as his body stiffened suddenly, with a curious crystalinity as the light burst out in eye-searing brilliance, and—died. A voice spoke, slumberous and deep, in the language he had used, as perfect in enunciation, in phrasing, in accent as his own, but it spoke, not from his lips, but from all his body.

"There is no place for you, nor your people with All and the people of All."

The man beside him recoiled suddenly, and body swayed slightly, slipped and shattered to a thousand pieces that cried out in brittle anguish.

Chu Liang bowed his head. "It is an infinitely greater god than ours. Lest we regret a decision, let his body and all parts of it to the tiniest scrap, be found and carried out to the center of the great court, and a guard be established for two hours at range of two hundred yards."

"You advise this, Chu Liang? Then, guard, let that be an order, and see that it is obeyed." The two saluted, and went away hurriedly. They were not among those who came to pick up the scattered fragments.

Torisuti turned again to Chu Liang. "What was your weapon?"

"An efficient and effective short-wave radio projector of unequaled power. It was very deadly. It was the best our science could offer."

"Their God seems peculiarly real. I—I cannot understand such a god."

Chu Liang smiled slowly. "The unwritten definition of a god includes the phrase, in every mind, that a god is one who promises, but never acts, and if he acts is not a God. There is no room in our civilization for a being above the known laws of cause and effect. We are unfortunate to meet one. Particularly one selectively opposed to our race, and one selectively helpful to theirs."

"Has your science nothing to offer which is selectively opposed to their race?" snapped Commander Torisuti.

Chu Liang shook his head slowly, then paused suddenly, as a thought came to his mind. "There may be, on second thought. But be it remembered that our science is in no way to be compared with the powers that their God has displayed."

"What then? The radio-weapon, perhaps. I do not understand that, but perhaps you may make it tune in on them, which is a thought my mind may grasp."

"No, the radio weapon is merely heat, excessive heat. That miniature set the man who has just been carried was a power unequaled in any hand-portable set in our science or, I would have said, in any science. For it gen atom and four hydrogens that act in many ways as killed nearly seven hundred horsepower, truly a vast amount to train upon an animal body, a disruptive power. Yet we know now that this must certainly have doubled, since the weapon burned out, and in all probability, trebled. Hence we say that the Staff of Life born by the Teachers is capable of generating two thousand horsepower, for the one who reported stated that the Flame of All increased but slightly."

"No meaning. The staff was damaged, and disintegrated within the hour. Tell me, too, how this may be?"

"I can suggest, but no more, and this is what my mind makes credible: that the staff is made, not of pure metal, but of an alloy, and the alloy is not one I can duplicate. There is a compound, ammonium, consisting of one nitrogen atom and four hydrogens that act in many way as a metal, silvery in color and very light. Now it may be formed in mercury to make an amalgam, which is very soft, but solid and, at low temperatures, somewhat stable. This staff then, may have been an alloy of platinum and ammonium, intended that we may not have the thing to analyze and investigate. Now when certain conditions were fulfilled, or certain time elapsed, or a hidden stud of the carving was not depressed, the stuff became unstable, and the ammonium freed itself as gas. The gas of ammonium in the presence of finely divided platinum burns with a blue light in air to a gas. If this be true, then the platinum would be dust finer than the motes in sunlight beams, and would cause the burning, while the metal would glow with red heat, and the blue flames with the red glow would be violet light.

"Thus it would be if it were science. But, Commander, we deal with a god, who is beyond laws as we know them, and may have destroyed the platinum. This, I suggest, for neither ammonium nor platinum, nor the gases released turn men to crystal that shatters, nor make the hands of men to crush solid, oaken beams." He nodded slowly to the crushed doorframe.

"Enough of that. It is, evidently, beyond your science, and I am beginning to fear that this thing is in truth a god, which is not good for the cause of the World Empire. Tell me though, what is that thing you mentioned, which attacks the Westerners, but not us?"

"I hesitate for two reasons; it attacks not the whites alone, but both races, though to a far greater degree the whites. However, many of our people will die. The other, that it will divide the whites from the Empire forever, if we point out that there is a god which protects and favors the Asiatic races."

"What is this thing?" demanded the Commander.

"Cholera. Asiatic Cholera. The white races are twenty times more susceptible, and if an epidemic of mild cholera be spread, nine tenths of the whites shall die, and one hundredth of our people."

"And those of ours who do die, I believe, will be the weakest of the race," said the Commander softly.

"Yes," said Chu Liang.

XII

The Four Servers stood before the thrones of the Five in the Temple of All, their faces grave and careworn. The First Server spoke. "The Lords know well the thousands who have besieged this Temple and been healed, till their five visits of the year are gone. And still they are sick, nor have they the thousand dollars to pay the Initiate Impost. So many as we will, we can heal, and so many as the Teachers can reach can be healed, so that cholera does not take them. But this brings trouble: that the healing by the Flame of All is not permanent, but merely a destruction of the disease as it exists, leaving the man open again to its dread attack.

"And the Empire is spreading and allowing the spread of the disease, while their people laugh at it, for having lived with it a thousand generations. We have not Teachers to reach every home in the time needed; we must accept as members the seventy-three thousand that are on our lists, and are capable of being made Teachers and of proven worth."

Lord Mens spoke. "This we could do, for the Impost could be met from the infinite resources of All, yet this would mean a·payment of seventy-three millions of dollars, many tons of metal, and the Empire would notice quickly. There are now in this country, some thirty-five million people of All, and due to the tenets of the Empire, there are neither feeble-minded nor insane nor recurrently criminal among them, though many are stupid drawers of waters and hewers of wood. Yet we must save them. So the Impost shall be met, and the Teachers shall join. But let them not all be Teachers, but only Members, whose Staffs are of the Sixth Order, capable of healing, but not of generation of All's powers, their powers dying with the day. Thus faulty members shall not lay open the mysteries of All to the Empire.

"And in this emergency the Flame of All shall burn at the Eighth Magnitude in all the Houses of All, day and night both. Now be it known also, to the Servers, that the Staffs of the Lords can bring life to the dead, and under the Staffs of the Lords, Lord Dis relinquishes his claim, if the body of the dead one be in condition to be again life's vessel, and not a thing of horror. So too, shall the Staff of the First Server be, and as soon as may be, the Staffs of the Four Servers, though the staffs of the Servers, save the First Server, are of a degree lower than the Staffs of the Masters.

"Now I, Lord of Wisdom, do find it time fitting, that the Servers and the First Teachers of the Houses know the full might of Dis, Lord of Death. Take thou, Dis, Lord of Death, these Servers, to the Crystal of All and teach them full the Services of Dis."

"Aye," said the Lords.

Lord Dis rose in a burning cloak of scarlet, and his staff flamed and licked with angry snake-tongues of fire; tiny crystalline trumpetings resounded from its lightenings as he led the way to the great Crystal of All. For the first time, the doors of the Temple swung shut, while the Lords themselves stood without, bringing health to the hundreds who climbed the mighty Singing Stair. Its song was a song of dread to the City of All now, for it rang day and night to the tread of hundreds afflicted with the cholera.

Lord Dis stood on the high altar of the Crystal of All, and to the Four Servers repeated the full service of Dis. The great crystal shimmered, and the blue of Mens and the Green of Tal faded as his voice rolled on, then the pearl of Shan, and even the silver starburst of All grew dim, and the sullen scarlet of Dis spread all the great crystal while trumpeting lightnings licked and danced about the altar and the crystal and the man. The scarlet floor wove and danced to foot-long streamers that writhed and muttered in angry murmur, and the long Service of Dis reached near its end.

And Lord Dis stopped. "Thus is the Service of Dis," he said, and his voice rolled in the Temple, powerful and deep. "But that is not the ending. Now these are the words of the ending, and they must be learned. I continue not the Service of Dis now, for the powers of Dis in his full might are not lightly to be summoned. Remember this, and remember too, that only in the ultimate extreme are the full words of the Service of Dis to ring in the chamber of the Crystal. Remember this, for their power is mighty beyond any powers of Earth, for

All, in his phase of Dis, strikes then with all his might, and it is not given that men should behold this thing lightly, nor much. And these are the final words, for the Service is broken now, and the Mighty Lord has retreated for the time."

As he had spoken the flames of Dis had died lower, and the floor of Dis was quiescent, flaming softly, and the silver and blue and green and pearl were returned to the crystal, tinged still with the angry scarlet of Dis.

Lord Dis spoke again. "The enemy attack, Lord Dis, and the walls resound to their march. Lord Dis, mightiest of the Lords, give answer now, to their threats, thrust forth thy banners, and thy flames of Death, snake-tongued to pierce our enemies, in the name of All, Lord of Life, strike, Lord Dis!"

The Service was broken, and not full in its power, but as his voice roared still in the stone-walled Temple, the light vanished, swallowed in rolling thunders of blackness, till only scarlet gloom remained, pierced and shattered with Titan lashes of scarlet fire, cold, the awful cold of the Dread Black Lord, Barmak, the Unseen, the Unmentioned, swept through the Temple, and the air was night, stabbed through by sunset rays of scarlet Dis, whirling, shrieking, trumpeting mad crystalline destruction.

And they died. White-faced the Servers stood; silence came at length, and Lord Dis spoke again from the altar. "Now these are the powers of Dis," he said very softly, so his voice was barely audible, and the silver of All crept in, and the blue and green and pearl. "The Lord Dis protects his own, but when the might of Dis is so great, the lives of even his people are as ants in the path of a warring God. Know this, then; within the Temple, when the full might of Dis is loose, let no man attempt to stand, save he be clothed in the scarlet robe of Dis, and wear the scarlet crystal of Dis. His staff must glow with the anger of Dis. Beyond the Temple walls, men of Western blood may stand, but if there be admixture of Oriental, his death is not less certain than the death of Oriental on that floor now.

"But this you must remember; let not these forces loose till there hovers danger above, men without, and enemies on every side, and that enemy attacks. For when the might of Dis is loose, nor All himself, nor Tal, the Lord of Peace may stay that anger. Only Tammar, Lady of

Mercy, has power then, and her power extends not infinitely.

"Now remember these things, and let the Teachers of each House of All and Dis know them well."

"Aye, Lord," said the Servers faintly.

XIII

"Your metal is pure, pure indeed, too pure. Server, we, the examiners of the World Empire, demand knowledge of this thing, and further, we demand admittance to this Temple in safety and peace!"

"That cannot be," the Server spoke sternly. "Lord All denies you admittance, and men cannot sway the will of All. The metal is good, so be it good, where is your complaint?"

"Then, Server, listen well. Emperor Nijihua himself takes notice of your Temple, having come to America this day, and this is his Edict; that any temple growing in membership more than ten thousand men in the last year shall pay an Impost of one million dollars for each member!"

The Server stood white-faced, his face stern as the mighty mountain ridges ringing the Temple. Finally Tornsen spoke again. His voice was soft and very low. "Return to your royal master and tell him then, this. That at each House of All, there must be a vehicle within twelve hours capable of bearing twenty tons of metal, and at this house a greater vehicle. Go."

The Oriental went, dazed and knowing not what to say, for in all the world, there was not eighty-four billions of dollars in hard metal.

The vehicles appeared as was ordained, and there were fourteen great freight planes in the City of All in the Valley of All.

Nijihua had not been troubled for he slept, it being night now, and only the collection service had been impressed. Uncomprehending men going in answer to an order. The Valley flamed with dull and ominous scarlet, hot with the warmth of the great fire-shot crystal of Dis, by the Cup of All.

The Collector came to the Singing Stair and mounted it, behind him the squad of laborers. The Temple flamed with the light of All, mighty and bright, a lance-flame that reached full hundred feet, steady and motionless with bursting stars of light, shattering crystals of light

138

that gave forth a low, ominous rumble of grinding sound. The floor of Dis wavered with a thousand thousand snake-tongued flames of angry scarlet.

The Collector halted, for on the great crystal floor were stacked ingots of metal. They were foot-thick bars, square of end and six feet long, and they lay rank on rank, three hundred feet they stretched, side by side, six feet long, and they towered twenty feet into the air, a mighty wall of precious metal such as man never conceived, all down one side of the great Temple. And down all the other wall of the Temple they stacked, save only at the far end, where men came now guiding other mighty bars, men in long lines, one behind another, and more behind, while another file returned empty-handed. One man moved those bars, those four-tone bars, and in his hand glowed the Flame of All, and the mighty ingots rested on it and floated, glowing faint with crimson light.

The Collector stopped, dumb-struck at the threshold. And shrieked, leaping back as the great Cubed Crystal spun savagely and the snake-tongued flame of Dis crashed a bolt of scarlet, licking lightning, to shatter in roaring crystalline wrath at the Barrier of the Threshold.

"Stop there!" ordered the Server. The Five Lords emerged through the jet wall, and their crystals flamed angrily, the Staff of Lord Dis crackling and shouting crystalline wrath, his robes and cloak shimmering under their angry licking.

"No further, Oriental," Tornsen rumbled. "It is Death, for the Lord Dis is angry this night. The ingots will be brought to you, and these ingots stand that you may see the infinite resources of All, Lord of Life. Beneath this floor lie the vaults of All, and they stretch a thousand and a thousand feet into the Earth, and a thousand and a thousand feet on every side. Now these are the metals of All, the Creator, and more he creates at will as he created those few scraps the world has know. These be osmium, osmium all. And in the vaults lie iridium and platinum, palladium and rhodium in vaster amounts, and there are all the metals of earth in what quantity we would.

"Now look you, the Flame of All is the essence of the Lord of Life, the Creator, and it is greater than any manifestation of his works, such as matter, or gravity, which it dissipates so that one man carries in his hands the great ingot. One of these ingots you may test."

The Server moved, and his Staff pointed toward the great wall of ingots, the Flame of All shot out, lancing, and a pencil line of intense violet pierced it through, leading it so it touched an ingot and the ingot burst into crimson, lifted and floated down the Flame. Tornsen turned his Staff, and the mighty ingot followed till it crossed the Barrier and hung above the salt-white stone outside. With a booming clang it dropped.

"Test that, Collector," snapped the Server.

The Collector moved swiftly and his tiny saw gnawed at the mighty thing, and a scrap came free. Swiftly with spectroscope and reagent he tested it. "It is purest osmium," he said at length. "Weigh it I cannot, for its mass is far beyond my scales."

"Then watch, Collector," snapped the Server. The crimson crystal of Dis glowed on his staff, and the forked tongue was keen as a knife's edge. It traced a line, and the ingot shrieked in tortured anguish, and—and became two, four, eight, sixteen pieces.

The Collector stared dumbly, and started forward. "Stop," said the Server. "What metal would your royal master have?"

"Gold—" said the Collector. "Gold—he has much platinum but men like better yellow gold."

"Stand back, Oriental, for All speaks his will, and he is Lord of All Things as well as Men."

The Flame of All lashed out from his crystal in mighty clashing discord, and struck the ingot and retired. The Collector looked at it dully, for it was yellow, yellow as butter of cows in lush pasture. And as he cut at it, it gummed his saw, so soft it was. With his knife he pared a great strip off.

Two ingots he loaded in the planes, and went away— the planes staggering with the concentrated load of mighty blocks of yellow buttery metal. The Server stood at the peak of the Singing Stair, and stared after them, while in the Valley, the Crystal of Dis pulsed mad scarlet flames that chimed and chattered and crashed angrily, and the clouding sky reflected their angry glory.

In two-score cities that night, two-score collectors looked upon vast treasures, while the Emperor slept.

He woke in the morning, and the clamour of his officers brought him out. The city, his city, roared and murmured with strange, riotous sounds, shrieks and howls and crying mobs of men. Careworn and brightened were his officers as he emerged.

"Lord Nijihua—Your Highness—The Temple of All—"

"What," snapped the Emperor in clipped syllables. "General Torisuti, report."

"Lord Nijihua the Temple of All replied that they would meet the impost—"

Nijihua started. "Would meet it! Impossible! For in the world, save in my treasury, such treasure does not exist."

Torisuti giggled softly. "Your Highness, they met it. They paid it with ingots of gold, platinum and palladium and rhodium, and the ingots were six feet by one foot by one foot, solid metal and pure. The Collectors returned with eyes dazed and blank, and they told of walls of metal in each Temple that stretched end to end and made of tens of thousands of such ingots! That—"

"There is not such metal on earth," Nijihua snapped. "They were plated base metals. What is the howling of this mob that disturbed my sleep?"

"It is the army and the citizens and the peasants, Highness. There may not have been such metal, but—look." Nijihua stared through the window of the corridor. The American Provincial Treasury building stood beyond, and it gleamed and glowed in the sun, like yellow butter, and its roof was fallen in, its mighty pillars slumped under their own weight. A half melted building of butter.

A score of men were fighting and howling and shrieking as they struggled to bear away a statue, curiously lifelike statue of metal, scarcely twenty inches high, made of yellow, yellow metal. But its concentrated mass was immense, and they fought savagely over it. A soldier came and his rifle blazed. They fell, or ran, and another shot the soldier down to draw away the statuette. And over all, the mad melody of the treasure-mad city howled.

"That thing was a treasury guard last night," said Commander Torisuti. "The Building is gold, purest gold, and they howl and fight to hack it away with knives and axes. And the soldiers fight with them for it. The War Department buildings are of iridium, pure and strong, too hard to cut, so they howl about it and cannot cut it away. The streets are bordered by curbstones of gold, and the bridges are sinking under their golden weight. The forts outside the city are lead, and the war-planes slump in ruin of leaden softness. The great coast defense guns at San Francisco and the bridges of New York run in liquid streams of mercury. The battleships anchored in the harbor burned last night with mighty tongues of violet flame and exploded in flaming ruin, and their solid metal ran liquid, hissing, burning on the water. All America is a mad joke on an insane, prankster god!

"And at dawn, when people woke to see the golden splendors a mighty voice roared over all the city, and commanded them to fight and slay and squabble for useless gold, for there were infinite resources in the treasuries of All. Over all the Province the cities are golden and platinum, and the weapons are leaden and mercury. Great forts slump like yellow, melted butter under their own weight."

The howling savagery of the city welled in at the windows, and shrieked about their ears. "Commanders, gather your forces. The Temples of All must be destroyed instantly. Are there any great guns and planes, remaining?"

"A score in the city, of planes, a half dozen mobile guns, with these we can attack—"

"Go, destroy the Temples, and every Teacher and Server in them." Nijihua sat in the windows of his palace, and stared at the city. Fire smoke climbed leaden into the sky, while the howls of the hunting packs drifted across the city. The city was no city, for a city is the center of an organized society, and Nijihua's heart was cold as he understood suddenly the powers of this mad god. His city was mad—mad as a lunatic howling his fury to the full moon.

Half a thousand men swept about the corner, a dozen trucks in their midst, armed soldiers. They opened fire as they reached the Great Court, and before they neared the Treasury Building, their numbers halved and none lived before them. They swept on howling, to the Treasury. A dozen power-saws squealed, and gunned down in the soft, clinging stuff. A hundred men loaded blocks and masses of yellow metal in the trucks. Then suddenly one collapsed under the vast load, and they distributed the loading better. But they could not stop. A wild mob of citizens, ten thousand strong, swept in from all sides with ax and saw and knife and pistol. There were gas shells there, and the soldiers died beneath hacking knife and ax. The peasant citizens swarmed over the trucks and loaded them further. They crunched and fell under the spilled yellow stuff.

Nijihua rose. An ordered roaring was coming from one end of the city. Presently he saw far down the Avenue of Nijihua the march of the organized troops coming, and because they were ordered strength, the peasant citizens were fighting them, fighting for the golden pavements and the golden houses with their golden people. But the troops wore masks and they were bathed in paralyzing-gas that stopped the citizens.

At the Palace, Nijihua joined them and went to the airfield. Planes drooped, lead color, like tired things on the field with broken wings, snapped stay wires, crushed landing gear and fallen engines. A score of saved planes turned over steadily with dull booming of death. Bombs lay in nestled racks beneath them. Mobile gas units were lined up. A strong guard surrounded the field.

And to the field came a Teacher, in silver cloak and gleaming headdress. The guards surrounded him in an instant, and brought him before the Emperor, smiling faintly.

"Well, man of All, what have you to say to your Emperor?"

The Teacher smiled slowly. His voice was easy and deep as he answered: "You are not my Emperor, Nijihua, for I obey but one ruler, All, Lord of Life. Now look you; All Lord of Life takes back this country for his people. It were best your men leave. You are greedy for the treasures of All, so in fullest measure he has given of them, to surfeiting and beyond, so that your people kill themselves for them and your army is disrupted by them."

"And," said Nijihua softly, "he has made them quite, quite worthless through their plenty. Aye, your God is a wise God, but I should like to know how this trick is done."

"It is done by All Things. It is not within the understanding of man. Now these things are done, and that is enough. Let your people withdraw, for this is the land of the people of All."

"In a day and a day," said Nijihua quietly, "there will be neither All nor people of All. So much I promise for the things you and your priests have done. Is that well within the understanding of man, such a man as you?" asked Nijihua.

"It is not to be. Lord Dis, Lord of Death, stands ready to defend his people, Nijihua. I will go now, and when you would speak again with All's men, seek the Temple of All in the Valley of All. The Five Lords await you. I go."

He turned to walk away. "No," snapped Nijihua. "You stay. Take him, guard!" The guards reached forward— and stopped. For the man was gone. In an instant he vanished from their sight, leaping upward slightly, and though they ringed their hands and closed in where he had been, he was gone. A voice spoke from the air and Nijihua stood calm.

"The Lord All protects his people, which is to be re-membered, and engraved in the scroll of your memory, Nijihua."

Nijihua turned to Commander Torisuti. "You will see that the planes take off at once."

XIV

"The planes come overhead, Server," said the Novice, returning from the threshold. His face was tense, and white with fright.

The Server nodded, grave of face and scarcely less firm within his heart. He stood in scarlet robes of Dis, and his crystal flamed with the red of Dis, as did the crystals of the Teachers within the Temple.

"Now go, John Kempson, and wait without, and see to that none attempts entry of the gates. For I summon Lord Dis in all his might."

The Novice closed the great gates behind him, looking back at the Server, who stood now on the golden altar of All and spoke in slow, rolling syllables. The air of the Temple was darkening, and red licked the flames of Dis about the Server's body.

John Kempson stood with seven of the Novitiate on the Singing Stair of the Temple facing the crowd of white-faced Americans below. "The Server summons Lord Dis," he cried out, "wait ye hear in safety. Lord All has maddened the Orientals with his gold and precious metals as he warned you, he has destroyed the fleet of the Emperor as was told you. Now the last weapons and the soldiers shall be destroyed, as was promised."

Behind him, the Temple glowed scarlet on all its faces, and the sapphire and emerald and pearl were gone. Only flaming angry scarlet remained and spread. Strange cold, like polar wastes, washed down from the Temple, and the sky grew dark, clouding swiftly. The clouds glared sullen in the light of the Temple, as it grew, and grew. The howling of the mob stilled over all the city, and the cold grew greater. Swiftly the black rolled up the sky, swifter and swifter, till all light was blotted out in rolling ink. Wave on wave of jet was rolling from the Temple, and it drank the light from all the city. The Crystals in the hands of the Novitiate were dulled and dim, and only the intense scarlet of the Temple pierced the jet that settled as Dis and Dread Barmak, Lord of Nothingness gained sway. The jet waves pushed out and the snake-tongues of Dis rolled and curled about the Temple. The great piling of the clouds above pressed lower and the cold of the Black Lord washed out in deadening waves that paralyzed heart and mind.

Abruptly, within, the last words of the Service of the Summoning of Dis were done. Thunderous trumpetings of angry sound washed in from all Infinity—and a mighty Being snapped into existence.

Dis, Lord Dis towered above them, scarlet in his cloak, a mighty Titan God, looming a thousand feet, dwarfing the great towers of the Empire's buildings, the vast cloak flapping in heart-chilling breezes of another world. In his hands flamed a mighty staff of red metal, tipped by a snake-tongued crystal that washed and sprayed the frightful flame of Dis. They roared through the heavens, sunset rays of Death. Ten thousand feet crashed out to the mighty bombers of the Emperor. The ships vanished in unbearable wash of scarlet flame piercing even the utter jet of Barmak's veil that held the city.

That day, Dis stalked a thousand feet high, his mighty flames roared down and the buildings of the Empire flared and vanished and boiled hot in the black and cold. The bombers vanished from the air and Nijihua's weapons crumbled on the ground; and thousand-foot Dis roared out his warning. "All, Lord of Life, defends his own, and I am Dis, Lord of Death, defender of All. Ye die, this day, invaders, and the country returns to the people of All, for All in his might, is angry. Now this is thy death!"

Mighty Dis thrust out the blazing crystal, and the flames from it rained down in hissing streams that rent the air, the rocks, the very waters. And as suddenly ceased. Stopped by a great glow of amber light.

Tammar, Lady of Mercy, stood before him, thousand foot high as he, in robes of gold, and about her wavered golden light that drove back the jet and scarlet of Dis and Barmak, Lord of Nothingness, who took much to him that day. Tammar spoke, and her voice rolled softly over the city. "Stop, Lord Dis. They shall go, for such is the will of All, but they need not go to the Black Lord. It be better and wiser and more just if they go to their own place, and their own gods. Cease thy wrath, and come again to the place of the Lords."

The jet and scarlet broke, and Mens, Lord of Wisdom,

came blue as sapphire. "Aye, Lord Dis. It is wisdom. I cannot halt ye, I have no power to stay ye, nor has any, save the Golden Lady. Come then, for it is wise as well as merciful."

Lord Dis' angry face calmed slowly. "Aye, I will go. And they will go. For if I be summoned by my people once again, I whip this land with the Flames of Dis till no thing lives save the people of All, and by my side shall walk the Black Lord, fully visible! By Mighty All I swear that, not shall Lady Tammar nor Lord Mens again stay our hands."

Thousand-foot Dis vanished, and the jet clouds that were with him vanished, rolling up before wave on wave of blissful heat, warmth God-sent. The jet vanished with the scarlet tongues of Dis. The sun broke through, so people were half blinded. And the city moaned, over all its streets and parks it moaned; then slowly the howl grew, and the shrieks of men that sought to escape on foot, in cars, in planes, in every way. For they dreaded death less than Thousand-foot Dis, of the scarlet lightnings, and the Unseen One of the black and cold.

XV

The great, golden plane of Nijihua settled to the landing sands at the City of All, among the mighty cliffs of the valley. The Temple glowed with the sapphire of Mens and the emerald of Tal, the pearl of Shan and, faintly the scarlet of Dis.

Nijihua dismounted from his plane, and a score of Teachers of All, in their robes of silver, bearing the crystal staffs, came down the Singing Stair that boomed softly in the great gorge, to their tread. Nijihua stood on the sands by the plane, only seven elderly men beside him, his Council. The first Teacher of the Temple advanced toward him, and spoke softly. "Nijihua, you seek audience of the Five Lords?"

"Yes, Teacher of All. I must make some peace for my people in this continent. They destroy themselves in their mad rush for safety, and my army is more disorganized than the people squabbling over useless metal, so it is impossible for me to save them and their goods."

"The Lords shall meet, and shall judge you, Nijihua. Come thou, then, to the Temple of All."

Nijihua and his seven councilors followed, eight elderly men, upright and straight in their robes of state, come to enact what peace they might. They mounted the Singing Stair, and halted at the peak on the salt-white stone of the threshold. Before them gleamed the mighty Crystal of All, such as they had never seen. And on its top stood the Five Lords before their Five thrones. The glory of the Temple impressed itself upon the Oriental, its beauty of simplicity and lighting. Gradually something of its peace seeped into him.

The Server stood before him, huge and straight. "You have come to audience with the Five Lords, Nijihua, and Tammar, Lady of Mercy has made promise for you."

Tammar spoke, and her golden voice rolled softly through the Temple. "It is death to Oriental who crosses the Barrier, but that these men may be truly and justly judged, it is best they be near to us. Wherefore, I do

148

promise them safety within the Temple for this time. Follow, Nijihua, in the golden light."

A star burst golden in the air of the room, a pinpoint of exploding light that expanded suddenly as it fell to a thirty-foot globe of golden radiance, settling light as a great bubble to the crimson floor, and halfway through it, till it was a hemispherical dome of golden radiance. Within its circle, the floor of Dis was dark black crystal, at the edge it shot tiny blue lightnings and over all the surface of the globe, blue lightnings played with a hissing crackle almost noiseless.

Nijihua and his Council were within it and they crossed the barrier, and walked a floor no Oriental foot had trod, till they stood near the great Crystal. The Five Lords seated themselves as the Server stood before the eight men.

"Now this is the peace with your people," said Mens, Lord of Wisdom. "That they leave this country with such things as they brought, and no more of goods, save only that they may take whatever quantities of gold and platinum and other precious metals as may delight them or be useful to them.

"But every man of your people shall leave, save those who have been in this country more than fifteen years. That is the peace with your people. All, Lord of Life needs no guarantee of non-aggression, no indemnity of materials for his resources are infinite, and no indemnity of goods, since it were better the people of All earn. The lives you have taken cannot be returned. That is the peace of All, Lord of Life, with your people.

"But All, Lord of Life, has further justice with you, Nijihua. Say first, Emperor and Council, are these terms with the people acceptable?"

Nijihua sighed softly. "Yes, Lord, these terms are acceptable, but what is this demand of Justice upon me?"

Dis, Lord of Death rose in his scarlet robes, and Nijihua shrank back. "Lord Dis!" he said softly.

"Lord Dis," answered the towering figure in scarlet. "I make this demand of justice. Without you and your council your people were good and earnest workers. With you, they became a deadly unnatural menace, a flowing ooze that crushed the nations of the Earth. Your life is forfeit for the many it has cost through heedless ambition."

The crystal staff in his hands dipped, and from it, snake-tongued flame lashed downward at the recoiling Emperor—and shattered on the golden globe about him.

Angry-browed Lord Dis turned to Tammar, Golden Lady of Mercy. "Tammar, ye builded better than I knew in this golden bubble. Shatter it, for his life is forfeit!"

Lady Tammar spoke then. "Nay, for as Mens has said, no taking of lives can return lives. It is not his life that brings trouble to the world, but his ambition. Now I say with you, that this menace to peace and happiness shall be, and must be, removed. But this I say; that it need not be his life. Let it be his ambition."

Shan, Lord Shan of the pearly robes turned to the Golden Lady grave-faced and sorrowful. "That too is a stricture great in its weight. Let the man choose which he would have, for it may be that he would choose the death Lord Dis advises."

"Aye," said the Lords.

"Then choose, Nijihua," said Shan, softly. "And remember in your choosing that these are the choices, and there is no alternate. You die without knowing, on the floor of Dis, or you be robbed of emotion, of ambition, lost to you then is both hate and love, both ambition and despair, and intellect alone remains unimpaired and undirected by any ambition, any desire, any emotion whatsoever. And these are for these and your Council to decide."

"Lady Tammar promised safety," called out one of the Councilors.

"Safety to cross the barrier and win fair judgment," the Golden Lady replied gravely. "This you have. Choose."

Nijihua giggled softly. "Naturally if this thing you promise be done, I would choose—intellectual freedom."

"So be it," sighed the Lords.

And from the air above the Crystal, from the Silver Flame of All itself, a blackness condensed. A Sixth appeared, the Sixth Lord, the Invisible Lord, Barmak, Lord of Nothingness. His throne was black, blacker than jet, for no ray, no sparkling returned from it, no faintest glint of light. It was the blackness of Barmak, Lord of Blackness and Lack, the Unmentioned Lord of Despair. He was robed in blackness, not black. He *was* blackness, having no face nor visible feature, only black form that was all essence of nothingness and annihilation. But from the blackness, a voice spoke, and from the utter night of this throne, Dread Barmak rose, towering tall, a hole of utter dark in the silver of All's flame, unillumined by even this flame.

"So be it!" His voice was a great rumble that echoed mournful through the Temple suddenly chilled by his presence. His staff of blackness tipped downward, and from it lanced a bar of solid blackness that touched and curled about the man, lancing through and swallowing the golden flame of the Lady of Mercy.

Shrill rang Nijihua's scream. "Ai—ai—ai—the cold—ai—" And the Emperor of the World lay stretched on the blackened crystal floor.

And the flame of All was whole; Dread Barmak, power of Nothingness was gone.

Lord Mens rose again. His blue staff gleamed, and its tetrahedral flame reached out a glow that penetrated and mingled with Lady Tammar's globe. And Nijihua stirred, and rose.

Nijihua spoke again, and his voice was clear and precise, utterly exact, as perfect as a perfect machine. "Very well. The thing is done then."

"Aye, it is done, Nijihua. Now say, Councilors, what choose ye?" demanded the Server.

"Life—life—"

"So be it," the Lords echoed soft.

And the heart of All's bright flame froze, and congealed in the cold and dark of Dread Barmak, the utter absence nodded its awful head and spoke. "So be it," and the cold dead ray of the Black Lord's staff lanced out, and the councilors fell crying with cold, and rose again as the Black Lord vanished and Mens' blue flame touched them.

"You will hold to the covenant of your word, Nijihua?" Lord Men's voice was low and grave.

"I will hold to the covenant of my word, and the people shall move out so swiftly as may be; what more, what other, can man do, before the powers of the living, eternal Gods? I dreamt I fought men, and the Gods walked and lived and acted. I am done. My kind is done. We go."

"This I say to you now, under seal of secrecy you cannot break, by intent or other," said Lord Mens, rising from his sapphire throne, "for I tell you under the Flame of Mens, and the channels of the brain that make this understanding expressible are forever closed. So always you will know, and understand, but never will you speak of it, nor write of it nor ever act by reason of it.

"Chu Liang who stands here now as your Councilor of Science said once that the God he fought was a greater god than his, his God of Science. That is true. The science of a knowledge of atoms and radiation undreamed before its discovery. Here in this vault we released the flame of matter, the flame of All Things, as America died.

"We learned its secrets, and one of its secrets is this: that radiation can be specific, even as chemicals can be. Close you came in your guess of specific chemicals and anti-bodies, but it was specific radiation. And under the crudest of these, Chu Liang, the plane-polarized light of the Moon, the mad grow madder. You tested, Chu Liang, and you found only ultra-violet in the Flames of the Lords, and never did you guess of their infinite variation of wave form and polarizations of unguessed types. For these no instrument you knew could detect, so safe you called them—and died. A thousand-thousand we know, for where drug must follow drug in difficult laborious synthesis, with the Flame of All Things, combination followed combination of polarization, hyperbolic and parabolic, and strange wave form as swift as control may be turned.

"Not unique are these specific radiations we use, for there are men who send powerfully, the powerful personality, the natural healer who by his steady gaze alone draws up the fires of life to fight again. In man these radiations form every nerve ending, and they bring unease or death to every other animal or living thing. So it is the dog looks not long in the eye of man, for man's radiation is powerful, and nerve-racking to all other creatures.

"Infinite power of them have we here, so that, specific to Western man, it sterilizes them of every living thing, and leaves only the man alive, uplifted by friendly, sympathetic vibrations. There be rays that speed tissue growth, and rays that stimulate heart and glands. These bring peace or sleep, joy or sorrow or death as we may choose.

"Such are the Flames of the Lords. And the Flame of the Black Lord brings death to the nerves that stimulate the glands, and death to all feeling of emotion!

"So, Nijihua, is All more and yet less than he seemed?"

"More," said Nijihua, "for his power is real and infinite, the power of all things.

"And—Less," said Nijihua, "for he obeys the Laws of Cause and Effect. Yet therein is his greatness, for all becomes dependable and understandable as Science, where he is whimsy and intractable as a self-will being."

"Dis—Lord Dis—the thousand foot—" said Chu Liang softly.

"By projection, projection of such forces as heard your innermost councils, they threw the image of Lord Dis of the Temple and Lady Tammar thousand-foot over Chicago. Remember, then, this too; in all the world there is no hiding from the sight of the Lords.

"So, go, Nijihua, and remember your covenant to keep it. For All is God, and more than God!" Lord Mens' Flame died and Nijihua shuddered slightly. His mouth opened, and sounds came forth, but no speech.

"You cannot speak of the knowledge, Nijihua, for the time of its revealing is not yet. Go, and remember in thy soul!"

Nijihua turned, and the Golden Bubble of Tammar followed him to the Barrier of the Threshold and burst in golden crystals that clamored soft in their extinction. The Singing Stair sang to his tread, and he went steadily, without emotion of despair, or regret, to turn the great organizing abilities of his perfect, unemotional intellect to the mighty task of evacuating America, the Land of All and the people of All.

For locked in his mind was the understanding that All *was* a god for all Lord Mens might say, and a mightier God than the man Nijihua who had entered that Temple had ever guessed.

Beside him walked his Councilors, seven elderly men, locked in silence of intellectual despair of questions that to them must ever be unanswered, unexpressed—microcosms of knowledge, forever incommunicable.

THE
SPACE
BEYOND

1

James Atkill stirred softly on the metal plates of the floor, and floated up some feet into the air. His face showed pale violet in color, his lips brilliant violet. His woven rubber jacket, which had once fitted him like a blue skin, was orange. His trousers were a nauseous green, his jet black hair an extremely deep green; his eyes alone remained black.

They opened now, and consciousness began to struggle up behind them. They opened wide with a jerk and his body whirled wildly in the air. A groan of pain escaped him, and a look of dawning, amazed understanding came over his weirdly colored face.

This feeling of falling meant he was weightless in the space ship they had stolen from Nestor's men. Weightlessness here simply meant they were not accelerating. With a rush the situation returned to him. The fight over New York City, the destruction of Nestor's four ships there, the sudden burst of violet flame from the last that had spelled doom to New York by atomic burning if it were not destroyed—his ship had caught the flaming wreckage, and carried it on a plane of pure force out to sea. The Release Flame, the flame that told of the utter destruction of matter to pure energy, had begun to eat at that plane, which no matter could penetrate, like a corrosive acid. Again he heard the cries of his criminal crew as their own Release Flame flared up, then died down under the lead even the energy of matter could not support—when it was controlled.

Then—something had happened, an awful wrench that tore each separate atom and electron of his body in a different direction, utter blankness—now awakening.

Instantly the quick mind missed the soft purr of the swirling iron atoms feeding into the release flame as they swept up in a miniature silvery whirlwind from the iron block. The Eternal Flame was out.

"That's one way to put it out anyway," he muttered. He struggled vainly for a minute to turn about in the air. He was facing the great control room window, and the roof. Weightless, with nothing to grip, he could not move.

Suddenly his eyes fixed sharply on the view from the window. The keen eyes narrowed abruptly, a low whistle sounded.

"Hello—now what does *that* mean!" He brushed his hand across his eyes, then stared at it astonished. Violet! His hand was pale violet.

"Good God! By the crawling worms of Luna! Where are we!" Abruptly he stopped moving his arms and legs aimlessly, and applied his knowledge of physics. In a moment, by intelligent manipulation of his arms he was facing the floor of the control room. A monstrosity that experience could never have named for him lay there, half under a seat. It was shaped like a man, but there was something horribly wrong with it. It might have been a man a long time ago, but from appearances it had been dead in the sun for a long time. Atkill shuddered and called.

"Tex—Texas, you long-eared jack-rabbit, come out of it." The long, narrow thing on the floor proved to be alive. It moved. In a moment it sat up, looked up, and its mouth fell open to reveal a set of broad pale, robins-egg blue teeth with dark blue trim in a deep violet cavity.

"My God, Tex, close that chasm. I'll forget you're human if I look at those teeth long. You look a lot like I did. Snap out of it and pull me down."

Texas hooked a large foot under the seat, reached up a long arm, and dragged Atkill down.

"Tex, I'm going to be busy. Do you burn?"

"Huh? Do I burn? Yuh got me wrong, hombre, I ain't no match."

"Does your skin hurt, is it sunburned?"

"Oh—it does. Say, that's right funny. I never felt this way since I was a two-year-old."

"Um. I thought so. Tex, there are seven others aboard here. They'll wake soon. They were all nearer the flame than we were, but they'll be waking. They've got guns, Tex, and they may try to use them if they're scared when they wake. Collect them, will you?"

Atkill turned to the window, and stared out for a long time, his trained mind taking in data and converting it to conclusions on which to base action.

The window opened onto a region of space such as he had never imagined.

It was scattered with stars as thickly as the Milky Way. But they weren't the stars of the Milky Way. They were stars so bright Sirius would have been dull and dim by comparison! They shone with a solid brilliance that was brighter than the full moon, a brilliant plate of blue-white, white, green and orange suns. The stars here were so obviously suns it was hard to look at them. And yet there were some that outshone all others. A half dozen perhaps, brighter than any star Atkill had ever imagined. And one lone star that shone as a tiny, blue-violet disc, an unwinking eye of impossible brilliance.

Atkill gasped. "Spectral class O or I'm a mackerel! Must be less than a light year distant. There are a dozen others must be Class B or O. Every doggoned one of them a class C supergiant! Sweet orbits, what a collection! Those darned things are so bright I bet I'm just not seeing a couple thousand little candles like our sun! That big one must be half a million times as bright as old Sol. And surface temperature around 30,000 degrees.

"A globular cluster—must be! Right in the middle of a globular cluster. And what a gang of big boys!" He stared silently for a few seconds. "We're turning," he muttered. "What's on the other end?"

The ship was indeed slowly turning about. The swelling of the midsection hid what might be behind them now, but in a few minutes it would be visible.

No wonder he had not missed the lights—with that vast congregation of giant stars flooding all this space with light. A globular cluster—perhaps 20,000,000 stars grouped in so dense a swarm, they averaged less than a light year apart!

A voice sounded behind him—a cry of horror.

"Jesus Christ—Holy Mary—what is it—what is it! He's dead! Take it away—it's dead!" There was terror in the scream.

Suddenly it mounted to an ear-piercing shriek. "He's dead—he can't move—he can't move when he's dead—Mother of God—stop him—he's dead." The shriek ended with a dull thonk and a sigh.

"It's all right, guy. You look the same, so don't get hot about it," said Tex's calm voice. "Take care of that

guy over there. Hold his eyes shut till he's awake enough
to get it all. Tell him first—everybody looks this way.
That fire done it when it did a fade-out."

Presently more voices joined in, gasps of astonishment,
and terror, then curses. Men began to filter up from the
back. Joe Keller, the leader of his gangster-friends,
showed up presently. He looked at Atkill out of the corner of his eyes and shuddered. He probably was the
equivalent of very pale. He looked down at his bright
blue-green shoe, and looked hastily away.

"Where'n 'ell are we, Atty?" he asked in a shaken voice.

Atkill grinned. "You may be right about that. It may
be hell, but my answer is where Warren went, I guess.
'Member we caught a message from him just before we
blew up? He was back again—said he'd been in 'another
space'. That's where we are."

"Yeah, maybe—but fer the love of gawd, what's wrong
with everything—this place ain't right—the whole damn
thing ain't right—I ain't right. Why's your face purple?"

"Remember the tricks that Release Flame could play,
Joe? Well we're in a place where similar things are
natural, that's all. The flame brought us here—it can take
us back, just as it did Warren, I guess."

"Well fer Gawd's sake hurry. This is awful."

"I've got to start the Release first, Joe. Come on."

Atkill wasn't any too sure he could get back even
if he did have the Release. In fact he knew he couldn't
do it right away. He cursed the fact that he had left all
the calculating machines in the laboratory when he set
out to that battle. It would take days and days to do
calculations those machines did in minutes. And he had
no assistant. The gangsters were unintelligent, and useless.
Texas, a strange human misfit, would be more help. Tex
had just never been able to settle down to real work—
he wanted adventure. Educated as he had been, he was
a real "maldito hombre." His curse was a need for excitement and action as strong as a doper's need for his
drug.

Now he alone of the gang was calm.

Atkill stopped on his way back to get some instruments out of the cabinet. He looked at them doubtfully,
and went on. In the engine room, among the massed
apparatus, he felt more keenly the reality of the situation. The Eternal Flame was out. The massive iron block,

a raw ingot of pitted rough iron, stood cold and lifeless in the midst of the mechanisms. The white globe of flame he had come to associate with it was missing. The top was a brilliant concave mirror of unbelievable polish. The Flame had eaten it smooth.

He looked at it for a minute while the half-dozen gangsters watched him closely. Finally he stepped forward to a cabinet in the side of the engine room and took out a square metal box. Carefully he lifted the lid. Inside was a miniature engine room with tiny apparatus set about a tiny block of iron. In the top of the block of iron was a concave, incredibly polished mirror—and *nothing more!* Atkil gasped. "It's out!" Even this was out. He sat down heavily on a massive metal brace

"It must have generated the quench field Warren mentioned—it wasn't just an overload that killed it," he muttered.

"Ey, wat'sa matter?" demanded Joe Keller.

"It's out," said Atkill simply showing him the inside of the box. "It went out with the big Flame. We haven't any flame left."

"Well, ya knew that didncha?"

Atkill shook his head heavily. "The big one—I knew that was out. But I thought these little ones would be going. They aren't. The fire's out, Joe, and we haven't any matches."

"What do you mean, Atkill? Can't yuh start that-air thing again?" asked Tex softly. Again Atkill shook his head. "Yuh started it once, back on Earth?"

"Twice," nodded the physicist. "Once with an eighteen mega-volt, 18 million volts that is, discharge between certain apparatus, and once with another Flame. With a Flame I could start it now. With an 18 million volt discharge and a week's work I could start it."

"Well, why can't yuh do the work, and make the discharge like yuh did before?"

"No room," said Atkill grimly. "Eighteen million volts needs a hell of a lot of elbow room—at least forty feet."

"This-yere ship must be a hundred and fifty."

"Long, yes. But it's got metal walls. It's only thirty feet in diameter. I can't possibly get more than a thirty-foot gap. I can't get that because my towers have to be fifteen feet in diameter, which would leave only about seven feet between the walls. The men that designed this damn ship didn't put in an airlock. We haven't any space suits. If we did have we couldn't get out of the ship without letting all the air out, and we can't replace it.

"When the Flame went out the air apparatus stopped working. The air is being used up now, and not renewed. I can fix that for about two months—I loaded on supplies for about a month when we took off.

"We're stuck."

2

"B—But how'll we git back?" Keller whimpered.

"We don't," said Atkill promptly. "That's an easy question to answer."

"We—we can't never go back?"

"This ship is like a car without an engine. It won't move. Only there's this difference. You can't walk home either, and there's nobody to give you a tow. In words of one syllable: we can not move, we can not get home, we are stuck right here now and so far from home they could not find us if they knew it back home."

A little man with bright green hair and two orange teeth, dressed in a neat, well-tailored suit of a nauseous yellow-green, began to shake. His face went several shades lighter in color, till it looked like sheets someone had used too much bluing on. He stopped trembling suddenly and went rigid. His face changed suddenly to a flushed violet, his reddish eyes narrowed to slits, and seemed to shine with a deadly light. "Killer" Hiney was suddenly stark, raving mad. He picked up a heavy monkey wrench, dug his toes into a joint between two heavy braces, and dived at Atkill mouthing something.

Atkill moved so swiftly no one saw just what happened, but Hiney dropped to the floor dead. Atkill left the room instantly, and went to the control room again. He barred the metal door, and sat down to think. He looked up as the light in the room became suddenly intensely bright. A thin streak of light was falling through the corner of one window, and hitting the opposite wall. The spot glowed with an incredible brilliance, so bright it hurt Atkill's eyes to look at it. It was a knife-edge of light that struck it, light of a deep blue that was almost violet. It was widening very slowly as the ship continued to creep slowly around.

"The color of radiated light doesn't seem to be changed much here." said Atkill to himself, looking at the light through narrowed eyes. "That means that the weird color effects are due not to the effect on light of this different space, but the effect on the coloring arrangements of dyes and colored substances. Then that is blue-violet light. To produce light of that color would require a temperature of at least 40,000 degrees. Now what kind of a star would give that light? That must be so loaded with ultra violet that it bakes a man to death in minutes. Uh—I feel it already." Atkill moved. The light-strip was an inch wide, and the cabin flooded with an illumination painfully brilliant. Further, the temperature was rising.

"Ah—that's not going to be so nice." The back end of the ship was windowless, practically, save for a few tiny peepholes for directing the deadly projector rays. The outside of the ship was polished steel that reflected the light like a mirror. As the ship turned the light came in the window, and instead of being reflected was heating the ship.

Atkill moved swiftly. He gathered every piece of paper, every bit of cloth, and everything that he could move which might be injured by the light, and moved them out of the room. A low panicky rumble of voices came from behind. He carefully closed the door of the control room, and went to his own cabin. This was equipped with a small porthole. Here he set up a spectroscope from his luggage, and examined the light that was pouring in.

Then he starting making examinations and measurements with many other stars, using little sodium flames for comparison spectra. He had no assistant, and it was hard work. But eventually he began to get rough results.

He looked at his results in unbelieving silence when he was through, and shook his head. "Must be wrong. There isn't any such class of star. It's something bigger and hotter than O. Mass must be about 400 times that of the sun. That's almost impossible to believe. It's radiation is, according to this, at least two and a half million times that of the sun. And I'm now some 75,000,000,000 miles out—and roasting under the heat. Good God what a star!"

He started to check his readings. In an hour he blew up over them. The radiation was half again greater than before! And had shifted further toward the violet!

He threw down his apparatus and went back to the men. There was something they'd be more interested in that he had to tell them now. Something he'd discovered shortly before he stopped his observation.

They looked up sullenly at his approach. They'd found

the bullet hole in Hiney's breast soon after he left. Texas had a gun. Atkill had one. They had none.

"Come on men, let's eat. We eat cold, but we can eat."

"Aw, t'hell wit it. I ain't hungry. But Tex says you won' let us have nuh booze and nuh smokes. How cum?"

"I didn't say that—but Tex is right. I should have. You can't have booze, because it will drive you mad. You can't smoke because the air is too thick already. I'm going to start working on it in a little while. In the meantime we can eat. And there won't *ever* be any smoking until—or unless—we get out of this. You can chew a crumb of tobacco. That will help."

Curtly he turned to the food locker. Two cans of corned beef, a couple of baked beans, a loaf of bread, and chocolate. Water to drink. And no heat.

They ate, most of them, because they were hungry. Atkill ate because he had an excellent appetite, and was most anxious to go back to his observations.

But after eating he started work on the air apparatus. The ship had been equipped with batteries. Ordinary Teril dry storage batteries. That was the work of the Power men, Nestor's men, who had built the ship. They had never heard of a power plant without some sort of reserve—they thought these batteries would be a reserve power perhaps? For replacing the titanic power of the Flame they were nothing, but their thousands of stored kilowatt hours would give the men air to breathe now. In three hours the physicist had proved himself chemist enough to rig an electrolyser apparatus that was turning out a steady stream of oxygen, and releasing hydrogen into space. To get rid of carbon dioxide he would use a physical method. It would have to accumulate till the air showed five or six per cent. That would not be fatal, by any means. Then a blower would force the air through chilled water. The CO_2 would be absorbed. When the sun's heat warmed the water the CO_2 would be driven off again, and could be released into space. He could afford no power for effective, constant-control apparatus. His batteries would last scarcely a month as it was. They had only one chance in a hundred billion at the best— but there was no reason for reducing that.

"There are," said Atkill when he returned to the power room, after demonstrating the oxygen apparatus to the quite un-understanding men, "at least four planets. Two are on this side of the sun, and at approximately the same distance from the sun as we are. One about 70,000,-000,000 miles, the other about 80,000,000,000. One of them might, by one chance in about 100,000,000 be inhabited. By one chance in another ten million or so, the inhabitant might have a ship capable of crossing space. By a perfectly impossible chance they might see us. Then by a similar chance they might be interested enough to investigate.

"That's our only chance. I'm going back and observe what happens about us." He stepped out, but stuck his head in a moment later. "Don't look at the sun. It will blind you instantly. Don't let the light fall on your flesh, it will cook it in five seconds."

He went to sleep soon, listening to the loud, tense voices of the men behind. They were quarreling and cursing. Their nerves were strung to the breaking point already. As he drifted off to sleep Atkill realized two things: His own death was certain, but he would certainly have a month, and probably as much as six months for observations; the men with him would not die of starvation either of food or air. They would all die violently, and they would all die insane—with the single possible exception of Texas. These city-bred gangsters, used to bright lights and moving, living crowds, used to conditions that left them full play of their own wishes, and utterly unused to amusing themselves or each other, would go mad as surely as they must die. Their minds were unaccustomed alike to loneliness and thought. Thought might have dispelled the loneliness, for him, study would make that six months of life all too short.

Of course, no one would know what he learned, no eye ever see his results, no meeting vote him acclaim. But *he* would know. He would solve mysteries no other man had ever solved.

When he woke the violent light was shining in once more. It reminded him of the investigation he had made the—night?—before. The light of that sun simply wasn't understandable. There were muttering, angry voices, drunken voices back of him now. Atkill's lips curled in disgust as he stuck his head into the room. Joe Keller and Texas sat playing cards slowly and carefully. Three of the others were sleeping drunkenly on the floor. The remaining three were quarrelling over a pair of dice.

"Lishen yuh blankety son of a show and show—thas my fi' dollur. Yush a li'r."

Atkill laughed softly. His five dollars. A five cent can of beans would be a lot more valuable soon. The physicist called Tex, and told him to go on to sleep. Tex slouched off to his bunk, and lay down with his gun in his holster. The westerner had substituted a hip holster for the neat shoulder device he had been wearing under his coat. He felt more at home with this style. His hand rested on the butt of the gun lovingly in sleep a moment later.

Atkill had gone back to the little machine room he had set up in the back of the ship. Nestor had originally meant this for a bomb-storage room. Atkill had thrown out the bomb-racks, and arranged the present machine-shop before he left Earth. There were three tiny slits in the walls here, and through two of these light was streaming like a fluid squirting from a nozzle in a physical stream. Atkill looked at them a moment, smiled, and stepped out to return in a few moments with a can of beans and a pot of water. The pot was tightly closed by a pressure lid for steam cooking, and so held the water in this weightless space. The physicist took a knife and ripped off the label from the bean can, smeared the shiny label with a mixture of graphite and grease, which was blacker than coal, and hung it in the beam of sunlight. He started to stick his hand in, but before the fingers had more than entered he snatched them back. Almost instantly he had felt the terrific ultra-violet of this light. He took a stick and a fan, and carefully pushed and blew the can into place. The grease melted in a few seconds, but stuck in place.

Next he got the water out of the pot. That was difficult, and he got wet doing it, but he succeeded, and blew it into a sphere in the path of light.

He set to work with his machines, and the pressure cooker. He changed the pan considerably, and added a small air pump to it. He used power in doing it, but he was willing to now. He knew he could restore it.

By the time the water was near boiling point he captured it in the rebuilt pressure cooker, added some tea leaves and let it brew. The beans were hot too, after he wiped the grease off. With the aid of the pump he was able to force out his tea when he wished. He gave up hope of making observations that day. Instead he made an apparatus. It consisted of a heavy fly-wheel (taken from one of the larger lathes) mounted on a shaft of a small electric motor. It was so supported that it could be turned in any desired direction.

In two hours he finished it, and moved into the power room with it. The men had left the room, and six heavy snores and two light ones from the tiers of bunks explained it.

Atkill set up his crude gyroscope-motor, and began operations. He had to tie the motor down with pieces of rope. It was slow, laborious work, but at the end of several hours he knew that the ship would have stopped its rotation, and would always face the sun with one side and the back.

He left the device in operation, and returned to the machine-shop.

In the course of the day he finished his very simple device. He had taken the motor from one of the power-presses that he no longer could afford to run, readjusted it, and connected it with a small four-cylinder air-pump. One of the smaller air-tanks was next worked over, and a quantity of heavy copper tubing. It ended up as a four-cylinder steam engine running an electric generator. The air-tank boiler was painted black above, and silvered below. A flat, closely wound spiral of copper tubing three feet across was similarly painted. The exhaust from the engine was led to a long copper tube simply laid down the dark side of the engine room, and emptying into a small tank.

The system was simplicity itself. The sun heated the tank and the coiled pipe. The steam turned the motor as a generator. The current could be led off to charge the batteries. He had to charge them half at a time, for the voltage given wasn't high enough, of course, to charge the whole bank. But—he had an unending supply of electric power within the limits of his needs for immediate life. Air at least they could have.

The men had re-awakened, and again were playing cards. They bothered him very little, for Texas and Joe Keller kept them away from him. The apparatus was sufficiently powerful to supply the necessary oxygen, and have power to spare. But it raised the temperature of the ship a little.

Atkill ate, and went to sleep again.

The next day he began his observations. He continued them the next. The first day he discovered the secret of the giant sun that seemed to vary in its power. It did. It was a gigantic Cephid Variable, with a period of little more than a few hours.

The days passed swiftly for him. Monotonously for the gangsters. A week went by. The eternal glaring sun in one spot, the eternal night in others. The knowledge that they were waiting for certain death, the weird coloring of the things and the men about them. And above all the monotony. The grinding steady monotony on men who has never learned to be self-contained.

"Whitey" Moran went mad the fifth day. He shot and killed Tim Farrell, and wounded Joe Keller before Texas shot him through the ear. He had stolen the revolver from Joe with consummate cunning.

Keller became delirious from his wound two days later and his mumbling incoherent talk gave a final push to the tottering reason of "Gink" Castonti. Castonti succeeded in killing him with a table-knife. Texas prevented his further murdering. There were only four men left now. Within a week, as Atkill had predicted, they were reduced to two —Atkill and Texas.

Texas helped Atkill when he could. He helped him with the gruesome work of disposing of the bodies. There was a refuse lock on the ship. It was meant for garbage and such waste—and it was six inches in diameter and eighteen inches long. They had to dispose of the bodies.

The second week Atkill called Texas with a sudden shout that echoed through the soundless ship in rattling clamour.

"Tex! Come here, Tex!" He had seen something that meant their chances of life were multiplied a thousand-fold. And more. In the three-inch telescope on board Texas saw the dim twilight region of a spinning world flashing with sparkling lights like a miniature lightning storm on a miniature world.

"Uh—storm ain't it?" Tex was speaking less and less

now. He was growing accustomed again to silence. The silence such as he had known before in open plains.

"No, Tex, it isn't. Dear lad, think a bit. That world is so far away you can't realize the distance. What kind of lightning would make that big a full? That's a battle, a battle so big you couldn't even begin to understand it. It's the size battle half a dozen of these ships would make if they were real angry—and knew all the things there are to know. Any race that can have a battle that big has space ships! All we have to do is wait."

"Uh. We've waited a bit now."

"We're coming nearer to them now. And—every day we're becoming more visible. We have a gigantic tail now. Hydrogen gas I've released in making our oxygen is showing up behind us like a comet's tail. They'll investigate if they've got ships, I swear they must have! That battle is too big."

And curiously, from that time Atkill's observations became fewer and fewer. He spent all his time in the machine shop now. Making something. Texas watched quietly, and played cards. It was evidently a release-flame apparatus—but a tiny thing. Scarcely larger than a book.

"Be any power in that when you get through?" he asked once.

"Not unless I can get it started somehow after we are picked up. Then about thirty thousand horsepower. The Flame could give more. A million or so. The apparatus wouldn't handle it."

Atkill worked on, refining and adding to the tiny mechanism, calculating fields and effects and building it into the apparatus. He changed the entire apparatus finally, and made it almost hemispherical, with a depression on the flat side. On one side however seven tiny openings appeared, and one cup-shaped device the size of a quarter-dollar. Nine thin wires dangled from it to a broad, thick bracelet of silver, set with a score of brilliant-colored bits of stone cut with infinite pains on a device he set up himself. The rings and stickpins of the dead gangsters had furnished those stones. His own magnificent emerald stickpin had gone into it too. And also several synthetic stones he made by fusing aluminum oxide and adding minute traces of various materials—chromium, nickle, cobalt—

He smiled to himself as he worked and hummed a tune softly. Week followed week as he worked lovingly over his little mechanism. He seemed to expect great things of it.

3

"I admit it," said Randolph Warren, "I admit it unreservedly and without compunction. It is, beyond doubt, the wildest, most hopelessly insane scheme I ever put forth. But, Putt, you've got to admit that one ground for making the try is valid. Hoping to find Atkill I have to admit is not much of a hope. But hoping to learn something about that other space that's worth knowing *is* a worthwhile hope. Particularly as we have learned so much more about our machine—and since that speed idea does work."

"That speed thing," groaned Putney, "lord, I wish you hadn't thought of it. Ran, I thought I was just about as good as you were till you made that thing. Faster than light. Einstein said it was wrong. Richie added to the statement in 1940. Moorehead proved Richie was right— so you go out and make the trip to Sirius and back over the week-end."

Warren laughed. "Hardly that, Putt, hardly that. We spent one of the most instructive months ever spent out there, as you know as well as I. It's perfectly obvious, though. We don't go faster than light in our own frame of reference. It's just that we go fast, and then slow up time more or less, with the result that we *seem* to go faster than light."

"Seem—blazes, we do! 'If A and B are two Flat-landers'" quoted Putney," 'living on the surface of a sphere, they will say the sphere is a plane. If the sphere rotates slowly, they move slowly and steadily into the third dimension, which appears to their consciousness as time. Time passes, they say. A is at the north pole, and recognizes two dimensions right and left, back and forth. Lines parallel to the axis of the sphere are time to him. If B is on the equator, he recognizes two dimensions, right and left, back and forth. Lines at right angles to the axis are Time lines to him. Now A and B agree that one of their two dimensions is a space dimension, but while A can walk at right angles to the axis, B can not, and thinks that is time. B however can walk parallel to the axis, which A cannot, for A thinks that is time. Then, if A moves, in whatever direction, save exactly around the sphere toward B, he walks through time to a certain extent, so far as B is concerned. This time-motion multiplies A's proper space motion to B's understanding. The same, in reverse, applies to B in A's conceptions.

" 'In Four dimensional space we have an example in the enormous velocities of recession exhibited by distant nebulae. Their motions are enormously amplified by their time motion. The further around the hyper-sphere of space they are, the more nearly they come to moving exactly at right angles to our three dimensions, and the more their velocity is amplified.

" 'This is the basis of my speed-device.' Ran, I have heard that simple lesson so many times I'm sick of it. I know it almost word for word. Word for word—but not thought for thought. The fourth dimension-time idea remains only time, and not an idea to me.

"However, I admit that does give you an enormous advantage in exploring that other space. You still won't find Atkill though. That space is larger than ours even."

"You're wrong, Putt." said Warren softly. "I've been holding back something. Atkill I know was sent through! I *know* it, I don't merely believe it. I made some experiments for data, and calculations on the data.

"Remember that Release Flame, when it went wild, gave off surges of gravity-fields, and certain other phenomena. I explored the thing before it finally burned itself out two weeks ago, and learned a number of things about it. I made experiments on a miniature scale and learned three important things: the reaction of a force-plane on the Flame is to produce a quench-field, and at the same time to throw any matter within the field into another space; the matter so thrown over is *not* thrown to the nearest part of the nearest other space, as we were by our field that time—but to the nearest, greatest center of mass in the nearest other space.

"Imagine yourself some super-being with a five dimensional consciousness. Looking about you would see an enormous number of four-dimensional spaces, looking like rough, dented globes whirling in space. A dent would be where there was little or no matter in the four-dimensional sphere. A protuberance would be where there was a particularly large concentration of mass.

"In the space between spaces there is no time, no dimension, no existence. That's why our Flame can destroy matter—it forces it into that timeless, dimensionless existence, and yet holds it bound to this space. When we were thrown across we were cut entirely free from this space, even repelled by the field we had momentarily set up. We fell to that other space.

"Atkill was similarly thrown across. Whereas we were simply thrown to the nearest point of the nearest space, which happened to be almost starless, he has been thrown to the nearest center of mass.

"There is one more point. Every one of the Flames he carried was extinguished. ,

"What do you think he would do?"

Putney had a mind that could analyze a situation with uncanny accuracy, weight the factors of character, and give an answer to the question of how the given man would behave under given conditions that was apt to be remarkably correct.

He thought silently for nearly ten minutes, puffing slowly at his pipe. Finally he spoke. "Hmm—nearest center of mass. A single star doesn't mean a thing. It would take a galaxy to produce a noticeably center of mass. That means he's near the center of a galaxy. But he's apt to be near a sun for several reasons. Near the center of a galaxy the star-density is higher, and once somewhere near stopping in that other space, the general region picked out in other words, a single massive star would attract him. I'll bet he's fairly near a monster star. In all probability a super-giant. They are apt to occur near the center of a galaxy. They are massive.

"There's always the possibility that he not only landed near it—but in it. That we'll—"

"No," interrupted Warren, "he didn't. The effect of the terrific concentration of matter in the center of a star, particularly a large one, with its unbelievable fields of force, make the approach from the fifth dimension impossible. He would land near but not in it."

"Then," continued Putney, "he has no power. He was moving slowly—only about twenty miles a second—no —he had the additional velocity of the sun's motion at that time. About thirty miles per second. A super-giant would rake him in in all probability. He has no Flames. His release generators are dead and useless. He can't start them because all his flames are out, and he can't get the necessary eighteen mega-volt shock, for his ship is only thirty feet in diameter, and has no air lock so that he could work outside.

"He's in an ugly position. Air—hmmm—Nestor, the old fool, put batteries in the ships for some unknown reason. We never did. They'd be useless, of course, if the Flame couldn't save us. But they may save Atkill. He can use them to generate oxygen. His water supply ought to last several months, they were using it for ballast I remember.

"His food supply I don't know anything about. His men—gangsters—city types—poor minds—bet they all go mad. They may kill him, but Atkill will expect madness and may poison them, or may just shoot them or let them shoot each other.

"If he's near enough to that sun to get any power, he'll use solar energy for generating electricity, and have air almost indefinitely."

Warren smiled and shook his head in wonder. "I'd be willing to lay money on that, Putt. We can about know his position then. Now, you see, it isn't by any means impossible to find him. I can guide the ship to the same position he is in."

"As you say, Ran. You know I'll be glad to come along. How about the men?"

"Wild to go. I asked them."

Putney smiled. "They would be. We will need but four. When do we start?"

"In just three days, Putt. Got the business straightened out?"

"No. No one ever will. Not for a century at least. Men don't know how to handle the power. Fortunate that we gave them only the knowledge of electric power to use. They've developed even that into weapons of a sort. Sooner or later some scientist will turn renegade for money and sell his brains and ability, and there will be a war with other weapons. Earth will need several centuries to learn she musn't play with matches that can set fire to the universe.

"As a business of course—just a money-maker—it doesn't need straightening out. You could have a firm of shyster crooks for lawyers, a bunch of embezzlers for accountants, and racketeers for executives, and the thing would still make money. The income is going to be so big this first year that the government will have to cut income taxes so the revenue won't be unholily great."

"I guess you can leave it for a while, Putt!" laughed Warren.

4

The Prometheus was a glistening, iridescent hull of pure berylo-tungsten alloy fitted with the most powerful engine ever known to man. The magnificent streamlined ship rested lightly in her cradle in the hanger built for her in northern New Jersey hills. She was stocked now for the trip she was to make into inconceivable space and inexpressible time. In her power-locker she carried 140 rough iron ingots, her fuel supply. They were arranged in racks that would automatically feed them into the power-room and the Eternal Flame as fast as they were consumed. Or as slowly as they were consumed, for the titanic energy of matter they contained was the energy they released as they burned.

In the power-room, set in the exact center of the ship, was a rough iron ingot now half used. Above it hung a globe of pure white light, like a globe of luminescent white quartz crystal. It seemed to be resting on a whirling, iridescent funnel of silvery atoms that spun upward from the iron mass with a gentle sighing. As the iridescent silver whirlwind touched the surface of the Release Flame tiny glowing sparks picked out the edge, like the display of pyrophoric iron dropped from a tube. They shone for an instant, then disappeared.

About the room were arranged solid, chunky-looking pieces of apparatus, squat and powerful things. From the Flame to three of these pieces stretched glowing, pulsing fingers of light that snickered softly as the air was alternately blasted out and let in again. Warren was here with Putney, working steadily on the controls, adjusting with a minute precision the things that would presently throw them through that fifth dimensional timeless infinity.

"To do the job we don't need that eighteen megavolt shock so much as the concentration of energy it means," Warren was explaining to MacLaurin, the Scots mechanic-physicist. He was a capable physicist in his own right, but above that he had the genius for constructing the apparatus of physics that is far rarer than the ability

177

of the physicist. "Remember that in following Atkill, we have to use the same method he discovered; unintentionally, it is true, but a method none the less. In doing that the Flames will be extinguished as certainly as ever the quench field could. That would leave us powerless in an unknown space—as he is now. But while we can't get that enormous concentration of electrical energy inside the ship, we *can* store magnetic energy. It will leak, but by storing 100 times the needed power, we can be sure of having enough when we get there. Further, I'm going to attempt to carry that little Flame over there wrapped up in its own insulating jacket of force that may possibly protect it. If it protects it it may keep it from going through, but I don't think so. I'm just making sure.

"At any rate, any sufficient concentration of available energy will do the trick. The Flame will start another Flame simply because it has the maximum possible energy concentration. We'll be ready soon."

Warren checked once more the settings, then went to the control room. The ship rose with the gentleness of a dirigible, backed soundlessly out of the hangar, pointed her nose straight for the zenith of the night sky, and shot upward with an acceleration that carried her howling out of the atmosphere in less than a second. Inside, in the acceleration-compensated ship, no slightest sigh of this terrific acceleration was noticeable. Only in the power-room where the sighing of the whirling iron atoms rose to a gentle hum, and the sparkling lights became a clear sheet of glowing light, did it show. That, and the dozen beams of radiance that stabbed to the heart of the Flame from various pieces of apparatus.

Behind the ship trailed a heavy ingot of iron, riding in a sphere of pure force similar to the envelope that had protected the weak metal walls of the ship as she crashed through the atmosphere that had resisted her passage like a solid body.

A million miles from Earth Warren stopped, and the forces suddenly fell to work on the iron ingot. In a second it was a sphere. A moment later it suddenly seemed a misty illusion, something twisted about it till the stars of space behind shifted and moved about like live things in pain. Then a spark of dazzling brilliance appeared, grew with incredible swiftness, and turned to a violet

Flame that swelled and fattened on the matter of the ingot. In three seconds it was fifty feet across. And simultaneously the ship began to lurch slightly to waving tugs of attraction as the Flame began to pulse. More and more rapidly it pulsed. It attracted the ship with a force that strained the titanic energies of the Release Flame in the power-room. The flame began to edge with red, and red crept to the heart of it. The whirlwind of iron atoms was a screaming tortured tornado, the sparks of contact were becoming a solid flame.

Then something wrenched violently about them, the Flame flared up for a single instant in blood-red light— and darkness and nothingness descended on them.

Slowly Warren opened his eyes, then clutched wildly about him in the absolute darkness. He struggled violently for a second, then as full consciousness returned he stopped, and listened. He was weightless only because the Flame had gone out, the artificial gravity was off. The blackness meant that the metal shutters had snapped down as they should have with the failure of the Flame. Someone else suddenly moved, and there was the thump of a fist hitting metal, a sharp exclamation of pain, and a curse.

"Don't be petulant, Putt. Only while it was a brilliant idea no doubt to have those shutters in case we stopped too near a giant star for safety, I might have thought of a flashlight."

Putney's chuckle answered him. Then a beam of brilliant white light stabbed up at him. "I did," said Putney quietly. "You are colored like the gayest bird of the air. You wave there in the air like the clumsiest walrus of the sea. Your teeth are blue, and your lips are violet. You have a most unhealthy color. Your ears are something to behold with awe and amazement. Your pants are the most virulent, shrieking red that 'twas ever my privilege to view. I'll have to censor your wardrobe."

Warren grinned. "I see you're in good health and spirits, my friend. Why not turn the light on your own rainment. I know just what your face will look like. I fain would comment on your dress."

Putney laughed outright this time, and did so. Warren sighed. "You would think of that. Black and white. All color and no color. The only things that can't change. You think of everything don't you?" Suddenly he burst out laughing. "Putt—I never told you and you never asked—how are we going to find our way back?"

Putney chuckled. "The Flames on Earth. They'll guide you back quite nicely. They operate through to this time-lessness."

"Foiled," groaned Warren. "Come on—haul me down and we'll start the Flame again. This condition of weight-lessness is ghastly."

Putney reached up a hand and pulled him down. To-gether they dived for the rear of the ship. Most of the crew lay in the bunk-room. Some of the men were stirring now; the light wakened them. As they entered at one end of the bunk-room, a light shone through from the power room, and in the stillness they heard a switch click. "Mac thought of the flashlight idea too," smiled Putney. Mac had a large incandescent bulb burning in the power-room. Before they reached the door more lights flashed on till the room was quite well lighted.

"The old son of a gun," grinned Warren. "I may be long on the theory of space, but he's got me beat when it comes to the theories of the behavior of light. Such things as the fact that it won't penetrate a three-inch metal shutter."

"Wait—" Putney grasped his friend's arm. They stood motionless, then Putney let out a gasp. "Whew—feel that heat!" He was right. Warren felt it now—heat beating in on him from the shutter over the bunk-room window. The greater part of the ship had double walls—three-inch inner coating that was merely a wall for the rooms. An outer wall of eight-inch berylo-tungsten alloy. The two-inch space between was a vacuum, so as yet heat had not come through the wall, but the solid shutter was sending out absorbed heat already. "Ran, do you realize that we couldn't live in that heat. If Atkill came that close, they must have passed out from the heat."

"Uh—that is wicked. We must be within fifty million miles of the sun. Let's start that flame."

They went rapidly to the engine room. The ingot of iron stood cold and lifeless under the light of the incan-descents. "Looks wrong," smiled Warren. "Come on, men." In minutes the trained crew of scientist-adven-turers had gathered. No makeshift crew was this. Every man was a genius in his own right: Carl Korbes, the astro-physicist; MacLaurin, the Scots mechanic-physicist;

Paul Wearing, the chemist; and David Miller, the electronics engineer.

"Magnetic energy's here, Ran." reported Putney.

"Don't need it. The shielded Flame came through all in good order. Hook on control field R-M 583 intensity energy concentration—oh, about 1500 megs per mu. Ready? Coming through."

The power room was suddenly filled with a shining sigh, the surface of the iron ingot began to shimmer, glow, and in the air above it a sphere of half-visible light appeared, strained, and space writhed about it, the corners of the room twisted and strained, then with a sudden sigh, the globe of light solidified into a glowing field of energy, the familiar crystalized light glowed and sparkled before them. Instantly the incandescents were drowned out in the flood of light from the glow tubes. Simultaneously the mechanisms about the room began to come to life.

"She moves—all right, Putt. Start setting up that field to reflect energy—here it is—231X—45-a-32-Y—"

In a moment the field of force was set up. Putney pushed the button that raised the screens from the windows. Absolute darkness beyond—all the energy was being turned back. Putney looked at his meters sourly. "That field's a good idea, but not very useful. The energy striking it is about six times as intense as sunlight—and we are using just three thousand times as much power to maintain that field at the present level."

"Oh well, give it a break. It's doing what we want. You might cut that field down gradually so we can see what we can see."

Putney began reducing the intensity of the field, and within a few seconds they were able to see the star that was shining on them. It was a dim disc of blue-violet light. Warren turned to Putney with a look of surprise. Putney was looking at him, and Korbes was looking at both.

"Ouch," said Putney, "it's hot."

"I don't know what spectral class that is!" said the young astro-physicist excitedly. "That blue-violet color is something I never heard of! That means a surface temperature of about 40-50 thousands! The radiation would be terrific. No wonder the ship was heating! How far are we from it?"

Putney went to the control room, while Warren set a few of the engine-room controls for more efficient operations under the present conditions. When he reached the control room Putney and Korbes were feeding the data of the various instruments into the calculating machines.

Presently Putney let out a gasp of amazement. "By the Gods of Space! That can't be! Forty billion miles distant! Forty billion miles! Jumping orbits! Forty billion miles and that thing's a disc! Not only a disc—but a blue violet disc six times as hot as our sun! That's a new spectral type for you, Carl. Spectral Class scXO. If Class c Oo is the hottest thing and the c stands for super-giant, tack in that sc to stand for super-super-giant. That thing would make S-Doradus look like a class M in the far red for heat, makes Antares look like a red dwarf for size—and it would take some million suns to give that heat! It would take a whole galaxy of suns to radiate like that! Forty billion miles! How big is the thing, Carl?"

"Seven hundred million miles in diameter, approximately! Has the mass of about 1000 suns rolled into one! Good God, that must be the left-over matter of a whole galactic center condensed into a single sun."

"If we take down that reflection field," Warren said softly, "the ultra-violet in that light would cook you to a nicely browned roast in about three seconds. If we leave it up we can't see the rest of the sky. Let's retreat. I'm going to use the speed drive device. In a space the size that sun works on, you need it. Do you realize that to be habitable a planet would have to be about eighty billion miles out? That a year of such a planet would be approximately 1000 of our years, despite the enormous gravitative pull of that monster?"

Warren took his place at the controls, and presently the space around them seemed to strain, change, and with a curious suddenness, the disc of the mighty sun began shrinking. It shrank visibly till a few moments later, it seemed, they were so far out that Putney said the radiation was bearable. Again the transient feeling of strain and change, and they were motionless again. They had come nearly fifty billion miles, far faster than light, and now they could lower the protecting field. As Warren threw the release switch, the men stared in amazement.

The heavens were like nothing they had dreamt of. A Milky Way of super-giant stars, suns every one of which seemed brighter than Sirius, far brighter.

"Sweet orbits! A globular cluster! What a center of mass that must make. It must have fifty million of those giant stars, and I'll bet right now we're looking at a lot of suns the size of ours and just not seeing them. What a mass that system must have—that whole cluster. Look—over there—you can just see it out of the window. Turn the ship a bit."

The ship rotated slowly, and came to rest in such a position that they could see another blue-violet star, a star so bright that they could see it was casting shadows in the brightly lighted control room.

"Whew—another one of the Class sc X-O stars or I'm a sinner. Carl, see if you can get readings on that with the instruments here."

Korbes got to work, taking readings on the delicate gravitation and space distortion instruments that would tell him just what distortion of space the distant star was producing.

"About three-fourths of a light-year distant." he announced at last. "Dr. Warren, this trip is going to produce more information that any research ever conducted before. I have just noticed something else. Look at the intensity-curve of the light from that star we're near now."

The two friends looked at it. Putney grunted in surprise, Warren whistled softly. "Cephid Variable—and what a variable. With that luminosity the period luminosity law would suggest a period of less than three hours.

"Well," he chuckled, "we can be pretty sure there aren't any planets here. To produce planets requires that a sun *larger* than the sun in question passes close-by. There ain't no such thing as a larger sun."

Korbes suddenly laughed softly. "Too broad a statement that time, Dr. Warren. I've detected five planets already! The instruments here show at least five major planets, circled by more or fewer satellites. I was—ah, here's another one. Big fellow too—about 100,000 miles in diameter. It's about 30,000,000,000 miles from us, 80,000,000,000 or so from the sun. Uh—nother one. Nearly 100,000,000,000 miles from the sun. It ought to be habitable. Size I can't determine, mass about .94 Earth's. One—two—three—four—I think there are four large satellites and one or more little fellows too small to more than jiggle the instruments at this distance. Dr. Warren, these field-detector instru—for the love of heaven, what was *that!*" He stared hard at the instruments. "Whoa—say, come here quick, will you! Something's throwing these field-detectors all over the dial!"

Warren and Putney hastened to his side. The needles of the four field-detector dials were jiggling and jumping, moving erratically and powerfully. "Good lord—from those motions you'd think someone was creating and destroying a planet the size of Jupiter every few seconds. Fifty-three—eighteen—back to sixty-two—Now what in blazes—" Warren jumped to his own instrument board, and quickly set up a tremendously wide-spread detection field, and connected it to the four necessary instruments. He waited for a maximum, then pressed a stud. The meters held rigidly steady as they were clamped in position. Rapidly he noted the readings, set four dials on a small mechanism beside him—and read the result. "From the dimensions of that field it is some kind of an electromagnetic field—the dimensions of both magnetic and electric fields occur, but in a peculiar way. As a magnetic field it has power enough way over here to effect a sensitive compass.

"I'm going fishing again." Again he released the instruments, waited for a minimum and read. "Just the planet that time. Try again." After some time they decided that there were, in operation, a titanic magnetic field combined with an equal electric field, the field of the planet itself, and some sort of force-field that was far weaker, so buried in the mass of the planet, magnetic, and electric fields as to be unrecognizable.

In about fifteen minutes the whole thing stopped, and peace reigned once more. "There's somebody there all right." said Warren with decision, "and they're no pikers. I couldn't set up a magnetic field that powerful myself. Personally I can't see why it doesn't wreck the planet."

Putney had been examining the instruments and data carefully. "I think you misunderstand the problem. It's not a spherical field. It's a ray—a beam."

Warren stared. "A *beam*. But, man, you can't beam a field!"

Putney grinned. "But, man, you can't make a field that strong!"

"Let's go look-see," suggested Warren.

"Maybe our friends will want to look-see what we look like turned inside out," suggested Putney. "Whether that's beam or field, it's super-potent medicine. What are you thinking of doing to it?"

"Use field T-549. That'll twist it through ninety degrees and send it back as a lightning bolt. The magnetic part anyway. The electric part will twist into a gravity field and pull us to the planet, and them to us. We can stay off the planet all right."

"All right, I would like to see what's happening."

Korbes interrupted them. "Something coming toward us. Strange body—small—density about that of water, little more. Moving about fifty miles a second. About 2000 miles away." A moment later. "Weight only about thirty pounds. Funny kind of meteorite. Let's rake it in."

Warren was willing. A density of only one—most meteors are either stony or metal, far greater than one.

They raked it in, and when it came, Warren shuddered, and went pale. Putney looked slightly sick, Korbes ran for his room. It was a mutilated human trunk. There were no arms, no legs, and the head was missing. But it had on the remains of a suitcoat. The coat was a dirty white now, for the glaring ultra-violet of the sun had bleached it and the exposed flesh was cooked.

"Human—good god—Earthy human. Atkill—Atkill was here. That—it came from the wreck of his ship. Without his force shields a meteor or something must have hit him and wrecked him completely. There's more coming. I'll throw out a field and see what I can gather."

It gathered unpleasant things. Thrown out for nearly a quarter of a millions miles in every direction, and then dragged slowly inwards, it brought a collection of the debris of space. Meteors, pieces of crushed and broken metal beams, obviously pieces of a ship, and—three heads, once human, four more trunks, several horribly mutilated legs and arms—

Warren closed them in a small shell of force, made the shell self-maintaining, then gave it a tremendous push toward the giant sun. The bodies of Atkill's crew would be cremated in the most gigantic furnace ever known.

"Well," said Warren sadly, "we found them, anyway.

The first part of our mission is done. Something wrecked their ship with a completeness almost unbelievable. Those scraps of metal were so broken and twisted they were almost unrecognizable as beams and plates. They must have hit an asteroid-like body at a speed of over 100 miles per second. It's a wonder the men weren't even more completely demolished."

"Uh—it was bad enough. I had no desire to examine them any closer. You saw the shoulder-holster still on that one fellow. Evidently my prophecy of their end didn't work out right. I didn't take that into account."

"Let's go on toward that planet."

5

Even while they approached from a distance they had seen the great, glowing red spot. Their instruments soon told them that the rock and soil was red hot. The size of the spot told them the terrific fury of the battle that must have produced it, and they circled downward toward the world with due caution.

Yet, though they rapidly drew nearer, they saw no slightest sign of a city on the surface. Putney grunted. "Don't like that. That means some forces we have to contend with. They must have their cities so far under ground that they are protected by sheer mass of dirt and rock against heat rays. But—even so one of them must have been destroyed."

A low soft whine began to mount in the loudspeakers of the Prometheus. She was entering an atmosphere. Slowly and cautiously she descended. "They must be watching," said Warren, "so they must be waiting for us with their whole armory. I'm putting out all the shields I can think of." Still the ship sank unhindered toward the glowing spot below. No sign of life either on ground or in the air had been observed. Even the instruments showed only a complete lack of activity.

Then the meters jumped off their scales, and simultaneously the Prometheus reeled to a terrific pull, a solid sheet of blue electric flame cascaded from her to strike at the bank of clouds off to one side like a jagged sword of light. The clouds split open to reveal a flight of winged ships. A hundred beams glimmered in the air as they stabbed toward the Prometheus. An instant later the force-shield rippled with light under titanic concussions.

The winged ships were suddenly spinning wildly, twisting as though out of control, rolling over on their backs, and yet falling upward toward the Prometheus, added to the attractive force that was drawing the planes upward, and then put some light into the invisible force plane so it became visible. The planes struggled in vain. Warren was adding a powerful magnetic field of his own, and increasing it. As the enormous field-strength built up, it acted as a tremendously resistant medium to all moving metal. The planes began to behave erratically. The glimmering beams of light began to curve this way and that as they bent under the magnetic field Warren was producing. Shells were exploding in midair as they too were stopped and heated by their resisted passage through the magnetic field. Warren stepped up his attractive field, and the planes moved more rapidly toward his plane of force. Presently most of them had landed. There was no visible propelling mechanism about them, only the wings for lift, but whatever it was, it didn't function, evidently, under the conditions Warren had imposed.

"Now we could just crush them with another force plane, but I think they had reason to attack. Evidently they have just gotten through with one attack on their city, and tried to destroy us before we did any damage." Warren began some difficult manipulations. In a moment a single, small plane came through a hole in the force plane, and rode toward the Prometheus. The other planes had stopped struggling now, and all had landed on the force-plane. The little plane was brought nearer, till Warren and Putney looked into its cabin. Two beings sat in there. They looked quite human. Their eyes alone seemed least human. With disconcerting ease they looked in different directions simultaneously. The left eyes looked at Warren, while the right eyes were traveling leisurely up and down Putney.

Almost at once the men appeared excited. One of them reached over and turned a small knob. A projector on the side of his plane turned, till it pointed down to one of the largest ships landed on the force-plane below. The projector began to wink rapidly and irregularly. "Signaling we aren't the enemy. We must look different," suggested Putney.

The second occupant of the ship had turned toward the Terrestrians. He had a device that looked like a flashlight with a bottle stuck on it by the neck. It was short about eighteen inches long, and apparently light, for he handled it easily. The air was evidently too rare up here for him to open a window, but he threw the thing somewhere behind him in the craft, and held out his empty hands.

"Pax vobiscum," murmured Putney. "What shall I heave away?"

"One of your shoes? That would be big enough to convince him it was a deadly weapon. Or if that suggestion doesn't suit, throw away a butcher knife. Anyone would know a knife was a weapon."

Putney did. Communications had evidently been established with the fleet of ships below, for they were flashing lights madly among themselves now, and the large ship was flashing a spotlight on the tiny ship before them with terrific speed.

Rapidly Warren eased off the attractive field that had held the fleet helpless, as they one by one fluttered a moment in the re-asserted gravity of the planet, and righted, he released the magnetic field entirely, and the last of the gravity field.

The little ship still held in their force-fields, Warren drew flat against the Prometheus, then with a terrific acceleration ship and attached plane dove toward the planet, passing the planes as though they were motionless. Five miles above the planet the ship slowed, at a mile they halted, and Wearing started a rapid analysis of the atmosphere.

"Inert gases, including nitrogen, 64%, oxygen 32%, carbon dioxide and water vapor the remainder. Rather dry air. Harmless to life, so far as a mouse and a tomato plant are concerned. By the way, I found out why the terrific ultra-violet from the sun doesn't destroy everything here. The upper reaches of the atmosphere have a tremendous amount of ozone in them that smashes that ultra-violet down to something bearable."

Warren nodded. "Good enough. I rather suspected something of that sort. In so far as the ozone went, that's understandable surely. The air is dry because there are few real seas, only great lakes here and there. Most of this planet is arid.

"Go let in your friends, Putt."

Putney went back to the lock, opened the inner chamber, closed the door behind him, and cautiously opened the outer door. A breath of their own air swept out, to be replaced in a moment by a dry, but invigoratingly cool breeze of this other atmosphere. As he glanced out he saw that the two men in the plane had already opened their door, and were coming out. They were walking along unconcernedly head down along the wing of the ship, which was equipped with a rail of some sort, evidently for this purpose. Their feet were bare, and equipped with a broad calloused palm, a strong, long and supple great toe, and the four lesser toes were all well developed and highly flexible.

To Putney's amazement one of the men let go with one foot, reached into his pocket with a contortionist motion that seemed easy and perfectly simple, and took out a heavy clip. In the meantime his hands had been busy unwinding a thin, strong line from his waist. The clip was fixed to one end of the line with the aid of one hand and one foot, while the other foot was engaged in holding him up, and the other hand adjusted the leather belt to which the other end of the line was fastened. Then with a single motion the man restored his foot to the rail, leapt, and landed lightly and safely on the threshold of the Prometheus' lock. He straightened up, and smiled engagingly.

"Praeul, threuw. Iiie Kwaer reen!"

The sounds were strange, but pleasant to Putney's ears, completely unlike English sounds. They could not be expressed as English sounds.

"Decide we didn't need killing?" said Putney, smiling. The second man landed as lightly as the first, and by the same means. Both looked Putney over carefully, paying particular attention to his feet and eyes. They shook their heads in wonderment. Then finally the larger of the two large men took something from his pocket. It was a device about the size of a large book. Pushing a catch on one side the lid flew up, and a three-foot telescoping column of metal stabbed upward. Simultaneously a little light began to glow through red to white. When it reached white the man spoke into it briefly. A voice responded from it in a moment, a voice with a tone of command.

The stranger answered, pushed the telescoping column back down, and caught the lid down once more. Then he smiled and handed it to Putney.

The Terrestrian shook his head and handed it back. From a rack in the lock he lifted a set they had made for use with space suits. It was twice the size, and equipped with a small funnel opening on one side. The Flame that would power it was out now, but Putney started it in a moment from the power-lead in the wall of the lock. The Flame glowed white and clear, half an inch in diameter in the center of the cabinet, under a heavy glass.

Putney pointed to a grating in one side, spoke into it, while pointing the funnel in the direction of the large plane that had by now descended to their level. At his words a dim haze of light appeared in the funnel, a haze that vibrated with the tones of his voice.

He put it back on the rack, pointed to himself and said "Putney." He repeated it twice, while the two looked on intently.

"Boed Nay," said the one.

"Bood Nee," decided the other.

"Bud," said Putney with a laugh.

"Who?" he asked pointing to them in turn.

"Moerkel," replied the smaller, and "Thaen," replied the other.

Something buzzed softly in Thaen's pocket, and he brought out the receiver. As the antenna snapped up, the speaker began droning softly. Three times Putney heard the name Thaen, twice Moerkel. The two conferred for a moment, then with inimitable grace Moerkel leapt back to his plane. He tried to start it, but it was still bound to the side of the Prometheus.

"Let him go, Ran, the High Muckamuck called him," said Putney in a conversational tone. Something hummed softly in the ship, and the flier fell away to soar up and toward the huge flagship.

"Come," Putney beckoned Thaen on, and through the locked door to the interior of the ship. As the inner door opened Thaen entered the power room and stopped in amazement. He was staring with both mobile eyes at the ten-foot Flame, a perfect sphere on which sparkled little winking lights. He listened to the soft sigh of the swirling, iridescent iron atoms. MacLaurin was looking at him interestedly.

"A queer body. His toes are long."

"Uses them for fingers. I envy him. He can untie knots with them or run four-dimensional controls all at the same time. And you don't know the half of it. He can move his eyes independently like a monkey—only he can see well out of both simultaneously."

"Hey, Putt—the ships are moving, they seem to want us to come along," said Warren's voice from a speaker. One of Thaen's eyes looked up, the other was wandering around the room excitedly. MacLaurin started. "Wall eyed! Now he's cross-eyed! Now he's like no man ever was! I dinna like those eyes."

Suddenly Warrent started the ship forward, and as the load came to the Flame it became a trifle more solid in appearance, the sigh of the glinting iron atoms increased to a low hum. Thaen looked at it with astonishment. The brilliant light was cold, cold and steady as though it were in truth a solid. No motion was apparent here, for there was no apparent acceleration.

Putney led Thaen forward, into the control room.

"If any one should ask, you might say those planes can *move!*" said Warren as they entered. "The air-speed must be close to what the meter says, though the air here isn't quite like Earth's, and it says 1000 miles per hour. That's moving with a capital m for an airplane. And I'd like to know how they drive them."

The area of red-hot rock was left far behind already, and barren, arid sand-hills were scudding backwards as the flight of planes roared along. Presently the character of the land changed. Hills began to grow taller, and rocks appeared in the distance, it grew higher, and they saw occasional snow-capped peaks, glinting strangely in the light of the tiny, blue disc of the sun—100,000,000,000 miles distant. Here and there they saw other cross-shadows, shadows cast by that other enormous and enormously brilliant star three quarters of a light year distant. It was plainly and brilliantly visible in full daylight. Several other stars were visible in the brilliant deep-violet sky. One of the four major moons rode high in the sky, another was low on the horizon, rising.

"They certainly must have a magnificent view here at night—four brilliant moons, one dim one, and that tremendous star outshining all the other brilliant suns. Guess they don't see it often though, if they live under ground," commented Warren.

"Ran—look! They didn't always! Look—in that valley —a ruined city!"

"Lord—you're right! And those aren't crumbling ruins! Look there—see how they've been fused! They were driven under ground by that other race!"

They swung high over the mountains, and the ruins of the city disappeared behind. Thaen had been watching

them intently with one eye, while the other roamed restlessly about the room.

Now, as they passed the mountain range, the character of the country changed entirely. It was brilliantly
blue, overlaid with growing plants. Streams appeared here
and there, and wandering erratically back and forth
across their path was a great river, growing constantly
as tributaries joined it. From the foothills of the mountains they crossed a vast rolling plain that leveled slowly
and the river became broader, and meandered in great
bends, like a giant Mississippi. Then on the horizon
beyond appeared a stretch of water that grew as they
approached, wider and wider, and always extending beyond the horizon.

"That big sea," said Warren briefly.

"There's a city under it!" exclaimed Putney. "That's
the place for a city! No heat rays would ever reach them
there, no bombs even. Why aren't all the cities under
water?"

"Not enough room probably. Also not all their eggs in
one basket. This is probably the capital."

The planes were slowing now, and as they neared a
low range of mountains that ran down to the lake, they
stopped. They hovered in tight circles above the mountains for a few moments, then suddenly one entire hill,
nearly a half-thousand feet in height, and fully 1000 long,
slid serenely out into the lake, seemingly floating on the
water. Beneath it was a vast cavern opening. The giant
ships sank into it three abreast, while the smaller ships
sank down whole fleets side by side.

"Shall we walk into their parlor, asked the fly?" mis-
quoted Warren.

"Um—I think so. If this ship be a fly, it must be a
Tartar fly. I suggest seven different ways of escape. One,
blow up the whole planet; two, escape by going into the
other space; three, construct a force shield like a cone
and plow out through the rock; four set up the transmutation field and transmute everything in the way to
hydrogen or oxygen and fly out; five, let loose a little
heat, and melt a way out; six, use the absolute zero field,
freeze the rock till it's hard and brittle and watch it
crumble under its own weight; and seven, use the oscillating field and crumble it to dust. This ship is a bit
hard to stop or to hold."

Warren was already in the cavern. It led straight down for half a mile, turned back toward the lake for a mile, then straight down for another mile. At the bottom were titanic lock gates of solid metal at least fifty feet thick set in great grooves cut in the living rock. The surface toward the city did not, at present, touch the surface of the grooves. Both were lined with thick layers of some dark substance, evidently similar to rubber. A quarter of a mile further on was a similar titanic set of gates. And with the first gates the lighting began. Heretofore great searchlights on the ships had illuminated the passages, for scarcely had they passed the mouth of the cavern when the mountain began moving back into place.

"There's one sure thing—these fellows have some source of power that beats anything earth had two years ago. Earth could never have dug this channel, they could never have moved that mountain around, and they'd have been plumb out of luck if anything like those ships came after them. Wonder what it is?"

"Efficient solar power? That sun would give plenty—even a hundred billion miles out. Maybe atomic power. We have the energy of matter, which is of course far greater, but even the energy of smashed atoms is enormous."

"Atomic is my bet," said Putney. "Look at those lights." The lights were growing more frequent now as mile after mile of the huge tunnel moved back. Lighted windows appeared in the walls. The lights were globes of pure radiance suspended in the air of the tunnel. They glowed with a brilliant, harsh blue light. "White to these men, I suspect. Our lights probably look red to Thaen." Thaen's left eye swung abruptly, and disconcertingly to Putney as he said this.

"Uh—those eyes," said Warren. "They must be darned handy things but they give me the creeps. Ever tried playing deck tennis with a cross-eyed man? Looks one way and sees the other? That's the way those eyes impress me."

Putney chuckled. "They get me a bit too—but I envy him. He'd be a darned bad man to fight in a ship of his own size. Be able to look all ways at once. His feet too—how handy they'd be with controls!"

The ships ahead began slowing to an even lower rate, turned an abrupt corner, and the Terrestrians suddenly came into a blaze of brilliant lights. A huge cavern widened out from the tunnel, a gigantic place with a dozen levels of metal floors on which, one by one, the planes began to settle. Thaen touched Warren's shoulder and pointed to the topmost one. "Yuarn," he said.

Warren nodded. "I don't see why this doesn't fall in on them."

"I'm beginning to. Don't go near those columns of light. I think the light just marks out the beam of force —yes, look at that magnetometer. A powerful beam. Probably they have projectors on the cavern floor, and on the various floors, and on the roof, that distribute the pressure. Look—see how that beam there widens at the middle—I'll be willing to bet anything that's how they drive their ships. Nasty weapon it would make too, if you didn't have any magnetic defense field. Just touch one of those beams with a weak field and see what happens."

Warren set some controls, and pulled a lever back gently. The surrounding columns of light swayed gently away from the ship, then gently toward him, bending at the joints. "Magnetic," he nodded.

Gently he landed his ship on the topmost level, beside the flagship of the fleet he had been following, and simultaneously rose from his seat. "Take over for a minute. Set up the zero field in a disc about fifty feet in front of us. I've an idea." He was gone only a minute, to come back with a small but powerful movie projector, which he set up in the control room window. Putney turned a little power into the zero field, and added to it till a cloud of white vapor collected before them. Men were coming toward the ship now, but fell back away from the space as the cold, damp fog rolled slowly down from the field. Almost at once pictures began to appear on the screen.

It was a field on Earth, with mountains rising behind green against a blue sky. In the center of the field was a huge, shining building. The Prometheus' hangar.

Suddenly field and background sank rapidly away, the horizon retreated mile on mile, till the whole world seemed laid out before them, and the blue sky changed to black. The lights of the cavern dimmed suddenly, and the scene on the screen became clearer. The bowl of the Earth inverted suddenly to the rounded swelling of a planet. It fell rapidly away, shrinking with amazing speed, and turning slightly reddish as it did so. It became a great round pumpkin floating in space, and occasional stars swam into view, then the moon, looking like a dull orange. The planet and its satellite swung, and the sun shown blazing on the screen. It too began to retreat, becoming redder and redder as it shrank swiftly, became finally so red it vanished. Utter blankness filled the screen.

Warren worked swiftly. He changed the projector, a pinpoint of violet light appeared, expanded swiftly, grew greater and greater—it was the sun of this world.

Thaen, beside them, gasped in amazement. The sun shrank again, and finally this world appeared, its four satellites visible. Then the picture broke off. The screen of mist began to fade as Putney cut off the power. But before it was gone, pictures began to appear once more, and Putney, in surprise, cut the power back. A projector outside was working.

6

A picture of an arid, dry plain swam into being on the screen of mist. Unlike an earthly moving picture it grew swiftly from a spiral till it filled the entire screen with a round picture with a peculiar suggestion of depth.

There was nothing but the level plain, and the clear violet sky with occasional clouds floating high in it. But somewhere a faint, heavy hum began to come into being; it grew till it was a majestic, full-throated roar echoing through all space.

As they watched, a fleet of giant battle planes swam into view from somewhere behind, moving onward and upward at an unbelievable speed. They climbed at an angle of forty-five degrees, yet their wings tilted back no more than thirty degrees. Some force other than pure air-lift was raising them. So swiftly they mounted that in moments they were out of sight.

Suddenly the ground cracked, broke, and a ring of squat, hemispherical metal domes pushed their way up through the sand. Several seconds passed, then from one, then another, broke a great flare of electric-blue fire that reached fanshaped to the sky, bent, and intermingled in a dome of solid fire above all. It fluctuated, wavered, twisted, and then steadied after a moment to a solid, motionless sheet. A constant, steady hum echoed through the great cavern.

Something materialized on the screen, a black dot high, high in the violet sky. It grew with accelerating speed, expanding rapidly to a torpedo-shaped body ten feet long, three in diameter, ending in a finned tail that kept it whirling with terrific speed, a gyroscopic missile that would maintain its orientation against any deflecting force.

Half a mile from the ground a stream of fire issued from it, and the giant bomb leapt forward with speed that must have reached miles a second.

At the last instant it swerved violently, landing finally in the exact center of the dome of blue fire. A single

197

stupendous flash of light, a titanic explosion sharp as the crack of a rifle, and it was gone.

It was merely a sighting shot. A hundred black dots appeared magically, and as they came into being, and grew from somewhere in the far reaches of that violet sky, blue-glowing cones of dim radiance reached up to them. They staggered, twisted in their paths as the beams touched them. Some jerked violently aside. All slowed visibly, and became red, many released their explosive energies harmlessly on the air, but a majority rained down on the protecting dome of fire.

Strangely, none seemed directed at the center of the dome, the force beams seemed engaged in directing them there. Most fell toward the edge of the protecting ring.

Other dots were appearing far above now. The planes were descending again, and now accompanied with long, slim ships, shaped like pencils pointed at each end. Lashing beams smashed out between them. The faintly glowing force-beams from the ships, long tubes of hazy light, some other beam, twin pipes of brilliant light that started from each other, and curved inward to meet at their object in a constant, terrific display of lightning. A dozen planes attacked each ship, the ships seemed content to sink slowly downward, dropping their gigantic bombs, and firing tiny, explosive shells toward the dodging planes.

The planes were not dodging successfully apparently, for a constant and growing rain of broken metal began to fall. From each of the hundred pencil-ships a ray reached out presently, something dim and half seen that exploded into a point of incredible incandescence if it touched a plane.

As at a signal, the giant attacking planes winged over suddenly, pointed their noses toward the planet, and descended in a terrific, shrieking power drive that must have raised their speed to nearly a mile a second. Their wings were folded into the ships in some manner, till only a knife edge projected from the fuselage. The great planes twisted and weaved as they shot downward, avoiding rays that sliced after them. They turned, leveled off, and streaked across the plain in a dodging course at a rate that carried them beyond the horizon in seconds.

The pencil-ships were not left to come on unhindered, for each great plane ship had spewed forth a great fleet of tiny midges that swarmed in darting, flitting motion about the ships, discharging brief bursts of that twin explosive electric ray. But somehow the ray always seemed to explode just short of the ships, leaving them unscathed.

Some signal was given. The hundreds of tiny ships all darted suddenly toward one of the pencil-ships, every ray burst forth simultaneously in a single blinding sheet of flame—and the pencil-ship was falling, white-hot wreckage. The midges scattered themselves as though fragments of an exploding bomb. Vengeful heat-rays lashed across the sky where they had been seconds before. The score must have been half a hundred—but by far the greater number escaped.

The battle was progressing on a level now, nearly fifty miles above the city evidently, for some telescopic device had been attached to the camera. Ships and midges circled steadily for the advantage.

Again the concerted rush—again white-hot wreckage descended streaming from the pencil-ship, and two score more of the midges followed it.

"The ships have some sort of screen—if the planes can get enough power over, the screen fails—when the ships don't have to use power for their screen, they can work those heat-rays," said Warren hastily.

"The ships will win—too many."

There was a sudden shift in the position of the pencil-ships. One rose half a mile above the rest, while the others set up a barrage of their heat rays about it, protecting it. The midges seemed suddenly to concentrate on attacking that ship, for fully a third of them rose to it, and poured their weapons against it—most of them to fall mangled wreckage.

For an instant the ship seemed unguarded. Then, from bow and stern, broke two new rays. They moved in a curve if the ship spun rapidly, their range was less than a quarter of a mile, but they seemed to stretch a web of force between them and around them that swept the midges from the sky like some gigantic broom. Only near the enemy ships were the planes safe, from this weapon, and there the heat-rays reached them.

The midges folded their wings and, like the giant planes, shot planet-ward with terrific speed. Not a full hundred reached the surface.

The pencil-ships descended in massed, close-packed

formation, majestically and slowly, toward the glowing dome of fire. At ten miles the forts went into action. For a single second, every one of the fan beams snapped out, to snap on as concentrated pipes of radiance smashing their way to the massed enemy ships. A wave of fire washed over the formation, it flowed like some squirted liquid, striking a solid glass plate. But it was like an acid, for it began eating holes that showed red against the blue flame, holes that expanded as some half dozen beams concentrated instantly on it—and a ship disappeared in flaming destruction beyond.

But presently this eating of holes stopped, the holes grew fewer, and smaller, ships avoided them in the meantime, and they hung motionless over the city.

Hours must have passed. The scene was at night, suddenly, and the ships showed brilliantly outlined by the wash of electric fire, the heavens were illuminated by the great, bright stars of this world, but they were overcast now, clouds were gathering.

The ships were no longer massed, their formation was a circle with a hub and spokes. But only half the ships were so engaged. The rest seemed moving about freely behind this shield. They began to concentrate above the hub, and the ships of the hub rose to join them. Blue beams began to reach from one to another, till all the ships were linked in a single network of power beams.

The center ship hovered over the center of the shield. A mistiness grew suddenly before it, a spinning misty globe of blue light. It attained size, then suddenly broke free, and went spinning erratically downward. It ate a hole through the shield. It drank up the blue electric flame on the other side, and grew fat on it. It jerked its way down and to one side. It acted like a light ball suspended in a jet of air. Suddenly a particularly violent jerk led it into one of the great beams. Instantly, with the speed of light, it followed that beam back to its source, puffed softly as it struck the dome-fort, and bounced aloft. The fort was a heap of powdery ash.

Frantic magnetic beams were jerking at it; they could deflect it when it moved, but only served to make its erratic motion more so. And another sphere was falling, jerking about like the first.

In minutes the last of the forts were gone. The enemy ships came slowly downward, cautiously. The spheres seemed repelled by them, and rolled swiftly away, out across the plane, moving erratically as ever, and every touch left a great, powdery scar, but every touch made them smaller.

The ships were pouring their heat beams into the rock. It was day once more, and a cauldron of molten rock half a mile across bubbled gently. It was night again—the cauldron of rock was three miles across. Day found it fully four, and bubbling gently.

The scene on the screen of mist vanished. It was replaced by a scene in a great subterranean city. Men, women, and children were hurrying about on moving ways, suspended on spidery bridges that spanned the great lighted tunnels. Each wall of the tunnel here was a great apartment house, and the great tunnels must have been a hundred and fifty feet tall, and fifty wide. The scene was at a "cube"—the three-dimensional equivalent of a city square, where four great tunnels intersected. Everyone seemed to be leaving. The reason was obvious. Above the spider-work bridges, above the glowing magnetic columns that supported the rock pressure above, a slow smoke was originating, and falling downward. The rock became dull red while they watched. The last hurrying people looked back over their shoulders with frightened faces.

Suddenly one of the great magnetic columns began to wobble erratically. It twisted, the upper section broadened, and seemed to be trying to slide off the lower. It did, its beam a cone that sharply deflected the four surrounding beams till they too began to wobble. The dull red rock was brightening. The beams were all spreading now; the first to fail suddenly went out as an explosion wrecked the projector. A great crack appeared in the rock, and with a terrific roar of sound the whole roof split wide. A river of molten rock came pouring through. The spider-work bridges and ways vanished in a puff of smoke and a brief sparkle of fire. A wall of white-hot rock moved rapidly toward the screen. The camera swayed, the picture went out of focus, and suddenly a flame obscured the screen.

An instant later the camera was looking down the tunnel from a distant station. The wave of rock was moving more slowly, cooled by surrounding rock, and by the great refrigerating plants that must have been cooling the city. A huge line of pipe had been hastily laid, and was spouting a sparkling blue liquid that hissed instantly into invisibility as it struck the rock—which cooled it. A dike was being built, a dike of frozen rock.

It was useless. The roof of the tunnel itself began to glow, and the pipes were turned on it. The Niagara of lava still flowing in from the original break overflowed the dike, and rolled on.

The city was doomed.

The screen went blank in a burst of flame at that moment, and stayed blank.

"Television—to another city," said Putney softly.

"So that's how it happened—that's what that pool of red-hot rock was," said Warren with a cold, deadly voice.

Thaen touched his arm. He pointed about him to the ship, the controls. He pointed at the screen.

"Naer liu muool raeneu?" he asked.

"I can guess what you asked. We will, Thaen," promised Warren soberly.

"Tex—Tex!" Atkill called softly. Texas woke from sleep with a start. Atkill was bending over his telescope, watching something with an expression of unholy joy on his face. "Come here, Tex, and look—we have visitors at last. I knew they'd come eventually. Three ships!"

Three thin pencil-ships floated in space, tiny things glinting in the harsh light of the great sun. Atkill watched them carefully, calculating their course accurately. They should reach him in a short three hours at their present velocity. He set to work rapidly.

In an hour he had set the controls in the power-room for starting the Flame, and had set up the little piece of apparatus he had made in the garbage-lock, with a long, thin tube of aluminum held in place by strings of insulators. The rod projected some twenty feet from the side of the ship. Along with the little apparatus he had made, there were three powerful magnets he had been making, and a little spark-gap of chorem-nickel blocks between the long aluminum tube and a heavy lead that grounded to the ship. Atkill had plans.

"Tex, sweet lad, we are about to be saved. The mere coming of our friends gives us once more, power, light and life! I can start the Flame!"

"Uhm—that's right good news. How come? Yuh couldn't before. They may decide to wipe us out instead of helping."

Atkill laughed cheerfully. "They've got to help. The sun's been doing the necessary work for the last three months! All they have to do is come near—and they will. Remember, Tex, the late unpleasantness we watched from space here that they were having on that planet? War. They want weapons—science. We've got it. We're a strange ship, a ship of neither their world or the enemy world. We are, apparently, a dead ship. They see in us a possibility of help. They will investigate."

"Uhm—but how come they'll have to help?"

"For three months that sun has been deluging our ship with ejected electrons. We've built up a tremendous charge. We haven't lost a bit of it. Those ships, just come from a planet, have a much smaller charge. We'll discharge to them, my lad, with a smash of about eighteen mega-volts—an extra two million. Really I need only sixteen or so. I said eighteen for safety—and I'll have it. My starting apparatus for the Flame is weak on magnetism and gravitational fields, but the extra electric will make it up, I suspect."

Atkill was busy with something else now. A robe he had made. It was made of the thick, strong silk sheets he had brought with him. They were pure white, beautifully clear, and the robe was made with a surprising skill. It draped about his powerful figure gracefully, caught at arms and shoulder with three clasps of highly polished stainless steel, set with more of the magnificent gems he had synthesized, and cut.

On one side lay a turban-like head-dress he had made, wound of silk dyed with a slightly fluorescent dye, with the result that in the light of this sun, rich as it was in ultra-violet, it shone of its own accord with a rich, brilliant scarlet. It was a magnificent headpiece.

Finally a sash was added, one of magnificent, deep purple, clasped with a metal device shaped like twin crocodile heads, their eyes four gleaming stones as deep in color as the sash, touched with a trace of pomegranate.

"I heard some sky-pilot say that Solomon in all his glory was not arrayed like this-here guy. I don't know who this Solomon was right well, but you sure got him beat," grinned Texas. "That what you been working on so hard?"

Atkill looked at him pityingly. "It's a shame to disturb his mind. Tex, brace yourself. You've got to wear a rig like this too."

"Me? Me wear that? Hombre, you got wrong ideas," affirmed Texas.

"Tex, if you don't wear one of these, we are extremely apt to die promptly and unpleasantly. I'd rather convince the populace that we are strange and wonderful gods than have them believe us strange and delectable foods, perhaps. You know, they may have a domestic animal that looks something like us, and is considered a delicacy—like chicken or something. In that case we would be in an unpleasant situation unless we could change their opinions.

"So stimulate that thing you call your ability to reason, and don these garments." Atkill extended a similar
turban and robe to Texas, but these were made of fine
linen instead of silk. The turban was not-unpleasant green,
and the sash black as night, held with a stainless steel
clasp set with a single blood-red stone.

"Take off your shirt, and put 'em on. You can keep
your pants, and shift that hardware to the shoulder-
holster. I've rigged this so you can reach it more easily.
Put this pouch on over your chest. You can carry
matches, tobacco, a flashlight and so forth in that."

"Uh—all right if I got tuh. But what all's the idea?"

Atkill smiled and turned back to his telescope while
Texas dressed. The ships were slowing now, approaching
cautiously. They were less than fifty miles away now.
Atkill could see them clearly with the naked eye now
as dots of light. He went back to the power-room and
started the gyroscope device. It had been improved in
the months that had passed, and was now a quite efficient machine for swinging the ship as he wished.

Anxiously he watched the ships approach. Finally a
lone, small ship came out of one of the three greater
spaceships, and approached slowly. It circled the earth
ship at a distance of a few hundred yards, then finally
came toward them. A long metal arm reached out from
the ship, and the machine came gently directly toward
the out-jutting terminal Atkill had arranged.

"Tex—get set as I showed you at the controls—one,
two and five switches closed, four and six open, three at
the midpoint. When the Flame starts, snap the dial seven
to 458–23. Got it?"

"Uh."

Atkill was working at the single, tiny lock. He closed
a switch and the magnets ground slightly in their sup-
ports, pressing away from each other. Swiftly he made
several further adjustments, and watched the ship. Absolute space—an almost perfect insulator. Would the
discharge-shock be sudden enough to give the result he
so desperately needed? Or would it be a slow leaking
that would be perfectly useless?

The discharge rods were less than a foot apart. Slowly
the pilot of the stranger ship maneuvered them skillfully
together. There was a terrific strain out there now—

enough to have started his Flame if he had been in position to use it.

They came within an inch—then suddenly they touched. A blinding, roaring smash of electric energy crashed across the gap between Atkill's discharge points. Less than two inches of separation, creating an electric field of terrific intensity. Atkill could feel the charge leak suddenly from his body—and cried out in exultant triumph as the clear white of the Release Flame suddenly sprang into being on his little block of iron. A tiny flame no larger than a flashlight bulb, a dazzling white point of light that pulsed for an instant, steadied, and glowed as it would glow for hundreds of millennia if left undisturbed.

Atkill yanked open the lock with a single calculated motion, whirled about, dashed to the engine-room, and snapped five ready leads into place.

"Ready!" Tex applied the switches as he had been directed. A haze of light accumulated over the great master Flame, the block of iron was stirring to life. A rustling of whirling atoms mounted; they became iridescent and whined softly as they reached the glowing haze of light; some began to sparkle. "Seven to 540–49," ordered Atkill. The haze suddenly intensified, the little glowing spot of flame in the tiny apparatus dimmed to reddish, and a protesting whine came from it.

A dull thud that did not originate in the room, but in space, answered; the haze of light crystallized in an instant of time to a solid glow, and about the ship the lights sprang up. The chuckle of the air apparatus working once more suddenly laughed in their ears familiarly. The motor-generator that had been charging the batteries was working madly, pumping air into the boiler.

A broad grin split Texas' face. Atkill straightened instantly, ripped off the five leads, dropped them into a box, and ran to his room—dove, rather, for the ship was still weightless. In an incredibly short time he had fixed his little rounded mechanism to clamps in the framework of the turban, snapped the lead-wires into their jacks, concealed the wires in his loose sleeve, and donned the jeweled bracelet.

Then he was at the control room window. The other ship had retreated suddenly to some miles distant, fearful of the sudden reawakening of the ship. Atkill stood at

the window, his arms raised above his head in a wel-
coming gesture.

He was a magnificent figure of a man, the white robe,
the brilliant turban glowing softly with scarlet light, his
tall, powerful body erect and commanding. His features
were powerful and rugged, his black eyes snapping with
life and energy. Slowly he lowered his arms and beckoned
to the strange ship.

The little machine moved cautiously toward him. Atkill
smiled at the creature he saw in the little ship, a queer,
slim man-like form, with arms four feet long possessed
of two elbow joints. The head was supported on a neck
at least eighteen inches long, supple and graceful as a
swan's, and almost as thin. The head seemed far too
heavy for the slim neck, a head possessed of two eyes,
capable of moving independently, a slim, bony nose, a
tiny round mouth whose lips could protrude and retract
as much as an inch. The whole face was tiny, set into
the lower part of the skull, rather than forming the
front of the head. The eyes themselves were set into
the skull as something entirely separate from the face
below them. The ears were curiously cup-shaped, and
protruded noticeably from the head on short necks, mus-
cular material that permitted them to turn and swing
about like those devices used for locating sounds of
planes high in the air. They were wondrously and disconcertingly mobile, as were the eyes.

"Now what in hell is that thing?" demanded the hor-
rified Tex.

"That is our new friend," replied Atkill calmly. "He
saved your life—course he didn't mean to, but he did.
Now remember what your mother told you, Tex, never
stare at freaks. Be grateful to the little—monstrosity,
shall we say? He did you a good turn, and I plan to be
the high Muckamuck among them presently. You are
about to see the powers of my new head-dress. Never
learned what it was for, did you? Watch!"

Atkill folded his powerful arms across his chest, and
scowled. He scowled at a chair that was clamped to the
floor near him. About his head a misty, bluish light appeared; it projected forward somewhat—but hung close
to his head. And suddenly—half the chair puffed away
into nothingness!

"Now that-thair's a right cute trick," said Texas in admiration. "If I didn't know the secret it shore would take me in. Got any more?"

Atkill's face relaxed, his arms fell to his sides, and he laughed. "Lots, Tex, lots. It will work a lot quicker when I want it to. And there are a number of other things. I have another little thing I'm going to start when I've time. Now—we follow our friend."

The ship, motionless, drifting helpless for so long, started slowly, turned, and began following the slow motion of the little ship. The scout turned abruptly and started back toward the home ship in haste. Atkill followed slowly, having first applied a number of protective devices. He approached the three waiting ships, and drifted motionless.

Nothing happened for a number of minutes. Finally Atkill turned his ship and headed for the second of the two planets he had seen, the home of these ships, as he knew. He went slowly. The three ships passed him instantly and fell into step, one before, one behind, and one above him. Together they went along smoothly.

Atkill accelerated slowly and steadily, and finally gave Texas charge of the ship while he went back to the machine shop. He returned carrying a bulky pistol with a stubby barrel of polished steel, and a heavy chamber mounted in a synthetic rubber grip. He looked at it lovingly and handed it to Texas.

"Throw away that hardware, and carry this. There are two studs on it. The one on the left side will take the starch out of anything living. The one on the right will take the starch out of anything—but don't use it anywhere near yourself. The left throws a concentrated pencil of invisible ultra-violet energy. It will of course heat, and isn't as easily reflected as infra-red. The other throws a similar pencil of radiation something like cosmic rays, only a little longer. It will penetrate anything to a depth of from 100 to 1000 feet, depending on the substance, and still be fatal. It will destroy the atoms in its path. And it will let loose so much secondary radiation that it will kill anything within fifty feet of what it hits. Don't use that unless you are more than 200 feet from your target—the ultra-violet is bad enough. Look." Atkin aimed it at the surviving half of the ruined chair. A blinding spot of incandescence appeared on the metal frame and flashed for an instant before it spurted away in vapor.

The pistol was shut off instantly, but a red-hot groove lay along the floor.

"There's an energy center—a Flame—in the chamber here. Feeds on the iron of the pistol itself. Good for about 1000 years of continuous operation I believe. If they attempt to disarm you—push this red stud in the base of the butt. It will fuse the weapon two seconds after you push it, and release the energy center. The center will burn for from half an hour to three hours afterward, but won't do any particular damage if no one tries to tame it. If anything but iron is shoved into it, it will simply knock it through into another space. If iron is supplied, both iron and Flame will move through."

"Oh," said Tex, and took the deadly thing unhappily. He was used to powder and lead, not these things. He stowed the heavy revolver he loved in his pouch and holstered the strange pistol.

Hours later, as the planet neared, the formation of ships about them was joined by a fleet of twenty or more, evidently called in from space.

The pencil-ships settled rapidly through the atmosphere, toward a small city with a huge spaceship cradle. The cradle consisted of huge metal beams protected by some form of buffers shaped like a semi-cylinder, the two ends of the semi-cylinder being closed by huge iron blocks. The whole apparatus was set on gigantic springs and pneumatic cushions. Atkill mentally noted that the ships must have exceedingly poor control on landing.

They did. One after another landed with a terrific jar, all power being cut off just before they entered the cradle. About half the fleet did not land however, but hovered nervously about the Terrestrian ship. The cradle was clear, men were waiting down there for them.

Atkill lowered his ship in a swift dive, then turned abruptly and landed like a feather just beside the cradle. Instantly a troop of guards arranged themselves about the ship, a small party of higher officers in resplendent clothes marched forward.

Atkill was busy. He was testing the atmosphere. He had few and poor reagents for this purpose, but he finally decided it contained sufficient oxygen, and no other known poisonous substances. Cautiously he opened the door. Air hissed out, for the pressure outside was some .

four pounds lower than within. The gravity on this planet was only about three quarters that of earth.

The air was breathable. "Tex—take charge, and keep an eye on me. If anything goes wrong, just push that stud I showed you, and you'll be half a million miles away before you know it."

Atkill drew himself up, and stepped out lightly. The blazing sun made the air uncomfortably warm; it was a blue disc in a violet sky, but there was little or no ultra-violet here, for the thick layer of ozone in the upper atmosphere absorbed nearly all of it.

The guards moved up quickly, stepped up beside him, and two prepared to march beside him to the officers. Two more stood on either side of the floor. Atkill walked calmly ahead.

"I greet you, High Rulers, but greet me, for I am Atkill!"

The officers looked at him skeptically, their eyes wandering over him disconcertingly. Their long, flexible necks craned in a way that required all Atkill's control to prevent laughter.

Atkill looked back at the ship suddenly. An officer of some sort was headed for the still open door.

"Stop!" roared Atkill. His voice was a deep, powerful bass, and the tone of command brought the man to a sliding stop. Atkill walked angrily forward. "Away!" he ordered, and waved the man away. The officer hesitated. A ring of guards had hastily drawn up around Atkill. The man seemed to make up his mind, for he bowed his long neck several times and started firmly forward.

Atkill folded his arms and scowled at the man's back. A glow sprang suddenly into being about his head, flashed bright for an instant—and died. The officer slumped slowly and gently to the ground without a sound. There was a sudden movement among the guards as they sprang toward him calling. Atkill merely swept his glance around them and they fell like ripe grain, to lie motionless where they had fallen.

Weapons were appearing now in the hands of guards further away, but now the officer, first affected, moved, rolled over, and jumped suddenly to his feet. Atkill waved him away with calm assurance and walked back to the assembled generals.

He had scarcely moved when a score of men rushed him from behind the curve of the ship. Their soft feet were almost soundless on the smooth metal. Atkill turned and scowled again, pointing his left hand at them in anger. They hesitated, slowed and vanished! A slight shimmer in the sunlight, a few sparkling dots of light, and the clink of metal objects that had been in their pockets was all that remained.

The physicist turned once more and walked toward the officers. The richly garbed men were fleeing rapidly toward the nearest ship.

"Halt!" roared Atkill. The men turned, jerking weapons from their pockets, and simultaneously a dozen crackling explosions sounded. Atkill had stopped with folded arms. He smiled, and waited. The air before him was suddenly filled with bright explosive flame, and smoke. It blew away and left him standing with eyes closed, his brows contracted in concentration.

The officers returned slowly at his gesture now. Frightened and worried. They came hesitantly before him. "Down!" snapped Atkill, pointing. They sank on their flexible, double-jointed legs, and looked up at him.

"I am Atkill!" he roared at them.

"Ahut-Kuhl!" they whistled uncertainly.

8

Warren looked at Thaen skeptically. The other evidently wanted the Terrestrian to come out. Warren looked at Putney, who finally shook his head.

"No. We stay right here till we can talk with them somehow. I wish to heck we knew some one of these wonderful systems of telepathy they talk about in stories. I can understand why the author uses them all right. Here we are in a situation that evidently requires immediate action. We don't know how to act, nor what to act against until we can communicate with these people. And in the meantime the enemy continues to operate unhindered. Till I know what this is all about, I'm not moving. They may have richly deserved to have that city wiped out, though somehow, looking at Thaen, I don't believe it. Nevertheless, I'm staying till we can communicate. That's the trouble with languages. They have to be learned, and before a complex situation can be understood, they must be learned rather completely. Months, perhaps, wasted. Nothing else to do.

"We'll have to investigate the language here, and find out how it works. If they go in for innumerable irregularities, passive, vocative and indicative voices, singular, dual and plural forms, nouns declined in singular dual and plural through eight or nine cases, we'll learn something else—or they can learn English. If theirs is easier than ours, all well and good."

Warren shook his head, folded his arms, and sat down firmly. He smiled up at Thaen. "When we can talk, we move," he said firmly.

Thaen looked at him in a puzzled way, and finally started back to the air-lock. Warren went with him and helped him open both doors. Thaen stood on the outer threshold and talked rapidly with some men below for several minutes. They looked worried and asked many questions. Thaen shrugged his massive shoulders finally, and looked at Warren questioningly, uncertain.

Warren beckoned him in and pointed down his throat, then looked questioningly at Thaen and asked, "Eat with us?" He led the strange man to the tiny dining room. First table was up, and the leaders were seated now; there was not room for all at once.

Thaen looked dubiously at the food, and sat down gingerly. He relaxed presently, and tried a bit of the grapefruit cocktail gingerly. Then he tried a little more. Then he drained his glass with a broad grin. Fish was next, and it puzzled him evidently. He watched the others manipulate knife and fork, then tried some of the food himself. This did not seem to please him as much. Potatoes he was not interested in. Beets seemed to fill a long-felt want in him. He devoured them endlessly. But the sweet acid pineapple that served as dessert seemed to throw him into ecstasies. Putney limited the quantity, however, as it might have disagreed with him violently.

Halfway through the meal a man of this world came up to the air-lock, where Korbes was standing guard, and started to climb in. Korbes called Thaen, and Thaen went and spoke to the newcomer. Thaen evidently didn't want him in just yet. The other went away. About half an hour after the meal he reappeared with two others. Looking at Warren, Thaen beckoned them in. Warren nodded. One of the men carried a good-sized pad of thin sheets of some material, and a stylus of some sort. There was an air about one of the others that somehow suggested an actor. The serious mien of the third, and a slight baldness at the top of his head, made Warren burst out laughing. "Putt—come here. Take one look, and I'll ask you who they are."

Putney looked and smiled. "They understand our difficulties. An actor, and an artist and a professor, or I'm unwound." He turned to Thaen and nodded vigorously. Thaen beamed as they set out extra folding chairs in the study or chart-room, as Warren called it.

Presently, as the three newcomers were settled, a fourth man came with a device that was evidently one of the magnetic-ribbon type phonographs with a stock of ribbon-records. He set it up at the professor's direction and left. Thaen settled himself beside it and the lesson began.

In half an hour Putney realized that this language they were being taught was no new language, and that the method employed in teaching it was very evidently a carefully prepared method. The records were graduated carefully. In that half hour they had begun to understand, from the artist's rapid sketches, and the actor's clever impersonations, the basis of the language. A simple system of twenty phonetic symbols constituted the written language, and a small dictionary printed on a tough, thin metallic foil was given them, three copies in fact. But amazingly it contained little more than two thousand words.

The sounds of this language seemed entirely different from those Thaen had first employed, and did not at all fit in with the names of the men. Their teacher, Haelieu; kept saying the word that meant full or complete in the dictionary, and after an hour Putney grasped the idea.

"Ran—no wonder this is so easy—it's a specially constructed language. It's simplified to the uttermost. Take their verb 'ascend.' It isn't that. It's made like the German verb *'abgehen.' Gehen,* to. *Ab,* up. They have taken a few dozen root verb ideas like to, be, see, talk, and made compounds with prefixes and such. They don't say descend, ascend, accelerate or decelerate. They simply say go down, go up, go faster, go slower and so forth.

"Further, the sounds are simplified for others to learn. They aren't like their own sounds. This was meant to be taught to other races."

"They've completely left out all sign of declension, thing, things. Big, bigger, biggest. That's about the only sign of change in nouns and adjectives. Not quite like some of Earth's languages, German for instance, with its *der-des-den-dem, die-der-der-die* for 'the' and so on for every single adjective in the language. No gender here, either. And their verbs! Two modals, two principal parts. Then you know the whole story, absolutely no irregularities. We can learn it in a day."

They did, practically. All that day their tutors worked with them, helping them, teaching them. Rapidly they advanced, till they could speak the language rapidly and readily. They listened to the records, which grew more and more complex, progressively. By night they could understand almost any sentence.

The language lacked nothing save beauty. It was terribly monotonous, for one "went up from the chair and went across the room, and went out the door and went down the stairs, and went through the corridor and went —everything," as Warren complained.

"Hmmm—maybe it does, Ran, but what we're most interested in is in learning their situation—and this makes it possible."

But not till the next day. Thaen, the professor, the actor and artist withdrew, leaving a collection of books for them to study if they wished. They did not—they wished sleep.

The day of the planet was some thirty-two hours, and the men were accustomed to about ten hours sleep, so it was nearly twelve hours later when Thaen showed up again. Haelieu was with him, and a third man, evidently another professor of some sort.

They began the business with a vengeance. First they wanted some idea of where the Terrestrians came from. To their surprise, Putney and Warren found they could not make them understand the idea of "another space." "World," not "space" the professor kept correcting them. "Yes, we know that, of course, but where?"

Finally Putney gave it up as a bad job, and explained that they had come a distance that was absolutely immeasurable. There was no measure. They could travel faster than light, indeed, but this was not how they came. These men had no idea whatsoever of space as Terrestrians knew it, a fabric made of mighty, titanic space-strains, the pulls and counterpulls of incomprehensible millions of tons of matter. "Space" to them meant "room" or "emptiness between stars and planets." Warren groaned and sent immediately for a scientist of this world, their greatest physicist.

The other professor, it appeared, was an historian. "You," explained Warren, "can no more understand what I must say than can a babe unborn." Thaen seemed a bit annoyed. It appeared that he was a physicist himself.

"While the scientist is coming, tell me your story," suggested Putney.

It was a simple story, in fact, made up of but three great elements, and one of these overshadowed their lives completely. Their great cities were not built underground to escape the enemies from other worlds.

"They, we could perhaps drive off or settle with in some manner were it not for the Great Catastrophe to Come," Thaen explained.

"Half a circuit ago (he meant half a year—their year was nearly five hundred earth years) we learned for the first time of the Catastrophe. Our sun is a changeable sun. It pulses with floods of light, and then dies down greatly. You must have seen that yourselves. But that is nothing. That we have known for all time, ever since man first understood the sun did not swing about our tiny world. At the time I speak of, once every day the sun flared up, and sank back, and flared up. A period of fifteen hours. Then suddenly it began to change. It has changed swiftly—for a sun. Now its period is but one fifth of that. It is rapidly shortening. Within a quarter of a circuit, it will flare up once more—in the Great Catastrophe. What it will do then, we do not accurately know. We have with our telescopes seen other stars flare up thus. New stars, they are called. Then gradually they sink back to nearly normal, to flare up once more in the course of half a circuit or more. We believe that eventually it will reach a stable condition not so bright as at present.

"About a tenth of a circuit after the first understanding of what was to come, the first of the Bay-Raonii came. It was a little ship. The mere nose of the huge machine that had started nearly a *raeth* (about seven months) before. It was driven by fire. These Bay-Raonii were welcomed. They had crossed space, a thing our people had been striving for since first we saw what was to come. They too knew of the Great Catastrophe, and were seeking escape. Their planet revolved far nearer the sun than ours. They had calculated that their own planet would be fused at the surface, red hot to a depth of ten miles. Ours would be red-hot at the surface, but cooling systems could be devised to keep the cities far below the surface livable. We had guessed that, and our cities were not being built up any longer, while the brains of our scientist struggled to find a means of drilling the hard rock swiftly and surely.

"The Bay-Raonii were merely explorers, and emissaries. They worked with our people till this language, Anlo-Raonii was invented. They cannot produce such sounds as we can, nor can we produce all their sounds. See, this is a picture of one of the Bay-Raonii."

Warren and Putney stared at the monstrosity depicted. A queer, skinny creature, with a neck like a giraffe. "So Anlo-Raonii was invented. They wanted room here. In exchange they offered certain things we had never had. One was the power of electricity. That was new to us.

Steam was new to us then. We accepted it. Their first ship was followed by more. Swiftly they improved their machines, till finally they could travel both ways. Before, a ship could come, but never return. Soon both trips were possible, if refueling was accomplished here. Their fuel was simply the active gas of air—oxygen, and the liquid fuel they compounded. It was made largely from water. We never learned how.

"They built a city. On the surface. It was an Anlonian who first devised the crumbler, nearly a fifth of a circuit later. Anything within five times my length crumbles to dust in its path. It is like our radio sets in many ways, but the wave goes in one way only. It breaks rock swiftly as a man walks, and powerful suction machines were used to carry it out, and blow it into the air. It settled as dust over all the world. In six months it was merely soil, broken by plants, and used for food by them.

"The first problem was solved. The cities moved underground. Further and further, till such cities as Pan-Lor here were built. Then we had no mountains over our doors, they were not needed.

"The Bay-Raonii rose. They attempted to destroy us. There were nearly a million of their people here then, and many young had been born, for they breed like rodents, very swiftly, as many as six young to one couple. On their own world strict control of this terrific fecundity was applied. Here they had bred swiftly, and it was our request that this be limited that finally caused them to start the war.

"Many, many of our cities were destroyed. We had but ten underground, and those alone remained, for terrible gases of death rained from their rocket ships and destroyed our people. All their cities were underground. We devised machines that settled noiselessly on parachutes onto their cities, and ate their way through the rock to the city below. Hundreds were dropped. If not destroyed within half an hour, they were beyond approach. Most were destroyed. But this was war, and more were made. Their cities were riddled by these, till they leaked in a thousand places. Then, like rats in a trap (*he used a different expression*), they were caught. We returned their gases. Some survived, not many. These were forced to flee in ships, and warned never to return.

"They did not, for nearly ten raenth. Then great battle-rockets appeared with the heat-ray. They started down our tunnels, and blasted our defenses as they came to them. Gas-dam after gas-dam fell, and they bored on despite our heaviest guns, for the shells were crumbled by terrific power even as they approached the ships. Some got through, of course, but not enough to damage the great armor plates on the nose of each ship.

"A chemist, one Rgiolin, saved us that time. Five miles of the roof of our cavern were blasted down with explosives, and at the head of the fallen part a terrific explosive charge was placed. Three more were buried on the way. The Bay-Raonii ships came on and started to crumble the rock away. The explosive charges shot them backward like shells from a gun. Most of the ships were destroyed in those first four attacks on cities. Some persisted with small ships sent on ahead which set off the charges, wrecking themselves in the process. The second charge in each city block destroyed the big ships which attempted to drill on.

"Our air was being derived from the rocks themselves by Rgiolin's process, and that was what permitted us to do this.

"After their losses, our own ships were able to beat off the rockets.

"All our cities moved underground. Their next attack found us prepared with the heat ray, which made it impossible for them to attack through the tunnels. They did not have enough power available to drill the entire distance themselves at that time.

"Raethe followed raeth, and they attacked again and again. They *must* have this planet. So must we. That is the situation. During this period they discovered the secret of the atom, but we learned it also from a ship of theirs we captured with a loss of nearly five thousand men.

"On their next appearance they met a terrific reverse. We were attacked by a huge fleet of nearly 100 great space-battleships, and nearly 1,000 lesser craft. We had stolen their atomic power—and attached a weapon of our own. See—this pistol here contains the basic discovery, this the modification. Examine them, and these diagrams."

Thaen handed the Terrestrians two pistols. They examined them carefully, and then Thaen went outside and demonstrated the first. It was a strange device, with a barrel like two ice cream cones stuck together mouth to mouth, and the two tips cut off leaving an opening of half an inch diameter at each end. One end was the business end. The other was set into a sphere some four inches in diameter, the whole mounted on a stock that made it balance easily in the hand. It was light, and manageable. The double-cone was made of a bluish, transluscent material, the waffling made by bars of silvery metal, buried in the insulating substance. The sphere was a globe of thicker insulation that gleamed faintly with an internal light.

Thaen pressed the trigger and a tiny ball of blue light sped out in a straight line toward the opposite wall of the cavern, nearly three hundred feet away. It struck it with a gentle hiss and the tiny globe expanded to a plane of lashing electric flame five feet across.

"Wicked little thing," said Warren.

"That is the first shot," said Thaen. "There are ten. The fifth and sixth are the most powerful, the ninth and tenth weakest. The tenth will barely kill a man. The fifth will kill fifty. Then the weapon is deadliest. After the tenth the weapon *must* be recharged. After the eighth, it *should* be recharged."

He took the other pistol, and raised it. It was a stock, surmounted by a sphere, glowing as the other, but the barrel here was a curious thing, a straight tube of the insulating material, with metal ribs running lengthwise, but surrounded by toroidal coils set at progressively changing angles. The barrel was nearly two feet long. This was a shoulder weapon, and a harness of stout leather belts bound it to the shoulder, as though a pull rather than a kick were expected.

Further, the sphere here was nearly eight inches in diameter, and set low, below the barrel. Thaen pointed it toward a block of iron that must have weighed some ten pounds, resting on a bench some other men had set up. He pressed the release button, and from the inch-wide muzzle a stream of blue-glowing rings sprang, rushed swiftly to the iron, and bathed it in soft light. Instantly the iron jumped, Thaen stiffened, and the weight leaped from the table toward the gun. As it reached the edge it fell, and the gun was dragged downward with it. It struck the floor, and traveled swiftly toward the weapon. In five seconds it was at Thaen's feet, and he shut off the device. The rings died out, the iron slid to a stop.

"A magnetic projector!" gasped Warren. "Jumping Jehosophat, I thought that was impossible, you remember. I begin to commence to start to understand. Are those boys clever! Get it, Putt?"

Putney shook his head. "Can't say I do."

"What was that first thing?"

"Ball lightning on a small scale," answered Putney at once.

"And that second one?"

"Thought it was the same with modifications at first—oh—it is! I get it—ring lightning instead of ball, and the rings are spinning about their common axis! A charge moving in a circle, makes a magnetic field—selenoid effect—with a long, long coil."

"How long will that operate?" asked Warren in Anlo-Raonii.

"About ten minutes on maximum load," replied Thaen.

"What if there is no iron?"

Thaen pointed his device at the wall of stone, and pressed the release. A sheet of blue flame appeared, and spread in widening ripples, some ten feet across. The wall began to smoke slightly.

"Pure electricity when the magnetic field isn't needed," said Putney.

"What range?" asked Warren.

"About a quarter of a mile in air, for this. Nearly twenty miles in space, but it isn't very effective against a man more than four miles off. The rings spread too much.

"The other is effective half a mile in air, and fully effective up to nearly a thousand in space. It re-condenses on striking its objective. The big weapons are effective nearly 100 miles in space. But the electricity is not very useful, unless it can be discharged destructively to some other object."

"How do you store that energy?" asked Warren.

Thaen shrugged. "We do not know. Only we know that under certain conditions, which we can achieve, metal plates can be put up against each other, and packed under enormous pressure, and yet they are insulated so that even thousands of volts will not discharge during weeks of time. A gas is first forced in under pressure. The metal plates put in position carefully, free of holes and cracks and lumps, and great pressure is applied. After that they will hold several horsepower-hours. Great batteries of these drive our ships. The magnetic beams are used to pull them through space, since planets are magnetic. In air, tiny points along the edges of the wings throw the electricity off, and drive the ship forward, or backward, or hold it in the air."

"What a gang! They must have some sweet condensers, Putt. Think of getting condenser plates so close together—perhaps only one or two molecules apart—and still have a dielectric strength capable of resisting thousands of volts! There are things in heaven and earth—! Horatio, and so forth. I never dreamt of a condenser like that—condensers capable of running those huge ships at thousands of miles an hour." He turned to Thaen. "Have the enemy these storage-devices?"

"No," smiled Thaen. "They have no spies, so cannot learn how they are made. To take them apart, at once destroys them, and all trace of their manufacturing processes. The gas escapes. They have analyzed it, but find only hydrogen and helium mixed. That is all we find. A scientist stumbled on the device by accident. It ruined his experiment, because he put hundreds of horsepower into a furnace, trying to make the two gases combine between the metal plates, due to a terrific arc. The power went in. Little heat developed. He thought he was successful, and the gas had absorbed the energy. He was very much afraid to break the circuit, for he feared the gas was unstable, and would blow up. He broke it from a long distance—and nothing happened. So he went back to investigate. Luckily he had used a voltage of but a few hundred, and the discharge through his body merely curled him up in a corner." Warren grinned. It probably did, he thought. "And then," Thaen continued, "he published his discovery. We also make bombs of them. You saw in the picture. Charged condensers are hurled as shells. When the plates are broken apart, they burst with stupendous force."

"Oh—they would," said Warren.

"You have atomic energy?" asked Putney. "How is it derived?"

Thaen scowled in disgust. "It is a disappointment. We had known of it for many raenth. Knew it existed. Vast energy. When we learned the Bay-Raonii had it, we trembled. It is worthless, for it is no better than coal, or oil. It simply burns atoms, and they give off terrific heat. The apparatus weighs tons. The heat is generated inside a great spherical boiler containing mercury which stops the rays and the flying particles swiftly, and is boiled. The heat runs turbines and generates power. The mercury is gradually transformed to heavy, useless gold, which dissolves in the mercury, and then is gradually built up till the stuff clogs the boilers and apparatus dismally, and must be scraped out laboriously, for the blasted stuff won't dissolve in acids. Usually the mercury is distilled off, and the boiler thrown away. Our mercury supplies are being used up all too rapidly. In ten raeth we will be helpless, unless we use gigantic boilers and empty zinc. Mercury atoms are heavy, and stop the radiation quickly. Other elements would allow it to pass and injure men. It is bad enough as it is."

Warren smiled ·in amusement. "Putt—that's rather good. Hear him cuss that gold? It *is* useless. Melts easily, soft, heavy, clinging." He turned to Thaen. "What do you use it for, if at all—the gold I mean."

"Oh, it does have one use. Other substances are as good, however. It can be made into very thin sheets, and is an excellent conductor. For condensers where weight does not matter, we use it. Aluminum works better for airplanes and hand-weapons, however, for it is far lighter."

"Thaen, have a great quantity of stuff brought—rock, scrap metal—even discarded boilers and old gold—and piled there." He pointed to a spot in the cavern floor.

Thaen departed instantly. In a few seconds Warren was in the control room. A set of forces set to work, and in thirty seconds, a hollow ten feet deep and twenty across appeared in the rocky floor of the cavern. The first load of scrap appeared within two minutes, on a large truck-plane. Warren lifted it with forces, closed an opaque wall of force about it, and set certain field-controls. The Flame behind him whirred gently, and a small hole opened in the bottom of the sphere of force. For an instant a terrible glare beat out that illuminated the vast cavern with a harsh glare. Then a spurting, tumbling stream of white-glowing vapor shot out to meet a cloudy patch of mist, and from the mist a steady, beating rain of shining liquid globules fell to collect rapidly in a pool in the hollow he had made. Warren set some more controls carefully, and went outside. A crowd of men had gathered already, more were streaming in swiftly from barracks about the hangar cavern. Thaen met him as he stepped from the ship.

"But—but, Wah-ran, you are making tons of mercury—that requires far vaster energy than we have ever possessed. Yet your machine is small. How can you get more energy than the energy of the atom?"

Warren smiled. "I will tell you later. Now see—that slanting plane of colored light? It is like a funnel. Tell that truck-ship to dump his load of scrap there."

Thaen snapped something to a man nearby, who ran off toward the circling truck-ship, and shouted to the pilot. The pilot looked doubtfully about, then maneuvered over cautiously. He dumped his load of scrap metal and rock cautiously. It landed on the plane of force, slipped swiftly toward the sphere of energies, and—through the wall. As it passed, each piece seemed to tear a hole in the wall, and for that instant an intolerable glare of awful violet light beat out. The pilot threw his hands over his eyes with a cry of pain and rocked back and forth.

"Oh lord!" gasped Warren, "I forgot that!"

But there were no more accidents, and the mercury continued to rain down in a steady stream till the pool was near overflowing, while pipe-lines were rapidly laid to carry it away.

9

That day Warren and Putney held a conference. Rejoicing men were swiftly draining away tons of mercury, while the great iron ingot beneath the Flame was slowly consumed. Warren looked at it a moment, and turned to Putney. "I think we can let these people have the Flame, don't you? It will mean life to them. They seemed honest, and likable."

Putney stood thinking long and silently. Finally he turned to his friend and spoke slowly.

"We give them the Flame. They will at once build a fleet of ships and attack the first enemy invasion with such effect it will be instantly and totally wiped out. Then scouts will come carefully and investigate. They will next lay a trap. How I don't know, but I do know that—say a thousand enemy ships—could capture even this if they went about it right.

"They would do that. Then both sides have the Flame —and this whole planet would probably be wiped out.

"Dozens of the ships would be sent through into that other space one way or another. I don't want that. I won't risk this ship of course. But they have atomic energy under control. I know how we can improve that for them in all probability, and have something nowhere near as deadly as this would be, and still give them mastery of the situation. Further, many of the weapons this ship carries would be suitable to that use. And I'll give them power for a magnetic beam that could pull that other planet out of position—and atomic energy that won't be so damned disappointing as Thaen said.

"The great advantage would be that the enemy would never find out how the trick was done."

Warren nodded silently. "You are, as usual, right. What's the scheme?"

"Lithium-beryllium alloy. They already have atomic energy under control, remember?"

Warren started. "Lord—sweet. But can they handle that?"

"Let's see. Lithium protons—or particles, I've forgotten, but it doesn't matter, when bombarded by alpha particles or protons, one or the other, but the opposite anyway. Alpha particles it is I believe. It gives off alpha particles when bombarded by protons. Beryllium, when bombarded with alpha particles, gives off protons. Mix the two, and you have a self-maintaining atomic explosion. But it's almost purely electrical in nature. And you'll have a potential of hundreds of millions of volts, if you want it. They can improve that magnetic beam. They can do things with their electrical weapon. They can add to their armament atomic bombs—using the lithium-beryllium mixture—and some of our things. We can make them an absolute zero field for instance, which will protect them against those enemy heat rays. And we can use this ship at least a few times."

Thaen appeared, with him a number of obviously important dignitaries. The ruling council of Anlo.

They were genuinely wise men. They listened to Warren, and they listened to Putney, and they agreed that this secret of the Flame was too dangerous. They would not accept it. But this secret of a greater atomic power? The scientist the Terrestrians had asked for had arrived. Would the Terrestrians accompany them to their laboratories and power stations?

Warren and Putney went, while the rest of the crew remained in charge of the ship. Down through the marvelous underground city, along spider-like bridges between the great tunnel walls, along moving walks that followed the main tunnel walls at one or more levels. The business district of shops and offices, then on out into the residential district. The tunnels were smaller here at first, with apartments lining the walls, lighted windows in the rocky walls looking cheerfully outward. On out, while their guides explained everything to them. These were the homes of the middle-class people, the people who worked in offices and shops, or owned small businesses. Young people, men with perhaps only one or two wives.

Polygamy was the rule here, for good reason. The men were the warriors, and were killed all too rapidly. For years monogamy had been "maintained." But it was not, for the women inevitably outnumbered the men, and the race would have dwindled swiftly. Polygamy had come; the fighting men were expected to marry; it was encouraged. These were the apartments where lower-rank men lived. Then beyond that the walk carried them to the low-roofed, broad "suburban" caverns. These were some hundred feet in height, but nearly three hundred and fifty wide. Stone houses, left standing quite separate from the walls appeared, surrounded by low-cropped lawns and shrubbery growing luxuriously in the artificial sunlight of the great globes. These were extinguished every evening, turned to a low, soft glow. Children played here, climbing through the trees in a way that made the Terrestrians stare, for their long, prehensile toes made them seem like monkeys.

Further still were the great estates, each in its own cavern, cut from the living rock, with half-lit tunnels that led to swimming pools, or planted grottoes.

Thaen led them to his own estate, to show them what was possible, and for the first time they realized that Thaen was no ordinary army man. They had picked the ship he rode as the most obvious of the smaller machines. It had been obvious because he, as a scientist, had drawn nearer to investigate. He had been called out to investigate the new weapon the enemy had displayed, he was the head of the Scientific Weapons Division of the Anlonian forces.

He had a beautiful house of carefully cut stone, set among trees nearly fifty feet tall. The main cavern was wide and large, and instead of the usual globes of light, a wavering curtain of bluish light hung over the entire roof. "It is something new—we are just trying it out, and it is not public as yet," he explained. Dozens of tunnels led to pleasant little grottoes set with trees. Somewhere near ran an underground river. Thaen had tapped it for his swimming pool, flowing water, clear and cool on this hot planet.

With wonderful skill these people had learned to advance all the pleasant aspects of subterranean life, and hide the difficulties.

At the house Thaen introduced his five wives, and twelve children—two were sleeping. But he led the Terrestrians presently to a large tunnel that ran back far beyond the house, nearly half a mile into the native rock. A series of laboratories opened from it, but at the last and largest they stopped. Apparatus banked the walls, a desk set in one corner, and a large bookcase. In the center of the room was a small atomic power-plant.

Thaen had been working on this, seeking to improve it. Quickly Warren and Putney examined everything. Finally Warren shook his head.

"They beat me. With all their science, mathematics seems way behind. Look, they haven't got a calculating machine of any sort. I wonder if they have even developed tensors?"

"What of it? You can laugh at their ignorance now—but they've had atomic energy for half a century—and you learned the control of space only a year ago."

"What indeed. Let's show them that lithium-aluminum though."

Warren had not come empty-handed. He had with him a small Flame apparatus, which he set up at once, and called for any matter. Thaen brought him half a dozen ingots of gold, nearly two hundred pounds. Warren looked at it, and laughed. He had to explain his laughter to Thaen, who laughed in turn. A world where gold had been used as money! A world where still, despite the fact that Warren's transmutation apparatus had made every element equally plentiful, people still persisted in hoarding all the gold that they could get!

Warren set to work. In a few minutes one of the ingots was a mass of pure aluminum. The other was changed to lithium, which promptly covered over with a coat of oxide. The next step was to alloy them. Warren mixed them in about the proportions he thought would work best, then fused them instantly in a large crucible Thaen had supplied. The next step was harder. He wanted a fine powder. They solved it finally by powdering the metals fairly well, burning them, and collecting the oxides. The fused, glass-like result, was cooled, then ground as nothing before ever was, between two force-planes that reduced it to a powder each grain less than one ten millionth of an inch in diameter. The needed elements were there. The fact that oxygen was in combination made no difference.

In the meantime, Thaen and his men had been setting up an atomic apparatus under Warren's direction in one of the laboratories. It was mounted on blocks of insulators ten feet high. Three feet from it was a solid silver shield a foot thick that completely surrounded it. This was suspended by insulators from the ceiling. A long, thin silver pipe led from a silver tankwell, and similarly insulated to the platform of foot-thick gold where the reaction was to take place. Here a standard atomic burner of very low power had been set up.

The silver tank was filled with the aluminum-lithium fuel, the tiny valve adjusted, and a minute stream of power, so fine it flowed like a liquid, fell freely onto the gold, directly in the path of the atomic burner.

Another, exactly similar system of fuel-feed was arranged, and a device added that let a stream of fuel into one feed, then cut off the supply when it was still nearly a foot short of reaching the scene of action. At once the other feed would start. Alternately, the two streams would supply it, so that if the Flame did try to strike back up the stream, it would not go far, nor release much energy.

Then they retired to safety. The television apparatus showed the young man calmly setting about his business. First he made the necessary adjustments on the regular atomic burner. Then, following instructions, he brought a pair of heavy carbon blocks within three inches of each other, and retired behind a lead screen. He started his atomic burner. A glare of blue ionization lit the room weirdly. Next he turned a small knob, and the aluminum-lithium combination began to feed. For perhaps a second nothing happened. Then with startling suddenness, an awful flame of ionization sprang up that blinded the television with its intensity; an earth-rocking roar came from the laboratory such that the rocks about them trembled. For five full seconds it lasted, and a blast of scorching heat reached down the corridor, then quiet resumed.

"Good God! There isn't any lower power for that thing! What happened?" demanded Putney.

"Forgot!" Warren was running. He leapt into the room, and behind the lead screen. He lifted the young assistant, and carried him out. A moment assured him the fellow was safe, only unconscious. The Release Flame cooled the room and the great silver screen in minutes. The silver screen looked tired. It drooped like a wilted flower, with down-hanging petals. The atomic burner was fused, and only a little puddle of glowing atoms revealed that the reaction was maintaining itself. Warren put that out with a force field generated by his Flame apparatus.

"The answer is, Thaen, that the ionization made the current better able to leap the foot gap to the silver screen than the three-inch gap across the carbons. I had forgotten that. The heat released in the enclosed furnace there, melted the apparatus. I know how to make it now. But the plan must be vastly different."

It was. For one thing, the entire apparatus was set up in a vacuum. Next it was arranged to work at a potential of nearly twenty-million volts. That eliminated the effects of the smashing speed of the protons and alpha particles thrown off. The voltage stopped them, leaving only the tremendous charge.

Thaen made the next improvement. The apparatus was reduced to a size that a normal space ship could contain, by use of some of Anlo's wonderful insulating materials. In the end it was scarcely fifteen feet in cubic dimension, and capable of generating power at a rate truly comparable to the Prometheus'.

Work was started at once on the ships. They were to be powered by this apparatus, the voltage being reduced to workable levels by means of a system of Anlonian condensers, charged in series and discharged in parallel. Curiously, within wide limits, no matter what power was wanted from the generator, it had the same cubic dimensions, for here it was the tremendous voltage that required elbow-room.

The remodeling progressed rapidly—but not rapidly enough. A week later, Bay-Raonii attacked again.

The Terrestrians were sleeping aboard the Prometheus that night, when the powerful, reverberating hum of the alarm signal sounded through the city. It was the low steady beat-beat-beat which meant a distant city was being attacked, not the roar of sound that would mean they were themselves attacked.

Warren leaped to his feet, to meet Putney's startled eyes. They dressed quickly.

"For one thing," Warren said, "we've got to know what it is the enemy have. I'm calling Thaen."

He picked up a Anlonian radio and snapped out the call for Thaen. Presently the rolling bass of Thaen responded. "I come."

Warren set to work. He had the ship in order, ready to lift when Thaen appeared. The Commander-in-Chief, Tepalor, was with him. The main fleet from the city had already gone.

"It is Twar Peuowl. You know the way out. The locks are cleared for you," said Thaen.

"Commander Tepalor, will you order that no Anlonian engage in the battle within ten miles of us? We wish to use weapons of much greater power than you have yet seen. We have never shown you our offensive weapons," said Warren. His fingers were busy directing the ship. He had established a resilient force-field about them, and was moving down the great entrance tunnel at a speed of nearly half a mile a second. As he finished his speech, he slowed, and shot abruptly upward and out. The stars of this world were beating down in wondrous multitude that lit the ground below them as the mountain slid silently behind.

Silently Thaen pointed. Tepalor was using his radio. The Prometheus leapt forward under an acceleration of nearly half a mile a second. In five seconds Warren shut down the power, for the world was rocketing by them at an enormous speed. Five minutes later they passed the fleet that had left before them. "Are you through?" asked Warren presently. Tepalor nodded, and Warren threw three switches. Putney was busy setting up fields at his board. Thaen pointed again, but Warren shook his head, and pointed to the instruments.

"Something is wrong," he said. "This shows a far greater disturbance over there." The ship had turned suddenly and was fleeing like a frightened thing.

"Stud 15 is the cold, Ran 1 is the pure force shield, 2 the radiation mirror. I'll analyze, and set up anything you need. Also work rays, of course."

Far ahead a glow appeared, the dawn-horizon. They rocketed across into light and shot around the world. The enemy came into sight, and they saw something huge and round and black that sat on the ground, a segment of a sphere, a black greyness with stars of illumination in it.

"An absorption field—energy drain. That city couldn't signal. Meanwhile they are trying to break them up, most of their ships are under that I'll bet."

Warren grinned, and moved the Prometheus into position. He was small, and close to the ground, and the enemy far above did not see him. "Putt, will you just pour a bit of energy into that field, and see if we can't open something up. They've probably got their apparatus radiating heat into space. Just pour so blasted much heat in there it will blow up, will you. Put two force-planes right in the field itself, and push 'em together. Use all the power the Flame will carry safely."

Putney smiled, and set up his constants skillfully. He pushed a little button. Behind him half a dozen relays clicked, and suddenly the Flame was whirring in deep-throated protest. Before them, the black dome of the energy-absorption field suddenly became a shining incandescent surface of light over its entire surface, and simultaneously the half-dozen ships far above all burst into instantaneous incandescence. The dome disappeared and two sheets of wavering, intolerable radiance fluttered where it had been.

"Oh, oh, naughty boy got his wrist smacked that time," said Warren cheerfully.

Very hard. The Bay-Raonii were getting along nicely, and everything had been going their way. They had put the blanket down while they were still so far away the men of the city had not detected them. After that they simply came over, and sat down on the city. The forts stuck their noses up through the sand, a terrific blast of electric fire stabbed right down through the Anlonian static sheet, and blew them up. That was something newer still. Further, their usual screens were protecting them against rays of all sorts with the usual effectiveness, simply sending the ray back where it came from. The Bay-Raonii heat rays had started work early, and were going at it hopefully by the time Warren arrived on the scene.

Then their screen evaporated in a flash of astonishing incandescence, and the planes out there that had been supporting it simply evaporated so quickly they never guessed that trouble was coming.

The Bay-Raonii weren't long locating Warren. Three huge ships started for him with everything they had. They opened with their heat ray, which simply disappeared silently somewhere in between the two ships (Warren had a cold field, which was simply an energy absorption field of an improved type), followed that with a few hundred high explosive shells, which stopped abruptly halfway between the two forces, and started back on their course with mathematical exactness, having been bounced from a force-wall like a sheet of the finest rubber.

The Bay-Raonii began to take notice of that impudent

little ship. Maybe there was a connection between the sudden and complete collapse of the force-wall and the appearance of the newcomer.

At about that moment Warren settled into his chair, snapped over a tumbler which locked his controls to hold him in position temporarily, and got to work. First he set up a sphere of pure force about two miles in diameter, then he maintained it and simply contracted it. One of the Bay-Raonii ships suddenly dented in like a broken can, tumbled end over end, and blew up in a terrific explosion. Three others followed it in rapid succession, and then all the enemy ships turned on Warren with all the unpleasantness they had in stock. Half a dozen simply redirected their heat rays; most of them shifted to the flare of electric flame that had wiped out the forts.

"What is that?" asked Warren as the electric flare turned sharply aside, and bent off a screen Warren had set up.

"Protons," snapped Putney. "Twenty-mega-volt at that!"

Warren immediately altered the constants of the force-sphere he had built around the Bay-Raonii, and it closed in rapidly, almost instantaneously. But nearly two hundred smaller ships were left! Though fully as many battered, crushed wrecks fell downward when he released it, the others floated quite unharmed!

"Putt—they weren't touched!" gasped Warren. Instantly he set up a plane that should have neatly bisected the nearest of the Bay-Raonii. The plane was given a faint blue luminescence, and it was quite visible. It was an absolutely flat disc half a mile in diameter. It ran exactly on a plane through the long axis of the ship— but it was not where the ship was. There was just a peculiar hole in the plane.

"Good lord, what does that mean?" Putney demanded. Warren was busy. He was setting up a test field, exactly in the center of that ship—or it should have been. His test field reported absolutely and completely nothing. Its very negativeness was a report. It showed that it was beyond time, and space. It had, in some mysterious manner, been cast into that fifth dimension, timelessness.

"That's that. But that just means our forces don't work. Uh. Say, Putt, do you notice we are getting warm? They've been slinging everything they had at us for the last five minutes, and now that heat is beginning to get through. Build up that field a little, will you?"

Putney looked at instruments and shook his head. "Can't. To absorb a certain amount of energy, that isn't too great, that field's fine. But under a concentrated beam of thousands of horsepower, it just won't carry power without losing its characteristics. Apparatus just won't handle it. Remember that is generated by mechanical apparatus, not by the Flame itself. Those ships are bigger, and carry bigger apparatus. We can't compete there."

"Those screens worry me. I wonder what will go through them? I'm going to try," said Warren.

Now there were five projectors on the nose of the Prometheus for the sole purpose of sending rays. Two were run by the great Flame in the power room. They were the lesser projectors, for they projected rays controlled by apparatus. But three were run by individual flames. Warren's fingers moved like lightning, and five terrific blasting streams of energy shot forth, five different beams. One was a cosmic ray concentrated in a pencil of atom-smashing power. It struck a giant Bay-Raonii battle-ship, and the vessel screamed in tortured agony; it shivered over its entire length as the awful stabbing tongue of cosmic energy washed through it. The atoms smashed into individual tortured protons and electrons under flooding billions of horsepower that smashed through their force-mirror as though it were not there. It crumbled to atomic powder, the atoms smashed to individual protons and electrons, and all reunited in a single intolerable burst of ultra-violet radiation.

And one beam was a beam of pure radio-frequency energy, not generated by apparatus, but in space itself, by a Flame that hurled nearly half an ounce of iron into pure energy. That lashed at the screen in a concentrated needle of searing power that blasted its way through simply because only 99.98 percent of incident energy was reflected. It struck the ship beyond, and in an instant there was an incandescent hole drilled through it. The shield fell, and the machine burst into white-hot gas.

The third beam was a strange thing. It was like the evil arm of a great, green octopus. It reached out slowly, drifting outward, and touched a ship's screen. It spread adhesively over the screen like a running glue, and ate through it to the ship behind. The ship glowed softly in green light, darted away, and escaped the beam; but the clinging radiance hung, and like rotting flesh the green spread and grew brighter, until the ship was torn open and fell a green-glowing rotten fruit to the ground ten miles below.

And the fourth beam alone did not have effect, for it was a pure heat beam that struck a ship's screen, and was nearly all reflected; and what leaked through the screen was reflected from metal walls.

The fifth beam was a true disintegration ray. It did not glow with the harsh, solid brilliance of a lash of cosmic force, nor with the sticky green of the other beam, but with a soft green-blue light that passed through the force-mirror with a slight sputtering and struck the ship. And the instant it touched, a stupendous explosion echoed that blew that ship, and two ships within two hundred yards of it to tiny fragments. The beam had released the molecular bonds that had held the steel of its walls as a solid, and the steel became a gas under a pressure equal to its strength, which was sixty tons per square inch. When nearly a thousand tons of gas under a pressure of that order is released suddenly, the results are awesome.

Bay-Raonii had had enough. The ships turned and fled into space with all possible acceleration. And the Prometheus followed easily, without a sign of strain. A great spaceship suddenly swerved from its path and crashed in a flash of light against its neighbor, and then suddenly all the ships darted upward far faster, toward a common point. They reached it with astounding speed, for the attractive field Warren was using caused an acceleration nearly fifty times as great as that of the enemy ships. In less than ten seconds a single great mass of smashed steel was falling to the planet nearly forty miles below.

Thaen was staring with wide eyes throughout. Tepalor sat stunned in his seat. Slowly he gasped as they descended gently to the city far below. For the first time Warren noticed that for miles around the ground was blasted and bare. Smoking grasses alone remained. Directly below the ground were glowing dull red, little tongues of flame licked up some five miles away.

Tepalor shook himself. "Grr—men of another world, we want no such thing as this. Urr. That was no battle. That was the loosing of the thunderbolt on the field of grain. Death reaping with his scythe. You fought them, and smashed them, and the waste energy has set the ground smoking for miles about, the diluted, reflected rays. That green ray—it ate like a blighting rot. It was unholy. This thing we cannot have. It is not meant for our people. With such, a world could be wiped out and left as nothing, as wholly vanished as the ship that hard, bright blue ray touched. A tongue of flame—and gone completely.

"And that other—a terrific blast, and only dust so fine it was not to be seen, mere dancing specks in the light of the sun, and glowing motes that were mighty atomic engines. Their shields fought, and crumpled as the strength of the ant before the tread of the unheeding man."

"Put very well, Commander of Anlo. That is the true case. As the insect is to the man, are those ships to us. Our power is as much greater, as the power of the man."

"I would look at this engine that has done this," said Tepalor.

MacLaurin showed him his engine-room. It was clean, and shining, and noiseless save for the ceaseless soft whirr of the glinting iridescent whirlwind of atoms vanishing forever. Tepalor stared for minutes. "This is the same block of fuel that I saw when first you came to this planet?" he asked quietly.

"Aye." said MacLaurin, and nodded. It was scarcely half gone. It seemed to have been just thus when the ship landed.

"Did you use all your power?"

"Far from that, Sir. Perhaps one thousandth."

The commander shuddered, looked at the smoking ground and heaped wreckage below, and went away. The air pumps chuckled contentedly, and the Flame burned softly, steadily, with a gentle sighing and a myriad whirling glinting sparks.

10

Back in the city once more, work on the new ships of Anlo was pressed forward. Meanwhile Warren was holding numerous conferences with the men of the Protective Science department.

Having seen Warren's terrible weapons in action, Thaen thought far less of their own weapons now. But he said, with reason, that he wanted none of Warren's weapons for which Warren could show him no defense.

"For were one of our ships to be captured, and the secrets learned, then those same terrible weapons would fight back at us, and there would be no defense."

Warren nodded his understanding. "Quite reasonable, Thaen. Now for the cosmic ray I showed you, I can give you no defense that purely atomic engines can develop. The power of a cosmic ray is so great it penetrates every atom and any screen of force within the strength of atomic engines. For the three weapons I think you can best use, I will show you defenses. These three are: the green ray of atomic instability. It is a sort of transmutation ray. It starts the process of transmutation, and the thing spreads swiftly. The atoms transmit it one to another, but the widening sphere soon loses power, and in a short time it stops, for there are always many atoms nearby to drink the power loosed in the transmutation of others. In iron, nickel and cobalt it is very slow and dies out almost at once. In heavy atoms it spreads swiftly and is hard to stop. In uranium, it is almost explosively violent and cannot be quenched by any force you have before the fuel is gone. In steel walls, the heavy atoms of tungsten, molybdenum and other metals supply the fuel. In atoms lighter than atomic weight 50 it will not maintain itself, for their energy is consumed.

"I will show you a simple screen which merely converts the transmutation—projectiles—into harmless electric charges. The beam is actually a stream of peculiarly warped space fields, or charges. They are, one might say, deceased electrons. I will show you a simple force-field that converts them to harmless things.

"The radio-energy heat ray you can use, of course, and no reflector of metal will stop that, for it penetrates the metal. A screen is easily built. Your power is greater now than the Bay-Raonii, and you can readily drive their screens to pieces with your power.

"Next and last of the three I now have, is the explosion ray. I will show you the secret of that, and I will show you how to screen. But do not put screening apparatus in your ships this first time. Not until they have actually been captured in some way, not until the enemy has samples of your weapons, are you to screen against them. Else you give him both weapon and defense simultaneously."

Thaen nodded in approval.

"Now one more thing I have to say. You do not yet know how you can protect your homes against the heat of the exploding sun during the Great Catastrophe. I will show you. I will give you a means of making the field of absolute zero, and before I leave, I will give you the Flame to run it."

"No. We do not want the Flame." said Thaen. "It is too powerful."

Warren frowned in thought. "I will give each city a Flame which will supply all the power needs for fifty millennia of earth time, for one hundred of your years. These Flames will maintain the Cold Field. They will maintain your supply of any element you need. They will protect your entire city with force fields that nothing on this planet could crush.

"At the end of that time the sun will have settled to stability. You can emerge in safety surely. The Flames will go out, for want of fuel. And I shall arrange it that no man may reach the Flame, nor the mechanism of the Flame, nor the mechanisms that the Flames support, save with the aid of a second Flame, until the fuel has gone, and the Flame has died. Will that be good?"

"How is such a thing possible? For one full hundred years! So vast a time?"

"In each city a great tower of solid iron will be built, half a mile in height. At the peak the Flame shall float, supporting about it on a plane of Force the apparatus that controls it. As the circuits roll on, the Flame will slowly eat its way downward, till it passes one after another of the marks we shall put on the tower, and at last reaches the floor of the cavern. When the last iron goes, the dying energy of the Flame will destroy the apparatus that has controlled it through the ages."

"That is good." Thaen nodded.

In less than three weeks time the fleet of the new Anlonian battle craft were ready. One from each of the ten major cities.

Ten huge ships that dwarfed even the greatest of their old machines, and each enormous in power. Their great new atomic engines gave until now undreamed of power. And each was equipped with the deadly beams Warren had made for them, and with small, rapid-firing guns that hurled shells some three inches in diameter that would, on striking any body, or having travelled a full ten seconds, release a horrific hell of blasting electrical energy, the energy of blasting atoms, pounds of atoms. One of these shells would blast a hole half a mile across in solid rock.

They were prepared now to resist any attack from Bay-Raonii.

11

Atkill turned a withering gaze on Texas in the privacy of their ship. He had made it their headquarters, and with reason. The Bay-Raonii had accepted him as a super-human, a being capable of destroying men and materials with a mere glance and a concentration of his will. But Texas was not living up to his part too well. He lacked the harshness Atkill demanded.

"Tex, will you please, dear lad, remember that you are not their friend. We aren't friends. We are masters. Don't even pretend to learn their language. They must learn ours. I have learned theirs, both their own Bay-Raonii, and that Anlo-Raonii thing. I understand everything they say—though they don't know it—but I never speak to them in anything but English. We won't condescend to speak with them in any language but the language of the gods."

"Uh. Right good idea, but I do like to talk now an then, yuh know," said Texas sourly. "Anyway, what's the plan?"

"I told you their situation. They want—have to have—that planet Anlo, but the fools out there are stubborn, and they haven't been able to drive them off. Just after we came, remember, we got reports of the very complete destruction of one of their fleets by some new weapon the Anlo had discovered. Now I'm going to be the Lord High Muckamuck. And to do it, I've got to give them someplace to live. So we're taking Anlo. I've got them started on the Flame ships now. I'm giving them only some of the weapons, but enough—more than enough. Meanwhile, I'm working out some stuff for this ship. And they are building me another. It will be nearly one thousand feet long. Fifty skilled workmen will be employed to install the private weapons. And those men will never tell what they installed, for—they will vanish."

Tex wrinkled in annoyance. "I don't mind that there heat thing so much, nor the knock-out thing. But that thing that makes a man burn like a barrel of gas gets me, and that thing that makes 'em just go poof and they ain't gets me, it makes my belly wiggle."

Atkill smiled. "Get over it. We are gods. The gods do as they will, and are not disputed. The knock-out is just a paralysis ray—and quite harmless. It is a warning. The thing that makes them burn is a cosmic that turns them into hydrogen and they burn. The other is just a simple transmutation field. I could make them change to hydrogen with that if I wished, but I usually change them to oxygen."

Tex looked unhappy. "What th' hell did yuh do to that guy that tried to stab yuh yesterday? Uh—he just turned stiff, and then went all brown, and glowed—and just blew away like a brown gas, and stank."

"That," said Atkill sharply, "was a warning. That was the tenth assassin I had after me that one day, and I was getting peeved. I have a little electro-static balance in the apparatus you know—an idea borrowed from War-ren by the way—that tells me when some one comes near. So when that fellow tried creeping up on me, I got peevish, and turned him into bromine."

Atkill suddenly stiffened as a red light began to glow on the panel before him. "Damn!" he muttered. He snapped on a screen, that glowed in dark, somber red, and black. Three strange long-necked Bay-Raonii were training some sort of a weapon on the ship. Atkill stepped to the open lock and through it, and looked toward the men. He could not see them in the dark, but suddenly they began to glow in weird, greenish colors. Their startled faces looked up stupidly.

"Your masters are stupid," said Atkill calmly, in per-fect Bay-Raonii. "I am Atkill."

The figures of the men began to glow more vividly. They stiffened suddenly immobile. The one on the left began to shake violently; his outline grew hazy and a scream rang out from his open mouth. Presently it stopped, and he slumped suddenly downward; but as he fell, the light that shone from him grew brilliant, and the clothes he wore, and the flesh of his body, melted like snow in the path of a heat-ray, and a skeleton fell to the ground surrounded by bits of metal and glass and crystal.

The one on the right shrieked, trembled, and melted as had the first, till a bare skeleton fell to the ground.

"Go, and tell your masters I am Atkill!" roared the Terrestrian. Something gripped the remaining Bay-Raonii in a vise of force and hurled him half a mile away, to land dripping in a small lake.

Atkill returned calmly. "They will never learn," he said shaking his head. "Sometimes I doubt whether even I can teach them."

"They don't seem bright," Texas said, and started toward his room.

But Atkill was at the works early the next morning, superintending the construction of his giant ship. He did a great deal of the work himself with the aid of a Flame he had started. At night the Flame was protected by a force-screen only he, equipped with another Flame, could enter. The great hull was shaping up quickly; it was a skeleton now, coated in places with heavy armor of six-inch beryllium plates, hardened with several other elements, all light in weight. He knew the power and results of the green beam of atomic decay that he would give his forces to use. The beryllium of which this ship was made he had transmuted for himself and no other ship would be so constructed.

That day saw the hull finished, and the next the control apparatus was being installed. The second night Atkill and Texas had moved into the new ship, and their crew of workers were locked in the ship. Those fifty workers would never leave.

A fleet of twenty giant Flame-powered battleships was being constructed by the Bay-Raonii, under Atkill's distant supervision. These Bay-Raonii, like the Anloians, had never conceived of space as Terrestrians had learned it. While Atkill had learned this quickly enough, he had made not the slightest effort to enlighten them. He had merely shown them how to make the necessary controls for their ships. They were being given only the lesser weapons possible to the Flame, and small flame apparatus, for Atkill had no intention of letting them even approach his ship in power.

In a month the fleet was completed, and Atkill's great cruiser was finished as well. And the great fleet of ships assembled near Forn-Karno, the capital of Bay-Raonii. The Emperor held court here, and his magnificent entourage appeared outside the palace to greet the ships. They sank gently to the ground in the great Pallada

Nuriol before the palace. They formed a giant square of ships, about the reviewing stand that had been set up in the exact center of the Nuriol. The Emperor's party was already assembled there, and as the crews of the ships stepped smartly to the ground beside their charges, the Emperor raised the ancient Ye-Raonii in salute. This was a shaft of pure, crystallized light, a wondrous shining thing of golden radiance, capped by an enormous ruby-colored stone, set in claws of pure iridium. The metal had been scratched with thousands of tiny lines, so that the surface gleamed with shifting, glowing colors.

The crews bowed down before the Ye-Raonii, and a great chant went up from the thousands of people congregated about.

Then from far above in space, a thin, ghostly radiance settled down on all the square, and the Ye-Raonii flamed suddenly with great shooting flames of golden light; it the entourage of Harum Dichir in glowing waves. A cry of entourage of Harum Dichir in glowing waves. A cry of wonder and anger rolled up from the assembled Bay-Raonii.

And out of the sky came Atkill's great ship. A plane of glowing golden force picked up the platform of Harum Dichir, and carried it through the air till it hung above the broad steps of the palace. In the exact center of the Pallada Nuriol there was a vacant square nearly two thousand feet across. In the exact center of that space, a structure of glowing forces appeared, forces glowing red, and gold and green and blue. A titanic dome a thousand feet high, mounted on a great base fifteen hundred feet across shàped as a regular octagon. A single great arch one hundred feet in height was left as an opening to the dome fifty feet above the ground as it opened onto the great base.

The sky that had been white with the eternal mists of Bay-Raonii suddenly was darkening over; a chill wing sprang into being, and in the space between the inner and outer force-walls of the Dome, a fierce glow was materializing, and a dark grey cloudiness. The wind increased, and roared shrilly about the palace and the great ships, and across the vast open space of the Pallada Nuriol. Rolling thunders and great jagged flashes of lightning tore from cloud to cloud far above, and the hot, damp air of Bay-Raonii was chill as the damp mist increased.

A thin shining layer was forming on the surface of the ground under the great octagonal base. Swiftly it swirled thicker, as a snow of dark metal fell to it, and welded under unseen forces. More and more rapidly it grew, and the shrill of the winds howled louder. Jagged lightning slashed downward in protest at the glowing gold of the giant force-dome. Where it touched, the gold of the dome glowed brighter, and the lightning was swallowed unheeded. A steady black snow of metal fell to the octagon base, and it built up swiftly to shining metal, silvery and bright. The clouds above were black now, sweeping in swift circles, a gigantic cyclonic whirlpool of clouds. A great black stem was reaching down from the clouds, reaching like the stem of a maelstrom for the very peak of the dome. With a shriek and roar it touched and held, and as the blackness sucked in, it vanished momentarily in a soft glow that shifted to black raining metal.

The whirlpool of energies grew, and the metal base was finished while now a shining layer of metal was filling the walls of the dome itself.

Swiftly this filled higher and higher, till the dome was completed, a shiny dome of solid, silvery metal resting on a great metal base.

And in an instant the whole great structure blazed white-hot, yet no heat reached out to the watching people. As swiftly as it had heated, it cooled once more and the metal was firm and smooth and shone with a soft, lustrous surface like velvet metal.

The colored forces vanished in a twinkling, and other forces set to work, forces that left shining, brilliant surfaces in their path. Swift forces that painted scenes and pictures on the walls with a gigantic brush. And over the arched entrance appeared gigantic, radiant characters, strange to the Bay-Raonii, that spelled out ATKILL.

And now those who were placed that they might see what went on within the Dome, saw a great solid ring of fully shining grey metal materialize on the smooth metal of the base, a ring a hundred feet in diameter.

And a giant voice rang out that could be heard over all the vast Pallada Nuriol. In perfect Bay-Raonii it spoke. "This is the place of Atkill. Those who seek me, shall find me here."

The great ship sank slowly, and settled to the metal base beside the dome, and a wall of jet blackness descended over both ship and Dome.

Behind that wall, Atkill and the fifty workers were busy. Great panels of apparatus were swiftly moved to the floor within the ring of iron Atkill had laid down on the surface of the metal base. In half an hour the apparatus was ready and connected. In fifteen, more forces had cut a clean plug of the fifty-foot thick metal out of the base and left a slanting tunnel ten feet in diameter that led down into the solid metal base. More apparatus was installed in the room that was cut out at the end of this sloping tunnel.

And a change was made in the ring of iron. It was lifted and a well sunk that it would fit in exactly, a well fifty feet deep that led down through the entire thickness of the base. The iron ring was built up until it was a hollow cylinder that slipped snugly and smoothly into this well, leaving some six inches projecting above the surface, and fifty feet below. A piston of force would support it and feed it upward as needed.

The apparatus in the center of the ring was covered over by a metal dais that rose in tiers. On the peak a throne of resilient forces that glowed deep violet would soon be established. The next step was completing the living quarters below the surface of the base, deep in the metal. The disposal of the great quantities of metal was not difficult; it was simply re-transmuted to oxygen, and escaped.

At last the Flame was established. Over the top of the entire great ring of iron, the Flame burned, arching in a roof of crystallized light a hundred feet above the dais. Reaching the control from the hidden branch passage below the metal surface, a slanting passage that, fifteen feet below the surface, cut through the iron cylinder that fed the Flame, Atkill came to set up the Force structures he wanted. First were the deep violet resilient forces of the Throne. Next was a throne, but was outside the Flame. This was the throne of Harum Dicher. And then two lesser seats, one blacker than space itself, one of continually pulsing golden light.

Then a wall of force to support the great dome, for

the metal alone could never have borne the strain. And from the peak of the dome a giant beam of deep crimson light stabbed upward. Now it was lost in the black of the screening field that hid their operations, but soon it would be a beacon visible for a billion miles in space.

From the floor of the dome to the roof, two great columns reached, one an angry crimson, and one of pulsing yellow. One was Death, and one was Life, a beam of stimulating, lifting radiation.

The dome was ready. Seated within that circle of the Flame, no conceivable force or thing could reach him. No heat and no cold could reach through, no beam nor ray, and no particle of matter. Atkill was ready, and the screen of black dropped away. A slow chant sprang up outside, and Harum Dichir came with his party up the great broad steps that Atkill had cut in the metal of the base.

"This is the place of Judgement and of Life and of Death," Atkill said through the great amplifier he had installed, and his Bay-Raonii was perfect. Not for nothing had he studied some fifteen languages on Earth. "Harum Dichir shall judge ye, with Bartir Kenlar and with Preylu Thilam. And they shall direct ye to Life or to Death, and if their judgment be good, and I concur, so shall ye go."

Harum Dichir was lifted suddenly in a mantle of white light that carried him swiftly to the great white throne, and the two other men, the Counselors of Justice, were whirled each to his throne, Bartir Kenlor, the prosecutor to his black throne, and Preylu Thilam to his pulsing bench of gold, whence he would argue in defense of the accused.

That day Pryd Wranlor, the Commander of Bay-Raonii's forces, was summoned, and the order for attack on Anlo was given. That night, when Anlo rose in the sky above Forn-Karno, the great fleet set out into space, two thousand great ships powered by the Flame.

And one more ship powered by a greater Flame, and with vastly greater weapons. Atkill was going to make sure the attack would be a success.

12

Warren was aroused suddenly by the steady throb of the great alarms sounding through the city. Putney was already swinging his feet to the floor as the hum of the Anlonian radio told them Thaen was calling.

"Yes?" Warren picked up the set with a single motion as he jumped from his bunk.

"They have not reached Anlo yet. Your detector field flung a hundred million miles into space detected them; our telescopes spotted them. They are coming slowly. They are like no previous Bay-Raonii ships; they are larger, and we can find no evidences of magnetic driving rays."

Warren was in the control room in a moment, setting up fields. In thirty seconds he located the direction of the ships, and Putney had joined him. In twenty more his face was pale and Putney was staring at meters. In that time they had learned one thing that told the whole secret.

"Thaen—Thaen—I gave you plans for the screen mechanism, you made it up and had it made ready to install?"

"Yes."

"Order no ship to leave the ground without it!"

Thaen was puzzled but he sent the order at once, then cut back to Warren. "Why?"

"The Bay-Raonii have the Flame!" Warren shouted. "How they got it I cannot guess—yes—by the Lord, I can! They have small Flames, their Flames are not as good as ours, but they are terrible none the less. Your ships must use all the power they dare on their screens, they must above all leave the magnetic beam alone! It will be more dangerous to them than to the Bay-Raonii now. Come, for I am going at once."

Thaen came within five minutes. The Anlonian fleet had not moved but men were swarming about the ships, cursing, struggling, working with bulky, powerful apparatus ready to install and which needed only three connections, but which was heavy and required time.

246

The Prometheus rocketed out the tunnel and into the open air at terrific speed. The ship shot out into space instantly, straight for the fleet, and when speed had been attained, Warren shut off the driving power and coasted outward.

From a million miles he explored the fleet. It did not take him long to learn that two thousand ships were weakly powered, for Flame ships, and that one was a giant of power. It had not the power of the Prometheus, for Atkill had not had time to experiment with the Flame, and had not learned the trick of control that permitted Warren to get nearly fifty times as much power from a given Flame. But Atkill's ship was larger.

Warren began to explore that larger ship. He had a television screen set up before him, and now there appeared on it pictures as of a glass ship, wherein the walls were bare, dim shadows, save where it was focused, and there perfect vision was obtained. Only about the neighborhood of the Flame was the device inoperative. Where, nothing showed beyond strange, distorted shadows. Atkill was in the control room at the bow.

"He escaped!" gasped Warren.

"I know it. I see where I was wrong—and right," nodded Putney. "The men with him went mad as I said. I should have had more confidence in my beliefs. They were dead. Atkill had to dispose of them. There was no lock on his ship, save the little garbage lock. The men had to be pushed out through that. The Bay-Raonii must have given him power to start again. Those fragments of broken ship that fooled us were fragments of Bay-Raonii ships. By some ill-chance we never got a piece of a Bay-Raonii. Or perhaps all Bay-Raonii dead had been collected by their own men.

"And he's given the Bay-Raonii the Flame—but a mighty weak one, I wonder why?"

Warren had been watching. Several Bay-Raonii were about, and he had seen their attitude toward Atkill. "He's set himself up as over-lord. He could, with the Flame. But he's not giving them anything free. And he's making sure they don't turn on him by only giving them half power."

Atkill had been manipulating instruments with sudden interest. Putney watched his a moment. "He's spotted us. Look—he's shocked. He realizes an Anlonian ship has him spotted—and has the Flame." Atkill was making more tests. Putney watched his instruments. "Examining the size and power of our Flame. Doesn't like it does he?" Atkill was pursing his lips thoughtfully. Suddenly dawning understanding spread over his face, and a wide grin split his features. His lips moved silently. "By God—Warren," quoted Putney, reading his moving lips.

Atkill was suddenly laughing, and turned to a radio set beside him. Warren snapped a tumbler that put his receiver in operation.

"Warren—Warren—Warren—James Atkill calling Warren—" Atkill's voice came through.

"Looking at you now, Atty," said Warren quietly. Atkill jumped, and looked around him annoyed.

"Don't jump, Atty, we won't bite you yet."

"Hmmm—you are watching me, aren't you. Warren, you are a good man. I don't see how you do it. I haven't spotted anything that will look through metal yet. Well—let's try this." Atkill's hand reached for a tumbler and through it. His image blurred, dimmed, and was scarcely visible. Warren increased his power a trifle, and the image was clear again. Atkill solemnly winked his left eye.

"The left," said Warren, slightly bored. "We call that field X-394-21. It won't stop this, though it will stop most radiation. Atkill, what are you doing out here now?"

"Going after some stubborn people that won't let these friends of mine land."

"Why—they were once allowed to land and they tried to kill off their hosts. That's not polite, so the Anlonians haven't asked 'em back. We are here trying to help the Anlonians."

"Oh, that's too bad, Warren. You know we have two thousand ships—besides this. You'd better hang off while we settle it, because that one ship of yours can't overcome my two thousand, and further, the Anlonians won't stand a chance now. I see they haven't the Flame. I've detected only one little one on Anlo. And the old atomic engines won't stand the chance of a cake of ice in a star's center."

"Call off your dogs, Atkill, and I'll show you how to get home. You'll never find out without calculating machines, which I see you haven't got," said Putney quietly.

"I have a home back on the planet. I've left my friends back there."

"Friend, Atty, friend?" asked Putney. "His name, I

believe is Texas. You didn't leave the calculating machines there, because you'd want those right under your wings, you know."

Atkill shrugged and grinned. "You're right, little man. That bluff didn't work. But here's one that isn't bluff. In the next five or ten years I can make calculating machines, and learn how to get home. In the meantime, I've got a darned nice time here, high Muckamuck stuff you know. I've always wanted to be a big frog in a little pond when I found I couldn't be the big frog in the big pond. I like it here, and when the Bay-Raonii move out here, everything will be fine."

"They won't," said Warren. "We're going to stop that."

Atkill laughed, and shut off his radio.

"I don't like that," said Putney.

"Do I?" asked Warren annoyed. He continued to watch Atkill, and signaled Thaen to call the Anlonian fleet. The fleet was not entirely ready yet, but some quarter of the ships were ready, and started. Warren told Thaen the best plan would be to have them wait in the atmosphere for the others. The Bay-Raonii were coming only slowly now.

In ten minutes the entire fleet reported ready, and were waiting directly below the Bay-Raonii fleet.

"Good," said Putney. "Have them maneuver laboriously and act as much as possible like only slightly modified atomic ships. Atkill knows we haven't given them the Flame. He has evidently warned the Bay-Raonii to watch out, however."

The Bay-Raonii entered the atmosphere scarcely five minutes later. They started for the Anlonian fleet, leaving Warren and Putney dangerously alone. Atkill hung on the outskirts of the battle, and sent his rays down. Warren and Putney were kept busy at first stopping those rays.

"Terrestrian or not, he's going *home!*" snapped Warren finally. The Prometheus withdrew suddenly the screen it had maintained to stop Atkill's rays, and turned everything it could muster into a driving, searing cosmic ray. It struck a screen that flamed into instantaneous fire half a mile in diameter. It was radiating so much pure heat that all the screens of the battling ships below flamed in defense. But it stopped the cosmic.

Warren sent a flat wall of force at the ship with a

velocity slightly less than that of light. It crashed into a sphere of force around Atkill's ship, and exploded into a blast of energy that half-fused the rock of the planet below. Momentarily both fleets below were forced to give up their battle, while the giants above clashed, for their own defense screens were required in full to protect against the waste energy of the greater struggle.

Warren's fingers were living lightning playing on an organ of cosmic forces. He tried his beam of radio frequency energy, but it was stopped in a terrific cascade of flying energy; he shifted finally to the simplest means of attack. He started all three self-powered bow reflectors on the radio-frequency energy and ran them straight up the spectrum. They reached infra-heat and slipped through Atkill's interference shield only to be bounced from a screen of pure reflection that coated his ship itself. The waste heat that leaked through was absorbed by a cold field. The ship and its crew were temporarily blinded with light. Ultra-violet light was absorbed by the metal a bit better than the infra-heat, but not too well. Next came X-rays, and they rebounded from the reflection-screen. Gamma-rays followed with the same result.

Warren snapped out a curse. "We've got his beams tied in there while he's defending himself, but we can't open his shell."

Atkill opened it long enough to send out a stabbing cosmic that made the Flame in the power room grumble, and exploded the thin traces of the atmosphere about them into a sea of ions and blue hydrogen flame. Then Atkill tried a little heat. Their cold field had been out, but it went through that in a sputter of blasted energy and struck the reflection screen Putney had been setting up. Simultaneously, the leaking energy that got through the reflection heated the metal walls through red heat so rapidly they were yellowish before Putney set up another cold field in them and chilled them once more.

Atkill went through the same performance on his own account. Warren smiled, and called to Korbes. "The repeater." A moment later faint shocks shook the ship, and simultaneously a seething hell developed around Atkill's ship, a blasting electric fire that reached out mile-long arms of fire. Atkill's rays stopped abruptly. Dimly, through the various layers of fire, they could see that his outer shield was being rapidly disintegrated. The force-wall did not like that blasting electric-field strain that was pulling it to pieces. Warren sent the hottest radio beam he could get down the channel of the terrific stream of atomic bombs the three-inch repeating rifle was sending. The lace-work in the screen became a distinct hole. The energy absorption screen behind it was sputtering violently, and beyond that white-hot metal began to drip off.

Atkill started to move. He went hurriedly at his best acceleration, and Warren followed. But even he could easily outdo Atkill's best acceleration, since the Prometheus was equipped with the artificial gravity acceleration, which Atkill did not know of, they could not use their repeater, since the shells were rapidly outdistanced. Warren set up a force shield in front of Atkill and put in plenty of power. Atkill simply blasted at it with all the energy he had, and succeeded in breaking through.

But it slowed him down—and a shell caught up with him. The rear of his ship was not completely protected, since his power was, necessarily, being used in blasting a hole in the force wall before him. A stream of some ten shells. The first eight or nine lashed out with their colossal electric and atomic fire, with the result that a hole was cut through the force-screen protecting the ship. The tenth got through successfully, weakened, but still there. It melted off about one third of Atkill's ship.

Atkill tried a last weapon. It was a half-ton block of iron mounted with a Flame—AND NO CONTROL! It came hurtling back toward the Prometheus, blazing higher in a terrible crescendo of escaping energy. Wild, free Flame of utter destruction of matter, releasing a stupendous flood of cosmic rays.

Atkill's crippled ship could still move. It moved quickly back toward Bay-Raonii, leaving Warren the pleasant task of taming that half-ton of wild material energy flame.

It was pulsing now, and had built up the fatal acceleration field that warned Warren it was preparing for an instantaneous complete release. Putney was establishing the quench field, which alone could handle it. But now, having knowledge of the results, he did not attempt to suddenly and completely quench it. He brought it under control first, letting it radiate at a stupendous rate in the pure heat range. Then he closed down his quench field. The Flame behind them turned angrily orange and roared in furious protest. The wild Flame before them turned violet and grew smaller. As it shrank the ship's Flame grew white and the roaring ceased. In a minute and a half there was only an incandescent cloud of iron vapor where the wild Flame had been.

"Hmmm—like the glass lizard. He left a wiggling tail for us to chase while he escaped," said Warren. "We tickled him anyway, and I don't think he knows just what those bombs were. He's afraid to use that wild Flame unless he himself is in mortal danger. Don't blame him. Bet he thought we couldn't handle it either."

"Our fleet—" said Thaen anxiously. "If they are fighting those Flame ships—"

The Prometheus was already streaking back toward Anlo. "I don't know how bad they'll be, Thaen. Those ships weren't powered with Flames as great as mine, and as the Flame of that other ship. Atkill set the control finer, and the Bay-Raonii I'll bet don't know how to handle the thing yet.

"A gun firing powder can send a bullet with greater power than a bow and arrow can develop. So a Flame ship can send more power than an atomic engine ship. But—a small gun cannot hit as hard as a giant catapult with huge steel springs. Those Flame ships have small Flames, and your ships—have gigantic atomic flares."

The fleets were in sight now. The two thousand ships of Bay-Raonii, armed with the Flame, were rapidly overcoming the atomic powered Anlonian ships.

Then Warren got in the center of things. At Thaen's order every Anlonian ship dived suddenly and simultaneously under their greatest power toward Anlo. When all were somewhat below the Bay-Raonii Warren established a disc of pure force between the two. The disc lasted for about ten seconds before the accumulation of Bay-Raonii ships blasted holes in it. In the meantime over one hundred giant space-cruisers became crumpled metal cans. The Bay-Raonii, seeing they could overcome at least one weapon of the Prometheus, started toward it. Warren released a flock of his terrible explosive shells. Nearly a hundred of them struck targets. Perhaps two score succeeded in blasting down the defensive screens by sheer concentration of explosively released energy. There is more power in a quart of gasoline than in a stick of dynamite—but the dynamite will do a lot more damage.

In the meantime Warren was trying out his five different projector rays. The cosmic blasted holes in five ships that go in line with it. The green ray of atomic rot ate through a screen, but Warren saw instantly that the screen was designed for it, and had simply fallen before superior power. The radio ray, and the steel explosion ray acted exactly the same. All successful—but all battled by the correct screen.

This took scarcely five seconds, and in that time the Anlonian ships were back. They fought easily on an equal if not superior footing with the Flame-powered ships of the Bay-Raonii. But the Bay-Raonii ships had cosmics, for which the Anlonian ships had no defense save speed, and the thick press of other ships. In return the Anlonian atomic bombs were deadly to the Bay-Raonii. With Warren's help it would have been a fairly easy victory. But the Bay-Raonii evidently got a signal from Atkill out in space. At least two hundred giant Bay-Raonii turned their enormously powerful heat rays on Warren. Not the radio-heat which he could have fought with his screen, and no doubt conquered, but the plain infra-heat ray. The reflective force-field turned about 99.9 percent. The cold field would absorb an enormous amount of energy. But when three hundred huge Flame-powered ships strike at once, even though they be weakly powered for a Flame-ship, no force-mirror will suffice. Warren had to retreat hurriedly, with red-hot walls. The flow of energy was so great he was not able to destroy sufficient enemy ships to relieve himself before his own metal walls would melt away.

He retired, to come back a moment later. Instantly three or four hundred more ships attacked him again. He retreated more hastily this time.

"That," said Putney, "is that! They've got to keep an eye on us, but they can keep us away while they do things to the Anlonian fleet. Further, our walls don't like that. But—we can do something." Putney was setting up a field. Presently he had it determined properly, and Warren smiled.

"What is that, Warren?" asked Thaen.

"It is a field which will disturb any Flame near it, acting as a damping control, cutting down their power. It has a greater effect than our own power would permit, since we are fighting their Flames in a highly efficient manner, while their Flames must fight back in an inefficient way. Let's try it. We can operate from some distance, and while it will cut down the Flames of the Bay-Raonii, it won't touch the Anlonian atomics."

Warren nodded. Behind them suddenly the great Flame growled and a shrill whine of torn atoms whirled into it. The Flame went from pure white to deep orange; it expanded nearly two feet, and a curious distortion of space about them became evident, as even space itself strained under the terrible, lashing force of the giant generator.

The effect on the Bay-Raonii a hundred miles below was evident. Their screens which had been colorless under the power of the Anlonian ships were suddenly orange, their beams which had been stabbing out at the atomic-powered ships were snapped off instantly, and all their power converted for use on the now straining screens. And—immediately the Anlonian fleet poured all their energy into smashing the under-powered screens. That put a further strain on the half-smothered Flames. The Flame of the Prometheus shuddered unevenly, groaning and wrenching at space.

"Mon—ye've burned two tons o' iron!" roared the Scot in the power room. "Ye can see the block move!"

A steady orange glare was beating out of the power-room to the control room. The Anlonian fleet was aiding the weakening process now—for half a dozen ships had failed and fallen as flaming wreckage. Their Flames snuffed out in a moment, and relieved the strain on the Prometheus by so much.

Down below in a thousand Bay-Raonii ships the frightened, uncomprehending men saw their two-foot Flames shrinking steadily, and turning from white to violet, and watched their power failing rapidly. They had almost no beams out now, and still their screens were turning to flaming, inefficient interference; holes were appearing, and waste heat leaking through. Their cold fields that had been protecting them were horribly inefficient anyway, and now, under-powered, were not absorbing energy as they should. All the ships were heating.

In desperation the Bay-Raonii flag-ship sent the signal to retreat. They could at least outrun these Anlonian ships which had so suddenly acquired deadly power.

They fled, gaining speed only slowly however, for the Anlonian fleet pursued them while pouring in their deadly rays, forcing the Bay-Raonii to maintain their own, power-drinking screens.

For two seconds Putney released the straining damping field, and threw the Prometheus' entire power into creating two sheets of force, and pushing them against each other in the center of the fleeing Bay-Raonii fleet. Quintillions of kilowatts of energy flamed into instantaneous heat radiation. The surface of the planet 150 miles below flared red-hot to the horizon—and nearly a third of the Bay-Raonii ships turned white-hot and flowed together in molten globules. The Anlonian fleet, some five miles behind, had put up screens at Thaen's order, and yet two of them had flared dull red. Almost instantly Warren cut off his flaring force-walls and restored the damping field. The Bay-Raonii were taking no more chances. They dropped half their fields, released the energy-wasting cold field, and fled under all the acceleration they could stand. They were out of accurate or effective beam range in ten seconds, fleeing wildly.

13

"We won, Thaen, but it was a costly victory, and a near defeat. You must have the Flame now."

Thaen nodded grimly. "We must, Warren. Who was the other Earth-man?"

"Atkill. A scientist of Earth who once before attempted to steal my invention from me, failed, and finally proved himself a man, even though not quite a moral man. He saved his country, and sacrificed himself. He was in a battle, and was thrown through to your world—your system, by the Flame of one of the ships he fought."

"Then he knows all the weapons you know, and will equip the Bay-Raonii accordingly?"

"Not everything we know." Putney shook his head. "And he has no calculating machines to help him. But therein lies our greatest advantage, Ran. We've got to get something absolutely new, even to us."

"So's he," Warren replied.

"Well—let's get to work. I have an idea for getting *real* power. Our greatest trouble is that we can't run that Flame as fast as it wants to go. We have to keep it half smothered. Isn't there some way we can let it run completely wild for as long as we want it to, and still direct the energies it releases? Perhaps the best way to stop it after it has run wild a while would be to overload it and quench it in the X-49 field then."

Warren grunted. "I can picture you. You can't control the energy it releases. How would you send it anywhere —you couldn't direct it."

"We'd not make the ship like this one—I'm thinking of a new ship, Ran. We'd have a couple dozen major flames. One for a driving engine, like our present Flame. That would also take care of the maintenance operations such as the ordinary force-field lock in the atoms of the walls that make them meteor proof, the air and light, that type of work, and our acceleration compensation. It would be a normal flame like our present one. The one semi-controlled flame to act as our screening. It would be easy to get it to throw a perfectly spherical field of

256

any of the types we know. Then—one or two dozen projector flames. We could have semi-controlled flames mounted for projectors. Normally they'd be just ordinary fully controlled flames, but when we wanted we could release them from control completely, yet keep them from running completely wild and consuming the ship by using power from our third main flame to direct their operations. So load them that they wouldn't have power to completely escape control—along development 586 that would be. That would give us at least 10,000 times our present maximum. They'd be a little slow starting, naturally, but once started they'd burn iron like a fire burns magnesium tape. And God help what got in the way."

"Ummm—we'll have to do some calculation."

They did. Within a day they saw it was possible, and the forces of Anlo were turned to building the monster ship they would need. It was to be nearly two thousand feet long, so big and so lightly built that speed might be made, that would make it incapable of supporting itself entirely; permanent Flames were built into its very structure, Flames that created a force-field within the metal of the walls and beams and made them stronger than any metal could ever have been. Without them, the great structure could not have borne its own enormous weight on a planet. With them, nothing less than a planet falling on it could crush it.

Week after week the Terrestrians worked. And the Anlonian workmen built not only this giant ship, but hundred of replicas of the Prometheus, save for the speed device, which would have enabled them to exceed the speed of light, for that Thaen's men could not understand, and could not reproduce even with the model before them. It was beyond the power of their minds to comprehend.

In building the great new ship, Warren and Putney and the Terrestrian crew had to install the necessary apparatus for this work. But most of the apparatus was built, installed, and set up by the Anlonians. One other thing Thaen refused to handle, and that was the wonderfully delicate apparatus that would control the half-mad Flames of the projector.

Week followed week, and no sign came from the Bay-Raonii. When Warren installed the tremendously more powerful penetrating television apparatus, he found that while he could reach to the surface of Thinal-Ren itself, the white-hot mass of boiling matter that circled the great sun at a distance of barely half a billion miles, and could look across 180,000,000,000 miles of space to Quaren-Ren, the third planet in, the nearest planet, Bay-Raonii always shied away from his apparatus in some way. Atkill had learned how to deflect the device.

Korbes brought them news one day. He had been working with the astronomers of Anlo, and had learned that they were convinced that Paarool, the giant class scA-4, the huge star that glowed like a second sun to this world only three-quarters of a light year away, was circled by planets. He had set up some apparatus from the Prometheus far from any of the cities, and had been projecting outward for days a gigantic detector field. The dimensions of the field and its characteristics had finally been measured with the minutest care, when it covered an area whose diameter was nearly a light-month. Then smaller fields were set up, and their dimensions carefully determined, and redetermined when all the effects of the planets of the system were known, and the irregularities caused by the works of the Bay-Raonii and the Anlonians in particular were accounted for. The result was that they knew now that at least five major planets revolved about Paarool, and further, that one was inhabited by a highly advanced race, for their instruments had shown powerful force-field effects that could not be natural. The sun itself, of course, caused some effects, but these could be determined fairly easily by using a far smaller field, one not sensitive to the minute disturbances of the artificial force-fields.

"That's not all," Korbes had finished. "They also show that—somebody or something is coming! Artificial force-fields of varying strength, and of those peculiar dimensions typical of Flames, are being set up somewhere between Paarool and us, and they are coming toward us at a tremendous speed, near that of light!"

Thaen looked unhappy. "Let us hope they are friendly," he said at last.

"We'll know in about one raeth," said Korbes. "They are not far off now." After a pause he added, "There must be nearly 1000 ships—and they are huge ships to affect the field from that distance!"

Thaen looked at his friends in despair. "No friend

comes to greet us with a thousand gigantic ships such as these must be."

Putney looked mystified, and he seemed to be thinking intently. "That race has lived in this space, and near this star for thousands of generations. They have built up a science that discovered the Flame. They know all about the variable status of this star, must have investigated it as intensely as you, probably more intensely. They have the power of the Flame to aid them in understanding the workings of the forces within the star, and you have not had it. Their detector fields told them long ago that your planets were here, probably that your people were here, for your atomic engines produce fields of force measureable from that distance if a spaceship observatory is used as the base for a detector screen fifty billion miles across. They must know that we are here with Flames by now—no, wait, the strains travel only with the speed of light.

"Knowing this is a variable star, and knowing what it consists of, they know it will explode. They are not coming to conquer your planets. They would not want to. Why they are coming I do not know. It may well be they are coming to make sure you don't try to conquer theirs."

"Whatever may be their purpose, Putney, they are just one more factor thrown into our already over-crowded battle front," groaned Thaen. "New science—new weapons—"

"Sorry, Thaen—we have more to give you too. I think I know all the weapons Atkill can have, but he may develop more. I made a fairly thorough examination of his ship, but the worst of it is that the power-room, where the apparatus would be, was absolutely unreachable. The Flame acted as a deflecting force."

"And we have some more weapons for you. I'm going to give you everything the old Prometheus had. Some of the things we have now you couldn't run. Not power enough."

Thaen smiled slightly. "At any rate the Bay-Raonii will get an unpleasant surprise!"

As a matter of fact, the Bay-Raonii had gotten an unpleasant and angering surprise last time. They had been driven off with terrific losses. Their tremendously powerful ships, more powerful than anything they had ever dreamt of had been unable to defeat the suddenly reinforced Anlonian fleet. Further, Atkill, the Atkill, had told them that Anlo had no Flame fleet—but they had certainly shown power enough for it and the terrible bombs they had had—

Atkill saw, even as he fled back to Bay-Raonii that he would have to act instantly and with decision. The Bay-Raonii were not going to respect their super-human for long if he came back with a badly crippled ship, and their fleet came in badly beaten. He watched anxiously as he fled, and saw that Warren and Putney had decidedly done things to the Flame power of his ship.

But at that moment he was more interested in analyzing the multitude of forces at work. He retired hastily about ten million miles, stopped, set up a detector screen, and began analysis work while his crew busied themselves fixing up the leaking ship. Unfortunately, he learned only two things. One was the dimensions and nature of the damping field Warren was using. That was so terrifically powerful that even at a distance of ten million miles it was noticably affecting his own Flames. Further he learned the peculiar twist-field Warren had developed which turned any field through ninety degrees of space-time, and changed its entire nature. The result was evident, but no further results were. Warren's two fields simply smashed out every other type of field around, save for the momentary burst of terrific electric fields with hints of a magnetic nature. His instruments wouldn't stand the strain of a detector field more than three centimeters in diameter, so his energy pickup was small, so small he could not analyze accurately.

"Hmmm—the boy is, as I have said, clever. Atty, my lad, calculators are in order. Evidently those are atomic bombs of some sort. They give off tremendous energy too —and they don't stop easily. They went through that energy absorption field of mine and just wiped it out till it wasn't. Now what might they be? I don't know— but I can guess."

Atkill stopped where he was, and started to work. With his little turban-wrapped Flame he transmuted some scrap metal to aluminum and lithium, and ejected about a pound of the mixture. Then with his Flame in the ship, he started the reaction. As he expected, he got a terrific burst of free flaming atomic energy.

"That," he said to himself, "would certainly do the trick—and several more for that matter.

"Now I wonder—could something else of an opposite nature be made?"

It took him nearly all the rest of the trip back to Bay-Raonii to work out the system of manufacture for his new idea, but eventually he got about half a pound of something that was absolutely black, the blackness of utter nonreflection—and weirdly, everything within two feet of it was darkened, and things beyond it were distorted in their outlines.

He threw it out into space, and pushed a small tumbler. It was floating about a mile away, visible only as blackness against the disc of Bay-Raonii. They were but half a million miles from the planet now. As he pushed the tumbler a ray of stupendous energy lashed out at the sheet of blackness. The black irregular sheet suddenly spun crazily away, and end over. Atkill caught it between some force planes, and held it. Nearly ten billion horsepower lashed at it, driving stupendous energy into it. Nothing whatsoever seemed to happen. For minutes he continued to burn it with his ray of concentrated destruction and nothing happened. He shifted to a cosmic. Nothing happened. He started down through the scale, and ended with long hertzian waves. Nothing whatsoever seemed to have happened.

He threw one of his new lithium-aluminum bombs at it, and set that off. There was a slight glow of dull red light. And the sheet of blackness was still there!

Atkill smiled like a contented cat and turned the most powerful ray of pure infra-heat he could get into it. He continued that for nearly five minutes, and at last a very faint glow began to appear. Instantly Atkill shut off his ray and turned visible light of a much lower intensity into it. It remained absolutely black. Minute after minute passed, then quite abruptly it turned grey. Atkill snapped off his ray. With astonishing rapidity the blackness faded through grey to a bright metallic glint, remained bright all over with shifting, whirling colors for an instant—then blasted suddenly with a stupendous violet flare of light that rocked the half-wrecked spaceship, and flared at the screens with a terrific shock. The screens were out, and the Flame in the ship shuddered once with a terrific thump.

Atkill looked startled for a moment, then his face settled to a look of thought. "That is not so good. As protective layer it would be fine—till it soaked up all it would hold. Well—"

The returning fleet was met sadly. Atkill was already back in the Dome. The Emperor, and various commanders of ships came to him there, angrily demanding explanations.

"Among the Gods," said Atkill slowly, "there are great Gods and lesser Gods, but for that they are yet gods, and greater than Man. I am great in my own world. I am so far greater than you that you do not understand the mechanism I make for you. But in my own world there was one who was as great as I. We quarreled. Through his vast powers he threw me and my friend from that world beyond what you know as the end of nothing, to this place. He thought he had destroyed me forever, but I saved myself to this extent: he hoped I should be destroyed as the iron that feeds the Eternal Flame. I was not. By forces he did not then know, I was able to escape to this space. For a year he believed he had destroyed me forever. In that time I have gathered strength to return and defeat him. Now he has followed me here. He has helped the Anlonians.

"You saw his ship attack me. He again tried to crush me, destroy me. This time I was stronger than before, though still he was somewhat the greater, for though he destroyed part of my ship, he did not harm me seriously, and he did not force me into that otherness. And I have learned another of his secrets. Bring me a small Eternal Flame."

A man hastened out, to return in a few minutes with a small Flame mounted on a little block of iron protruding from a single gigantic crystal of ruby that Atkill had made for the Emperor.

Atkill looked at it and nodded. "That is good. Put it on the stand." He turned to the assembled Bay-Raonii leaders. They were less angry now, somewhat more thoroughly awed. A battle of the Gods! Their God and the God of the Anlonians!

"I have learned to quench the Eternal Flame—see!" Atkill stood upright, his eyes staring at the little pinpoint of white flame over the gigantic ruby. An aura of faint violet light built up about his head as his brows drew

together, and his chest heaved. His breath came harshly
(to cover the slight sound of the straining Flame within
his turban) and his cheeks paled. The aura of violet light
intensified; it seemed to lengthen from him toward the
little Flame, and grew reddish, while suddenly the tiny
Flame was mounting through white to blue-white, to
blue-violet—violet—and with a sudden sobbing wrench
of space, it was gone!

The Bay-Raonii stood suddenly upright as the blue
glow appeared about Atkill's head, then disappeared as
he slumped suddenly in his seat.

"It is done. I can make apparatus which will do much
the same thing. That is why the power of your ships
failed you.

"I said the Anlonians had no Flames, but you, fools,
say they must have. Their power was terrific? It was.
Too great for atomic engines to produce, for apparatus
to handle? Such as you know, yes. This War-Ran, the
Great One who opposes me always, did not give them the
Flame because he knew something else that approached
it in power.

"He felt the Anlos not fit for it. He gave them a
greater atomic power than ever you dreamt of. You
have not the metal whose number on the atomic table
is three have you? Neither has Anlo. But War-Ran could
make it—as I can—and he did, and with it he made a
new atomic engine that gives terrific electric power instead of more heat.

"Those terrible bombs—bombs so powerful they succeeded in penetrating to me, are made of this new
atomic power, which I will give you.

"But I will give you something else he has never
thought of. It is a substance through which no ray can
go, no energy can penetrate. It will soak up energy as a
sponge soaks water.

"Each ship shall be coated with it, and no ray, even
such rays as the Eternal Flame generates, can penetrate.

"But this I must tell you: it will not stop the damping
energy which chills to lifelessness the Eternal Flame. It
will not stop magnetic energy, and it will not stop electric energy. But it will soak them up if they appear as
heat.

"You can coat your ships with this. See!"

And he demonstrated to them the terrific absorbing qualities of his new blackness.

And while all Anlo strained to build giant Flame ships, Bay-Raonii built similar great Flame ships, freed now, however, of the restrictions Atkill had imposed on their Flames, and—their outer walls were solid sheets of the utterly black energy sponge. They would need no screens to protect against most of the rays!

That meant that while they could drive rays at the Anlonian ships, they need not worry about their own defense—for their ships were invulnerable!

The sponge material was made of iron—but iron that had been treated in a peculiar type of Flame. The Flame released the energy of the iron not as in an ordinary Flame, but it worked on all the iron. When the iron had been about two thirds destroyed, the Flame was quenched. The remaining iron was also there—but yet not all there. It was a skeleton of iron atoms from which most of the energy had been extracted. Any entering energy was simply soaked up to restore the iron to true iron once more—and the instant the entire atom was complete, the artificially strained and tortured iron atom released all its terrific energy. As Atkill had seen. To protect against this happening the ships were being coated with two-inch shells of this weird material. None of it became saturated until all was, so they had hundreds of tons in all to be converted before any would fail. In the meantime they were free to use all their power for deadly rays, while the Anlonian ships divided theirs, and finally would be forced to use all theirs in defending themselves. Then —Atkill expected that a steady rain of his huge lithium-aluminum bombs would break the walls of force protecting the Anlo ships!

"Only if their power is vastly greater than ours, need ye fear, for otherwise in the end we will prevail. Under no circumstances can you lose greatly, only another retreat may be necessary.

"And with the vastly more powerful Flame your ships are now equipped with, you will easily overcome any atomic ships that may attack. As soon as your new fleet is ready, we must attack," Atkill had said.

He left them to the work of reconstructing their ships, and his, while he calculated. He had glimpsed something else—and finally he saw the derivation in the equations his crude machines had given him that he must follow. It took a week of almost continuous work to derive the equation, and hours to convert it to terms his apparatus could handle. In the end he used the little flame in his turban—and suddenly he was wrapped in a dense cloud of utter blackness that extended around him in a sphere. And when Texas turned one of the great projectors of his ship on him, even then he was protected, for the terrible ray seemed to bore harmlessly into the blackness and vanish. It was a strange field that concentrated all energy entering it on the spot at its center where rested a half-pound block of the partly disintegrated iron, and all energy was absorbed harmlessly by it.

In his ship the half-pound block was replaced by a huge ingot that had weighed nearly fifty tons. Nothing he felt, would ever reach him now.

14

Warren looked down on the new ship that Thaen had had constructed for him. It had been built in a special pocket of the great entrance tunnel, for it was too large for any hangar in the city.

"It is finished—all we can do," said Thaen.

"I have been working on it too, with my men. We have everything installed. And—several new pieces of apparatus. We have borrowed something from your strange ball-lightning device, Thaen, and we have something now that will be very unpleasant. We are prepared. I am going to test it today."

"I will accompany you, as you asked," said Thaen.

Together the two men entered the huge ship. The control room was in the exact center of the ship. There was a huge cubical space here, and at the center of the cube floated the control compartment. It was supported on solid planes and bars of force, and half a dozen great snaky cables led from it to the apparatus ranged around the gigantic power room.

No single Flame dominated this room. There were four Flames. One burned quietly now above them on a gigantic ingot weighing close to a hundred tons. Automatic forces would keep a steady supply of those gigantic blocks of energy, while others would feed fifty-ton ingots to the three smaller Flames on the floor of the room below them.

The control room was equipped only with television devices. No direct sight to the outside was possible—but if one set of apparatus was burned out there were a dozen more to take up the load.

Putney was in the control room now, the Scottish engineer with him.

"Okay, Mac—Ran's here. Go on below and watch over your pets—they are a bit less tame now, you know."

"Aye. That they are."

"Ready, Putt?" asked Warren.

"All set—all the Flames started. Everything set for operation. Going to Il-Anlo?"

"That's—yes, that's moon five, isn't it? That's what I was thinking."

"Good enough. Take over."

Warren seated himself at the vastly greater control board, and Putney seated himself beside his friend, Warren glanced over the instruments swiftly and gingerly applied the power. The walls outside moved slowly across the television screen. There were seven screens so arranged that Warren could see what was happening exactly as though he were actually looking through glass windows. "She's sensitive," he said. The ship suddenly shot forward, turned abruptly, and rose rocket-like through the open tube to free air outside.

The sun was shining with blighting blue light; it was at a maximum and at noon, but it sank swiftly as Warren headed his gigantic ship out to Il-Anlo. Presently the little moon appeared before them, suddenly expanded swiftly, and a soft hum came from below. As quickly it whirled to a side port, then was suddenly shrinking in the rear-vision screen. It was a point of light in seconds as one of the great Flames roared angry protest to the terrific acceleration. They were accelerating under about fifty thousand earth gravities—yet no one could feel it here in the force-shielded control room.

Abruptly the moon stopped shrinking, whirled crazily, and was before them, and expanding. In fifteen seconds they were cruising gently over the surface of the tiny planet—scarcely 100 miles in diameter.

"Going up the scale on projector 27," said Warren. He started in long radio, and the rock below was suddenly a boiling inferno. The incandescence spread to a white-hot pool ten miles across in five seconds, and Warren snapped off the projector.

"That," he said softly, "was one tenth power. I'm trying the full power of projector one on Cosmic. One is our biggest gun." His flying fingers set up three protective screens, lest rebound rays damage them.

Then he threw a tumbler, and simultaneously pushed a little slide to the extreme end position. He just barely reached the end before he snapped it back. The television screen had flared violet and winked out in blackness. The side screens showed a terrific glare and a rushing cloud of bright violet gas. Warren retreated half a million miles and set up a new television sender by touching a stud.

A globe of blue-violet gas was expanding swiftly in all directions, some two hundred miles in diameter now. It was the remains of the moon. Thaen gasped, Warren whistled softly, and Putney nodded gently. He looked at a dial before him. "Five pounds of iron, Warren. I expected that. Fix it up again."

Warren grinned, and set his new machine to work. Humming whines came from the Flames beneath and around them as a great wall of force condensed around the moon—nearly three hundred miles in diameter now. It was cooling swiftly both by reason of its enormous radiation and because of its expansion. Warren cooled it even more swiftly creating a cold field that sucked out the energy of the five pounds of iron he had thrown into it. In ten minutes the moon was a perfect sphere of mathematical regularity, and at a temperature of absolute zero. Thirty pounds of iron had been consumed.

"Let's make it look like a normal moon," said Warren. A slowly reaching finger of green touched it, and a bright green light flared from it, and spread like a foul disease across the surface. It lasted perhaps three minutes, and a great cavity of dust was there. The "Anlo" as the ship had been named, rocked to a sudden explosion as a single hundred-pound atomic bomb smashed toward the moon. A titanic flare raised half the surface to a red temperature.

"That's the old ones—try the new ones."

Twelve hours later the Anlo settled back in the berth under perfect, gentle control, and with shining eyes Thaen stepped from her to report to the council—

The council also had something to report. A scout ship Anlo had sent out—the first they had ever been able to send out—had vanished suddenly that day in a single sudden sparkling of light as reported by the television screen. And it had been a Flame ship!

"That means an invasion is on its way," said Putney slowly. "I suggest we prepare. Evidently both sides have been preparing to fight with the utmost speed. Bay-Raonii had to rebuild her fleet, but had hundreds of new craft to train her new men. We had to build new ships, and train men. Apparently we have been successful at least in equaling their speed."

"They were powerful last time, thanks to the Atkill.

What if they now have even more?" asked Paernol, the Coordinator of Anlo.

"What indeed?" Putney shrugged. "There is nothing to be done now. I do not think they have, for we have calculating machines, which are, Paernol, a vaster weapon than any ray or any Flame, for from them came the Flame and all rays. And Atkill has none."

But Atkill did have some, crude to be sure, but sufficient for his purpose. They had shown him one last trick—

Far in the night of space, the probing television of the Anlo found the Bay-Raonii fleet. It did not take long to find that every ship was powered with the greatest possible Flame, and that they were all equipped with some field of force that stopped the television dead at their jet-black outer coating. But it was evident that they too were relying on indirect television viewing now, for no windows or ports of any nature broke the smooth, black walls, save for tiny lens-holes.

Atkill's greater ship was equipped with ports and windows, as well as television lenses, and there were black metal shutters hung before them. His walls too were impervious to the probing beam.

Putney looked worried. "I don't like that, Ran. There isn't the effect of the deflecting field there. It looks more as though that wall were opaque to this beam, and yet we know that no matter can be opaque to it!"

"I want to go out there and make some tests."

The Anlo was already out of the atmosphere now, on its way toward the fleet. The Anlonian ships were waiting back in the atmosphere, where defensive screens were more effective. Warren was forced to parallel the Bay-Raonii and Atkill's ship at a distance of ten million miles. Nearer he did not dare to go, lest Atkill throw out detector-deflectors and prevent his study.

Something seemed to be preventing it anyway. Time and again Putney built up a minute, delicate field and maneuvered it toward one of the Bay-Raonii, and time after time it entered the wall unharmed, but the instant he tried to change the field in any way to get useful readings, the entire field collapsed instantly and completely. More and more worried, he turned to Warren. Warren was grinning, watching with entranced interest.

"The old son of a gun! That boy is good. He's got

something I never thought of—and will it raise hob for Thaen's boys! Don't you see what that is? It's a sort of half-destroyed matter that can re-absorb all the energy it's lost. Remember that for the last weeks Bay-Raonii has been deluging Anlo with tremendous rays, rays that were absolutely useless and perfectly ineffectual—representing thousands of tons of iron, and we wondered why they were using them, and not making tight, mildly annoying rays that would have required defense? They've been throwing off energy and that was how they got rid of it. That half-destroyed iron will drink energy like space itself, till it's all rebuilt. Then of course—of—mmmmmm—I'll be, it blows up *all* the energy!"

Warren turned sudenly to his notebook, and began reading rapidly and carefully. Finally he reached out a hand blindly to a stud, and threw it over. "Thaen—Thaen—Thaen—"

"Thaen speaking."

"All the ships have those big accumulator stacks they used with atomic engines still in place, haven't they?"

"Yes—I believe so. It wasn't considered necessary to remove them."

"Listen carefully, and take this data down. Field 589-634. X-754, Y-34-92-1, Z-583-21, T-4 to T-27. Have every ship set that up in spherical shell about them, by means of the C^5 auxiliary Flame. With the C^6 auxiliary set up field 935-B^8. You know that one. Place tap apparatus from the atomic generators in position to collect and feed power to the accumulator banks. That field will protect you against any *radiated energy* attack so long as the accumulators will take it, and that would be about fifteen seconds if no load is put on them. On the other hand, if you load them with the various electrical devices you have for everything you can, you'll find the first field will absorb any radiated energy attacking, and will release it inside the ship—directly in the Flame that makes it—as an oscillating electric field. The second field will convert it to magnetic to rectify it, and give it off as direct current your—Good Lord! Putt—listen—how about using only that first field, and tapping it with the magnetic semi-inverter field, and then re-inverting that! You'd get your oscillating electric field split into two halves, then back again, and would arrive just half-phase off—and at the same center! Result: two bright lights make a great darkness! Within wide limits, it would require very little power, because the ray-energy would kill itself!

"Thaen—get that? Set up that first field in your A-2 Flame. Your A-1 you need for driving and acceleration compensation. Your A-2 can handle that collector field. That keeps both your main Flames busy. Then you have six class B Flames. You had best use B-1 for the field I'm giving you now—"

Rapidly the men of Thaen's fleet were setting up the field Warren called for. One of the greatest advantages of the Flame ships was that the Flame required only control apparatus of one sort to perform any desired function in the realm of space-fields. It was the knowledge of these space fields, and what control would produce them, that hid the complete knowledge of the Flame.

Warren was himself setting up such a control field, but he was using two class scA flames, two of those half-tamed Flames, and felt no ray could penetrate.

"Ran—Atkill's been listening to you," said Putney presently.

"Uh-hu—expected that. That's not helping him any, just telling him we have a means of defeating any ray he sends before it starts, and that we have his own absorbing material beaten for protective power. Ours won't get soaked and explode."

"But you gave him hints, even if he doesn't know your control code."

Warren shrugged. "Had to tell Thaen."

The Bay-Raonii fleet had turned slightly, and was heading for Warren. He estimated a fleet of no less than three thousand huge ships nearly one thousand feet long! The Flame had certainly been at work in constructing those monsters. Detector fields could pick up little sign of activity outside the walls of absorbing material, but from the windows of Atkill's ship more signs were detectable. Atkill's machine at least carried ten full-powered Flames.

"Thank you, but I do not mind running just now," said Warren firmly, putting the Anlo into reverse, so that she moved away from the Bay-Raonii and maintained their separation. The Bay-Raonii came on steadily. "We may have ten thousand times the power we had," said Warren, "but that doesn't say we can fight a couple hundred of those babies."

The radio buzzed sharply, and automatically switched

itself on. "Warren—Warren—we are coming out into space since our screening need no longer worry us. These weapons are too great to use near a planet in safety."

The Anlonian fleet was shooting swiftly out toward the Bay-Raonii—and using a terrific acceleration. They would arrive in a matter of minutes. The Bay-Raonii were shifting about wildly into battle order, and several score suddenly leapt forward under what must have been a crushing acceleration to come to grips with the Anlo. Atkill was not among them. He refrained temporarily! Warren retreated easily in his acceleration-compensated ship, and in doing so laid a few hundred hundred-pound atomic bombs equipped with a simple rocket drive that would drive them toward any force screen in the neighborhood. As a second line of unpleasantness he dropped several hundred fifty-pound material energy Flame bombs that would automatically escape control and become centers of unbearable attraction at the moment a force screen touched them.

The Bay-Raonii ran into the first line of defense, and an intolerable sheet of atomic flame suddenly sprang up as the protective force-screens met them at head-long speed. The bombs, their concentrated energy suddenly released, ate huge holes in the screens; the great ships plowed into them—and the bombs went out like snuffed candles, leaving only a faint murkly glow on the wall of the ships.

"Jumping orbits—what stuff that energy sponges it! It soaked up those atomic bombs like thirsty sand drinking water! Let's see what happens when—ah!" The first of the Flame bombs had felt the touch of a force-plane, and went off. Instantly the entire Bay-Raonii fleet heeled sharply, the Anlo even stopped abruptly and reversed its motion. No tangible acceleration was produced, for everything was affected similarly, men and machines alike. For perhaps a tenth of a second the acceleration endured, before a ship hit the bomb. The bomb went out as quickly and as quietly as the atomic bomb; only a dull blue glow flowed over the wall of the ship that struck it. Instantly it seemed half a dozen more bombs started action.

Some half dozen ships were wrecked slightly by their mutual collisions, then no more bombs went off. "Quench field killed 'em," said Putney. "He's learned that."

Warren shifted in his seat. "A bit of action, brothers."

The Anlo darted toward the leading Bay-Raonii under her full acceleration, and was among them in an instant. The force-plane that had attempted to stop her had flared in one instantaneous coruscating flame of light, and vanished as the half wild Flame in the Anlo gave a single heavy thump that shook space, then quieted.

Warren started with ten cosmic rays concentrated on one small spot of one ship. All the near hundred Bay-Raonii had instantly poured their entire power into him, with the result that their rays died abruptly some two hundred feet from the walls of his ship, and the screen Flame whined slightly. The energy of the rays was fighting itself now.

The ten cosmic projectors each consumed about thirty pounds of iron a second, a total of three hundred pounds of metal. Now there was one effect Atkill had forgotten in his calculation of the resistance of his absorbing material, for such rays as Warren was using were not beyond the power of a big ship using normal controlled Flames. And this was the fact that cosmic rays have mass, real mass, and when three hundred pounds of cosmic rays, traveling at 186,000 miles a second strike any wall—though that wall may be able to drink up the energy—it *must take care of the momentum!* No material could withstand the blow of those rays, rays like solid streams of liquid. The projectors on the Anlo were anchored by force planes and bars. The walls of the Bay-Raonii were punctured as though by a white-hot needle. A hole appeared as though by magic, and a terrific flood of cosmic rays entered the ship, battered for an instant of time at the opposite wall, and went out—leaving a white-hot wreck wrapped in a shell of utterly black, utterly absorbing half destroyed matter.

Warren smiled firmly, and turned his terrible pencil of rays on another Bay-Raonii. The second ship crumpled like the first. Two more followed it—and then Atkill appeared, while the Bay-Raonii retreated hastily.

Warren turned his terrific knife on Atkill's ship. Nothing happened, save that the rays disappeared somewhere between the two ships, and the attacked ship lumbered away gently. She was feeling that terrific push, but standing up to it.

"He doesn't depend on his walls," said Warren.

Atkill tried a few Cosmics on Warren. He sent over

fifteen pencil-rays, which were promptly absorbed and defeated by their own powers. He tried half a dozen material energy bombs. Warren smiled dreamily as the first struck, and ate at a force screen.

He pushed a stud and something like a deformed sphere grew suddenly on the side of the Anlo. It moved outward with deceptive appearance of slowness, and as it moved two long, pale-blue arms reached out and enveloped the nearest four or five Flame bombs—and the bombs were gone, and the strange deep-blue thing moved on—toward Atkill. It reached out for his ship; it felt the screen that had drunk in the energy of the cosmic rays; and ultra thin streamer reached out, seeming to seep through the screen while a pale violet light emanated from it constantly.

Atkill had sat frozen in amazement. With a cry he gave an order, and an instant later a thudding echoed through the ship. A stream of black lumps struck into that weird blue thing, and they drank in its blue life—and it died. Half a dozen more were starting, and a terrific solid bar from all twenty of the Anlo's projectors. It was a solid bar of ultra-violet heat energy. It faded out abruptly ten feet from the wall of Atkill's ship, but there was a hazy mist of light for ten feet about it that outlined the thin film of the screen.

Almost simultaneously from Atkill's ship there came a crushing force-wall that closed suddenly on the Anlo. It crushed down, and smashed through the Anlo's great force-screen as though it were a tissue paper wrapping. It crashed into the actual wall of the ship itself, and the two hundred and eighty-five separate Flames that locked the atoms of the metal wall immovably suddenly shrilled menacingly, and turned a deep red. An awful wall of pure energy was flaming outward where the two forces conflicted.

Automatically and instantly the protecting, energy-absorbing field had rushed in to drink out the waste energy and to cool the metal. In the infinitesimal fraction of an instant before it acted, the metal walls became invisible, save for a very dull violet glow. There was an inner wall of metal, and this too became white-hot, although the cold field was maintained in it. The third and innermost wall of metal was smoking; the men felt a sudden beating wave of heat. And Warren acted. He sent out a field of force that would break down the control of any force-wall, cut it off. It was a circular disc a mile across, and instantly it was a mass of flame, as the awful vice of force released its hold on the Anlo, and she quieted once more as screaming Flames died down. His fingers like the pistons of some marvelous engine, Warren set up the outer force-screen, and put one of the scA class flames behind it. Then he released his failing control damping field, and Atkill's force instantly attempted to return. It failed this time. Warren's face was pale as he adjusted a tiny dial off to one side. As a projector up on the front of the ship strained at its mooring forces, a driving beam shot out that devoured the iron that fed into it at a rate nearly a hundred times as great as before. It was increasing. Warren cut back the dial to zero. The beam fluctuated slightly, and increased once more.

The Flame that ran it was completely wild! In an instant Warren had cut off its fuels supply, and at the present rate the 100-pound bar of iron it fed on was exhausted in a fifth of a second.

"His power increased till it easily equaled ours!" said Putney.

"We're feeding him!" gasped Warren. "The sweetest little thing yet. I make him stop his own rays—and he turns mine around and sends 'em back with his compliments! Let's try forces—"

The projectors snapped off. The load on Warren's force screen fell to practically nothing, scarcely more than a few thousand tons to the square inch. Warren ran the force screen back by sending out one of his own. He started closing his in. At ten feet from Atkill's ship the screen stopped dead, and Warren failed to push it nearer. But Atkill suddenly blossomed forth with a projected magnetic oscillation that passed Warren's screen because it was not radiation. It heated the walls with tremendous speed, and Warren pulled his force shell off with burned fingers.

"That's a better screen than we've got!" said Warren. "I'll have to—"

A great green snake, some two feet in diameter, and a thousand feet long issued from the Anlo like smoke coming out of a hole. It writhed gently, and undulated a moment before it began to break up in a thousand little sections, each about ten feet long, and a few inches thick.

Each was headed by a speck of white light, and each began to glow faintly. They all started rapidly toward Atkill's ship. They fluoresced slightly when they struck Atkill's screen, and stiffened into rigidity—but they went through. Like a flock of pigeons alighting, they nestled on Atkill's ship—and sank into the metal. Instantly the deadly green atomic rot set in where they were, and spread.

Another snake had issued from the Anlo. Atkill was busy trying to stop the atomic rot the first had started, by adjusting his screen to work in the walls. The atomic rot screen was a sphere, and the ship was not. He could not reach all parts at once. The second crop of the green terrors was on its way, and Atkill wisely started out to stop that. His screen failed to work on the seed of the rot. They glided unharmed through that screen too. He sent out his black shells—and the snaky filaments glided through them—and the shells glowed green! Atkill looked unhappy. He was unhappy, for if these shells could not stop it—

Half a dozen of the green monsters swam out. A deep violet globe appeared shortly after the last of these, and it started toward Atkill's ship with a business-like efficiency. It hit the energy absorption screen, bounced, hit again, and broke into millions of minute specks of violet light that filtered through the screen unharmed—and joined once more on the other side! It settled on the wall of the rotting ship, and—the Flame broke out! It was actually the heavy metal behind the half-disintegrated shell that was going, and it was the damping effect of the black shell that made it possible for him to quench the Flame. Dozens of the violet globes leaked through, and frantically Atkill set up his quench field and maintained it. The atomic rot he could not control, till his ship became a sphere, so he had set up his field, and pressed it rapidly outward, till it just included the outerwalls at the greatest diameter of his ship.

The ship was rapidly crumbling away, leaving only a useless dust held in place by force-planes. Grimly Atkill reminded himself that the force-walls were the real walls of the ship. Though the metal vanished, the strength the walls was there.

The violet globes stopped appearing, and fearfully Atkill groaned. "That ship isn't natural—those things aren't weapons—they're diseases. What more has he got?"

The new thing was small; it looked like a small cup, some three inches across, a hollow hemisphere. It was almost invisible, individually, but after the first one floated out, thousands sailed forth. All were rotating rapidly so that alternately their closed and opened sides faced the ship. They reached the screen like a swarm of buck-shot spreading, and they touched the screen, Atkill sighed. They vanished. Then he groaned. They were taking bites out of the screen, and vanishing, while a peculiar shimmer appeared that the cups seemed to enter easily, and safely. The screen itself was scarcely two feet in actual depth, and it was mere seconds before the cups had carved a hole through it, leaving a channel of curiously shimmering light. Atkill drove a tremendous cosmic down that path, followed it with a complete gamut of frequencies, tried an atomic bomb, and watched the cups eat the bomb before it went off. He could destroy the cups momentarily by his beams, but invariably, the instant the beam was off, they all appeared—each *with a cupful of cosmic rays!*

Atkill turned his ship and ran for home. A whole flock of those deadly cups, all that had been near him, clung about him, and thousands more were trailing after him at their best speed, each faithfully rotating. Those behind presently wandered erratically and fell away. Those actually within the screen, several hundred of them, began to eat at the walls of the ship. They swallowed the black half-disintegrated matter and disappeared as rapidly as they had eaten the screen. They ate out the force wall behind the material wall, and—he could not replace the force at that point.

Warren was smiling tensely. "I should have started with that. How's the fleet getting on?"

"About even. They have slightly better ships. And they've been using the individual fields of the atomic rot successfully. But the Bay-Raonii are more numerous. They've all been handicapped by having to look out for your beams."

Warren placed the Anlo suddenly in the midst of a group of Bay-Raonii, while the far more mobile Anlonians retired. Instantly, from five great ports, a great stream of the green atomic rot fields shot out, the great snakey fields breaking down into smaller force-fields quickly, fields like the ball-lightning of the Anlonian weapons, which carried their power locked within them, not loose as in a beam, with the result that a screen would not stop them.

The concentrated energy of the Flame fields, the violet spheres that reached out and set the Eternal Flame to any iron spouted forth, then the "cups"—hemispheres of concentrated space strain where the strain was so great that when any additional strain, such as the space-strains of matter, or of a powerful shield, came within their compass, they were precipitated half through to that fifth-dimensionless timelessness. But only half. The other half clung stubbornly to this space with exactly the energy of the space-field the cup enclosed.

Warren dropped a tremendous group of these strange bombs, and of the pale-blue glowing field of force that, when it touched matter, transmuted it instantly to hydrogen.

Entirely released of control now, they repelled each other, each its kind, violently, particularly the cups; but each was attracted violently by matter—and the forces opposing, each sought a ship, and to avoid its kind. Occasionally two would meet, two different types. A soundless explosion, or a sudden flickering, and they were gone.

Ship after ship of the Bay-Raonii was suddenly burdened with these flying, searching, indestructible things, and disappeared in tattered, torn metal. Only the Flame itself could consume them all. Only Warren and the Anlonians could control them at all, and then only by making such a concentration of them as to send them away by mutual repulsion.

The Bay-Raonii were beaten not by beams and screens, but by devouring, individual space fields, each a separate, individual enemy, which, multiplied by the tens of millions, ate their fleet.

AFTERWORD

by George Zebrowski

When he became editor of ASTOUNDING in 1937, John W. Campbell, Jr. already had behind him a career as one of the best writers of the large-scale, super-science adventure story. His new position at Street & Smith Publications curtailed the further publication of new stories, as these could not be permitted to appear in competing science fiction magazines. SF in hardcover was very rare in those days, and paperbacks as we know them did not exist. Later, in the 1940s and 50s, Campbell's work was gathered into hardcover editions by Fantasy Press, Shasta Publishers, and FPCI.

The Space Beyond was written for *Amazing Stories* (the title page of the manuscript proclaims this); *Marooned* was written under the pseudonym of Karl van Kampen, which Campbell had used in *Astounding* before he took over from F. Orlin Tremaine. The story might have been intended for *Astounding* or a competitor, but the ploy was never carried out. *All* was signed Don A. Stuart, who had been published to great acclaim in the November 1934 *Astounding,* and who continued to appear for a time after Campbell became editor, until the publishers put a stop to it. The background of *All* was later given to Robert A. Heinlein, who wrote a much longer novel based on it (*Sixth Column,* currently known as *The Day After Tomorrow,* Signet). These three short novels are the only original stories by Campbell to appear since his last story in the 1950s. They reveal a young, enthusiastic author in his mid to late twenties, in whom we can discern a serious stylist, as well as the unabashed storyteller striving to go one better than his universe-spanning contemporary, Edward E. Smith.

There is much of the 1930s in these stories, as concerns science, politics and social attitudes; they also reveal the unpretentious patterns of the pulp genre tradition. But these forms were fun and permitted the exercise of much originality, as Isaac Asimov's vast autobiographical anthology, *Before the Golden Age*, Doubleday, 1974 (the golden age being the first decade of Campbell's editorship of *Astounding*), reveals so well.

The pattern to be noticed in *Marooned* and *The Space Beyond* is one in which the protagonists find themselves in a difficult situation and have to invent hardware, processes, theories, to get themselves out of danger and back home. The pattern is capable of surprising refinement, as Frederick Pohl's recent novella, "The Gold At the Starbow's End", brilliantly demonstrates. The formula differs from SF written in the nineteenth and early twentieth century in that the characters do things in a systematic way to solve their problems. In Campbell's early story, "Piracy Preferred", a lone-wolf mad scientist type, Wade, is captured and "professionalized" by becoming a part of a scientific-engineering research team.* The earlier pattern was set by Goethe's *Faust* and Mary Shelley's *Frankenstein*, where the problem is to escape or destroy the products of knowledge. The excitement of the later formula lay in the intellectual understanding of hypothetical inventions, their logic, plausibility and capacity for generating large action scenes; and the characters were not helpless victims, but agents of ingenuity and heroism.

In *The Space Beyond*, atomic energy is regarded as an imaginary but imminent source of power; the story shows us how the SF writers of the 30s were looking forward to it, in much the same way as we look forward to fusion power. In *Marooned* we are shown a continuous-thrust atomic rocket—a torchship—one which is quite modern even today. A spacecraft of this type could take astronauts across the solar system in weeks rather than the years required by rockets injected into unpowered trajectories today. The story also shows us a primitive mechanical arm for making repairs on the outside of a spaceship. The

---

* See Leon Stover's fine essay, "Science Fiction, The Research Revolution, and John Campbell", *Extrapolation*, Vol. 14, No. 2, May 1973, page 142-3.

arm is controlled by an astronaut from a pod much like the one in 2001: A SPACE ODYSSEY; but the observant reader will recognize the prototype of Heinlein's "waldoes"—the name given to remote-control manipulators for use in atomic research—from the *Astounding* cover story of August 1942, titled "Waldo."

Another interesting detail in *The Space Beyond* is the use of computers, called "calculators" in the story. Campbell was one of the few SF writers, if not the only one, to describe the usefulness of computers in research at such an early date. *The Space Beyond* also shows us an arms race, in addition to considering the ethics of placing decisive weapons in the hands of a people at war. *All* reflects the use of atomic physics in medicine, which many forget was the earlier fruit of atomic science—radiation therapy through isotopes—predating the atomic bomb by at least a decade and a half.* The natural inventiveness of Campbell's scientists and engineers is a constant reminder of the group which gathered in New Mexico to produce the reality of atomic energy. In later years Campbell was often credited with instilling the enthusiasm and curiosity that led many young scientists into a career.

In their description of new energies, new technologies, new building materials of great strength, and the use of these to create a better world despite misuse by villains, Campbell's stories make tangible reference to many elements of the postwar world, as well as showing us something of the social and political climate in which they were written. For example, *All* expresses the pre-war fear of Asia, especially Japan, as well as presenting the idea of America as a "sleeping giant" of great scientific and industrial potential. In both Heinlein's novel and Campbell's original there is the sense of the coming struggle with Japan (Heinlein's story appeared in 1941). There is even a hint of the Nuremberg trials in the weighing of the fate of the Eastern conquerors after their defeat by the Western atomic scientists. This is probably a view of hindsight,

---

* The healing powers of the atom were a popular subject during the 30's. In THE INVISIBLE RAY, a film starring Boris Karloff, the hero restores his mother's sight using a radioactive substance. This reminds us of the highly private therapy performed on his ailing mother by the great American physicist, Ernest Lawrence and his brother, John, using a neutron beam from a cyclotron. (See *Lawrence and Oppenheimer* by Nuel Pharr Davis, pp. 76-77)

but the postwar world seems to cast its shadow back over these three stories. This is not surprising, since the SF Campbell accepted for *Astounding* during the 1940s shows an even more accurate aim in depicting the world of the 50s and 60s. Campbell's technological forecasting became a guiding method (in a fictional mode) for Heinlein, Asimov, Kuttner, Moore, Blish, Williamson, and others; at the same time the method bore a richer fruit through its application by more than one writer.*

Marooned is probably the best of the three stories in this collection. It is a good example of the modern hardcore SF story—almost. I say almost because the final invention which saves the day for the explorers owes much more to a space opera like *The Space Beyond* than to the fairly realistic narrative of the rest of the story. Although the characters in *Marooned* are the familiar, extraordinarily competent men, predominantly Northern Europeans, they are more filled out and believable than the characters in the two other stories, especially Corliss—a big tall fellow of the kind so admired by John Wayne movie fans; Campbell makes the point that his size makes him less well suited for space travel than the smaller men in his crew. Corliss even worries about dying in a fairly mature way. The story gives the appearance of shifting to Don A. Stuart for a few moments, then back to the style of a very realistic John Campbell (writing in the manner of the later *The Moon Is Hell!*), then back to the universe-spanner of *The Mightiest Machine* when Corliss invents the solution of the story's major problem.

The world of the story (not filled in, but seen in bits) is the familiar, neo-capitalistic one of free enterprise—individualistic scientific entrepreneurs and technological companies; yet it seems fairly real. It follows, of course, in such a world, that anyone attempting an expedition to Jupiter will do so in a competitive spirit. Science and hardware are well integrated with the story, becoming necessary parts of the drama as well as acquiring and exciting

---

* The wedding of religion and technology also appeared in another Heinlein story, "If This Goes On . . .", and in Fritz Leiber's *Gather Darkness! All* may be the unpublished ancestor of these stories, including the religious satire in Heinlein's *Stranger in a Strange Land*, in the sense that Campbell mined his own story in discussions with these writers, even if he did not show them his own effort.

interest in themselves, since the fate of the expedition rests on calculation and inventiveness. The narration (author-omniscient, relating past history) is more sophisticated than in the other two stories.

The point of still current interest in the story concerns the view Campbell developed of the major scene stealer—the planet Jupiter. At once the interested reader will compare the story to others about the giant planet—stories by Simak, Blish, Anderson, Clarke, and others (all can be found in a fine collection, *Jupiter*, edited by Carol and Frederick Pohl, Ballantine 1973). The story dates from the same time that Campbell wrote a major science article on Jupiter (1937). The sheer visual-scientific interest of *Marooned* will be enough to interest readers. I refer the reader to Isaac Asimov's introduction to this volume for a discussion of Campbell's view of Jove.

The Space Beyond may have been intended as the first of a series, since we learn at the end that the villains are badly defeated, and no more. We know that Warren and his group can return home at will, but this is not shown. The story must be read as an early kind of SF adventure. The excitement, tension and emotional impact do not derive from the interplay of characters *and* ideas, as we expect from modern SF, but from (1) the description of new technologies and what can be done with them, (2) cosmic battles involving large fleets of extraordinary spaceships, and (3) the spectacle of alien worlds, large distances and astronomical vistas.

Both the hero and the villain of *The Space Beyond* are fascinated by each other's technological tricks. There is a fair amount of campy fun to be found in their posturings and dueling. Except for the fact that one is power mad and wantonly cruel, the two men could almost be taken for brothers. I suspect that if Campbell had written a series from *The Space Beyond*, the villain might have been "reformed", in the manner of Wade, who became a permanent character in the trilogy of novels, *The Black Star Passes*, *Islands of Space*, and *Invaders from the Infinite*. E. E. Smith developed this same problem with his super-villain, Blackie DuQuesne in his Skylark tetralogy,* as

---

* Smith finally wrote a last "Skylark" novel, *Skylark* DuQuesne, which finished serialization in *IF* just two weeks before his death in 1965. Blackie DuQuesne is reformed more than thirty years after his first appearance.

did Robert Louis Stevenson with Long John Silver. These kinds of villains tend to be more interesting than the heroes. The problem goes back at least as far as Milton's *Paradise Lost*. If approached for the kind of story this is, the reader will be rewarded with many fascinating action sequences that are of cinematic quality. Campbell was a heavyweight in this kind of storyteller's fun, and took it just about as far as it could go long before the invention of camp. The interested reader might wish to compare *The Space Beyond* to Campbell's other work in this subgenre.

All is an entertainingly written fairy tale about an oppressed group winning freedom with the aid of mighty powers (atomic energy of a mystical variety). The story seems curiously nationalistic, but this can be excused on the grounds that the situation involves an invaded country fighting for its freedom. The story suggests the work of A. Merritt, in its color and pageantry, and reverence for the vast forces of nature. In Heinlein's version, the characters treat their invented religion pragmatically, as a cover for the resistance movement; but Campbell's scientists seem almost to believe their own Platonic myths. Heinlein was perhaps commenting on this aspect of his editor's version when he showed us a character who goes insane thinking he has become a diety.

Each of these three stories has at least one brilliant scene. *The Space Beyond* has the awesomely beautiful spectacle of the giant blue suns. The sequence of descriptions becomes almost hypnotic. Campbell was very fond of the color blue, and used it often as part of his settings and as details (see, for example, *Who Goes There?*). *Marooned* has a wonderful scene showing us a storm of giant snowflakes as the exploratory ship drifts in Jupiter's atmosphere. *All* gives us the sight of a thousand-foot giant, dressed in priestly robes, striding across America. Heinlein retained this figure in his version. These are all potent images, both entertaining and satisfying dramatically.

A few words about the state of the text. *The Space Beyond* seems to have been in a first draft, and needed smoothing and cutting to bring it to the version in this book. *Marooned* and *All* were virtually finished texts and only minor corrections were necessary. As I went over

these stories, it occurred to me suddenly that I was edit-
ing a John Campbell who had been about my age, in his
late twenties, when he finished these stories. I thought
back, remembering how I had come to meet him, and
how my views of him had changed and developed, and
what I had concluded about the man and his effect on
science fiction. These conclusions, I thought, might help
make a fitting context in which to place the stories in
this book.

As a teenager I called John Campbell on the phone
once or twice in the early 60's. I heard a big man, speaking loudly, yet ready to talk as much as I wished. I rang
off after a polite minute or two, probably out of shyness,
not really believing what my feelings told me—that he
would have talked gladly as long as possible. I met him
at the World Science Fiction Convention in Washington,
D.C. in 1963, where he signed his introduction to George
O. Smith's *Venus Equilateral* for me, in his usual large
fluidly curved handwriting. I still own that book.*

When next I met him in 1970, I was already a published writer. We sat in the *Analog* office on Lexington
Avenue as he picked up a copy of one of the best known
continuing collections of SF and said, "The trouble with
these writers is they can write, but they can't think
much!" We both agreed that was why *Analog* had so
many lesser stories in it with interesting ideas. He preferred to publish them because they would provoke dis-
discussion, disagreement—thought—while the well-written
ones usually had little else in them.

But that was the extent to which Campbell and I could
agree. He asked me what I thought thinking was, and
refused all answers, including his own. Generally he did
not like to agree, probably because he felt it led to lazi-
ness. He told me that his editorials were meant to provoke discussion, and that a week after publication he might
disagree with himself. I glimpsed the sight of a man who
had lost the environment of productivity; his old writers

---

* I met Isaac Asimov at this same convention. I was so over-
whelmed by my recent reading of *The Foundation Trilogy* that
I stumbled over my words as I shook his hand. "Er, would . . .
you ask me a question?" I asked. "Of course!" he shouted, "What
would you like me to ask *you*?" I went red and my knees shook.
To this day he thinks I'm someone else when he sees me.

had left, and he had to be his own adversary. It brought home to me the importance of content in science fiction, criticism, and the environment of colleagues. This may be one of the reasons why *Astounding/Analog* declined in the late 50s and 60s.

A year later John Wood Campbell, Jr. was dead, and as editor of the SFWA Bulletin, the official publication of the Science Fiction Writers of America, I put together a memorial issue for the man I had always suspected had provided at least one of the major ingredients for a good theory of science fiction, and more. As Don A. Stuart, he had been a "new wave" all by himself; and that writer, who was lost to us in the new editor of *Astounding,* might have been able to do it all—style, content, everything we would like to say belongs to a high, enduring science fiction. The writers he trained, however, started on this path for him. The work of these writers, together with his own best work, makes a fitting monument.

We have to say today, to adapt a comment made by John Brunner, that so-called "hard core" SF, to truly be itself, must be well *thought out* and well *written,* in terms of the standards one must apply to the best fiction. It must be novelistic in the best literary terms, as well as science fiction in content. When he became editor of *Astounding,* Campbell instituted a higher standard for the *fiction* that he would accept, as well as demanding a development of science fiction's unique potential. But no editor can maintain any kind of demanding standard indefinitely. Campbell held to it for less than a decade, just long enough to create modern science fiction and see his writers go on to better markets and publishers. Some came back occasionally, but there never seemed to be *more* of them—no new names comparable in stature. The lesson to be learned is that the supply of first-class talent is always limited, and can only very rarely be increased by conscious effort on the part of editors. The true heirs of Campbell (and this may seem heretical) are writers like Ursula K. Le Guin, Gene Wolfe, Stanislaw Lem, Gregory Benford, D. G. Compton, and others who have a sense of unified values, literary and science fictional. They have not forgotten the special beauties which can be found in these three stories, the oft spoken about "sense of wonder." In their own way the newer writers are trying to serve it better, perhaps more intensely and with more depth of feeling and intellect. This is the further vision we can see standing on John Campbell's shoulders.